PRAISE FOR LAWRENCE LIGHT AND *TOO RICH TO LIVE!*

"A lickety-split-paced tale of mystery, mayhem and greed."
—Steve Forbes, *Forbes* Magazine

"With a cast of vibrant characters set in the wildly adventurous New York City boroughs, *Too Rich to Live* is a perfect rainy day read."
—Fresh Fiction

"Light provides an insider's view of Manhattan's financial world while crafting a fine, engrossing story."
—*New Mystery Reader*

"[F]ans will appreciate this intense thriller."
—*The Midwest Book Review*

BEHIND THE DOOR

Karen peeked around the door to see what the obstruction was.

She slid sideways into the apartment and knelt over the form on the floor.

"What is it?" Linda said behind her.

"Don't come in here." Karen felt for a pulse in the neck. None. The body was dead-cold and clammy. The head was bent at an odd angle, as though belonging to an unloved doll.

Linda edged in anyway and gasped. "Is he dead?"

"Looks like it." Karen felt her stomach churn. She choked back bile.

From her crouch, Karen scanned the cramped apartment to be sure they were alone.

"I wonder if Goldring is here," she said hoarsely. She roamed through the seedy little studio apartment and saw nothing resembling it. "He has a lot of computers, but…"

"There should be a gold ring embossed on it, an old IBM ThinkPad, a replica of Daddy's friendship ring to Flo," Linda said, frozen to her spot, transfixed.

Karen examined the computers and delved through drawers, in the closet, under the furniture. "Nothing."

Then they heard the thunder of feet from the stairway. Feet that slammed down the hall toward them like some many-hooved beast. Fear-frozen, they watched as a brace of powerful guns appeared in the doorway, pointed at them….

Other *Leisure* books by Lawrence Light:

TOO RICH TO LIVE

FEAR & GREED

LAWRENCE LIGHT

LEISURE BOOKS NEW YORK CITY

To my beloved Meredith, the center of my life.

A LEISURE BOOK®

November 2006

Published by

Dorchester Publishing Co., Inc.
200 Madison Avenue
New York, NY 10016

ISBN 0-8439-5742-5

The name "Leisure Books" and the stylized "L" with design are trademarks of Dorchester Publishing Co., Inc.

Printed in the United States of America.

Visit us on the web at www.dorchesterpub.com.

ACKNOWLEDGMENTS

Many thanks to Don D'Auria, my excellent editor at Dorchester, whose story sense and love of the thriller genre have added so much to the Karen Glick series. Don's guidance and wisdom are unparalleled. He gave me my start and I am forever in his debt.

And I would be nowhere without my extraordinary agent, Cynthia Manson, who believed in me from the start. Her marvelous insights were key to making this book work. They just don't come any better than Cynthia.

My wonderful and gorgeous wife, Meredith, helped me enormously in the characterization. Her deft advice made Karen Glick and the Reiner sisters come to life. A mystery writer herself, she also has a sense of comedy that is echoed in Karen.

Special thanks go to Steve and Tim Forbes for all their help and encouragement—and for running a terrific magazine, where it has been my privilege to work. A fine set of people have helped shape me as a journalist and writer: Bill Baldwin, Steve Shepard, Dave Wallace, Bill McIlwain, and Vivian Waixel.

Trying to get readers' attention is not easy for a new author. My good friend Elizabeth Hunter has done so much in getting the word out about Karen Glick.

FEAR & GREED

CHAPTER ONE

The Reiner sisters had created a computer program that did the impossible: it predicted the stock market. Very suddenly, the program made them enormously rich. They called it Goldring. And they kept it a secret. But Linda Reiner couldn't resist courting publicity. Being rich wasn't enough, Linda told her two sisters. You had to be celebrated, too.

A young reporter's interview made the Reiner sisters famous. The world read in Karen Glick's *Profit* magazine article that the sisters had become ungodly wealthy over just a few months by cannily investing in the stock market. The story, however, didn't say *how* the Reiners had spotted their winning stocks, beyond a few platitudes about finding unappreciated companies with big futures.

The photo in the magazine showed them in their office: smiling Linda Reiner, the glamorous stockbroker who had pitched the story to Karen; her serious-looking older sister Ginny, a college math professor; and scowling Flo, the youngest, a prototypical computer geek. The picture was telling. Linda reveled in her newfound fortune, Ginny was indifferent to it, and Flo . . . "Money," sourpuss Flo told reporter Karen, "can't buy you happiness."

"Yeah," Karen said. "Well, it can sure make you comfortable while you're miserable."

Karen Glick had a reputation for writing well-crafted, often witty profiles of interesting folks in the business world—soft, positive stories that everyone liked, that made no one mad. This was why Linda had chosen her. On the brink of divorce from an investment banker and feeling miffed at the testosterone-laden financial crowd, she was delighted to write about successful women investors.

Guarding their secret the way a society dowager does her age, the sisters made no copies of the stock-picking program and stored it on an innocuous old IBM ThinkPad, which no one would bother to steal. The magical laptop, one of several computers in their office, had a discreet golden ring embossed upon it so they could always identify it.

Wall Street pros, forever scrambling to learn the last scrap of information to gain an advantage, would die to get their hands on the Goldring program, Linda warned her sisters.

What she didn't realize was that some people would kill for it.

The intruder waited unseen in the Reiners's office at night. The loft held only three widely spaced desks, each in a pool of spot lighting. The rest of the industrial floor had a reception area, a gym, and a coffee bar. Tonight it was as dark and empty as interstellar space. Reiner Capital lay behind a teak door in a building populated by tech start-ups with names like Cyborg Gameworks and Dimento Digerati. The intruder held his breath, watched, listened.

Flo Reiner was alone that night. Her voice filled the loft space as she ranted at an immense TV near her desk. She was talking with someone on speakerphone. A laptop, the one with the golden ring embossed on it, sat closed on her desk.

"Are you looking at this?" Flo exclaimed. "My God, could her skirt get any shorter? And here comes the hair toss. Yes, flip. She's not too obviously flirting."

Linda Reiner was on CNBC, chatting with a sappily smiling male interviewer. Linda with her wondrously flowing sweep of honey-colored hair. Linda with that sultry, throaty delivery that sounded like the young Kathleen Turner in *Body Heat,* the intruder's favorite old movie. He sighed.

Linda was saying, "We only run our own money, and we've made buckets of it." She gave her practiced laugh, full of melody.

"Oh, great, buckets," Flo cried mockingly.

The interviewer, acting like a teenage boy trying to impress Jennifer Lopez: "Too bad you don't take outside clients. A lot of folks watching us could use that kind of magic in their investments. Tell me, you and your sisters function as a team, don't you?"

"Oh, yeah," Flo said. "A real team."

Linda, touching the interviewer's arm: "Why, yes, Cliff. My older sister, Ginny, is a distinguished mathematics professor at Columbia. She figured out the algorithms for our investing system. I, of course, have the background on Wall Street. That's where"—she laughed brightly—"the rubber really hits the road. And our younger sister, Flo, does what computer work is necessary."

"Do you hear that?" Flo shouted. " 'What computer work is necessary'? Like I'm just another techie. Without me, there'd be no Goldring. I'll hit her road with the rubber, all right."

The interviewer, almost sheepishly: "What is your investing secret? You can tell me."

Linda, holding up a teasing finger: "Cliff, if I could tell anybody, it would be you." She put a finger to her full lips.

"Tell me," Cliff pleaded,

Linda leaned forward with the smile she used when insulting someone. "Buy low, sell high."

After the forced laughter subsided, the interviewer turned to the camera and intoned: "Linda Reiner, part of an investing trio of sisters that, in a few short months of trading, has produced an astounding seven thousand percent return."

Flo turned off the TV with a contemptuous stab of the remote. Then she did a dead-on impersonation of Linda, with every Kathleen Turner lilt. "Oh, yes, Cliff, you big hunk of man. Why don't you drool over me some more and let me tell you how terrific I am?"

"You're not being fair to Linda," said her sister, Ginny, on the speakerphone.

"Ginny, she's going to get us in trouble going to the media," Flo said. "She has always been such a damn show-boat." Flo brandished a copy of *Profit* magazine. "And it all started when she went to that reporter, Karen, bragging about our 'astounding seven thousand percent return.' We should've kept this under wraps. Linda's so hot to be a celebrity she'd run the New York Marathon naked."

"I do worry that the way Goldring works isn't quite legal. We're breaking all kinds of securities laws. But Linda says—"

" 'Linda says'? It's always 'Linda says' with you. Linda will get us caught."

"Please, no more," Ginny said. "She hasn't told anyone about the details of Goldring, or even its name, and that's how it will stay. To the world, it's some vague 'system.' Linda is very shrewd."

"Tell me one time you haven't taken her side."

"I'm taking no sides," Ginny told her sister with weariness. "Listen, I have a student outside waiting for me."

"Why bother being a professor anymore?" Flo said. "You can buy the math department now."

"I'm hooked on academia," Ginny said. "Besides, I don't need the fancy new penthouse or the clothes that Linda does. My old place and a new pair of Birkenstocks are sufficient for me."

The intruder started forward, then stopped.

The instant the Ginny call ended, the phone rang. Linda's sultry octaves filed the loft.

"Wasn't that great?" Linda said over the speaker.

"You still at the studio?" Flo asked, belligerence gone when confronted with the real Linda.

"No, Flo, I'm at home. We taped earlier. Cliff is a good interviewer. No tough questions I couldn't turn aside. He's one of those chiseled-chin boys. All surface, no substance."

"You did a number on him."

"What was that? I can't hear you."

"Nothing. Mumbling again. One of my bad habits you always are criticizing me for."

"Nonsense," Linda said. "I never criticize, just offer well-meaning suggestions. When are you coming over to my new place? The views are great."

Flo took a deep breath. "Linda, is it smart to keep seeking publicity for us? First the magazine story, now TV. Shouldn't we keep our success to ourselves?"

Linda laughed. "The whole point of wealth is to be lauded for it. I'm getting invited to the really good parties, the kind I used to get to only as arm candy for some guy. Now I've got Astors and Whitneys practically lining up to invite me. And today I was asked to attend the masked ball to celebrate the opening of Faff Towers. You know, Jack's latest, the luxury condos overlooking Central Park? This is *the* party."

"Jack, huh? You're on a first name basis? Jack Faff's a pig."

"Obviously. Jack wants to get in my pants, but that's nothing I can't handle."

"He always ditches his wives when they hit thirty-five. You're getting dangerously close to thirty-five."

Linda's breezy delivery suddenly turned a bit chillier. "I'm not interested in him."

"You'd never tell anyone about Goldring, would you?"

"Please. Never. And don't discuss that on the phone. I'm not alone."

"Who are you with? That new boyfriend of yours, the married one?"

"No," Linda said. "And he's getting a divorce. He's picking me up in an hour. No, right now, Stefan is giving me the most intense full-body massage. Hitting every muscle."

"You're there with a man? And you have no clothes on? And he's giving you a massage?"

"Don't worry," Linda said. "Stefan is dependably gay. Aren't you, Stefan?"

"I'm dependable, Ms. Reiner," came a male voice.

"You should get a boyfiend for a change," Linda told her sister. "Anna was nice enough to call and tell me she gave you the best haircut. Use it."

"Your hairstylist told me she wanted my hair to resemble 'a field of waving wheat,'" Flo said. "What Anna gave me was a crew cut. Maybe it looks good on her. I look like a Marine drill instructor."

"Your hair looked like something a bird would nest in. Listen, Stefan is finished. I must go."

"I'm going to church. I can cover my hair there." Flo hung up. "Bird's nest, my ass."

This time, the intruder rushed from the shadows.

Neighbors down the hall later told police they thought they heard Flo's cry for help but weren't sure where the scream came from. People were always acting hysterical in geek land. They definitely heard the gunshot. But the sound could have come from a video game.

No one saw the man in the ratty jacket with the laptop under his arm bolt down the metal stairs and into the windy nighttime street.

CHAPTER TWO

The day wasn't starting out well for Karen Glick, feature writer for *Profit* magazine, soon-to-be divorcee, and resident wiseacre. She didn't feel too wise this morning.

"I think you missed something crucial on the Reiner sisters story," said her best friend, Frank Vere, with the sorrowful air of a doctor delivering the bad news about the biopsy.

"I missed something crucial?" Karen said. "And here I figured you were going to tell me how nice I look this morning."

Frank Vere had the awe-inspiring, if annoying, habit of always being right. One of the premier investigative reporters of the age, he had exposed the misdeeds of, as Karen put it, "many mighty miscreants" and sent them to jail. He knew everybody from street hustlers to homicide cops to Wall Street Masters of the Universe, and they all fed him stories. He had won every prize but the Nobel, and that was only a matter of time. The only prize Karen had ever won was from the sixth grade talent show for her imitations of Porky Pig and Scooby-Doo.

"What did I miss, Frank?"

"I hear the reason the Reiner sisters have done so well is they've invented a computer program that can correctly predict what stocks are going to take off, every time," Frank said. Tall and gangly but always slouching, he looked down at her. "They buy the stocks, watch them rise, then sell for a huge gain. It's a foolproof system. They call it Goldring."

Karen sighed. "Give me a break. Sure, they have some kind of system they wouldn't discuss with me. Foolproof, though? That's impossible. A computer that can predict the future is like a perpetual motion machine, or a potion that turns lead into gold, or a spell that turns water into wine. Good for our parties, that last one, but impossible. My husband, if you'll excuse the expression, says that a dozen monkeys throwing darts at the stock tables can out-predict anybody on Wall Street."

"I also hear you are taking on Jack Faff." Frank could switch subjects faster than the White House press secretary. He'd won the right. Hardly handsome, Frank had this way of inspiring confidence in others, much like a homely dog can gain affection. So people told him everything.

"What *don't* you hear? Listen, I have to go before the Star Chamber on this now."

Karen went into the conference room. The managing editor, Calvin Christian, started in on her first. Christian's toadying sidekick, senior editor Gene Skeen, reinforced each of Christian's objections. Christian, who spoke in a monotone and always wore a bow tie, and Skeen, a know-it-all with a Pinocchio-length nose, belonged to the cowardly school of journalism.

"If we print that Jack Faff is on the brink of financial disaster, he'll sue us," Christian said.

"Faff won exactly $5.3 million in his lawsuit against the *Wall Street Journal* last year for their story on his most recent divorce," said Skeen, whose rapid-fire nasal delivery made him sound like the obnoxious Saturday morning cartoon characters Karen used to watch.

A loud throat clearing came from Karen's editor, Eudell Mancuso, a large black woman of indeterminate age, who defended her charges like a she-bear. "We've got the dope on Faff," Eudell said. "This is a great story. Great magazines do great stories. It's our duty to tell the thousands of innocent shareholders in Faff Enterprises that the company is about to hit the wall."

"It's not our duty to keep getting sued," Christian shot back. "Frank Vere's stories have gotten us into enough trouble."

"Over the past three years, defending against the three libel suits Vere provoked has cost us $1.2 million in legal fees," Skeen said. "Printing these kinds of stories is getting expensive for us."

"Big deal, Gene. We won every one of those cases. And those stories of Frank's sent crooks to jail. Crooks who prey on people."

"Moreover," Christian pressed on, "I find it impossible to conceive that a man of Jack Faff's stature is in financial trouble. Gene shows me he has reported consistently rising profits."

Karen, no longer able to contain herself, said, "Well, conceive of it. The numbers Faff reported are fake. That's a violation of law right there, which they'll be real interested in down at the Securities and Exchange Commission. Investors depend on those reports; they've bought Faff stock based on fraud. I've got an internal Faff Enterprises document showing he doctored the books. Yes,

Calvin, a man of Jack Faff's stature. And by the way, he's on the short side."

"You don't have a full set of documents to prove your case," Skeen said.

"They're coming. That's why I'm going to Atlantic City."

"At least," Christian said, "Vere is an experienced investigative reporter. Glick only knows how to write fluff."

"You're a real inspiration, Calvin," Karen said, trying not to show how his remark had stung. "You may recall how I broke the Billionaire Boys Club story."

"And risked her life in the process," Eudell added.

Karen's cover story that summer had shown how the legendary buyout firm, known as the Billionaire Boys Club, had cheated on taxes—and had been targeted for death by a vengeful former subordinate. Bill McIntyre, the editor-in-chief, had pronounced it "a powerful piece of gutsy journalism." It also had produced a federal probe of the Boys' investment bankers, Dewey Cheatham, thus far without any consequences. But it had gotten Karen's estranged husband, Tim, a Dewey Cheatham banker, in trouble at work because his wife had written the story.

"Karen Glick got lucky on that story and was out of her depth," said Christian, who had ordered Karen back to the feature-writing ranks. "Dewey Cheatham may sue us yet over this."

"The Faff story is my call, and I'm going to let Karen run with this," Eudell said. "That's how a reporter grows." After Christian and Skeen skulked out, Eudell turned to her reporter. "Honey, you don't have all the proof?"

Karen felt her forehead grow as hot as it did when, home from college on spring break, her mother found condoms in her backpack. "I'll have the documents I need by the time I interview Jack Faff."

Eudell's face betrayed a steaming gumbo of emotions. "I'm going out on a limb for you here. I'm letting you do another investigative story, which really is far from your area. Frank would never go in, hoping to get the evidence at the last minute, right before confronting Faff."

Weighed down by Eudell's skepticism, Karen walked through the nondescript mass of cubicles on dung-hued industrial carpeting. The newsroom was like a good college filled with friendly, smart, fun-loving people, most of them her friends. She exchanged greetings with them as she passed, ducking her head to dodge a Frisbee, not stopping to listen even to the Three Musketeers—a coterie of economists who clustered around the Bloomberg terminal, examining the latest market data. Oddly, they seemed to be talking about Jack Faff.

Eternal pessimist Milton Brainard, the wild-haired chief economist ("It's not morning in America for big real estate stocks, my friends, it's midnight.") was locked in intellectual combat with Phil Sarkasian, the optimist ("The gross domestic product is an apt phrase: it's so fat, it's obscene. So now is the prime time for real estate development. Build a luxury condo tower like Faff's and they will come."). Meanwhile, the ascetically thin Thomas Dailey defended the middle ground by repeatedly saying to them, "Neither of you knows what he's talking about."

As Karen glided away, she heard Brainard say, "Fear and greed drive the stock market. Greed drives you to take chances. Fear holds you back. We're about to see fear."

Wearing the down expression of the class slacker asking the smart kid for help right before the final exam, Karen stood over Frank's cubicle. "What do I do if I can't get my hands on the documentation?"

Frank, his lanky body sprawled in his ergonomically correct chair, thus nullifying the benefits, gave her his owlish stare. His Adam's apple jigged up and down. This meant he was thinking hard. She knew she had messed up big-time.

"How reliable is your source?" he said at last.

"Very. I met him when I was tagging along to parties with Linda Reiner. He's very close to Jack Faff." She hadn't yet met Faff, the star casino operator, real estate developer, and crook.

"Why does he want to betray Faff?"

"Not sure. But he's very angry," Karen said. "Look, Frank, I'm dying here. I've got to make this story work. I'm tired of doing cute features."

"Sure, you're getting a divorce and you need to make changes," said Frank, the bionic insight machine.

"Yeah, divorce is like getting food poisoning at your favorite restaurant," Karen said. "Was the Billionaire Boys story a fluke, Frank? Do I have the stuff for investigative work?"

"Of course you do," Frank said.

She smiled, buoyed. "How do I deal with Faff?"

"Keep in mind that, to Faff, the sun, moon, and stars revolve around Faff. Also know that he's in cahoots with this Russian mob boss. That's the rumor, anyway. Tough to prove. Organized crime ties would cost Faff his casino license."

"Who's this mobster?"

"A mean snake named Mikhail Beria. He loves to cut people with a knife. He's had his teeth filed to be sharp, like a wolf's. Story goes that, in a turf meeting last year with the traditional Italian Mafia, Beria showed how tough he was by biting off the head of a live rat. Not a little, bitty mousey. A huge six-incher."

"Nice."

"Be careful. Bad things happen to people who get on the wrong side of Faff. He owns the cops in Atlantic City. And the prosecutor and the politicos."

"What if my source doesn't come through with the documents and I have this meeting with Faff?" Karen tried to sound business-like and unafraid.

Frank's Adam's apple bobbed. "Bluff."

The police called Linda early. Having gotten in at 3 A.M., she was sleeping soundly when the phone rang. Since she was still interviewing for live-in help, there was no one else to answer the phone. The gruff cop at the other end of the line, Dick Friday, said a serious crime had occurred at her workplace and she'd better come at once. He would give no details.

Holding back the fear fluttering in her throat, Linda threw on a sweater and jeans, pulled her hair into a ponytail with a tortoise-shell clip, and grabbed some Jimmy Choo high heels, the most prevalent footwear in her walk-in closet, which Ginny said was the size of Low Library. Her doorman gave a piercing whistle that summoned a cab quickly.

Waving a hundred-dollar bill at the driver, she told him to move like a madman. That wasn't hard for him. Cursing in Arabic, he dodged through rush-hour traffic as if the 82nd Airborne pursued him. Wracked with worry, Linda barely noticed the five near-collisions. He safely deposited her at the Meeker-Grubman Building.

Police cars and vans lined the street, their roof strobes pulsing blood red in the long shadows of morning. Two uniformed officers, busy complaining to each other about their meager vacations and rapacious ex-wives, stopped her at the door but let her proceed once she had identified herself. She asked them what had happened.

"See Detective Friday," the beefier one said. He turned back to his partner. "And then she had the balls to call me when I was out on the boat with Sheila."

On the third floor, T-shirted techies crowded the corridor, buzzing among themselves. They parted when they saw it was Linda. Their eyes were wide.

"Shit, man, it's her," one kid said.

"Do you think she knows?" another asked.

"This is horrible," one girl said. "In our building. My God. This is like a reality show."

Linda ran toward her office, pushing past the shoulders and elbows. Ahead, an authoritative voice shouted for everyone to clear the hallway.

Ginny was just outside their teak doors. She wore one of the several dozen Columbia sweatshirts she slept in, taught in, and all but showered in. And her face was crazy with tears and grief. At the sight of her sister, she lurched to hug Linda to her thick body. Ginny tried to talk, but only sobs and wails came out. Linda held Ginny while casting about for someone who could tell her what had happened.

Approaching them was a man in a polyester tie and a short-sleeved shirt that showed his thick, tattooed forearms. "Linda Reiner?" he asked with the flat delivery of one who had done this often. When she nodded, he introduced himself as Detective Friday. "Come with me, please."

Ginny disengaged. Her face two inches from Linda's, she cried, "This can't be happening, Linda. For the love of God, this can't be happening."

A dozen police officers were drifting around the office, some in uniform, some not. They talked among themselves and touched nothing. River, the Reiner Capital receptionist, sat in the corner with his head in his hands. Molten light poured in from the long window, outlining everything in stark relief. The desks were as Linda had last seen them: hers piled with corporate quarterly reports and stock prospectuses; Ginny's spare, orderly, and immaculate; Flo's strewn with electronic gizmos. Then Linda noticed Flo's huge flat-panel digital TV had been overturned.

Next to it lay a human form covered with a sheet. An oblong lake of reddish-brown extended from it across the concrete floor. In the lake were clumps of meat. The people in the room edged past the human form as if it were a sacred object, the center of their attention, but too potent to touch.

"Where the holy hell are the lab guys?" Friday was saying to someone else in a low, funeral-parlor tone. He was out of Linda's vision. She only had eyes for the human form on the floor beside the reddish lake.

"First statements we got from neighboring offices," another cop said, more loudly. "Last night they heard screams and a single gunshot around seven P.M., but didn't know where the noise originated from." Friday must have motioned to him that Linda was within earshot, because he quickly added, "Damn it. Sorry."

The cops' voices, the footsteps on the concrete, and the hallway talk merged into a fierce buzz in Linda's ears, like the static when the cable goes out.

She opened her mouth and nothing emerged. Then she managed to say with difficulty, ". . . Is it Flo?"

"We need a relative to identify the body, Ms. Reiner," Friday said from some other dimension. "We normally wait until we get it to the medical examiner's, but they're really backed up today. Your receptionist, Mr. Treysor over there, discovered it when he arrived this morning. Your sister Virginia isn't up to doing this."

Every part of Linda began trembling. Friday took her arm to steady her. She tried to walk and couldn't in her teetering high heels. She stepped out of them. The concrete floor was fiendishly cold against her bare feet.

"Sean," Friday said to another cop, "could you?"

The cop gently pulled the covering halfway down the human form. Then he retreated, mincing.

Linda put her hands over her gaping mouth.

Flo's face was a mash of blood, skin, and bone. The red lake seemed to have geysered out of the top of her head, which was close-cropped the way Anna the hairdresser had wanted. Flo wore the Armani man-tailored suit that Linda had picked out. It had been right for Flo's field hockey goalie body.

"This is your sister, Florence?" Friday said. More statement than question, the sentence hovered buzzardlike in the air.

Linda pulled her arm away from Friday and knelt beside her sister. She reached a shaky hand toward Flo.

"Don't touch nothing," Friday said.

"Pull . . . the cover . . . down more," Linda managed to say as she withdrew her hand.

At Friday's gesture, Sean the cop gingerly obeyed.

Flo's nails were jungle-red, a color Linda instructed her was always hip. The ring was in place on her right hand, where it had been for half her life. In the mirror, Flo had joked, it seemed like an engagement ring.

"That's her ring," Linda said so softly that only Friday could hear. "Daddy got it for her in high school. He called it their friendship ring. Flo was the youngest. I was in college, Ginny in graduate school."

"This is your sister, Florence?" Friday repeated in an attempt to sound kind when kindness wasn't his native language.

"Yes, Detective Friday," Linda said slowly, gaze locked on her sister's body. "This is Flo. This is Flo's haircut. This is Flo's suit. This is Flo's nail polish. This is Flo's ring . . ." She trailed off and closed her eyes to think.

"Is anything missing?"

"Ring," Linda said and got to her feet. She bent over Flo's desk, pulled out drawers, delved under piles of computer discs, poked into Flo's Kate Spade bag on the floor.

"Don't touch nothing, Ms. Reiner," Friday warned.

Linda cold-footed it over to her own desk. At Friday's direction, several cops hustled to stand in her way.

"Detective Friday," Linda said, "you want to know what's missing. How do I know if I can't go through the desks?"

"Not until we do, ma'am," Friday said.

"Never mind," Linda said. She crossed over to where River sat.

Sensing her approach—River, like most men, was entranced by Linda—the receptionist removed his hands from his handsome, tear-tracked face and said, "It must've happened right after I left last night. If only I'd stuck around."

"River, did you notice whether . . ." Linda stopped when she saw Friday had followed her. "That's okay."

"Flo didn't like me much," River said gloomily. "I tried, but . . ."

"You're famous, right?" Friday said to Linda. "Didn't I see you on the *Today* Show?"

She made for the front door and said over her shoulder to Friday, "I'd like to speak with my sister, Ginny. Alone, please."

In the hall, which had been cleared of onlookers, Ginny was holding herself, fragile and alone amid a bunch of tall policemen. She looked at Linda expectantly, as though she might hear it was all a nightmare.

Linda put a supportive arm around Ginny and led her away from the cluster of cops at the door. She gently told her sister that Flo had been shot in the head and was dead. She comforted Ginny through a round of sobbing. Ginny told her, "You always were the strong one, Linda."

Finally, when Ginny's grief subsided, Linda said, "They took Goldring. It's gone."

"What?" Ginny said as if on the distant end of a dream.

"It's not in the safe next to my desk, which is open, and I could see inside. We're supposed to keep it there after hours, but it isn't there. It's not on Flo's desk, where it usually is. That's what they were after. Flo's wallet is still in her bag."

"Why did they kill her?" Ginny's question had a haunted quality.

"We can't tell the police what it does," Linda said.

Jack Faff knew about Goldring. It was going to bail him out. And that made him feel better.

He had wavy hair and piercing eyes. He still had the same bounce in his walk from his days as a championship college wrestler. His face adorned billboards advertising his casino. Women in call-in radio shows said they fantasized about him. One typically fawning press account called him "the golden boy with the golden looks."

He stood five foot two. He blamed his father's genes. Pop-pop was six feet, but small men were hung through the Faff family tree like tiny, distasteful monkeys. Pop-pop never let Jack forget how small he was. So Jack learned at an early age to compensate. "When you're rich," Jack would say, "you're always eight feet tall."

Confident as a dragon, Jack Faff didn't just talk. He projected at top volume so that every sentient being would catch every choice word. Standing by his office's panoramic window, he surveyed the gaudy gaming strip he dominated. Faff's casino was Atlantic City's jewel, the first stop for the gamblers' buses from New York and Philadelphia. It was like a giant roach motel, good for the owners, not for the guests. Casinos are a fine business since the odds favor the house. In the old seaside resort, money flew out of wallets as easily as bombast flew out of Faff's mouth. He scanned the tiny creatures that plodded along the boardwalk and the sun-sparkled water beyond.

"Who says money can't buy happiness?" he boomed. "Well, check out the smile on my face."

His brother, Solter, as meek as Jack was brash, stood a few paces behind. "You only smile in public, Jack." Solter was as tall as Pop-pop. But Solter stooped, trying not to offend Jack.

"This reporter is a first-class bitch. She thinks she can prove I'm about to go bust. Do you realize what that'll do to our company's stock?"

Solter laughed nervously. "But you are about to go bust," he said.

"What?" Jack Faff got on his toes. "Perception is reality. I have a temporary problem the world doesn't have to hear about."

"Jack, your problem isn't temporary," his brother said.

"The hell you say," Jack Faff declared.

Edging away as a crab might from danger, Solter said, "Yes, Jack."

Jack Faff held up a well-manicured hand to greet a newcomer. "Ah, Mikhail."

The gangster slid into the ornate room. He ignored Solter and shook hands powerfully with Jack. "We're ready for her," he said. He smiled with long, fang-like teeth.

"I've got some negotiations with this Glick. If they fail, I'm delivering her to you. Then I'll leave. Best not for me to know. Just do it."

The gangster's carnivorous smile faded. "You're forgetting one big piece of business, Jack."

"I forget nothing." As the most important person in any room, the developer would let no one reproach him.

"You owe me a hundred thou for Glick. Half up front, whether we do her or not. Cash."

Jack Faff shrugged. He clicked a computer mouse and consulted his screen. "Got some technical glitch at the bank." Mikhail didn't have to know that the glitch was a near-empty account.

"Some of my best hard-asses I got to handle her. They want to be paid."

"I'm good for it. Check the dictionary. The name Faff in America means money."

Mikhail mulled proceeding with no down payment. "Okay, but we need all the money tomorrow."

Now came Faff's turn to smile—at his negotiating victory. "Then there's the second job we talked about. Finding the Goldring computer. That means more money for you."

"How much?"

"Later on that." Jack's smile widened. "As for Glick, do it slow."

CHAPTER THREE

Special Operative Trixie Logan knew about Goldring, too. That was why she went to her own funeral. But she didn't enjoy the experience. Not one little bit.

She had met the priest who officiated at her burial mass numerous times and rather enjoyed his learned homilies. But Father Fahey today was impersonal, merely going through the motions. He called her Trixie, when she preferred Logie. She hated the name Trixie, which her demented mother had foisted on her; Logie had given her own daughter a much more pleasant name, Alexandra. One befitting a princess.

Little Alexandra sat in the front pew, next to her father. The poor sweet thing looked hollowed out, almost drugged. She was transfixed by her mother's coffin.

Logie wanted to scream out to her husband, "Put your arm around the girl, Jeff. She's only six. Comfort her." Alexandra was, like her mom had been, a sad little girl. She seldom cried. Logie worried about Alexandra, who was friendless and quiet. And who now had lost her mother.

Beneath his frown of mock sorrow, Jeff Lupa seemed ebullient. The church, just a mile from their home in Arlington, was hardly crowded—mainly his coworkers and clients from the brokerage showed up—and he had greeted everyone as if this were a party. Well, he now could be less discreet about his visits to Pam Moxley down the street from their house. The Widow Moxley, as Logie referred to her, wore garish lipstick and had teenage sons who sold marijuana. Occasionally, Logie had found traces of the lipstick and the pot smoke on her husband's clothes. Thankfully, the Widow Moxley wasn't at the funeral mass.

"Trixie Logan was a dependable federal employee of many years," Father Fahey was saying, in his robes from his pulpit. "Our prayers go out to Jeff and Alexandra in their hour . . ."

The real source of Jeff's good cheer, though, was the $100,000 insurance payment that Logie's death had triggered. That ought to stave off his financial trouble for at least three weeks. Given his penchant for ripping off his clients, it was a matter of time before Jeff found himself a guest of the county. Logie was in a position to know such things.

"She smashed her car into a bridge abutment," said a woman in the pew in front of Logie's. It was Nanette Carnes, one of the brokers in Jeff's office. Her affair with Jeff had ended a year ago, when he took up with the Widow Moxley. Logie used to spy on the smutty e-mails Nanette and Jeff wrote each other. Nanette, with her industrial strength nails, had scratched up Jeff's back.

"But they didn't rule it a suicide, which would rule out an insurance payment?" said Mick Morris, the man next to Nanette. "She was kind of weird."

Logie could pick up their whispered conversation thanks to the tiny directional mike she wore in her brooch. It fed into an earpiece that her hair covered. For Logie, eavesdropping was as perilous to her self-esteem as it was enlightening.

"I didn't like her, either," Nanette said. "So sarcastic. Must've hated her life."

"What'd she do again?"

"Something with computers for the Pentagon. Jeff can find better. Everyone here is his friend. She had no friends. Lived in front of a computer screen, even at home."

"Jeff has no friends, either," Mick said. "They're here out of business courtesy. I don't trust him. What a sleaze bucket."

"Her husband tells me," Father Fahey was saying, "that Trixie was a fine and loving mother."

Logie didn't take communion. After the mass, she lined up to give condolences to her husband and her child.

"Good of you to come," Jeff said to Logie and gripped her hand with a salesman's faux warmth.

"I was a friend of your wife," Logie said. Jeff's lack of interest was palpable. He'd dropped the frown. He already had hootch on his breath. She hadn't seen him smiling this broadly since the day he had finally won at blackjack in Faff's Lair casino.

Alexandra stood next to her father in a heartbreakingly dark little dress with a lace collar that Logie had bought her, though not for a funeral. Up close, she looked still more numb, her mouth open.

Logie bent down and said, "You be a brave little girl."

Alexandra looked at Logie's face and her expression widened in surprise.

Logie put a finger to her lips. "Ssh. Someone loves you very much, sweet princess." And then Logie strode briskly out of the church into a bright early fall morning. Who would tuck Alexandra in now, telling her she was all snug and safe and warm? Who would read her *Winnie the Pooh*? Who would sing her their favorite song ("The more we stay together, the happier we'll be")?

Logie removed the earplug and was thinking about doing the same for the wig when the limousine with tinted windows pulled up beside her. A rear window slid silently downward.

"I wouldn't do that this close to the church," said Wooton, who they said could read minds.

"Can't I have some time to myself?" Logie asked.

"No, you're operational now," Wooton said. "Get in."

She obeyed and closed the door behind her. The car moved away quickly. She couldn't see the driver because the passenger compartment was sealed off.

Wooton sat across from her, conspicuous for his brilliance and his girth. He never was seen without a three-piece suit and a silk tie and French cuffs. Back in his CIA days in the 1960s and 1970s, when he assassinated Viet Cong cadres and enlisted KGB agents as moles, Wooton had been slender. Lately, he enjoyed good food, good clothes, and living off his legend.

"How does it feel to witness your own funeral?" Wooton asked. His basso profundo, they said, resembled the voice of God. He did nothing to discourage the comparison.

"Awful," Logie said. "My poor daughter. I wanted to reach out and hug her and tell her Mommy would come get her soon."

Logie had wanted to remain nonoperational, to do the mission as if it were a normal job, to stay in her life with her daughter. No interruptions. Wooton had insisted otherwise. And he had leverage.

"How soon that is," Wooton said, "is up to you and your

considerable computer hacking skills. Right before the police arrest your husband, we will bring your daughter in, as I have promised."

"At least tell me where she's going to be," Logie said.

"You do not have the need to know," Wooton said with finality.

"Too bad your funeral sucked," said Dirk Donner, sitting beside her. He looked like a prizefighter who had taken one too many punches—broad face, broken nose, tree trunk neck, dulled sensitivity toward the pain he meted out. "I had a blast at my funeral. All my lady friends showed. They cried their heads off. I ate it up with a spoon." Senior Operative Dirk Donner, who Logie knew could be quite sweet, had these recurrent bouts of machismo, which came on unexpectedly like asthma attacks.

Logie pulled her skirt down. "I have qualms."

"Qualms?" Wooton said, as if he smelled a foul odor.

"My funeral was ten years ago," Donner said. "I've been operational ever since. And never looked back."

"I don't mean about going operational," Logie said. "I mean about what we are doing."

Wooton pursed his lips in annoyance. "I will have this conversation one time more and that is it." His voice belonged to a burning bush. "As the director of the Authority, I can do what I want with impunity as long as I don't embarrass the president. As far as anyone is concerned, we are embarking on a national security operation. The money we chance to make from it will be totally legitimate."

"I always lost my shirt in the stock market," Donner said. "I can handle betting on a sure thing."

Wooton said, "The three of us—and only the three of us—use that freedom judiciously for our own benefit. When we start making money in the stock market, anyone suspecting we are traitors taking bribes from a foreign government can easily be shown that our wealth is untainted."

"I have qualms," Logie said.

"I strongly encourage you to lose them," Wooton intoned.

"I know, but—"

"My dear woman," Wooton said with royal impatience, "your husband is *this close* to ruin. Your life hacking into others' computers for your government is a dead-end job."

"No, but—"

"And you had knowledge of your husband's shenanigans. You prepared your joint tax return, which neglected to include the money he skimmed from clients. If you went to prison along with your feckless husband, who would take care of your daughter? The Widow Moxley?"

How did he know Logie called her that? "I understand," said Logie, who liked the stability of federal employment and feared the layoff-prone private sector, which had destroyed her father's life and wrecked their family finances. "I could use a big wad of money for my Alexandra. But—"

"Come on, baby," Donner said. "Don't you fantasize about all the stuff you'll be able to buy? Cars, houses, boats. I'm gonna get the world's biggest hot tub at the place I'll buy at the beach."

"Don't call me 'baby,'" Logie said, and ignored Donner's exaggerated display of holding up his hands in sham surrender.

"I seldom choose one of our computer hackers to go operational," Wooton said. "You are the best. You agreed to go along with our plan. Now you are getting cold feet. This is unacceptable."

"I was fine until, right before the funeral, Dirk here told me we may have to hurt people to get what we want."

"I assure you we will hurt no one. Does that satisfy you?"

Logie mulled for a moment. "Yes."

"Are you aboard?" Wooton said.

"Yes," Logie said. "I am aboard, Director."

"Good," Wooton said with finality. Moving swifter than

his obesity would suggest possible, he grabbed her left hand and yanked off her wedding ring.

"What are you doing?" she shouted at him.

Wooton whirred down the window and tossed the ring out into the suburban woodlands rolling past. "That's done," he said.

"You go operational," the grinning Donner said, "your past is behind you. Way behind."

The director proceeded with his smooth discourse: "Our next move is to take possession of Goldring. We may have a complication involving Jack Faff."

"Do we get to kill Faff?" Donner said, mainly to upset Logie.

Wooton's heavily armored limo cruised south from Arlington along the asphalt river of I-95. Traffic was thick, but it moved. Behind and ahead of the director's vehicle were gun cars, each with four operatives like Donner and enough firepower to level an armored cavalry squadron.

"No one in the Authority outside the three of us will know what the true purpose of this mission is," Wooton said. "We will have the assistance of the entire organization in what is billed as an investigation of a possible terrorist operation. Do we understand each other?"

"Damn straight we do," Donner said.

"I understand, Director," Logie said tonelessly.

"Both of you will live at headquarters for the duration," Wooton said. "We have a special command post for this operation. Should the need arise, we have an alternate command post set up in New York, where our subjects are."

They sailed past the Washington Beltway and the roadside woodlands grew dense. The turning leaves had reached New York, she knew, and soon would hit Virginia. Logie loved to take Alexandra strolling through the woods in fall, with its impossibly intense palette of yellows, reds, and greens.

The motorcade veered off at the Valhalla exit and thundered along country lanes until it reached a fortified entrance with a smallish sign saying, FEDERAL RECLAMATION AUTHORITY. The first gate slid open and let them in. Then a guard in a blue, insignia-free uniform opened the car door and inspected everyone's right eyeball with a reading device. Even the director's. Their procession cleared the final gate and drove past the two watchtowers bristling with M-60 machine guns.

"I appreciate that you're not accustomed to being at headquarters," Wooton said to Logie.

Normally, she worked behind a steel-vaulted door in the Pentagon, where the Authority maintained a satellite office devoted to computer surveillance. Headquarters resembled a huge concrete flying saucer come to land in the Virginia woods.

"Know who built headquarters?" Donner said. "Jack Faff."

"That was a long time ago and he was kept out of the national security loop," Wooton said, sounding annoyed. "He had no idea what this was for."

"Let's hope so," Logie said, which earned her a hooded look from the director.

Once the car stopped in an underground garage, Logie and Donner trailed Wooton at a respectful distance through long corridors and numerous security checkpoints. Several top aides silently joined their procession. Wooton walked with regal aplomb. There were two guards outside the command post; inside was a phantasmagoria of computer and communications gear. Three blown-up photos covered much of one wall—photos of the Reiner sisters.

"Last night, Goldring was stolen and one of the sisters, Flo Reiner, was killed," Wooton said.

"Blew her head apart," Donner said.

"I have much to do," Wooton said and marched away operatically, his other minions in tow.

When they were alone amid the electronics and the Reiner pictures, Donner said to Logie, "So your husband and kid were there today?"

"Uh, *hello?* Yes. It was my funeral." Then she tried to be less touchy. "My plan is to relocate with my daughter once this is over. Wooton insisted I go operational. He has this control complex—maybe you noticed? Just as well, I'm deceased. I don't want my husband to find us once he gets out of prison. I'll have a new identity. Where's the bathroom?" She followed his thumb and walked to the adjacent room.

She stood over the sink and peeled off her foam latex nose and chin. She noticed that Donner was in the doorway, well-muscled arms folded.

"If you could shape a new life, what would you do different?" he said.

"Get a bigger bladder and better taste in men." She gave him a forbearing smile. "What the hell did you get me into?"

"I was only trying to help. I'm your friend, remember?"

"I'd better come out of this as rich as you say. My daughter deserves a good life."

"Once you agreed to your own fake funeral"—Donner made the shape of a gun with his hand—"the director could, at any time, arrange for you to have a real one. In the interests of national security." He gave a worried smile. "In the car, when you started to have cold feet, it was a good thing you came to your senses. Be careful, Logie."

Albert flipped open the laptop and lit up its screen.

He ignored his sister's worried phone call. The answering machine took the message and devoured it like a bug zapper. He never would listen to it.

"Oh, ho-ho, yes, yes, yes," he exclaimed as he delved into the mysteries of Goldring unfolding before him.

Goldring's screen told him to buy Corsine Industries, which very shortly would enjoy a huge price surge. Buy Corsine stock now when it was cheap. He cackled as he envisioned the dollar flood that would pour into his small apartment and lift him to heaven. First item he'd buy: the Barry Manilow boxed CD set. Manilow sung love tunes. Linda would like that.

"Rich, rich, rich. I'm going to be rich."

The window to his shabby apartment framed him from the outside like a TV screen.

Outside, eyes studied him as he giggled and murmured over Goldring. A perfect target.

CHAPTER FOUR

"How's it going, Rocky?" Karen said as she fished out a couple of quarters for the beggar, who seemed unusually glum. "Something wrong?"

"You in some kinda trouble, Karen?" Rocky asked after he palmed the coins. The beer was redolent on his breath, as usual, but he was far from his customary mellow self.

"I'm always in trouble, Rock. I'm in the trouble business." She had returned home to deposit the original copy of the Faff document there for safekeeping.

"Couple of guys was asking questions about you this morning, is all. I figured you was in a bad way with the law," said Rocky, who had had his scrapes with the gendarmes.

"The law? Why do you say that? What did these guys look like?"

"Like detectives. Dressed in suits, ties, like that. Maybe could be FBI. I didn't ask for no badges or nothing. As a second-class citizen, I know not to provoke them bastards with no smart mouth."

Sweeping her eyes along the street, Karen asked, "What were they after?"

"They asked if I knew you. I said yes. Then it was what times you came and went from your apartment building. I said I had no earthly idea. They didn't believe me and kept asking me and then said if I was lying, there'd be problems for me."

A frisson of fear crackled along her spine. "Would you be able to recognize them again?"

"Damn straight. They big mothers. You remember them good."

"If they show up, beat feet. I doubt they're the law." But who were they?

The Ford Escargot, the nickname Karen had for Frank's battered old Ford Escort, wheezed out of the city and down the Garden State Parkway. With fall arriving and the New Jersey beaches empty, traffic was thin. Storm clouds boiled overhead. A few drops speckled the windshield of the senior citizen car.

A New Yorker unused to driving, Karen hunched behind the wheel and poked along with the bravado of a Buddhist monk, ready for bad karma. Frank was a good friend to lend her his car. And a trusting one. Cars barreled past her as if daring fate. She already had passed two crash sites, full of flashing lights and ambulances. In America, according to polls she'd seen, the average person thought he was an above-average driver, in a class with Dale Earnhardt Jr. She marveled at the foolhardiness of the other drivers zooming past Mr. Escort. But then, they weren't foolish enough to be confronting mobbed-up Jack Faff.

Karen's husband, a Wall Street hotshot named Tim Bratton, drove a BMW. And because he was an above-average driver, Tim had managed to total three of its predecessors. In their divorce, Karen wanted none of Tim's possessions—

not his BMW, not their apartment, not his sailboat. She was settling for a nice but hardly sizable amount of money she'd put into a retirement account.

The cell phone trilled. It was Eudell. "Honey," her editor said, "you sitting down?"

"I'm behind the wheel of Frank's Ford Escargot, Eudell. Of course I am. What are Christian and Skeen up to now?"

"Well, you better pull over."

A rest stop came into view. She veered off the highway into its parking lot and stopped. "Okay. Done. What's the matter?"

That was when Eudell told her about Flo's murder. "Motive unknown. Cops aren't releasing any details. Once you get back from Faff, we want you to get on the murder story. The Reiners aren't talking to the press. But they know you and might open up to you."

Once the call had ended, she sat for a long while with the motor running and stared at nothing. A massive thunderclap rent the sky and a sizzling lightning bolt lit up the lot for a neon-white instant. Then a hard rain pelted the asphalt, making little silvery explosions on impact.

Flo was the least personable of the sisters. She thought the world was an evil place full of scoundrels out to get her. Ginny, the professor, existed on some extraterrestrial plane of integer fields. A lesbian who distrusted most men, she liked Karen a lot. And with Linda, there were always many men around. Linda was the one every non-gay woman wanted to murder. Men's heads were programmed to swivel like heat-seeking missiles in her direction.

Still, why would anyone want to kill any of the Reiners? They weren't that bad.

Linda sat with her elbows on the gunmetal-gray table and massaged her temples. The cops had Ginny in a nearby room. Given her older sister's trauma, Linda wanted to be with her during the questioning. But Detective Friday said procedure demanded that they be interviewed separately. River was somewhere down the hall.

For a full half-hour, Linda had been sitting alone in this room with the dark glass panel—obviously, from the TV police shows she'd seen, a two-way mirror. She had been sitting there with her thoughts of Flo and the horror on Reiner Capital's concrete floor. And with her thoughts about Goldring.

The door opened with a haunted house creak and Friday entered. He carried a Styrofoam coffee cup. "Want any? We just brewed a pot."

"No. No, thank you. No." Linda ran her hands over her hair. If the coffee cost less than four dollars and wasn't prepared by an overeducated barista, she wasn't interested.

Friday moved around to the other side of the table and straddled the turned-around chair he'd left thirty minutes before. "Sorry for the interruption. Something came up."

"Related to Flo?"

Disregarding her question, Friday continued with his own. "So this laptop computer is missing from your office, you say?"

They had been over this ground repeatedly. Linda had decided to report Goldring missing, figuring that the cops, thus alerted, might be able to get it back.

She looked at him dully as he sipped his substandard coffee. The short-sleeved shirt showed off his burly arms, one of which had a military tattoo with a grinning skull, a parachute, and the words: *Kill 'em all and let God sort 'em out*. With his round face, balding head, and rubbery belly, the detective wasn't an attractive man. But he certainly was a dogged and tough one. "Well," she said, weary, "since I haven't been able to do a thorough inventory of the office, I can't say nothing else was taken. But I didn't see the laptop."

At long last, Friday had a new question. And it set alarm bells ringing in Linda's head. "What was on this laptop?"

Linda tried not to vary her tone. "Oh, records of our trades. That sort of business. We'd really like to retrieve it. It's an old IBM ThinkPad. Nothing fancy. As I've indicated, it had a gold ring embossed on it, a replica of the ring Daddy gave Flo." She added, in hopes of steering the conversation in another direction, "My father is dead. My mother, too. We have no other relatives."

Friday's eyes narrowed. "Records of your trades, huh?" He stared at Linda as if she had said she weren't pretty at all.

"Yes, detective. Records of our trades. And we'd also use the laptop to place orders with E-Trade. That's an online stock brokerage service."

"I know what it is." Friday drank some more coffee and contemplated Linda silently for several painfully long moments. No, this wasn't the gaze of a man enjoying the sight of a beautiful woman; it was the gaze of a cop facing down a liar. Then, "Why would anyone want to steal an old laptop? And nothing else, not even your sister's wallet?"

"I wish I knew. Poor Flo."

"You wish you knew, huh?" More silent staring.

Linda drew herself up in anger. "Yes. Why are you treating me this way? Do you believe I killed my own sister? Should I bring in my lawyer? Is that it?"

Friday drained his cup with maddening nonchalance. "You have an alibi. We located Stefan the masseur, the man you said you were with around the time of your sister's death."

"Yes, and if you check phone records, you'll see that Flo and I talked to each other just before . . ." Linda shook her head. "I loved my sister."

With a palpable indifference to human sentiment, Friday pressed on. "We'll return to the laptop. Let's go back to possible enemies. We see you have a restraining order out on a certain individual."

"Yes. That's right." Linda felt relieved to move away from Goldring. "His name's Albert Niebel. Lives out in Queens. He met Flo at her previous job. They both were on the computer help desk at Formdex Corporation in midtown. When we set up our investing office, he'd come around to hang out. We thought he was harmless until he developed this crush on me. River told him to stay out, but Albert started sending me bouquets of roses. Usually five a day. Once, as many as ten."

"That's quite a crush," Friday said.

"Somehow, Albert got my home number, which is unlisted, at my old apartment. He kept calling, leaving long, rambling messages telling me how much he loved me. This got so bad I never picked up the phone at home. I had the number changed, but he found the new one. I can't say how. Nor could the phone company."

"Clever guy."

"Excuse me, detective," she said with queenly indignation, "it was frightening. River stopped him from coming by the office. Sometimes, Albert would follow me in the street. Once, I yelled at him to leave me alone. He slunk away and I thought that was the end of him. That night, I got another message on my machine from him. He called me a bitch and a whore and threatened to hurt me for 'torturing' him. His word. That was the last straw. I went to court and got the order. This was a month ago. Haven't heard from him since, thank God."

Friday nodded. "We're trying to track him down. He got fired at Formdex. But seems that, right before you girls set up shop in the stock biz, your sister Flo got fired from Formdex, as well."

Sighing, Linda said, "Flo had a checkered work history.

She had difficulty respecting authority. Once, her boss criticized her for not meeting a certain goal. She told him, 'Which one? The stupid one, the impossible one, or the one you forgot to tell me about?' "

"No kidding." Friday rifled through some papers in a folder on the table. "Flo served three months in jail for computer hacking." He arched an eyebrow.

"A harmless prank." Linda laughed without humor. "She broke into a government network. She was working for this agency and got angry at them for some reason."

"The agency, says here, is called the Federal Reclamation Authority. Never heard of it."

"She was in their trainee program. They fired her and prosecuted her. She was an angry misfit her entire life."

With a shake of his head, Friday said, "Why do I get the feeling that more's going on here than meets the eye?"

"I don't know what you mean, detective."

"Don't you? Maybe you can tell me why the front door of your office was unlocked around seven P.M. last night?"

"Excuse me? I don't follow you. We usually keep the door locked after business hours. Flo would be there into the night, typically. I'd pop in and out of the office during the day. Ginny would show up occasionally. You say the door was open?"

"Uh-huh," Friday said. "One of the girls in a nearby office was leaving around seven P.M., before anyone heard any shots. She noticed the door hanging open a bit. Your neighbors know about how it's usually closed and locked."

"I suppose. We don't mix with them much." Linda shook her head. "That makes no sense. River is very meticulous about keeping it locked."

"Uh-huh." Friday's phrasing reeked of skepticism. "Why do you need a receptionist if you do no work for anyone else, only invest for yourselves?"

"People come see us. Media mainly, after the magazine

story on us. I want us to appear professional. River looks nice. He's an actor. He can sing, even. This is about image."

"Image?" Friday stuck a tongue in his pudgy cheek. "He sing for your media visitors?"

A loud explosion erupted overhead and Linda jumped. "What the hell was that?"

Friday, who hadn't even twitched, offered a shrug. "Thunder. Bad storm was forecast. Maybe God's angry with somebody. I wonder who."

Driving through rain toward the shimmering facade of Faff's Lair, Karen felt her apprehension grow. Faff's casino grew larger as she approached in the rain. She had to admit that the tycoon's buildings were architecturally striking. While the critics dismissed them for their ostentation, Faff creations had remade the New York skyline. And here in Atlantic City, his massive casino hotel stood out among all the other gambling palaces lining the boardwalk like a McMansion in a trailer park. The Escort crept through the decrepit blocks leading up to the seaside gaming strip.

Jack Faff's casino dominated like something out of Fritz Lang's *Metropolis*. It was an eclectic mishmash: Oriental arches, Mideastern minarets, vast sweeps of glass, strange patches colored pink or green. The front entrance appeared to be the gaping maw of a dragon.

While Karen never had met Faff, she had read plenty about the man. How Faff had launched himself out of Long Island, where his father had made a pile constructing suburban tract housing. How Faff, using family contacts and financing, had bought a rundown Manhattan hotel in the depths of the city's 1970s fiscal crisis, when everyone thought New York was dead. How Faff, barely out of college, rammed the project past city zoning officials, crooked construction unions, and other obstacles to remake the old dump into the glittering Faff Crown Hotel. How Faff then went on from triumph to triumph until he had made more money than his father could have dreamed. And how Faff collected beautiful women the way boys do baseball cards. That wasn't hard, considering Faff was handsome, famous, and rich.

Karen knew she wouldn't qualify as a Faff girl. Most people called her cute, not beautiful—big dimples, big smile, thick dark brown hair and a gamine air. She hadn't lost that slight winter pudge before swimsuit season, and now it was October. Her husband used to call her pretty, yet hadn't for a long time. Frank, in his analytical way, had termed her attractive, a middle ground between beautiful and cute. She wanted to believe him.

Karen nosed Frank's car into the dragon's maw and out of the rain. The car stalled once it stopped; the moisture had gotten to the electrical system. A milling throng of gamblers was moving in and out of the wide door. The gaudy interior beckoned with its siren song of big money to be made at the tables, where the free booze sharpened the players' wits.

An old black man in red livery took her keys and assessed the battered heap with an amused, tight-lipped smile.

"In New York, we call this a city car," Karen explained. "You don't get the dings repaired because you don't want anyone to steal it. Guess what? This works."

"I bet it does," the parking attendant said with avuncular kindness. "Will you be staying long?"

"That depends on Jack Faff."

"Oh, are you that reporter? We've been told to be on the lookout for you."

"I'm her. I'm really early."

Shortly after the attendant made a call from a red wall phone, Solter Faff came out the front door. More nervous than usual—and usual was quite nervous—Jack Faff's younger brother gave Karen a limp handshake. "Jack will be down in a minute."

"In a minute? I need time to review the package of documents you have for me."

Solter licked his thin lips. He jerked his head around to ensure no one overheard. "Now's not a good time for that. I think Jack suspects me."

"He'll never know, Solter. I swore that to you and I keep my pledges." What must this poor guy have suffered from his brother to make Solter so willing to sabotage him by leaking company documents?

"Listen . . ." Solter bowed his head and pondered. "Get out of here, Ms. Glick. It's dangerous. Leave. Now."

"What?"

One of the casino-goers cried out in almost religious joy, "Hey, look! It's Faff. Jack Faff!"

Faff moved along the regal red carpet through his mirrored, gold-trimmed lobby, an immortal come down to mingle with badly dressed earthlings. The gamblers were in that unpleasant transition from middle-aged to elderly, but they behaved like teenagers around Faff. In his casino to lighten their wallets, they applauded what amounted to a free show. And all he did was walk and smile and wave tepidly. The assorted sordids kept clapping after he passed, their grins broad and genuine. The men with their globular bellies, the women sagging like month-old Christmas trees, they would tell their friends and relatives back home how they had been *this* close—*this* close—to the great Jack Faff. A few gamblers touched his sleeve. For luck.

Tonight Faff had dressed to show his wealth—an English-tailored suit on the compact frame, a silk handkerchief in the breast pocket, a rep tie around the multimillion dollar neck. Faff was two inches shorter than Karen, but he acted like a giant out of a Grimm's fairy tale. He sure seemed big on those billboards.

"Major Darcy," Faff boomed to the old parking attendant, "you're looking well tonight. How am I looking?"

"Very well, sir," Darcy said with dignity. "Your car will be right out."

"I got a thought for the evening, Darcy," he said. "Don't believe what you read."

"I'll keep that in mind, sir."

"It's all lies," Faff roared.

"I'm not into lying, sir."

Karen thrust herself forward and offered her hand. "Jack Faff," she said, "I'm Karen Glick."

Faff's eyes registered Karen for an instant with no expression. Then he turned to his brother and made a turning motion with his hand.

The gamblers, clustered about as though watching a play, murmured among themselves.

A cream Jaguar XJ8 growled up. Its sleek body gleamed in the galaxy of casino lights. A young attendant jumped out and held the driver's side door.

Jack Faff turned his attention to Karen. The tycoon's eyes, bloodshot from late-night indulgences, weren't friendly. Nor was his forced smile with its bleached-white display of Hollywood caps. His handshake was far too aggressive.

"Nice shake you got there," she said.

Faff kept pumping her hand, painfully increasing the pressure. "This the hand you use to write your lies?"

"I type with both," Karen said. "You can let go now."

Solter and the attendants were herding people back inside.

Faff released the reporter's hand. "We're going for a little ride. Hop in."

"It's raining and slippery out," Karen said, Solter's warning flashing in her head. "Wouldn't we be better off in the casino?"

"I paid seventy grand for my new Jag and I want to see how she performs," Faff blared. "I'm a busy man with little time to waste. You want an interview, you ride with me."

Major Darcy held the passenger-side door for Karen, who slid into the leather bucket seat and snapped on her seatbelt. Hard rain popped on the pavement beyond the casino entrance.

No sooner had Faff jumped behind the wooden wheel than he blasted the Jag into the soaking night with a dual-cam V-8 vroom. He slammed through the gears and the car flashed along the streets, sending up great geysers of spray when it hit puddles. Guffawing grandly, Faff fishtailed around corners and stomped on the accelerator. He wore no seatbelt.

"Shouldn't you slow down?" Karen shouted. The wipers had trouble keeping up with the torrent of rain.

"Why?" Faff shouted back.

A cop car's siren and flashing lights came up from behind. Faff slid the Jag over to the side. When the slicker-clad officer appeared at Faff's window, Faff said, "Is there a problem, Harry?"

"Oh, I didn't realize it was you, Mr. Faff. Have a good night, sir." He touched the bill of his hat and retreated.

The Jag zoomed off like a rocket launch. Karen's head jerked back at the sudden acceleration. "So the way out of a ticket is to ask if there's a problem?"

"I hear you made Linda Reiner famous," Faff called over the motor.

"Yes, I . . ."

"Linda is beautiful."

"She's . . . cute. Now—"

"Shame about her sister. Why are they so successful?"

"I don't know. Now if we could . . ." She fumbled out her notebook and pen. Taking notes would be tough under these conditions.

"Linda's a hottie. She's coming to my new building opening. A masked ball. Party of the year. Party of the century. A hundred bucks says I bang her that night."

Karen had to restrain herself. "I don't care about your personal life. I want—"

"You just want to ruin my life, that's all."

"Let's talk about your financial situation."

"Let's talk about yours," Faff said over the engine and the rain and the wind. "You drive a piece of crap. Your husband has money, but he's divorcing you. You couldn't be making much as a reporter. Let's say I paid you ten grand for consulting services. How'd that be?"

"You had me looked into, huh? So I'd write a cream puff story about you, saying you are in fine financial shape. This the idea?"

"You're not that dumb," Faff said. "I can cut a check when we return to the casino. We got a deal?"

"No deal. I don't take bribes. Now, about your finances. I sent you an e-mail with my findings and I'd like you—"

"Are you nuts? Make it twenty grand. Everyone has a price."

"Let's talk about the debt on Faff Towers. I understand—"

"I guess you *are* that dumb," Faff said. "Too bad. Your last chance. We keep driving."

They had cleared the decayed urban wastes of Atlantic City and were heading deep into the country in warp drive. House lights became fewer and fewer. Dark pine stands lined the two-lane road. No one else was out.

Visibility was minimal. Heavy raindrops pounded on the car roof like bullets. The headlights played madly over the pine branches, which moved closer and closer to the road.

"Where are we going?"

"You're doing this because of what I represent, aren't you?" Faff shouted at top volume, over the rampant rain and the roaring RPMs.

"What are you talking about?"

"Your husband's on Wall Street, and he's throwing you out of the good life. No more big apartment, no more BMW. So you're getting back at him, using me as a proxy. Sick."

True, Karen now lived in a cramped studio apartment beneath the thunderous tread of her overhead neighbor. True, she used to live in a soundproofed luxury floor-through, where the only noises were the burble of the brass Gaggia cappuccino maker in the well-appointed kitchen, the clink of silver on fine Lenox bone china in the baronial dining room, the strains of Bach from the omnipresent Bang & Olufson speakers—and the obnoxious utterances of her husband, Tim.

"I'm doing this because I have evidence you're in big financial trouble, Jack Faff."

"How dare you doubt my finances." Faff was screaming now.

"And how dare you cheat your investors," Karen shouted back.

"You're nothing." Faff pounded the steering wheel each time he hollered the word: "Nothing, nothing, nothing!"

The wet pine branches enveloped them in a green instant, and the Jaguar lost contact with the ground. The airborne car rolled over and over at an insane speed, headlight beams spinning. Right before impact, Karen found herself thinking of her husband.

CHAPTER FIVE

The warmth of the blood that trickled over her lips. The cold of the rain against her skin. The dark that wrapped around her. The smell of oil burning.

As she slowly let the sensations sink into her brain, Karen realized that she should get moving. Her hands explored around herself to regain her bearings. She was still in her car seat, still buckled in. But now she faced upward at a forty-five degree angle. There was broken glass all over. A massive object had protruded into the car. She pawed it. Rough stone. A wet boulder had smashed through the windshield. But it came no more than a foot into the car.

She was so tired.

The acrid burning smell had grown more intense.

She groped to her left and found a body. Suit fabric. Skin. Slippery wetness—blood. It groaned.

"Jack?" Karen said.

Another groan. Then, "Shit."

The burning smell intensified. Now Karen could see a

glow from beyond the smashed windshield. She could hear fire.

"Jack, you've got to get out of here." Karen's right shoulder ached. She popped her seatbelt open. The harness snapped back like a lash.

In the growing glow, Karen now could see Faff draped over the wooden steering wheel, facing away. The passenger compartment seemed to have shrunk. Karen tried opening her door but it would budge just a few inches. Bracing her legs, she shoved with her entire might. The door resisted for a while, but at last, with a creak, slowly folded outward. She could see the ground three feet below.

She turned back to Faff. "Can you move, Jack?"

"Lemme alone," Faff slurred.

"The car's on fire. I've gotta get you out." Karen maneuvered behind the man and hooked him under his armpits. Grunting and jerking him—hell, he was small, but not light—she slid Faff past the gearshift. Faff's head lolled back as Karen hopped to the ground. There was blood on his chest.

Small flames were dancing along the passenger compartment carpet, where their feet had just been. The fire beneath the crumpled hood was like a cauldron's. It crept out and started eating the paint job. Very shortly it would reach the gas tank in the back.

Karen hooked Faff under the armpits again and, cradling the lolling head against her non-aching shoulder, she yanked the man out of the car. They toppled together to the sodden, pine-needled earth. The rain wasn't coming down as hard now.

Faff moaned.

"Jack, can you walk?"

"Lemme alone."

The seats they had just occupied were now burning.

Karen was sopping, though more from sweat than rain.

Ignoring the pain in her shoulder, she dragged him back, back, back. Past whipping pine branches and spiky bushes. Once, Karen almost lost her balance. She stepped over the log and bumped Faff's feet across it. Back, back, back.

The flaming silhouette of the Jaguar wasn't far enough away. Karen tried to drag her burden faster. She panted wildly. The entire car had become a blazing pyre of—

"Christ." Karen dropped Faff and leapt atop him. Then came a Hiroshima-size explosion. She tried to cover both her head and Faff's with her arms. Fiery meteors of flaming metal fell on either side of them.

Calm followed, broken only by a slight hissing from the car's direction and small flame crackles and the rain's *pitter-pat*.

Karen looked around. "Rain won't let the fire spread," she said. As she watched, the car fire swirled hungrily. "Hey, maybe someone will see it."

Faff moaned again.

Gently turning him over, Karen asked, "You okay?"

Faff opened his bloody mouth before speaking. It hung ajar for a moment. Then, "I'm pretty damn far from okay."

Karen squeezed Faff's limbs, clad in shredded tailoring. "Does this hurt anywhere?"

Faff's eyes bugged. He let out a scream and pulled himself into the fetal position.

"What is it, Jack?"

"My heart," Faff said through gritted teeth. Veins bulged in his neck and forehead. "This is the first spasm. More on the way. It happened before."

Karen jumped to her feet. "Listen, I'm going for help."

"Sit down," Faff gasped. "We're miles from nowhere. Stay with me. I'm dying."

"You're not dying. Now you wait while I . . ."

"Sit down," Faff managed. "I want to talk about Goldring."

* * *

"His name is Albert Niebel," Logie said. She passed the director a replica of Niebel's driver's license, which contained a photo of a fish-faced man with sparse, straw-like hair and squinty eyes. Niebel didn't look like a killer. A stalker, maybe.

A large, comfortable, overstuffed chair had arrived at the command post, right before Wooton's visit. It was clear only Wooton would sit in it. From his chair, the director examined the picture and frowned. "We have him under surveillance?" he asked Donner.

Donner, who leaned against the wall like a cowboy, grinned with confidence. "One operative has acquired him. He's outside Niebel's apartment in Queens."

"One?" Wooton said, deep voice resonating through the room.

Cocky grin wavering, Donner said, "Yes, sir. A full team is on the way."

"Why is a full team not in place now?" Donner's face darkened.

"Uh, well, it's like . . . You understand . . ." Donner's grin had vanished. He removed his hands from his pockets and stood erect.

"We didn't immediately know where he lived," Logie said from where she sat quietly beside a computer screen. "The driver's license and other identification I uncovered had him living at his sister's address. She subsidizes him. Pays his therapy bills, which are considerable. And his rent. Where do I get a sister like that? I had to access his real address from his tax returns on file with the Internal Revenue Service. That took me a while."

"We have to be a lot tighter," Wooton intoned. "The New York Police Department will be after him for questioning."

"The police will have trouble finding Niebel," Logie

said. "The restraining order has him living at his sister's, also."

"A lot tighter means a lot tighter," Wooton said.

"We also know," Logie added, "that Niebel opened an account with Merrill Lynch Direct, using ten thousand dollars he borrowed from his sister, Mimi. And we know that he just bought a huge amount of Corsine Industries stock with that money, making the trade online from his apartment. He doesn't get out much, except for shrink visits and stalking."

Wooton smoothed his silk tie. "When Niebel does leaves his apartment, our team will gain surreptitious entry. They will take Goldring."

"Will comply, Director," Donner said.

"His cockroaches will leave before he does," Logie said. "I'm telling you, he's into this laptop. He hasn't been offline the entire day."

"Hey, I got an idea," Donner said, grin back in place. "Why don't we start cashing in on Goldring? Why don't we buy a batch of Corsine shares, like Niebel's doing?"

"We will not tip our hand early," Wooton said. The director made a show of consulting his Philippe Patek watch, the last present his wife had bought him. It was three years old. "I'm late for dinner." After he left, two workmen under armed guard came and removed his chair. Then Logie and Donner were locked in the command post together, alone again.

Donner hovered over Logie as she tapped on a computer keyboard. "Thanks for helping. Wooton is a pain in the butt."

Logie sighed. Sometimes she feared that if Donner blew his nose too hard, he'd blow out his brains. "Nobody's going to hurt Niebel, right?"

Faff was probably right. They were far from anyone else. Driving in the car, they hadn't been past any house lights for miles. Still, if Karen ran back along the road, maybe a car would pass she could flag. Eventually, she would reach a house.

"Nobody uses the road we were on," Faff said after hearing her suggestion. "I brought you out here for a reason."

"Where were you taking me?"

"Never mind."

Faff said the chest pain was dull now. Maybe that was a good sign. Karen had elevated his feet with a log to ensure he got sufficient blood to the heart and head. Removing his torn jacket, Karen said, "How about I construct a lean-to shelter to keep the rain off you?"

"Forget that," Faff said. How odd to hear him speak softly. "Rain feels good. It's not coming down hard anymore."

"I don't want you to get cold. How about I bring you back beside the car? The car won't explode twice. Keep you warm."

The car fire leapt and crackled with demonic energy, sending shadows flailing. Ghostly mist twisted coldly around the pines. The spooky night lay heavy with rain.

Faff waved away the idea. "I had you looked into, all right. They say you're a lightweight. Doesn't make sense you digging into my life, stirring up trouble."

"Enough with the compliments. Your snoops missed that I broke the Billionaire Boys Club story. Did you send some guys to my neighborhood asking questions?"

Faff said, "They call this forest the Pine Barrens. There's a local legend. Ever hear of the Jersey Devil? They named a sports team after him, like he's a joke. He's no joke. He haunts these woods. He flies above the treetops by night. He swoops down from the sky and carries people off. This is an evil place. Evil. And I'm dying in it."

"Jack, I'll be right back."

"Sit down, damn you," Faff barked and grimaced from the effort. Then, more gently, "Sit down, please."

Karen, who was halfway up, reluctantly complied.

"You know about Goldring and how it can predict the market?" Faff said.

"I've heard. And I believe that about as much as I believe I could win a fortune at your roulette table."

"Linda's shrewd about human nature, but she's no stock market genius. The college professor sister is into higher theoretical math or some bullshit. Not stock prices. And the one who got killed didn't have a lot on the ball. How did they do it?"

"Maybe they hired the Jersey Devil as a consultant and he brought a kit."

Faff patted his aching chest. "A computer program that predicts what stock is going to rise? That's impossible. But these girls created that. Goldring was going to save my ass. Now someone has stolen it, and I needed to get it"

"They stole the laptop? When Flo was murdered?" Karen said. Faff nodded. "So you admit you are in the soup financially?"

"Hell, yes. I owe a ton of money to the banks for the casino, and the casino is barely bringing in enough money to handle the interest payments. That'd be okay if I didn't have Faff Towers to worry about. See, I borrowed a whole boatload to build Faff Towers. I can't cover that interest tab and I'm not getting the buyers. The damn condos cost too much. Every one has Italian marble in it. I can't drop my prices, though. How would that look? Hell, you know all this. You sent me that e-mail with your questions about my finances."

"Jack, I didn't have enough evidence on you. Just a preliminary worksheet." She wasn't sure why she was admitting this, but she felt an odd compassion for him.

"Before I die," Faff said, "tell me how you found out

what you did. I don't understand that. Did someone betray me? Who?"

"Jack, I'm going for help. Just wait here."

The sound of engines came from out of the darkness.

"Someone is coming," Karen exulted. "They must've spotted the car fire." She ran, slipping past the trees, heading for what she took to be the road and calling, "Help, help!" Vehicle lights shone through the branches and made more shadows.

Several flashlights bobbed in the distance.

"Over here," Karen called.

Five men appeared, specters wafting amid the pines. One put his beam on Karen's face, dazzling her.

"Over here," she cried and ducked out of the beam. She waved for them to follow. "A man is hurt. We need an ambulance."

The flashlights played over Faff's huddled form.

"You hurt, Jack?" one of the men shouted with a foreign accent.

"Mikhail," Faff said, "what does this look like to you? Nap time?"

Mikhail aimed the flashlight at his own face for Karen to see. He was a large man in a black leather jacket. In the hobgoblin glow of the flashlight, she saw he had a fierce black beard and slicked-back black hair and very long, sharp teeth that could bite off a rat's head. He advanced toward her, walking as if he enjoyed stepping on things.

His men followed him, a wolf pack with smoldering coal eyes.

"This," Karen said, "is not Triple A, is it, Mr. Beria?"

"You that smart-ass Glick bitch, huh?" Mikhail said, serpent-sly. "We been waiting to meet you."

CHAPTER SIX

Faff regained some of the old force in his voice. "Get me out of here first," he said.

Mikhail Beria turned to his men. "Vlad, Leonid." He gave instructions in Russian.

Vlad and Leonid, both hulking creatures, helped Faff slowly to his feet. Beria was tall, but his two gangster underlings were taller. They began to walk slowly away.

"You forgot one thing, Jack," Karen called after them.

The developer looked over his shoulder. "What?"

"To say 'thanks.'"

"You had your chance," Faff said. They shuffled onward.

Mikhail pushed his bristly face into Karen's. The Russian's breath was rank. "You keep your big mouth shut." Karen's nasal passages wished that dictum applied to Mikhail. "We was gonna do you at a place down the road until we saw the fire. But we do you here." He gave instructions to one of the two remaining brutes, called Nikita.

Nikita carried a satchel that the other thug rummaged through. The satchel clinked—metal on metal.

"I got a better idea," Karen said with more bravado than she felt. "Let's don't and say we did."

"Shut up," Mikhail said. "Josef?"

Josef produced a long pair of garden shears from his bag.

Karen's mouth had become incredibly dry. Could she make a break into the woods?

"Nobody writes bad shit about Jack," Mikhail said. "Josef?"

The bear-like Josef circled behind her. He was the biggest of them.

"I hope Jack has paid you guys up front," Karen said, talking in a vain bid to buy time, surprised at what she heard her dry mouth saying. "He's having a hard time with money."

Josef's huge paws clamped her upper arms. Karen's heart raced so fast she barely noticed the pain Josef's grip sparked in her hurt shoulder.

Mikhail fondled Karen's right ear, almost lovingly. "Doesn't seem you hear too good. Told you to shut up. Maybe your ears don't work. We gonna take one off and give it good inspection."

"I can hear you fine," Karen quavered.

"You got a smart mouth," Mikhail said. "Woman do not talk back to me."

"Maybe it's time—" That was when Mikhail punched Karen in the stomach. Josef let go of her. Karen dropped to her knees on the soggy earth, wheezing and fighting for breath. She heard commotion overhead, punctuated by Russian curses. In her pain, she imagined that the Jersey Devil was hovering above them, talons ready to pounce.

Then at the edges of her agony-squinting eyes, she saw the flashes of new lights. When she could unbend herself, there was a uniformed guy with a flashlight crashing through the brush toward her. No one else was around.

"You all right, miss?" The guy was a cop. His shoes were patent leather.

"I've been better," Karen wheezed.

"An ambulance is en route. Where are you hurt?"

"I'm fine. Wind knocked out of me. Where's Faff?"

"My partner is tending to Mr. Faff," the cop said. "You two are lucky. A camper off in the woods heard the crash and saw the fire. He phoned in to us on his cell. Had good grid coordinates for us on his map. The fire was like a beacon, driving out. Lucky."

"Yeah. Lucky. Where'd the other characters go?"

"Can you walk?"

Holding her aching stomach, Karen haltingly followed the cop through the trees and up a hill to the road. The patrol car's roof strobe was bright, rivaling the burning Jaguar below. The other officer knelt beside Faff, who sat on the ground holding his knees.

Faff eyes flared when they caught sight of Karen Glick.

"Where are those two men with Mr. Faff?" asked the policeman accompanying her.

"It's funny," his partner said. "Three other white males came charging out of the woods. They told me they were going for help. I ordered them to stand fast, but they didn't comply. I decided to stay with Mr. Faff. They all five jumped in a four-by-four and took off." He read the other cop's disapproving expression. "Listen, I got their plates. If we need them for witnesses."

"Forget them," Faff said. "They were good Samaritans. The real problem is this scum here—Karen Glick."

Karen straightened up at this. "What are you talking about?"

Faff jabbed an index finger at the reporter, as if shooting psychic bullets. "This piece of garbage. She insists on driving my new Jaguar, which I let her do to be nice. Tells me she never gets to drive a decent car and her husband is taking the BMW in the divorce. I feel sorry for her. But she starts driving my new Jag like a crazed weasel. Way, way too fast. Especially on a rainy night. I tell her to slow down. She keeps shouting how much she hates me. Then the wack job drives off the road and smashes up my Jag. You'll pay for this, lady."

"What are you saying?" Karen looked at the cop beside her to see how this information registered. The cop kept a stoic face.

"You're pathetic," Faff continued. "Then the car catches fire. She starts to panic. I haul her out before the thing explodes. I get a heart attack from the effort. And does she help? All she can do is cry. She'd have died if I hadn't saved her."

"How can you lie like this?" Karen said, and took a step toward Faff. "My God."

The cop clamped a restraining hand on her wrenched shoulder, which hurt some more. "You'll get a chance to give your statement after you're examined at the hospital, miss," he said. The sarcastic twist he now gave to the word "miss" showed that Karen's status had dropped faster than a first-time gambler's stake at the blackjack table.

"You'll pay for this," said Faff, the king of Atlantic City. "Pay till it hurts."

The swarm of doctors summoned from their homes kept everyone out of the hospital's VIP suite for hours. At last they finished, and Faff ordered them to go. Only Solter and Mikhail could come in.

Faff, wan in his medical gown, was sitting up in his chrome-railing bed. First light seeped through the drawn blinds. The developer felt restless, caged. "I hate hospitals," he said.

"We've got the A.C. mayor, county freeholders, the county prosecutor, state legislators, outside hoping to convey their best wishes," Solter told his brother.

"Let them wait," Faff growled. "I pay them enough." He swept his hand dismissively at his white-walled surroundings. "How much money did I give this stupid hospital? Damn doctors insist I only had mild angina, maybe brought on by the crash, exacerbated"—he winced at the fancy word they had used—"by bruised ribs when my chest hit the steering wh—the dashboard. Glick was driving. No heart attack, they claim. But our family has a history of them. Pop-pop died of a massive coronary. Uncle Stan dropped dead at the racetrack from another one. Hell, I've had pains before."

"That was never substantiated as heart disease," his brother said. As usual, Solter was maddeningly unable to say what Jack wanted to hear.

"Don't argue with me, Solter. I want some real doctors. New York doctors to check me out."

"Yes, Jack." Finally, Solter delivered what Jack wanted: slavish obedience. "I'll fly them down here right away."

"Now, what's happening with that chick, Glick?"

"Minor facial lacerations from windshield glass and a shoulder bone bruise," Solter said. "Treated and released by the hospital."

"Released? I gave explicit orders—"

"Jack, Jack. She's in police custody. They're holding her pending arraignment on charges stemming from the accident."

Making a fist, the developer said, "I want the locals to throw the book at her. Since Mikhail didn't take care of her." He gave the Russian, who had been standing pillar-like next to the reedy Solter, a withering stare, as though Mikhail were to blame for the car crash. "The cops saw you out in the woods."

"We are in good shape, Jack," Mikhail said. "No problem with the law people here."

"They got your license plate when you got the hell out of Dodge, back in the woods. I don't want your name linked to mine. I could lose my casino license if that happened. Are we clear?"

The gangster, not used to kowtowing to anyone, hesitated a moment. Then, acquiescing to Faff's superior economic position, said, "We are clear, Jack. Not to worry. The SUV we used was stolen. Been ditched, this SUV."

"None of the officials, like the prosecutor, spotted you coming into this hospital room, right? Casino owners can't be associated with criminals."

"I'm glad to see you, too, Jack," the gangster said, getting back some of this own. "No, I slipped in like a spirit."

"Like a spirit," Jack said impatiently, beginning to tire of trafficking with underlings.

"Jack is afraid of ghosts," Solter said. "Has he ever told you about the Jersey Devil?"

Jack silenced his brother with a glare. "Well, it's a good thing this reporter was just bluffing me, but I want to keep her bottled up. Let's get to the most important stuff. What's going on with Goldring?"

Solter started to speak, but Mikhail talked over him. "We located this Albert Niebel. We got our boys in his neighborhood in Queens, ready to take the laptop computer from him. But here we might have some problem."

"Problem?" Jack Faff roared, the old arrogance fully restored. "Problem is not a word I understand. What's the big problem about breaking in and grabbing the laptop?"

"It is not that simple, Jack. We are not alone. A bunch of other men are staking out the place. Not good."

"What?" Faff exploded.

"Jack, keep calm," Solter cautioned. "Your condition—"

"Shut up, Solter. Is it the New York cops?"

"Not the cops," Mikhail said. "We got a good spy with the cops, and he says the cops do not know where this Niebel guy lives. We think feds are involved. These men look like feds."

"For Christ's sake," Faff yelled.

"Maybe you can tell me what's in this computer," Mikhail said.

"Maybe you," Faff said hotly, "can concentrate on grabbing the thing before anybody else does. What am I paying you for?"

"You pay me nothing."

"Get to work."

The Atlantic City jail wasn't what the likes of Mrs. Tim Bratton was used to. But then, Karen told herself, she no longer ran with the high society types, who were served drinks at bars, not serving time behind bars. The concrete floor held a suspicious-looking puddle and the long wooden bench where she sat was coated with an odd sticky substance. Karen's pants had so many rips and stains from the crash that she didn't care what she sat on, provided that it didn't seep through to her butt.

"What you staring at?" demanded the only other inmate in the female holding tank, way down the bench. She had spiky hair and stringy arms, covered with a swirl of tattoos. The well-illustrated arms held her knees to her chest.

"Nothing," Karen said, hoping she remembered some moves from her days as a teenager boxing in a gym with her tomboy pal. Not that the tattooed woman would obey the rules of the Marquis of Queensberry.

"You calling me nothing?" the woman barked. But she hadn't budged yet.

"I didn't say that."

The beefy guard trudged by, a woman with sufficient

upper-body strength to bench press three hundred pounds. She gave the two prisoners the fish eye, and the tattooed girl responded by flipping the guard the bird. The guard lumbered off.

"Jesus, your face," the tattooed girl said to Karen. "You been in a cat fight?"

"Car accident."

The tattooed girl uncoiled herself, sauntered down to Karen's end, and plunked down a little too close. She had toxic BO. "You drunk?"

"Not me driving."

The girl's face lit up like a crack bong. "Hey, wait. You're the one who wrecked Jack Faff's Jag."

"Jack Faff wrecked Jack Faff's Jag."

"Hoooooooo-ey. You are totally fucked." The tattooed girl got up and moved away. "I was gonna mess with you a little, but I don't want to touch your skanky self. You are bad luck." She retreated to the bench's far end. "I want none of that, babe."

The guard hulked into view. "Your lawyer and your editor are here to see you," she announced to Karen.

"Eudell Mancuso?" Karen said.

"Name of Gene Skeen."

Karen turned to the tattooed girl. "You might be right about my luck."

Drained, Linda paced around her patio and tried to think straight. Sleep had been impossible. The sun was warm and friendly, but occasional breezes kept gusting past, chilling her through her thin T-shirt, then departing like a bad lover. She leaned against the balustrade and surveyed the spires and rooftops of the city, vast canyons of sun-gleaming glass, a kingdom of giants. The Faff buildings stood out.

Trying to get the police to release Flo's body for burial

was difficult enough. Linda's lawyers would get back to her on that. And her sister's remains were the least of her problems.

The cell phone, sitting on the wrought-iron table, trilled. Linda reluctantly took the call.

It was Ginny, not the lawyers with more excuses. "Are you sure we're safe?" her sister quailed. "If Albert, or whoever killed Flo, could get into the office, he could get in anywhere."

"I told you to come stay with me," Linda said. "This building has a doorman. There's security here. Your walk-up apartment has none. Nor does your campus office."

"I have a duty to my students not to cancel class or office hours," Ginny said with the maddening self-righteousness she had learned from their mother.

"We need to be together at a time like this," Linda said. "It's us against everyone."

"What about that new boyfriend of yours?" Ginny said. "Can he help?"

"He's busy."

Ginny liked her world to be one of certainties, much like math. Irrationality and chaos threw her more than most. "Detective Friday kept going on and on about why the Reiner Capital office door was left open. I mean, why was it? River keeps it locked at night."

"Listen, if you won't come here, I'm coming up to Columbia to be with you. How about that?"

"I never trusted River," Ginny said. Unable to appreciate male good looks, Ginny had objected to Linda's hiring an ornamental male receptionist. Flo, although she treated River poorly, liked having him around to ogle. Ever the actor, River had bathed his three bosses in charm. With Flo, that was tough.

A police helicopter, lights winking, scooted over the thrusting towers of New York power. The visible symbol of

the cops, who should be protecting the well-fed folks working below. Detective Friday had shrugged off Linda's fears
about the possible Albert threat.

"I'm sure we can trust River. Flo's death devastated him."

"He's an actor, Linda. Remember that. Maybe he *acted*
devastated. He was around us every day. He could have
picked up what Goldring does. Maybe it wasn't Albert.
Maybe River took Goldring and killed—"

"Don't talk about it on the phone, for God's sake. And
make sure you don't talk to the press. We want nothing
about you-know-what in the media."

"Isn't it suspicious how long the police kept River for
questioning?" After Ginny and Linda were finished at the
station, Linda had insisted they wait for River. They did until one cop told them River would be staying for a long time
and they'd better go.

"I'm sure the fact he was the last to see Flo alive has
more to do with that," Linda said. She had to admit River's
behavior had been odd; after returning home, she had left
a message on his machine and he hadn't called her. River,
like all men, jumped to obey Linda's every whim.

"River is bigger and stronger than Albert," Ginny said.
"I'm scared, Linda. Are we safe from River?"

"What do you mean?"

"Well, Danielle, one of my students, told me she saw
River on the quad. She'd met him before, when she
dropped off a paper at Reiner Capital. He asked where I
was. She said he was real worked up, crazy, wild, scary. She
gave him wrong directions, but—"

"Call campus security."

"I did, a half-hour ago. Nothing yet."

"Hold on. I'm on my way."

CHAPTER SEVEN

Ginny's study overlooked the Low Library dome. Low's sweeping steps were swarming with students. A lemony late-afternoon light gave the campus an odd luster. Autumn shadows cast by Columbia's fine buildings lengthened and deepened.

"Still no campus security guard?" Linda said.

"I called back and got voice mail."

"River's probably harmless."

Plunking a mug of tea before her sister, Ginny said, "River gives me the creeps. He's too vain for a man. I was glad when he went crazy at Albert, because that kept Albert away from the office. But think. What if it was River who killed . . . ?"

"Come on," Linda said, and sipped the tea. Too hot. She put it down and smiled for Ginny. "We don't know for sure who did it. All we know is that whoever it was took Goldring."

"Linda, this River is a nut. He has that little mirror he

preens into. And what about that story he sent some guy to the hospital for questioning his sexuality in a bar?"

"Ginny, my gaydar would've spotted him for non-hetero. As for the nut part, River is a little high-strung. He's a nice fellow. Performers are performers. Most of them don't have two nickels to rub together. He needed a job. One better than waiting tables."

"Remember that funny reporter from *Profit*—when she took us to the restaurant and we weren't getting any service? She called out, 'Actor,' and a waiter came."

"We need a plan to get Goldring back," Linda said.

"Why?" Ginny put down her mug. "We already have plenty of money. Let the horrible person who stole it, keep it. I consider it cursed now."

"Cursed? This from the rational mathematician. This is about more than anonymous comfort, Ginny. We should be legends. And the only means of achieving that is to keep winning in the market. Year after year."

"Maybe you want to be a legend," Ginny said. "Not me."

"You wouldn't mind a few flashbulbs going off as you pass by," Linda said teasingly. "With people saying, 'Gosh, there goes Ginny Reiner.' I've sat in on your classes; you love being the center of attention. Don't tell me you don't."

"My students aren't taking my picture for the society page," Ginny said. "I had qualms from the start about Goldring. Linda, we are breaking securities laws with this program. We could go to prison."

"If Detective Friday retrieves Goldring for us, how would he ever find out how it works?"

"Why are we talking about Goldring and not about Flo?"

"You're right," Linda said.

Freddy, Ginny's student assistant, barged in without knocking. "You need me for anything else, Professor Reiner?" He wore Army surplus camouflage pants, a flannel shirt, and a sleepy-eyed expression best suited for hanging out at the mall, eyeing babes. His droopy eyes fixed on Linda.

"Knock, please, Freddy," Ginny said, not for the first time and not for the last. "No, I'm fine. See you tomorrow." Freddy went into excuses why he'd be late, which involved an overdue paper or some such. Ginny waved him away. After he closed the door, Ginny said, "He wants to be a mathematician."

"He looks like he'd have trouble counting his toes."

"No, the future isn't bright for Freddy. The other day, I asked him what were the chances, if there were twenty-three people in a room, that two of them had the same birthday. He didn't know."

"Hell, who knows the answer to that? Who cares?"

"It's fifty percent . . ." Ginny began. The door swung open. "Freddy?"

It wasn't Freddy.

River stepped inside. He looked unkempt and evil.

Ginny let out a yelp of terror.

"You want me?" he snarled. "You want to screw with me? Well, I'm here to screw with you."

"River," Linda said, trying to be calm, "no one wants to—"

"One more word out of you and I'll kill you, bitch."

Kingman Wooton lived in Georgetown in a superbly boned old house from the 1830s. William Seward, Lincoln's secretary of state, had lived there. Wooton settled his portly self into his favorite Eames chair in the drawing room and watched the rosebushes outside the French doors, once a lovely September batch of flowers. They were wilting now. A wedge of Mont d'Or festered beside him, slowly shrinking as he dissected it.

A laptop, far more advanced than Goldring, sat next to the death-on-a-plate cheese.

The house had been bought with his wife's money. The

Colonel, as they called Erica's father, never let Wooton forget that old Southern wealth supported their lifestyle. "Lucky for you, boy, you're a god on my daughter's dollar," said the Colonel, who liked his whiskey a little too much, to his son-in-law every Christmas. Thankfully, he was dead. But after the Colonel passed on the year before, Wooton learned that the old fool had been profligate and his depleted estate had very little to pass on to Erica.   •

Wooton could hear his wife repeating over and over: "What are we going to do, Kingman? Your government job doesn't pay much. What are we going to do?"

Her answer was to throw herself even more enthusiastically into her latest dilettante project, a high-toned take-out store called Ratatouille. She claimed it would be "a goldmine, because people like to eat well. Look at you." Wooton, sensitive about his weight, replied that the venture was "money down the ratatouille hole." She was not amused.

Not that Erica devoted hours at the shop, elbow deep in chopped tomato. She seemed to spend a lot of time gadding about with her manager, who was half Wooton's age. When Mick smiled, the left side of his upper lip curled in a sneer. Erica found Mick to be, as she put it, "gor-Jesus." When she came home, she acted as buoyant as someone who has just had great sex. Wooton could have had surveillance photos made of them, but didn't for fear he'd lose luster within the Authority as a cuckold.

The sun had begun to sink behind the gables of the neighboring house, which belonged to a political chat show host who never deemed the Wootons important enough to invite to his frequent parties. Erica was not very impressed by her husband either; she knew only that he had some job in the CIA, and that she shouldn't talk about it. Erica found the state-of-the-art alarm system in the house a hassle. She never noticed the four-man gun car parked outside.

Periodically, Wooton was tempted to tell Erica that indeed he was a very important man. That he had private audiences with the president. That he possessed the power to order people killed. Like her Mick. That at the Authority, he inspired soul-quivering awe.

His mind strayed to his last meeting with the president, who was about to leave for a weekend at Camp David. Starting with the first Bush, every president had taken Wooton with him to Camp David. Not this president. "You've given admirable service, Kingman," the president said from behind his Oval Office desk. "Now it's time to push on. Say around the end of the year?"

"You need anything, Director?" It was Frohlich, one of the operatives on his detail, standing at the door.

"That cold you're coming down with," Wooton said, as he placed another paste-like glob of cheese on a cracker. "Why don't you get a replacement and go home before you infect others?"

"Mmm, yes, sir." Frohlich, who had been trying to control the symptoms with antihistamines, seemed astonished the director had found him out. You drew double pay for Wooton duty, but the director insisted no one be contagious around him. The abashed Frohlich withdrew, thunderstruck by another demonstration of Wooton's telepathy.

The phone rang. It was his wife. "Kingman," said Erica, in the dreamy tones he used to hear after they'd made love, "I'm going to be a little late. Why don't you go on to the party without me?"

"Very well," Wooton said into the receiver and hung up. He ate more cheese.

The party was at the Russian embassy. The caviar would be exquisite. Strolnikov, Moscow's chief spy in the U.S., surely would be present. He and Wooton had jousted often during the Cold War. Wooton looked forward to seeing Strolnikov, who knew what a big man he truly was.

* * *

The phone rang yet again. Albert should have shut off the ringer. He reluctantly picked up.

His sister, overwrought as usual. "Why haven't you returned my calls? What's the matter with you?"

"Quit bothering me."

"I lend you ten thousand dollars and you tell me to quit bothering you?"

"You'll have the money back in a week. With interest. I'm going to be a very rich man."

"You worry me," she said. "You haven't been keeping your appointments with Dr. Whetstone. Are you taking your medication?"

"None of your business."

"Albert, FBI agents came by and asked questions about you," Mimi said. "What kind of trouble are you in now?"

"I have to go." He sat entranced by the laptop before him.

"Did you hear that Linda Reiner's sister was shot and killed? They were interested in that." Mimi got shrill. "Did you have something to do with that, Albert? Tell me now."

He hadn't been listening and perked up only when she mentioned Linda. "Who was killed? What's this about Linda?"

"Did you do it?" Mimi blared with enough force to crumble the wax buildup in his ears.

He slammed down the phone. What had she been going on about?

The night gleamed through Albert's window, all that smug light from others' apartments. A mosaic of yellow-white windows from the nearby buildings spoke of happy men and women with love in their lives. Dominating the wall next to his sole window was a massive silkscreen he had made of Linda, lifted from the magazine story. That cost a lot of money, but was worth it. He devoted hours to looking at the picture worshipfully.

Albert ran his hand over the smooth plastic of a closed-up Goldring. "Corsine stock, Linda," he said. "For you and me." His first extravagant gift to her would be this exquisite gift he had found on eBay. Something called cubic zirconia.

Then he realized he was hungry. Albert checked the tiny kitchenette. Nothing left of the deli meat he kept in the mold-encrusted refrigerator. The cereal box was empty. His wallet had a few bucks, which would buy a couple of pizza slices. Where did he put his jacket?

That was when the soft knock came on his door. Who could that be? No one outside of Mimi knew he lived here. Could it be . . . ?

"Linda?" Albert called, tentatively. Then with surging hope, "Linda? Is that you?"

He flicked open the deadbolt, but kept the chain on. You never knew in his seedy neighborhood.

A dapper gentleman in a striped suit stood in the dark hallway—the overhead lighting had burnt out when Giuliani was mayor. The man in the hall, partly illuminated through Albert's cracked door, looked pleasant, with silver hair and a small smile.

"Who are you?" Albert asked.

The man whispered in an English accent, "Message from Linda."

"Linda," Albert exulted. He undid the chain.

CHAPTER EIGHT

River Traysor was wired, jittery from malevolent electricity. His handsome face had a desperado's manic quality. With wildly gesturing arms and fiery eyes that jigged around the study, he berated the sisters. "You're trying to pin her murder on me, aren't you? Tell me the goddamn truth." He was shouting now. "Don't lie."

Ginny, her hands to her chest, cringed in her chair. But Linda sat straight-backed, meeting his eyes.

"Answer me, you bitch," River roared at her. He stood over Linda, who looked up at him as if at a bad movie.

"River," Linda said, "I want you to calm down."

"I'm not gonna calm down. Not when the cops are putting the squeeze on me for something I didn't do. You know I've had trouble with the law."

"Assaulting that man in the bar. Yes, I know. Sit down, please."

"He thought I was a fag." River subsided. He pointed at Ginny. "I'm no pervert freak."

"Sit down, please," Linda repeated.

The note of command in her voice got through. He sat on the hard wood chair where Ginny put her less favored students.

"I did nothing to hurt Flo," River said with a little boy's truculence.

"What I told Detective Friday," Linda said evenly, "was that Flo rode you. That is true. I also told him you handled it well."

"Flo started out putting her hands on my shoulder and shit," River said. "I showed her I didn't like that. Nobody touches me unless I want them to. Then she got huffy. She started treating me like I stole money from her. I mean, Christ."

Linda said nothing, just kept sitting there serenely.

River completed the transition from belligerent to whiny. "Then this chick down the hall—I bet it's the one with the pockmarked skin who kept coming on to me—told the cops I left the door open after I left. I told that girl to keep the hell away from me. I bet she's trying to get me in trouble as a payback. Like I'm in on some conspiracy to leave the place not secure."

"Did you lock the door behind you?" Linda asked.

River nodded his bowed head vigorously. "I always do. The cops treated me like I was a werewolf, kept me there forever, going over every detail, again and again." He brought his head up and looked at Linda beseechingly. "I was in a hurry last night. I had to be somewhere. But I locked up behind me. No one believes me. No one."

Shaking her head, Linda said, "Here's what I've got, River. You can't behave in this manner around my sister. Or me."

Ginny mouthed the word "no" but didn't utter it. She braced for River's next eruption.

"Hey, I'm sorry, Linda," River said, meek instead. "It's just I've been through a real bad time."

"A real bad time? You have no idea. You didn't lose your sister," Linda said. "River, we no longer need your services. I'll send you a check for what you're owed. And we'll ship you any personal belongings from the office."

"You're firing me?" River exclaimed, astonished.

"River, go home."

"But, Linda—"

"Now, River."

He quietly got to his feet and shuffled to the door. A small whimper escaped as he closed it behind him.

"I don't know whether to believe him," Linda said. "This doesn't add up. If he did lock the door, how did the killer get in?"

"Maybe Flo knew him and let him in. She used to be friends with Albert."

"Correct—used to be. I've been worrying—what if the police don't find the killer . . . and Goldring? We've got to find Goldring and get it back."

"But it got Flo killed," Ginny said.

Karen sat at her grandmother's table. Emma, Karen's mother and a devotee of world peace, kept cooing over her daughter. Karen's grumpy father, Maury, deep into middle age and defiantly jobless, still toiling at his Sisyphean doctoral dissertation, had put down the newspaper to obey his wife and come to the table. Gran, sometimes lucid, sometimes dotty, sat with a pencil and paper, working on her recurrent hobby, anagrams.

"And they kept you waiting in that hospital forever," Emma said, unable to admit out loud that her daughter had also been in police custody.

"That's why they call us patients," Karen said. "Ma, I can easily cover the facial scratches with makeup. They'll go away. My shoulder feels better already. Even where that goon hit me in the stomach is okay."

"The pigs threw me in jail once," said her father, a Flower Power-era radical.

"That was for drunk driving," Gran said to her son-in-law.

"I don't know what to do," said Karen, who had been released after the Easter Island-faced judge had arraigned her. Karen had endured the drive back to New York with Skeen in eerie silence. "I can't tell if the magazine is going to back me. Skeen was not talking. I called Eudell and she said she can't talk to me right now and to come to a meeting at the office tomorrow."

"They wouldn't fire you," Emma said. "You've been a loyal employee."

"It's the capitalist system," said Maury, whose grad school thesis concerned how socialism hadn't really died, but was simply on vacation. A psychedelic relic of the 1960s, he had managed to string out his student years for decades. He loved to regale younger students with how he had fire-bombed the ROTC building in 1972. He didn't mention how his Molotov cocktail had gone off in his hand, giving him second-degree burns, leaving the ROTC building unscathed. Out of economic necessity, he and Emma, a low-paid social worker, lived with Emma's mom in her elegant old West Side townhouse.

"The meeting is with Calvin Christian," Karen said. "He hates me. He thinks I'm insubordinate."

"Why would he ever think that, dear?" Emma asked.

"Because I am."

Gran scribbled furiously to rearrange the letters. "Calvin Christian . . . I, Carnival Snitch."

"If only Frank Vere would get back to me," Karen said. "I left a message on his voice mail. He knows what to do, always."

"Frank Vere," Gran said. Her pencil danced. "Freak Vern." She'd done that anagram before.

"See, there's a connection somehow between Faff and

the Reiners," Karen said. "It's hard to believe a computer program can predict the stock market, but—"

"The stock market is rigged," Maury said. "The biggest crooks are on Wall Street."

"That Linda Reiner is lovely," Emma said. "I saw her on the *Today* Show."

"Linda Reiner," Gran said as she jotted an anagram. "Linen Raider."

"Another crook," her father said.

"Pop, please," Karen said.

"If the shoe fits, wear it," Maury said.

"If the shoe fits," Karen said, "Linda would buy it in every color."

The phone rang, and Emma crossed over to the kitchen to pick up. "It's Frank Vere."

"Freak Vern," Gran said. "Is he your boyfriend?"

"I'm off men for now, Gran." Karen perhaps had detected a subtle shift in Frank's interest toward her during the summer, yet wasn't certain.

After she finished talking to Frank and felt a bit better, Karen sat with Gran and watched an old movie on TV. Karen had recommended that her grandmother get video-on-demand, a luxury that Karen no longer could afford. This movie was about a casino heist, and Karen liked the part best when the intrepid robbers masked their escape from pursuing guards by throwing money into the air and causing a pandemonium among greed-crazed gamblers.

"I wonder if they have the old silent films," Gran said. "Like *Robin Hood.*"

"I should have insisted on staying in the casino, not getting in that car," Karen said. "I really screwed it up with getting the documents from Solter Faff."

Gran jotted rapidly on her paper. "Solter Faff, Flat Offers."

"I'll say. God, money has bought Faff this incredible power."

"I used to hate rich people," said Gran, who in her Marxist days had some shadowy connection to subversive activities. Then she had become a Republican and, to Maury's dismay, a landlord. "My financial adviser called today to say I should diversify into mutual funds. I have money in everything else, it seems."

"Sounds like a good idea," Karen said. "If you get good ones, they're professionally managed, so you don't have to worry about tracking individual stocks. That's the manager's job." Karen planned to salt away her divorce settlement in mutual funds for her retirement. She didn't want to end up penniless like her parents.

"Talk about power," Gran said. "These mutual fund managers have a lot of power over the stock market, don't they?"

"Sure. When they buy a stock en masse, its price moves higher. They try to do their buying discreetly, but everyone seems to know." Karen recalled the times Tim had cursed the funds for pushing up a stock just as he was set to buy it. "But seriously, Gran, Faff is one devious creep with a lot of money and power. How do I top him?"

"When you were a teenager, you were good at outfoxing your parents."

"That didn't take too much doing."

"You can outfox Faff."

"I love you, Gran."

The next morning, as the sun cleared the misty horizon and glinted off the mirrored massiveness of Manhattan's towers, Karen stepped warily off the elevator. Rose, the sweet old receptionist, told her to hang in there, that everyone believed in her. Karen's friends crowded around her to express support; they said nothing about her scratched face. The Three Musketeers informed her that history showed that wealth didn't always buy justice. The Razz, as the magazine's reigning wordsmith, called Faff "a retromingent cur"—meaning a backward-urinating dog. Mombo, her favorite loopy photo editor, said he had pictures of Faff picking his nose. Wendy's parrot, riding her shoulder, kept repeating, "Faff's a liar, Faff's a liar." Its best trick was, when near Christian or Skeen, to make a strangling sound. Another reason Christian had tried to get pets banned from the office.

The morning papers were full of stories about how Karen was charged with wrecking Faff's car, and even told how he had saved her from the burning wreck. There was nothing about Karen's side of the story. The magazine, through Calvin Christian as spokesman, had no comment. "The damn media," Karen said as she scanned the papers at her desk.

The editors' tribunal awaited Karen in the conference room, where the mood was far less welcoming than from the staff outside. Calvin Christian and Gene Skeen sat scowling across the long table from Eudell, who offered Karen a small encouraging smile and patted the chair to her right.

Christian greeted her with that patented management intimidation phrase: "Close the door, Karen."

"You don't want folks out there to hear what you're up to, Calvin?" Karen said, and then swung the door shut.

"You're in enough trouble already," Skeen said. "If I were you, I'd—"

"Well, you're not her, Gene," Eudell said. Karen smiled at this show of support.

"The face scratches will vanish soon and my shoulder feels a lot better," Karen told Christian and Skeen. "And I'm generally fine emotionally, despite all the trauma of the car wreck and the gangsters. Thanks for your concern."

As the managing editor, Christian ran daily operations—scheduling stories, allocating pages for each issue, enforcing deadlines, and overseeing administration. The last duty encompassed budget and personnel. He didn't like smart-aleck reporters. A joyless man, he had tried and failed to enforce a strict dress code, saying the staff should be "more corporate." In a newsroom where people's garb tilted to the casual side, that had provoked a rebellion. Christian thought most reporters were little better than juvenile delinquents. The editor-in-chief, Bill McIntyre, mainly wanted him around to serve as a brake, a note of skepticism about seemingly good stories that might be less solid than advertised. Christian misinterpreted this mandate to mean he should shovel responsibility for any mishap onto subordinates. For him, it wasn't whether you won or lost, but where you placed the blame.

"Give us your version of what happened," Christian droned at Karen.

"It's also known as the truth, Calvin," Karen said. She went through the chronology of her visit to Atlantic City.

"Do you mean to tell us that these two so-called witnesses, who supposedly saw Faff driving and not you, can't be found?" Skeen said. "How can that possibly be?"

Christian had hired Skeen, who had exasperated everyone at the many places he'd worked, to take up arms against one of the most formidable foes in journalism, the freewheeling staff of *Profit*. Skeen, whose editing talents were minimal, served as Christian's all-purpose trouble-maker. Skeen surely had heard from office snitches Karen's crack about how he should be arrested for impersonating an editor.

"Well, Gene," Karen replied, struggling to minimize the sarcasm, "it probably has something to do with Jack Faff's clout in Atlantic City. Major Darcy, the parking attendant, works directly for Faff Enterprises. The cop who stopped us, named Harry, works for a city government whose politicians take generous campaign contributions from Faff."

"Sheer speculation," Skeen said with a flip of his hand.

"Remind me, Gene," Eudell said. "Whose side are you on?"

"That's not the issue," Skeen said.

"The issue," Christian said, coming to the aid of his stooge, "is that Karen Glick has embroiled us in another expensive legal mess. And worse, she has embarrassed the magazine in the light of Jack Faff's statements to the police."

"His *false* statements to the police," Karen said.

"Why don't the two of you use a little common sense here?" Eudell said. "Has Karen ever been proved wrong? Her facts always check out. Faff has every motive to lie his head off."

"Common sense?" Skeen shot back. "Glick's telling us that Faff wanted to get his hands on the Reiners's computer because it can predict the stock market? Nonsense. No one can predict the stock market. Or horse races. Or what cards will be dealt. Or whether it will rain two weeks from today. Her contention is preposterous."

"Karen Glick's execution of this entire story has been questionable, certainly," Christian said.

"If you put the matter to a staff vote," Karen said, "I'll predict, certainly, that the folks would like to see a couple of executions."

Skeen lunged part way across the conference table, his long nose flared at her. "I'm warning you. You stand very close to dismissal."

Karen shoved herself across the table, too, her face just a couple of feet from Skeen's. "And I'm warning you, Skeen. Quit going after your own staff like they're criminals."

"Please, please," Christian said, restoring the order he prized above all else. "The question of whether we fire Karen Glick or place her on leave without pay or some other remedy—we will come to that decision judiciously."

"Those are the options?" Eudell said. "What kind of kangaroo court is this?"

Christian gave her an owlish stare. "We are under a lot of pressure. . . ."

The door swung open, and a hush enfolded the conference room. Bill McIntyre slouched into the head chair and swung his feet onto the table. "How y'all doing?" the editor-in-chief drawled, his words redolent of Carolina's piney woods.

"Bill," Christian began, "we have to decide—"

Bill's upraised hand silenced him. "We-e-e-e-e-e-ell, you don't have to decide a blessed thing. I already decided." Although his bald head was mostly below the tabletop, his sorghum speech rang clear. "Karen, I do believe every little last word you say. I don't want to hear any more talk about punishing you. Okay, fine, we can't print a story on Faff right now about what we know of his finances. We can't prove it. It's his word against yours about what he said about the Reiners's computer—said when he thought he was a goner. First, we gotta get you exonerated. You're tainted and the Faff finance story is tainted by the legal charges against you."

"Bill, I . . ." Karen wanted to pour out the whole experience again directly to the editor-in-chief. But Bill already knew.

"Don't work on anything else." Bill hauled himself up a tad from his recumbent position, making his bald dome and crooked grin visible. "You've got my blessing," he said to Karen, "to find this Goldring computer whats-is gizmotron, and prove you're right. This computer sounds like a pipe dream to me, but my gut tells me that Flo Reiner's death and this computer are linked up somehow—and Faff's part of it. That there's an even bigger story than Faff's shaky finances. My gut, you see, is always right."

"The newspaper story of her murder said a laptop was the only item missing from the Reiners's office," Karen said. "The Reiners have said nothing to the press."

"You go out and make us proud," Bill said.

"I will, Bill," Karen said, her emotions showing in her ragged whisper.

Back at her desk, Karen launched a swarm of phone calls. She got voice mail at Reiner Capital. The home phone number she had for Linda had been changed to another unlisted phone; by now, Linda would have moved into her new palace. Ginny's home number yielded an answering machine. The Columbia math department secretary told her, with the icy manner reserved for unqualified job seekers, that Professor Reiner was taking no media calls. Then Karen phoned companies in the Meeker-Grubman building and heard that the cops had told them to stay mum. She tried calling the one cop she knew, a girlhood friend named Marcia Fink, who had worked on the Billionaire Boys case, but Marcia was on some kind of leave.

The phone rang. Karen grabbed it, hoping one of the Reiners was returning the call. Instead, she heard the cigarette-raspy voice of Sasha, her lawyer. Sasha wanted to set a date with her husband and his lawyer to finalize the divorce settlement. "Are you sure this is all you want from him, honey?" Sasha said. "He's worth a helluva lot more. You can get half. You can put his balls through the Cuisinart."

"I wouldn't do that to my Cuisinart. No. I want only enough to set up a decent retirement nest egg, putting it in good mutual funds. Tim can keep his BMW, and keep buying another new one every time he crashes the old one."

After she hung up, Frank Vere slouched by her desk. "How's it going?"

"You intervened with Bill, didn't you?"

"Somebody had to. Christian and Skeen are out of control. No loyalty."

"Well, thanks. I'm okay. But otherwise, it's going rotten. I can't find a way in to the Reiners. They're sealed off, tighter than Linda Reiner's heart. Though, come to think of it, it's only a rumor that she has a heart."

Nodding, Frank said, "I met Linda Reiner once, before you made her . . . before she became famous. At a reception hosted by Oracle. She was Larry Ellison's date." The mega-wealthy Ellison, head of tech powerhouse Oracle, always had beautiful women. "She actually talked to me. She was charming." Frank, while a world-class reporter, had the looks and sex appeal of two-day-old cod. "But no . . . uh, sparks. From her, anyway. I was sparking like a Roman candle."

"Sparks? Linda's as cold as they come. The ultimate control freak. Has to be in charge. She makes Donald Rumsfeld look like a geisha girl. Cross her and she gets as vicious as Mikhail Beria with a migraine. But she sure can turn on the charm. Linda knows how to beguile men. Women are less enthusiastic. Flo once told me this great story. Before the Reiners got rich, Ginny wanted her sisters to help paint her apartment. She lives in this dumpy place provided by Columbia, where she is a professor. Linda doesn't do painting, unless it's her nails. She tried to wiggle out. Ginny told her to just put on some old clothes and come over. Linda said, 'But Ginny, I have no old clothes.' "

"You need to dig everywhere, and not only with the Reiners."

Karen grimaced. "Easy for you to say, Frank. You've got more sources than the Mississippi." She pursed her lips. "Say, can you call some of them for me? Like the cops?"

Frank glanced about furtively, then leaned down so his voice wouldn't carry. "To appease Christian and Skeen, Bill McIntyre ordered me not to help you."

"Those retromingent curs."

"However," Frank said, eyes clicking to and fro, alert for nasty editors and other beasts, "I made a few inquiries anyway." He related what Detective Friday's investigation had unearthed about Albert Niebel and about River Treysor, the receptionist who may have left the office door unlocked. "Treysor's story doesn't add up for Friday. Where did he go after work? A mystery. Did he leave the Reiner Capital door unlocked?"

Karen was jotting down notes faster than Gran did her anagrams. "This is great."

"I'd use what I told you to bait the Reiners, make them talk to you," Frank said. "Also, I made some calls on the Atlantic City front. I know you had no luck tracking down the witnesses. I had a bit more, but not much. The cop who stopped you is Harry Estrada, but he filed no traffic-stop report and insists you're lying. He'll be hard to crack."

"Why am I not surprised?"

Frank nodded. "But hold on. Major Darcy, the parking attendant, is getting cold feet about toeing the party line about what happened that night. I hear he has toyed with the idea of changing his statement about Faff not getting behind the wheel. They say Darcy is a man of integrity."

"A man of integrity works for Faff? Next you're going to tell me you had an Elvis sighting." She smiled wanly. "Hey, thanks for your help, Frank. You're a prince."

"You might go to Atlantic City to find him. Darcy, not Elvis. That has obvious risks."

"I'd like to get another run at Faff, this time with a tape recorder. And this time in public. Maybe in a Burger King. Why not? They both serve up whoppers." She sipped the tepid office coffee. "Well, can I interview your sources?"

Venturing an enigmatic smile, Frank said, "Sorry. Too sensitive."

For someone as well plugged-in as Frank, Karen knew sharing a source was akin to sharing a toothbrush. "Thanks anyway. You can have my space in the refrigerator once the house begins." They and their friends shared a summer house in the Hamptons.

"If I hear anything else, which I'm not supposed to pass on, I'll pass it on."

The phone rang again. It was her mother, wanting to know how the editor's inquisition had gone. Emma, who liked to see the bright side, was cheered at the news. "I'll tell your father and grandmother. She's busy talking to that financial adviser. I don't know about these matters. Your father says he's a con man and you should review his recommendations. He wants to run something called a 'stock screen' for Gran. She told him she wants to make money like the Reiner sisters."

"A stock screen is where you do a computer run to see what stocks fit your investment goals—money for your kids' college, for gifts to charity, for retirement, on and on. The Reiners did it with Goldring on a bigger scale. They showed me the trades that made them rich. They screened for 'value stocks.' Those are stocks that don't go anywhere because Wall Street doesn't appreciate their virtues. One day, the bet is Wall Street will wake up to them. It did for the Reiners, to beat the band."

"Your father thinks this money-grubbing is rather seamy."

"Which is why he has none." After her mother's call, Karen recollected that Linda had given her a cell phone number. She rummaged through her old notes and found it. Would Linda have changed this, too? Linda, with those smooth-flowing octaves, answered on the second ring.

"Linda, Karen Glick. I'm sorry about Flo. I need to . . ."

"How did you get my . . . ? Well, we're not speaking to the press, thank you." Her brush-off, long practiced on insolvent and other unsuitable men, had a heartless formality.

"Linda, I know about Albert Niebel and his stalking and that he's a suspect," Karen blurted at the speed of a carny barker, hoping to beat her hanging up. "And I know about the office door being unlocked, maybe by River Treysor."

The ever unflappable Linda was flapped. "What? Who? Where'd you hear that? This is confidential." Then she composed herself. "I have nothing to say." Linda hung up.

Unsure whether she'd done herself harm or good, Karen made the last of the calls to techie kids in the Meeker-Grubman start-ups. Yet again, she heard how the cops had ordered silence, from a young person whose every other word was "like" or "y' know." Then Karen's phone rang.

The caller's voice made her push back from her desk and spill her coffee over her papers.

"It's me," her husband said. "We have to talk."

"No, we don't." Karen would have preferred hearing from Mikhail Beria.

Tim Bratton displayed that preppy finesse found at the best squash courts, the best Episcopalian parishes, and the best Republican fundraisers. "I'm calling on behalf of a friend."

"A friend?" Tim ranked his friends by status and bloodline. He would do nothing for one unless it benefited him.

"Linda Reiner. She's quite upset. Her sister was murdered. Please leave her alone."

"Hey, thanks for your concerned call after my car crash." Everyone in Karen's life had gotten in touch, with one big exception. "Why didn't you call?"

"And open myself up to more of your snide remarks? You seem to have gotten yourself in quite a pickle. But I'm serious about Linda."

"Well, you're familiar with car crashes. How do you know Linda?"

Tim paused. "We're, you might say, seeing each other."

"Linda Reiner is my husband's girlfriend?"

CHAPTER NINE

Tim Bratton sat in the magazine's tatty reception area as the receptionist chatted on the phone about an upcoming family wedding. He shuttled between the cell phone in his right hand and the personal digital assistant in his left. His cell and his PDA were as sleek as Linda. Sandy blond and tastefully tan, Tim had the bearing of a man used to getting his way. To Tim, life consisted of well-deserved victories, whether on the Merion Cricket tennis courts or in the wood-paneled offices of Dewey Cheatham. His Philadelphia Main Line pedigree and savoir faire entitled him to everything good. And when, like the occasional Democratic presidential victory, life didn't obey the rules and turned up bad, he could become very upset.

Karen's big investigative story exposing the Billionaire Boys Club as crooks had gotten Tim very upset—because it had gotten Tim's superiors at Dewey Cheatham very upset. The Billionaire Boys had been important, well-paying clients of Dewey Cheatham. The fact that a maniac had killed off most of the Boys, making future business with Dewey Cheatham impossible, wasn't what annoyed Tim's bosses so much. What really bugged them was that Tim's wife, estranged or no, had uncovered the crookedness and thus tarred Dewey Cheatham by association. At least the federal probe into whether Dewey Cheatham was complicit in the Boys' tax evasion seemed to be going nowhere. "Your wife," said Lewis Joffrey, the partner who oversaw Tim, with a tight barracuda smile, "has been making waves, we see."

Tim pretended not to recognize some of the magazine people going past. They noticed him, but kept moving without comment. There was that loon, Rasmussen, whom they called the Razz; he liked to lie on the summer house's floor and quote Rudyard Kipling. And the bone-slender woman with the parrot on her shoulder. Wendy? And then the other woman—as chunky as Linda's sister Ginny—who burst into arias from Wagner. Sally? Karen's friends.

"The late Tim Bratton," as his wife called him obnoxiously, had arrived fifteen minutes later than he had promised Karen, and she was letting him wait for her for a change. He tried to recall what she looked like the last time he had seen her. Other than angry.

He had met Karen at the end of his senior year at Princeton, when she was a freshman. It was lust at first sight. He took her to bed (her first time, not his) and promptly forgot about her for ten years until they met again in the Hamptons. He was even more polished then; she was even funnier. He quickly charmed her out of her resentment at being loved and left. The year they married, he felt very miffed at his parents, having learned that he wouldn't have full control of his trust funds until forty. Maybe out of some delayed adolescent rebellion, maybe because the sex was spectacular, maybe due to her pervasive sense of fun, he proposed to Karen Glick, the irreverent daughter of left-over New Leftists—and not the debutante type everyone assumed he would wed. Tim's mother, never one to act ungracious or betray a hint that all wasn't well, told him: "This Karen, she's so . . . New York, isn't she?" While Karen's mother was nice to Tim, as she was to every living entity, Karen's father treated his son-in-law like a member of the Waffen SS. "Too blond," Maury said.

With his meticulously tailored suit, the pinstripes of which met at the seams like the uninterrupted lines of a distinguished family tree, Tim knew he projected poise, dignity, and self-confidence today.

"You wanted to see me in person? Here I am," he heard his wife say. Karen, face scratches badly concealed by makeup, emerged from a side door, projecting annoyance. Tim gracefully rose to his feet from the cracked vinyl couch. They, by some tacit agreement, exchanged no handshakes, smiles, or greetings. Karen eyed him as if he were a maggot on a knish.

Tim knew he had a negotiation on his hands. But Bratton men through the ages had been skilled at such maneuvering. An ancestor had signed the Declaration of Independence too small for George III to read. So when British troops occupied Philadelphia, Josiah Bratton could claim he had nothing to do with the Revolution and went on to pad his fortune by supplying the redcoats with strong grog and loose women. The same gifts had allowed Tim to do well as a young investment banker at Dewey Cheatham—at least until recently—making stumblebum corporate clients, with new offerings of stock to peddle, feel their company was the next Microsoft.

"We have a small problem," he told Karen with his well-modulated voice. "Yet I'm sure we can come to a resolution. Linda wishes no publicity in her time of grief. I'm sure you understand. She will consent to see you at some point after her time of mourning"

"A resolution, my Aunt Fanny. I don't know why Linda insisted on sending you here."

"This was my idea. Some matters are best handled in person."

"Well, handle this: either she meets with me today or I write about Goldring. I have a hunch she doesn't want that made public."

"Karen, be reasonable," he said, poise beginning to fray.

Interestingly, she thought, Tim didn't ask what Goldring was or even how to spell it. "You like reason? How about a reason why my husband is going out with Linda Reiner."

"None of your damn business," he said with the asperity she knew so well.

Smiling that she'd broken through that poise barrier once again, Karen said, "I'm done here."

"How about a reason you screwed up my career," he shot back.

"Career problems? Well, that makes two of us. But your biggest problem is telling your new girlfriend"—she drew the word out, sarcastically—"that her secret is going to be all over the news if she doesn't cooperate."

"Don't forget that meeting we have with the divorce attorneys."

"The highlight of my year."

Linda grabbed the phone at the first ring. "Well?"

"Well . . ." Tim's hesitant tone mingled with the street sounds from his end. "I can't talk her out of it, Linda."

Simmering, Linda stopped herself from remarking that silver-tongued Tim, able to charm corporate plutocrats out of their money and socialites out of their clothes, should be able to convince his unaccomplished and ordinary-looking wife to stay clear. "Then I'll simply ignore her."

"That might not be easy. If you don't meet with her today, she threatened to write about Goldring."

For a moment, Linda felt she was in free fall. Then she regained her aplomb. "Gold what?"

"Come on, Linda. Everybody on Wall Street knows that's what you call your stock-picking system." He sounded pleased with himself to be blatting her deepest secret. "Rumor is that the sole copy is on the laptop that Flo's murderer stole."

Linda sat down heavily on her Le Courbusier lounge. "Everybody on Wall Street?"

"You can't keep a secret like this," Tim said, so cheerfully she wanted to throttle him. "Wall Street is gossip central. I don't buy that it makes a hundred percent infallible predictions, but it must be pretty good. Not long ago, you had no money."

"How thoughtful of you to remind me. Set up a meeting with your wife."

Jack Faff sprawled in his hospital bed after the hotshot New York doctors had left, grouchy about their indecision. Was this a "minor cardiac event"—as one of them phrased it— or just the result of his ribs hitting the steering wheel? Um, the dashboard. The tests were inconclusive. No one wanted to make a call.

"And I feel fine," he told Solter, who stood fidgeting by his bedside, arms full of reports and documents. Jack held a schedule of the gala opening party for Faff Towers. "I'm sick of being cooped up here. The masquerade party is on top of us."

"These doctors are the best, Jack," his brother said.

"The best, huh? In my line of work, we step up to the plate. We make a decision. I've got work to do."

"They're top of the line, Jack," said Solter, who wasn't. Solter never had been good at anything, and never would have made it outside the family business. As Jack often reminded him. He backed out of the hospital room.

The best. Top of the line. At least some of his older brother's pet phrases had rubbed off on Solter. Jack, in his utterances to the media or sales prospects or investment bankers, used a cascade of superlatives for his business ventures. Faff Towers wasn't merely another swanky condo building with a good view. It was "the premier residential address in New York." He never employed an architect who was well-respected. The architect was "the greatest visionary since Frank Lloyd Wright." And Faff's casino couldn't be just a popular day-tripper's destination. It was "the number one gambling establishment on the planet."

Faff's father had been equally immodest. When Jack challenged his old man's judgment, Pop-pop would weigh in with: "Never forget that I created Long Island. I put up the tract homes for all those GIs coming home from the war, looking to start families. Think twice about who you're talking to, idiot." Solter, five years younger than Jack, tagged along behind Pop-pop like a pathetic puppy. He frequently ratted out his older brother to Pop-pop for infractions ranging from undone homework to dope smoking. Every time Jack hit Solter, the dip reported it.

Among his family, Jack preferred his mother, who kept as much distance between herself and Pop-pop as possible. On Jack's winter visits with her at their Palm Beach place or summer sojourns at the Bar Harbor house, he sat for hours listening to his mother go on about his destiny. "You're smarter and tougher than your father," she said, daiquiri before her. "You can spit in the eye of a lion."

Out of college in the late 1970s and newly employed at the family firm, Jack tried to convince his father that they should buy up a decrepit dowager of a hotel, which languished in bankruptcy court, and make it grand again. From that success, Jack argued, the Faff firm would next build a luxury apartment building on Fifth Avenue. And from there they would . . .

"You've got your head up your ass as usual, moron," Pop-pop replied, and took a long pull from his illegal Cuban cigar. "New York is dying. No one wants to live there. Companies are bailing out. Crime is the only growth business. In ten years, the city will be a ghost town."

"But Pop-pop," Jack said, "New York is the premier city in the world. Not a chance it won't come back."

These were the feverish days of disco music, copious drugs, and abundant sex. A regular at Studio 54, Jack could have settled into being a rich gad-about. But he restricted the partying to the night and devoted long hours to learning his father's business: how concrete must be mixed, how construction crews should be treated, how zoning restrictions could be skirted. And then when a heart attack left his father bedridden, he went beyond Pop-pop's purview by cultivating politicians. Not local yo-yos on Long Island, but city and state bigwigs. Once he secured the deal to buy the broken-down hotel, he told his father.

"You stupid shithead," his father yelled from his massive bed. "We don't want to get involved in that cesspool. How dare you."

Jack had locked eyes with him. Pop-pop was pale and drawn in his monogrammed silk pajamas. "How dare you stand in the path of our company's future." He too was shouting.

"You ungrateful little bastard—" Pop-pop stopped and clamped both hands to his chest. "Jesus," he wheezed.

Jack stood statue still while his father writhed and gurgled. Pop-pop whimpered that he should call for aid. "Help me."

"All you've ever done for me is deposit some sperm," Jack said. "Why should I help you?"

Pop-pop reached out one clawed hand beseechingly to his son. Near the end, his mouth gaped wide, jaw switching from side to side, wide enough that Jack fancied he could see eternity. Only when the old man had subsided, his chin resting on the tuft of gray hair protruding from his silk pajamas, did Jack call for the servants. A wind rustled and thrashed the cash-green leaves outside.

Since the funeral back in the 1970s, Jack never had visited his father's grave. But he kept having the same dream: being chased through the graveyard, not daring to turn around, hearing the beating leather wings of the Jersey Devil behind him. Then standing before Pop-pop's headstone and saying, "Who's the idiot now, huh?" And then Pop-pop stepping out from behind the headstone and, grinning evilly, pointing to his left. He was pointing at a headstone bearing the name Jack Faff.

Faff awoke with a start. His heart was pumping as if he'd been in a race. But he had no pain. God, he hated that dream.

Mikhail and Solter were coming into the room. Solter's rounded eyes showed more panic than normal. Mikhail's glowering face had an especially dangerous cast.

"There's been an unforeseen development," Solter said, as if afraid his brother would rise up and strike him.

"What the hell are you talking about?" Jack demanded.

"Somebody killed Albert Niebel, Jack," Mikhail said. "And took the Goldring laptop."

They stood at the foot of the bed and braced for an outburst. Instead, Faff's skin grew crimson. "What happened?" he asked, trying to contain his anger.

Solter glanced anxiously at Mikhail. "Jack, it wasn't my idea to tell you this now. In your condition—"

"You shut your mouth," Mikhail told him.

"No one tells my brother to shut up but me," Faff said. "Now tell me. What happened?"

"Our guys see the men who look like feds go into Niebel's apartment building," Mikhail said. "They were agitated plenty. A half-hour goes by, they come out and one of my people hears two of these pricks talking about how the computer is gone. They leave and my guys go for their own look. Niebel is dead, no computer."

"Wait a minute," Faff growled. "If they're FBI, wouldn't they still be there? Maybe bring in the NYPD to keep everybody away from the crime scene while they dusted for prints or whatever the hell they do? You're the damn criminal. You tell me."

"That's why we think they maybe are not feds after all," Mikhail said.

Faff's expression was murderous. The veins stood out on his neck like blue ropes. "Well, considering I'm paying you a fortune, who in the name of Christ were these assholes?"

"A fortune? We are working on finding out these guys, Jack."

Unable to contain himself any longer, Faff shouted, "You're damn straight you better be working on it. Instead of trying to screw everything in sight." Mikhail had a beach place nearby called the Bang-Bang House, where he indulged every earthly delight. "How in the hell did someone sneak in and kill this hump Niebel?"

"Whoever, he moves like a spirit."

"Like a spirit again. Wake up. I have a hunch a real live human being iced this creep. What kind of idiots do you have working for you? Are they blind?"

Mikhail's beard bristled like a porcupine's quills, although he kept his own rage in check. "Not idiots. But we need to be paid. How about a quarter million?"

Faff had that merciless negotiator's air. "Make it two hun-

dred thou. And put some of your hard-asses on the casino
payroll as security. That'll pay for part of it."

"The Casino Control Commission requires criminal
background checks for any casino employee," Solter said.
"I doubt they'll pass."

"I just gave them the test, and they passed," Faff said.
"Now move it."

Logie tried to console Donner, but he wouldn't listen. Donner paced the room like a caged carnivore.

Finally, the director's retainers brought the chair. Minutes
ticked by painfully. Donner paced still faster, pausing occasionally to make a call to his New York team.

They both froze when the door opened and the director
entered. He betrayed no emotion and sat. First he looked
at Logie, then at Donner. "Report," he said.

"Director . . . I really . . . You understand, we had no—"
Donner addressed the ceiling, as if explaining to the
Almighty.

"Do you mean to tell me," Wooton said, "that somehow
an unknown person got into Niebel's apartment house,
broke his neck with one blow, and made off with the laptop? And you caught no good sighting of this person? And
he sneaked out of the building without your team detect-
ing him?"

"The angle of the door was such that—from outside we
couldn't get a good perspective through the window. . . . It
happened very fast. Neibel was about to leave and we were
going to enter his apartment to get the computer—"

"Brilliant," Wooton said.

Donner passed a hand across his chin. "The unknown individual who terminated Niebel—it was a pro job. He
switched off the lights when he scooped up the laptop . . .
kept his back to the window . . . We couldn't get a good

view of him. Our operatives stormed the place at once—
gone. Like a ghost."

"A ghost?" Wooton said, wearing his disdain like food
spilled on his fine suit.

To Logie, the most dismaying thing was that this screwup meant her reunion with Alexandra would be delayed.
Perhaps forever.

"Let me listen to the recording of Niebel's visitor,"
Wooton said with ominous calm. "You did employ a para-
bolic mike, I trust?"

Donner scrambled to comply. Rock concert loud, the
taped conversation filled the room.

The killer whispered, "Message from Linda." A thump and
crash followed. Then came quick footsteps. Nothing more.

"I have independent sources of my own," the director
said. "A Russian gangster group, hired by the developer
Jack Faff, is after Goldring, as well. Your operatives didn't
detect them, but they were posted outside Niebel's building also."

"Huh?" Donner said. "We would've seen other operatives."

"Evidently not," Wooton said.

"So the gangsters took Goldring?" Logie said.

"Maybe, maybe not," Wooton said. "Maybe someone else
took it."

Logie and Donner needed a moment to process these
revelations. Logie asked first: "If not Faff and the Russians,
then who has Goldring?"

The director closed his eyes for a spell. "That voice on
the recording is familiar. It's an English accent. Cross check
it with London. Anyone who left the MI-6 payroll since the
Cold War ended and set up shop for himself. The British
will cooperate."

"What else can we do, Director?" Logie asked.

"What is the security on Neibel's apartment now?"

"We withdrew our team," Donner said.

"Bring them back," Wooton said. "The person who took Goldring may reappear. Maybe he forgot something. Maybe he wants to cover his tracks more. You are authorized to use deadly force."

"Director," Logie protested, "you said we wouldn't do that."

Wooton left the room.

CHAPTER TEN

Karen stepped into Bryant Park a little early and stood beside the coffee kiosk. She checked her reflection in the kiosk window. The makeup was doing a pretty good job hiding the facial scratches. You didn't want to meet Linda Reiner looking as if you had just bodysurfed through a threshing machine.

On time, Linda glided into the park, which a few weeks before had been the site for the spring fashion show, held each September. Linda would fit in at that. She wore a butter-soft, short black jacket that Karen thought was an Azzedine Alaia, over a Miu-Miu T-shirt, with baby-blue cigarette trousers. Linda lit up one of her incandescent smiles, which made the nearby Times Square signage seem like a flickering twenty-watt bulb. Karen knew about Linda's smile and didn't feel special to be the recipient of one. Linda used them on her dry cleaner.

Karen didn't smile back, gave her a tepid handshake, and started right in. "Goldring will target in on a stock that is about to take off, right? There are thousands upon thousands of stocks. How does it single out a particular stock?"

"Let's not get into that." Linda's smile clicked off. "What do you want from me?"

"Look, whoever took Goldring killed Flo. I know you and your sisters better than any journalist. The Goldring theft will come out. I can tell this story better than anyone else. With more sympathy."

"Sympathy," Linda snapped, all vestiges of the smiley babe gone. "You want a story to redeem yourself after the Jack Faff car crash fiasco."

Karen felt the ire rising within her. "Tim told you that? Your new boyfriend."

"The crash was all over the news, Karen, and kind of hard to miss. And I'm not discussing my private life with you."

"Oh, isn't that special? He's the perfect man for you, isn't he? Personable and presentable, with money, but not so rich and important that he overshadows you. You don't want corporate hotshots like Larry Ellison anymore." As soon as she'd spoken this, Karen wished she hadn't. Her big mouth, she always realized too late, seldom was her friend.

Linda turned to go. "You write what you wish." She marched imperiously away.

"Jack Faff is involved in this somehow," Karen called after her. "When he thought he was dying after the crash, he told me he wanted to get Goldring to cure his sinking finances."

Stopping and half-turning, Linda said, "Really? Then tell the police."

"They wouldn't believe me. Not after what happened between me and Faff." Karen hustled up to her side. "Do the police know about Goldring?"

"Seems everyone else does. My big secret, huh?"

"Linda, I'm in the doghouse at work. Tim's right. Let me help you find Goldring and who killed Flo. Then I'll write the story. With sympathy."

"Karen, sweetie, you're not exactly Woodward and Bernstein. And we have the police."

"Who are clueless. Flo is yet another murder to them among dozens. Frank Vere says if they don't get a suspect very soon, odds are they won't ever. They'll move on"

"Frank Vere?"

"Frank Vere is helping me." Karen decided not to tell her that Frank's assistance must be under the table.

"Frank Vere?" Linda was genuinely impressed. "I've met him. He's a legend."

"He's my best friend."

"Only a friend?"

"This question from the woman who puts a lid on her personal life. Yes, only a friend."

"He's not very good looking," Linda said, as though Karen didn't deserve any more handsome men after Tim. "You're right. The cops aren't doing a great job. My lawyers say to hire private detectives, but I've heard mixed things on that." Linda nodded, as if confirming a decision to herself. "Please don't be angry about Tim and me. We met at a party. He said he was the soon-to-be ex-husband of the reporter who made me famous."

"Tim always had the lines," Karen said. "He'll be ex as soon as humanly possible. Depend on it. I wish you luck with him. But the hell with Tim. Do we have an arrangement?"

"Yes," Linda said slowly. "That's what we have. Don't ask me, though, how Goldring works. That, at least, will stay a secret."

"Great." Karen whipped her notebook and pen out of her bag. "Now why bother getting back Goldring when you're rich enough now?" She listened while Linda told her how she wasn't content to rest on her accomplishments, but needed to be out and trading and winning—and famous for that. "But why only one copy?" Karen persisted.

"For security reasons. The fewer of them available, the

less chance an outsider would get a hold of one. And our plan was that all three of us had to agree to invest in a particular stock. Then the stock would be bought online in the name of Reiner Capital."

Despite the great strain she felt, Linda was composed on the surface. Karen knew that now she must proceed gingerly. "When is Flo's funeral?"

"Tomorrow," Linda said. "At this church she went to. The cops finally released Flo's . . . body. I don't expect many people to show up for the funeral mass. She didn't have any friends."

"Maybe I should be there. I liked Flo."

"Nobody liked Flo."

"What about you? Did you like Flo?"

"Not always. But she was my sister."

"Linda, someone who is a key to her murder may attend. Maybe Albert."

She stopped and clasped Karen's shoulders, giving her injury a twinge. "I'm putting my trust in you, Karen. Do you understand that?"

Mired in thought, Karen silently accompanied Linda out of the park. She recalled how, at the beginning of interviewing for the Reiner profile, Linda had recounted the sisters' harsh upbringing. Linda had told her about how "Daddy" was a stern disciplinarian and how her mother wimpishly backed him, no matter what he did. She came from a well-off family in small-town Ohio that lived in a large Tudor and belonged to a country club bounded by a white rail fence; her mother was active in the local Catholic parish and her father sold insurance.

"Daddy" cruelly criticized each of his daughters for sins—real, imagined, or exaggerated. To him, Ginny was "an unattractive pig no boy would want to get near," Linda "a little sexpot trying to get by on her looks and her flirting, not on hard work," and Flo "a loser whose only friend's a computer."

• "You told me once about your childhood and how you three coped."

"Yes," Linda said, "the three of us, my sisters and I, we stuck together."

"What a wonder you're as well balanced as you are," Karen said. Coming from an odd home life herself, Karen could sympathize.

"You know, I tried to straighten Flo out," Linda said. "The poor kid was plenty messed up."

"Because of your father?" Karen asked. "There must've been a time when Flo, as the youngest, was the only one left at home with you and Ginny off at school. No you, no Ginny to protect her."

"Let's change the subject."

To Karen, that meant press forward from a different direction regarding her background. "Your parents are both dead, right?"

Linda was getting eyed by the male pedestrians like Lady Godiva. "Mom died of leukemia four years ago. It was horrible. Daddy died twelve years ago."

Karen waited for more, and hearing none, asked, "Of what?"

"He was murdered, Karen. Okay? They never solved it. No more about this."

"Why don't we focus on one thing?" Karen said as they walked. "Finding Albert Niebel."

"Albert." Linda clasped herself as if suddenly chilled.

"Your stalker. What do we know of his whereabouts?"

"He supposedly lives with his sister, but doesn't really. He has some apartment in Queens. She is very protective of him."

"Do you know Albert's sister?"

"No, but she knows about me. She paid for his legal counsel when we got the restraining order on him. The papers were served at her home, his legal residence. He was there for dinner."

"What do you know about the sister?"

"Her name is Mimi. She's in a wheelchair. Lives alone. Divorced. Does computer work from home. Must run in their family. Albert is a real computer whiz, you see. Just like Flo was. That's how Flo and Albert met, working for Formdex. That's how he came . . . into my life."

"Small chance she'd tell us where to find Albert."

"Zero chance," Linda said. "And my name must be a curse word with her."

"Would she give out his location to the police?"

"She'd plead ignorance. She's devoted to the poor bastard. Maybe she really doesn't know where he's living."

"I doubt that. Do you have her full name or address or phone?"

Linda plucked a scrap of paper out of her handbag. "Mimi Niebel. She went back to her maiden name. It's all here."

"I'll bet she knows." Karen pulled out her phone and called the office. "Frank? I need some help tracking down an address." She gave him Albert's name and what information she had.

Linda's eyes widened. "That's Frank Vere?"

"Told you."

They walked in silence and Frank called back after a few minutes. "I've got what most likely are Albert's number and his address," he said. "Mimi paid her brother's phone bill, which is how my phone company pal traced it down, using her billing address."

Karen took notes and thanked him. She disconnected and relayed what she'd learned to Linda. "I'm going out there."

"The phone company? Isn't that illegal? Won't the police think of the phone company?" Linda asked. "You're going to Albert's?"

"Maybe you're right that they're not working the case very well. The number is unlisted and in a name other than Albert's."

"What name is that?"

Karen hesitated. "Godfrey Reiner."

Linda looked scared. "That was my father's name," she said. "Daddy's name."

Freddy's desk sat right outside Professor Reiner's office. Although the door was shut, it wasn't thick. And the professor's voice traveled. Perfect for him. Freddy fastened his ear to the door crack like a leech.

His part-time job stepping and fetching for Professor Virginia Reiner didn't pay much. And the Ecstasy he did regularly had gotten more expensive. He didn't require Professor Reiner's Fourier series, harmonic analyzers, or floating point notations to work out how much more money he needed. And fortunately, he had a means of getting it without much actual work.

"Will you be safe going to Albert's, Linda?" the professor was saying into the phone. "He's very unstable. . . . Yes, I'm glad Karen will be with you, but if he did kill Flo. . . . Is Karen qualified to judge he's harmless? . . . I realize your presence might have an impact on Albert and make him talk, but— . . . I'll be right here. Please be careful, Linda."

Freddy scribbled notes. These were more thorough notes than he ever took in class, where he tended to doze.

"Yes," the professor continued, "all the arrangements are made. I just spoke to the priest. The flowers will be there half an hour early. . . . Closed casket is wise. They tried their best at the funeral home, but the damage to her poor head was— . . . No, I think Karen should come to the funeral mass. . . . But don't change the subject. Are you sure you'll be safe going to Albert's?"

Her light blinked off on Freddy's extension. She'd hung up.

Freddy pelted down the stairs, jostling a girl who yelled at him, and bolted onto the quad. Licking his lips and dodging his head about to be sure no one was within hearing distance, he stabbed out the number on his cell phone.

"Talk to me," a voice said at the other end.

"This is about Professor Reiner," Freddy said. "I mean, like, about her sister. The beautiful one. Like, Linda? She and this Karen are, like, heading for Albert Niebel's apartment. . . . Right now. . . . I don't know how they found where he lives. . . . When do I get my money?"

Linda gave the decrepit Ford Escargot a look of wry amusement. "Perhaps we should hire a car. This one doesn't look like it'll make it two blocks."

"It's not a BMW," Karen said in mock apology. "Linda, I know you like to be the boss. But let me call the shots here, okay?"

"Your car is very . . . cute. Still, I can get us something much better."

"Mr. Escort is Frank Vere's car."

Linda reexamined the old junker with BMW respect. She wiggled onto the passenger seat, where stuffing peeked out in spots. She pressed her knees demurely together and gave Karen a brief smile. Karen got in her side and drove out of the parking lot.

Albert lived in a six-story walkup in a bad part of Jamaica, Queens, psychic worlds away from Manhattan's glitter. Albert's neighborhood rivaled Tijuana for homeless people, derelicts, and beggars. His apartment building's windows were caked with several years of grime. Overflowing garbage cans stood like fetid sentinels beside the front door.

"What a cesspool," Linda said. The only pools she dealt

with sat next to palatial cliffside second homes in the Caribbean. "And look at all those homeless people. Wretched." Clearly, Linda wasn't offended by an unjust society that had produced such pathetic folk. She was offended by the sight of them.

"Yeah, I'm used to a better class of bum in my neighborhood. They have the courtesy to lie about what they'll use your change for—college courses, granma's nursing home. In your neighborhood, you don't have that problem. They're shot on sight."

"On second thought," Linda said, daunted by the neighborhood squalor, "let's call Detective Friday and let the cops take care of Albert."

"Forget that. I'm calling the shots, remember? Albert may be a strange guy, yet as I said, he has no past pattern of violence. You can get out of him what Friday never can."

For Linda, who typically insisted on calling the shots with the vehemence of General George Patton, reluctantly ceded Karen the lead on this outing. She clasped her hands under her chin. "He wouldn't harm me. I hope."

Inside, Karen felt a growing panic, as though she were poised to enter a burning building. She kept telling herself this is what Frank Vere would do.

Karen pressed Albert's buzzer. The one marked Reiner. No response. He lived on the fifth floor. Then Karen noticed the front door standing ajar. "Great security. Lock's busted."

One lightbulb dangled obscenely in the downstairs hallway. That was the sum of the building's interior illumination. Karen went first up the gloomy staircase. It was as if they were miles underground. Linda trailed her warily.

At the fifth floor landing, they paused. "Hard to see the apartment numbers in here," Karen said. She delved through her bag and found her pocket flashlight.

Linda gripped her arm. "This isn't such a good idea."

"You wanted to come."

They inched down the stygian hall, which was littered with indistinct clumps of filth that resembled dead toads. Karen shined the flashlight on the door numbers. Albert's was at the end, in the most cavernously dark part of the hall. Rapping on the door, Karen called out, "Albert?"

She inched the door open. It, too, wasn't locked.

"Albert," Karen called again, and eased the door inward.

Hazy light filtered in from a single window, light that glinted off the computer gear sitting on a few tables and on the floor.

The door stopped midway. Something blocked it. Karen shoved and called Albert's name once more.

She peeked around the door to see what the obstruction was.

"Jesus Christ," she exclaimed. Karen slid sideways into the apartment and knelt over the form on the floor.

"What is it?" Linda said.

"Don't come in here." Karen felt for a pulse in the neck. None. The body was dead cold and clammy, the head bent at an odd angle, as though belonging to an unloved doll.

Linda edged in anyway and gasped.

"Is this Albert?" Karen said, trying to sound collected.

"Yes, yes, yes. Is he dead?"

"Looks like it." Karen felt her stomach churn. She choked back bile.

From her crouch, Karen scanned the cramped apartment to be sure they were alone. Then she caught sight of the huge silkscreen on the wall, the one of Linda's face. Hanging there like a bizarre icon. She wasn't going to point that out to Linda.

"I wonder if Goldring is here," Karen said hoarsely. She roamed through the seedy little studio apartment and saw nothing resembling it. "Albert has a lot of computers, but—"

"There should be a gold ring embossed on it, an old IBM ThinkPad, a replica of Daddy's friendship ring to Flo," Linda said, frozen to her spot, transfixed by Albert.

Karen examined the computers and delved through the drawers, in the closet, under the furniture. "Nothing."

Then they heard the thunder of feet from the stairway. Feet that slammed down the hall toward them like some many-hooved beast. Fear frozen, they watched as a brace of powerful guns appeared in the doorway, pointed at them. The muzzles had coin-sized circles, as dark as oblivion.

CHAPTER ELEVEN

"Holy guacamole," Friday shouted. Then he commanded, "Lower your weapons." He bellowed at the two women, "What the hell are you broads doing here?"

Karen, recovering herself as best she could, said, "Broads? Nice."

"I'll show you nice," Friday said, and slid his gun into the shoulder holster that his sports jacket concealed. His badge holder was draped from his breast pocket. In the soupy light cast from the apartment, the two other detectives out in the hallway did the same.

Friday stepped into the apartment, bent over Albert Niebel, and frowned. He looked at Karen and Linda and frowned some more.

"No," Karen said, "we didn't do it."

"Didn't say you did. Victim went to his maker a day or two ago. Let me ask again: what the hell are you two . . . *ladies* doing here?"

"Can't tell," Karen said, recalling her father's tales, likely bogus, of standing up to the cops in his protest-filled youth. "I'm on a story. I'm a reporter"

"Karen," Linda admonished.

Friday turned to the other detectives. One was as burly as Friday, the other as lean as a Doberman pinscher. Each had the sour look of someone tired of taking crap and able to do something about it.

"Well," Friday said, "my story is I'm booking you for obstruction of justice."

"We had no idea he was dead till we got here and the door was open," Karen said. "How is that obstruction of justice?"

"Your attitude is one big piece of obstruction," the detective said.

"Karen is a reporter for *Profit* magazine and my friend," Linda said.

If Karen was Linda's friend, then so was the old crone down the block who was rooting through the garbage pail. Karen decided to curb her wiseacre urge for the moment.

"You need to watch who you pick as friends," Friday said to Linda. "Both of you stay away from interfering with this case or there will be trouble."

"Did Albert kill Flo?" Karen asked him.

"Get out of my sight."

Going through the door into the dark hallway, Linda said, "Detective Friday, where are you on solving the murder of my sister?"

"Ms. Reiner," Friday said, "you and your sister Virginia are keeping something from us concerning that missing laptop. And this River character, your receptionist, isn't the picture of openness, either. He won't say where he went after he supposedly left Flo Reiner alone at the office. And there's the business about your unlocked office door. N.G.—not good."

Swallowing, Linda said, "You might as well know since everyone else seems to. The stolen laptop contained the only copy of our stock-picking system. It's very valuable."

Friday rubbed his jaw as if nursing an old wound. "Well, what a sunburst. I'll let you amend your statement outside. Without the Fourth Estate present, that is."

Karen preceded them downstairs and waited by the Escort while Friday reinterviewed Linda in his unmarked car. She felt entirely clueless about what to do next.

Then her cell phone rang. Frank. She quickly told him what they just had found.

"The cops," Frank said, "located two guys who work in the Reiners' building who saw someone answering Albert's description, right before the time of Flo Reiner's death, on the same floor as their office."

"But Faff and his mobster pals are the obvious suspects in Albert's death," Karen said.

"Nothing's obvious," Frank said. "See, the reason the cops haven't made much progress is that they've been hobbled in tracking down Albert. They got the word from the FBI to stay away from him and all else to do with the Reiner murder because it was part of a national security inquiry into terrorism."

"Huh?"

"Huh is right," Frank said. "The FBI always involves the NYPD in any New York terrorism investigation. Routinely. When my police source told me this, I called a pal in the Bureau. He said the FBI has to stay clear, too, that the whole thing is a cover for a spook operation."

"Spook? As in CIA?"

"Or whatever. Friday, who's a real hardhead, said, 'Screw it,' and refused to back off. He went to see Mimi, Albert Niebel's sister. After protesting they were picking on the handicapped—she's in a wheelchair—she told Friday that the FBI had been over to question her about Albert's whereabouts. She gave them zip, too. But they weren't FBI. We know the FBI guys have been nowhere near her place."

"A federal case?" Karen said. "Ridiculous. Linda strikes terror into the hearts of most women, but how would the Reiners's laptop be involved in terrorism?"

"Unclear. There's another wrinkle: Flo Reiner's links to the spook world."

"Flo, a spy? She was such a scatterbrain that she'd forget to pay her bills for months on end. And her taxes. Linda had to bail her out all the time. The closest she got to government work was as a trainee as some kind of computer nerd. She got arrested for hacking into a government network. Served time for it. Somehow, she got a job at Formdex after that, where she met Albert. I always suspected she got the Formdex job by wiping her record clean of the jail time by hacking."

"I know. Did you see that the government work she tried to get was at the Federal Reclamation Authority?"

"What do they do, make old furniture ready for flea markets?"

The lordly rumble of a jet sounded far overhead, slicing through the Queens sky. "On paper, they review claims of damages against Washington, like Navy destroyers ripping through fishing nets. It's really a super-secret offshoot of the CIA. Word is that the Authority is the agency that is waving the cops away from the Flo Reiner case."

"Wow. Do you have any sources in the spook world?"

"A few."

"Come on. Let me talk to one of your sources."

"Maybe someday. They say the Authority freaks out everybody. An old friend of mine, ex-CIA, says, 'They can get away with murder.' That's a direct quote."

"Murder?" The word dropped off Karen's lips and hung

in the air. "Murder, as in murder? Could the Authority or someone in it want Goldring, and terrorism is a ruse?"

"That's what I wonder," Frank said. "There are heavy-duty dogs jumping in here, heavier than Faff and his goons. You better watch your back."

"How am I supposed to do that? I don't even know what I've got in front of me."

With his creamy Merchant Ivory English accent, Siegfried Wolfe, professional assassin and man about many towns, made dinner reservations in the Plaza's lobby for dinner later. He cut an elegant figure in his tailored suit and gray hair, just the sort the hotel liked as a patron.

"How many in your party, sir?" the concierge asked.

"I'll be dining alone this evening. There won't be any party."

The computer carrying case swinging at his side, Wolfe left the storied hotel, where he always stayed in the same special room. He headed west, past Jack Faff's latest architectural monstrosity, which was soon to open. The Catholic church lay long blocks beyond Columbus Circle in a grim neighborhood dedicated to selling and repairing badly engineered automobiles. Old by American standards, the church had a stone exterior darkened by years of car exhaust. Inside, Our Lady of Perpetual Suffering was much more grand, with afternoon light filtering through the stained glass windows depicting martyrs getting slaughtered.

When Wolfe entered the confession booth, the priest was waiting.

"Don't bless me, Father," Wolfe said. "For I have sinned."

"That's the laptop with you?"

"Certainly. Aren't you going to ask me why I don't seek absolution?"

"Maybe because you're not a Catholic," the priest said.

"Worse. I sold my soul to Satan," Wolfe said. "And I'm not being metaphorical. I signed my name in blood, renouncing all good works, the whole bit."

"Okay," the priest said evenly, putting up with this for a moment. "What's he like? Satan."

"He's rather like you, Father."

The priest peered through the aperture at Wolfe's computer case. "And I suppose you've met God in your travels, too?"

"Yes, once. He tried to talk me out of joining the other team, actually."

"Oh, and what's He like?"

"British, of course. Very upper class."

The priest's face pressed lustfully against the screen. "Enough nonsense. I want the laptop now. Hand it over."

"I don't know anything about computers, even how to turn one on. But I assume this has to do with the stock market if it comes from the Reiner sisters. What a shame I know nothing about the stock market, either. But I do know about women. And Linda Reiner is a divine example. This coming from a man who is damned."

"Give it to me."

Wolfe didn't budge. "Father, do I really have to kill both the remaining Reiner sisters? That Linda is too lovely for such a fate."

"Yes, I'm paying you a lot of money for them. And you have that reporter to deal with, as well. Now give me the laptop, for God's sake."

"I'll do it. But please, not for His sake."

The next morning, with the funeral looming ahead, Linda decided she and Ginny needed pampering, so she made an appointment for Antonio's. Ginny, who thought beauty treatments were folly, agreed to go along. "Forget me," she said. "I'll just watch and commiserate."

Certainly, Linda needed commiseration. They were headed up Madison Avenue in the Sixties toward Antonio's salon. "I couldn't sleep all night," Linda said. "Dead bodies—my good God. First, Flo. Now, Albert. Horrible beyond belief. The sight of poor Flo's face. And the way Albert's head was twisted. Horrible."

"I never felt scared living alone before," Ginny said. "Now I do."

"I want you to stay at my place. You're much safer in my building."

"I'd rather stay close to campus. It's good that you've got Karen helping."

"Karen? She's how we tap into Frank Vere's sources. I don't know what to make of this spy business he found out about. I had no idea Flo was trying to join an intelligence agency. And these Authority people are investigating her death? Or maybe they want Goldring for themselves? And we know the cops aren't going to solve Flo's murder with this terrorism problem."

"I tell you, Karen has more on the ball than you realize," Ginny said.

"Jury's still out. Maybe I should hire private investigators. She almost got us arrested at Albert's by shooting off her smart mouth at the cops. I do have to wonder how effective the cops have been on this case, terrorism or no. Friday arrived at the apartment only because of an anonymous phone tip. He wouldn't say more."

"What did Karen say about that?"

"Vere couldn't find out about the phone tip beyond that it was a man's voice and the call was made to Friday directly. Well, I told Karen she could come to the funeral mass." Linda crossed her arms over her chest.

"What about Tim? Won't having both of them at the church be awkward?"

"Who cares? If Tim even shows up, I'll be surprised. He treats all this like it's a roof leak or a flooded basement. To him, it's my problem." Linda shrugged. "He came over last night and made me feel good for about twenty minutes. Then he went to sleep. At dawn, he was up and off."

"Typical man," Ginny said.

"That priest of Flo's, he's an odd guy. Weird, really. But nice."

"Priests personify the male hierarchy. So I don't go to church anymore. Haven't for years. Remember that we're due at the lawyer's for the reading of Flo's will."

"The one responsible thing she did on her own was to prepare a will. I didn't even have to push her to do it."

Antonio greeted them at the door with hugs and kisses. He offered his effusive condolences over Flo's death. "Anna gave her the most becoming cut, *cara*. Looked like a field of waving wheat."

"Anna's not in today?" Linda asked, moving Antonio away from the Flo subject.

Tossing his leonine mane, the hairdresser said, "Young girls these days. Anna is all the time out at the clubs, dancing her behind off, getting mixed up with crazy boys and coke and Ecstasy. She hasn't been around for a couple of days at least. I'm going to give that young lady a severe talking to." He threw his hands flamboyantly into the air. "And then welcome her back to the nest."

Fronted by a large glass window that gave onto Madison, the salon was a statement in chic. Blond wood flooring, spot lighting, chrome-lined mirrors. The staff was an exotic mix of ethnicities. The clientele—high-toned women with perfect noses, who took money for granted—sat in ornamental chairs, wearing capes and drinking from gold-edged demitasse.

"I will personally tend to you, of course," Antonio told Linda. "And your lovely sister here. Let us begin with you, *cara*." He smiled at Ginny.

"I'm not in a lovely making mood today, thanks," Ginny said.

"Oh, but, *cara* . . ."

"Who's that man?" Ginny exclaimed.

"Who? Where?" Linda followed her sister's gaze to the front window. No one was there.

"Distinguished-looking. In a suit. Gray hair. He was staring in at us from the street. Like he knew us."

Linda, used to men staring at her, patted Ginny's back. "He doesn't sound dangerous."

The news was good, and when Donner heard it, he pounded the desk like a chimp in heat. "Oh, yeah, the snotty bastards came through. Love those Brits. Love them to death."

Logie arched an eyebrow.

Donner grabbed the hotline to the director's office. "Tell him I got some top-notch intel for him. Thanks." He strutted around his desk. "Back in the game."

The door opened and the chair bearers entered with their cargo. Wooton was right behind them. He sat down and said, "Well?"

Donner's grin grew still wider. "The British ID'd the voice of the guy who killed Niebel and absconded with Goldring, Director."

"His name is Siegfried Wolfe," Wooton said.

Deflating visibly, shoulders rounding, grin collapsing, Donner said, "How did you know?"

"By listening to the tape several more times. We first met in Prague, after the Russians had invaded, when I was starting out in this trade. I saved Wolfe's life. How about that?"

The director folded his hands over the vest that encased his paunch. "He's a remarkable man, in many senses."

"Oh," Donner said.

Wooton told him more he didn't know. "Wolfe left British Intelligence after the Cold War," the director said. "Eliminating drunken chieftains in the Irish Republican Army held little appeal for him. He has done quite well freelancing. So we have to pinpoint him and whom he is working for. It's not Faff, I can assure you."

Donner cleared his suddenly dry throat. "Did you know Wolfe has this wacky routine about selling his soul to the devil?"

"Yes, yes, yes. Everyone's heard about that." The director waved impatiently. "Did you get a list of his most recent aliases?"

"Uh, a couple of them."

"He employs several dozen aliases. Get them. Call London back and ask for Jeremy Wrigglesham and use my name. Jeremy and I go back—the Plain of Jars, Laos, nineteen-seventy. Those were the days." He turned to Logie. "Once Mr. Donner has managed to complete this taxing assignment, I want you to find Wolfe."

After Donner had drifted back to his desk, Logie said, "Director, you realize how worried I am about my daughter?"

"No, you can't see her until the mission is successfully concluded. I keep telling you. Are you becoming as dull-witted as Mr. Donner?"

"Uh . . . well . . ."

Wooton tapped his forehead and gave a sage look reminiscent of the Amazing Kreskin. "I know what you are going to say before you say it, Ms. Logan."

Logie wanted to hoot at his claimed telepathic powers, which were simply a matter of observation and common sense. If he could read minds, then he'd know how everyone thought him a fat cuckold soon to be unemployed.

But it didn't take telepathy to see that Wooton considered himself God's superior officer.

Swallowing Wooton's latest insult, Donner said, "Oh, Director, we did make inquiries about that reporter, Karen Glick. The one who did the Reiner story and got the tip from Solter Faff about Jack Faff's financial problems."

"Oh, yes," Wooton said, "that silly girl who got involved in the car crash with Faff. She's sidelined in disgrace."

"Not totally. We may have to deal with her."

Logie looked at Donner in alarm. "Deal with her how?"

Karen, like any sane person, was no fan of funerals—and especially not of this one. At the office that morning, the Razz encouraged her to have a few drinks first to give her courage.

"I'm a cowardly drunk, myself," Karen said.

Karen made the long walk from midtown to the church, whose stone walls were dark with soot. Gazing up at it from the sidewalk as she slipped into the plain black pumps she'd carried in her bag, Karen felt Our Lady of Perpetual Suffering had the welcoming warmth of a medieval fortress before a siege. Inside, the trappings were more pleasing, with complex stained glass windows that sucked in light and an ornamental altar with a golden cross. Flowers fanned out colorfully from both sides of the altar. Flo's coffin was centered under the cross. The pews, though, were as empty as a bad marriage.

Linda and Ginny stood in the vestibule, black clad and solemn. Linda kissed Karen on the cheek and gave her a brittle smile. Ginny hugged Karen like a family member.

"Anybody else here besides us?" Karen asked.

"She had no friends," Ginny said.

"Tim should be along," Linda said. "At some point."

"I see he hasn't changed," Karen said, then wished she hadn't, as she often did.

Ginny glowered impatiently. "Where's Father Finagle? Time to get this under way."

Karen looked outside in the vain hope that someone, anyone, might materialize to join the party. Surely the Reiners could hire some mourners. "That's the priest's name?"

Putting an arm around Ginny, who had placed her hands over her face, Linda said, "The priest is Father Finnegan. He's very nice."

Ginny dropped her hands to reveal tear-tracked cheeks. "The lawyers told us he's the executor of her will. And she left him a million dollars. And she left this parish another million. And she left the rest of her money to a trust fund overseen by none other than . . . Father Finagle himself."

"Now, now," Linda said. "We don't need the money."

"That's not the point," Ginny shot back. "He used her. She spent a lot of time here. Too much time. I know they were having sex. I do. Religious fraud. Vow of celibacy, my ass."

Karen would have preferred to be on an airless asteroid. The only way it could be worse would be if Tim showed up. But she was present for a reason and paid the sisters rapt attention. "Do you know for a fact they were lovers?" Karen asked them.

"Both of you—this is her final mass," Linda said in a way calculated to yank everyone back to the proper posture of funeral-going rectitude. "We have no proof of any of this."

Karen, however, was on the scent. "But," she said, "Flo could have told him in the confessional or wherever about Gold—"

"He wouldn't reveal a confession." Linda, very much in charge, put her index finger across her lips. "Enough such talk. Each of us loved Flo in our own fashion. Ah, Father Finnegan."

Wearing a white robe and a thin smile, the priest eyed them with the caution a meat deliveryman would a slavering pack of wolfhounds. His forehead was crinkled as if in a constant state of worry. His eyes flicked from person to person. After introductions, he suggested in a reedy voice that they begin. "No one else coming?"

"Maybe one," Linda said.

"He'll be late, as usual," Karen said.

Indicating for Ginny and Karen to follow, Linda led the way into the church. Ginny buzzed at Karen how glad she was to see her, and reminisced about the time Karen had cooked for the sisters. "It was so tasty. Linda wants to order in tonight. Could you do the meal instead?"

So now I'm the Reiner's servant, Karen thought. Still, this was an awful day for them and they needed support. "Sure. You guys like peanut butter and jelly?"

Having reached the church's front ahead of them, Linda gave an impatient look. Ginny whispered to Karen that they had better hustle. "You know how mean and sarcastic Linda can be if she doesn't get her way. My sister, the boss."

Linda gestured for Karen to sit in the front pew with Ginny and her. An organist and a singer sidled in. Karen, as the lone non-Catholic, followed the others' lead in sitting, standing, kneeling, chanting, and singing. When Karen was young and her father denounced organized religion as "the opiate of the masses," she thought churches and synagogues were places they sold drugs. It would be an improvement on this endless ritual. Maybe the Razz was right about those drinks.

Throughout the interminable mass, Karen stole glances at Linda, who stared straight ahead at the cross or the priest, avoiding the coffin. Ginny kept her head bowed as if in prayer or shame.

Father Finnegan addressed them from the pulpit. "Flo Reiner was a true child of God," he said. "Disappointment dogged her. Love, she felt, stayed away from her. But in her final days, she came to terms with herself and her faith."

"And you came to terms with her money," Ginny muttered. Linda shushed her.

"Flo knew great joy from her investing success," the priest continued. "At long last, she could do something well. And she talked to me often about how proud her beloved father would be of her now. 'Daddy's watching over me from heaven,' she'd say."

"From heaven?" Ginny whispered.

"Yes," the priest said, "she always wore the friendship ring her daddy had given her when she was a girl."

Ginny sighed audibly. "I can't stand this." That was when she turned around and said, "It's him again."

Karen swiveled her head to the back of the church. A distinguished-looking man in a suit sat by himself.

"Who?" Karen asked Ginny, sitting next to her.

"Be quiet," Linda said.

"The man who was watching us in the hair salon today," Ginny said. "Who is he?"

But when Karen turned to look once more, the man had vanished. As might a ghost.

Father Finnegan rattled on about God's love. Then he gave communion to the two Catholics. Ginny went up to the rail grumbling. The mass concluded, the three mourners stood at the church door. Ginny groused that the hearse was late. The funeral home-provided pallbearers kept the casket in the church until it arrived. Linda talked quietly to the priest, who smiled guiltily. Ginny stood glaring at him.

Gingerly, Karen drew Linda aside and whispered what she needed to do.

"No, no," Linda said and vehemently shook her head.

"I have to see everything. Nothing left out."

Ginny, brow lowered crossly, joined them. "The hearse just pulled up. What's wrong?"

Fed up, Linda said to Karen, "Okay, okay, but be quick. Ginny, come with me."

Karen's steps echoed as she moved along the side of the church, past the confessional, to where the coffin sat. She requested that the pallbearers stand in front of the casket, to shield it from view. "One last time for a sister," she told them.

"We understand," the chief pallbearer said. "Allow me." The latch to the lid opened easily. "Jesus Christ," he said. Then, "Sorry."

Flo was dressed for eternity in the scruffy clothes she liked before Linda remade her look: a sweatshirt, baggy jeans, sneakers. Linda had told Karen about Flo's new haircut, from Linda's chi-chi hairdresser. It was short and odd. The funeral director hadn't bothered to restore Flo's face. Perhaps that was impossible. It was a bloody vision from a nightmare.

Forcing back the gorge in her throat, Karen motioned for the man to close the lid.

Linda met her as she stumbled outside into the welcoming sunlight. "Well?"

"I wasn't sure what I was looking for," Karen said. She watched them wheel the coffin to the waiting hearse. "I needed to see—but I noticed a missing . . . Well, it's not on her finger."

"A missing what?"

"The friendship ring your father gave her. It's not on her hand."

"Flo had that on constantly. That's why she called the laptop Goldring. The friendship ring was on her hand when I identified her body at the office."

Karen was the first to spot the woman in the wheelchair as she rolled furiously toward them. She aimed straight at Linda. Her face was a tight fist of rage.

"You," she yelled at Linda. "You lured my brother to his death, you bitch from hell."

CHAPTER TWELVE

"You tell me why you did it, damn you," the woman in the wheelchair screamed. "You answer me now."

Karen jumped in front of her and stopped the charging chair by grabbing its armrests.

"Get out of my way." Her screaming directly in Karen's face was among the most intense experiences she'd had that day, right up there with viewing Flo's mangled face.

Tim chose that moment to make his belated appearance, resplendent in his bespoke suit. "Who is this woman?" he demanded. "I'll call the police." He whipped out his phone.

Linda put a hand over his as he started to punch 911. "No one is calling any cops. Let's go." She gestured to Ginny and Father Finnegan. "Come on."

"And why are you here?" Tim demanded of Karen.

"Not to see you," Karen said. "Nice of you to show up on time."

Linda ordered Ginny, the priest, and Tim to pile into a waiting town car. Their driver quickly closed its doors. Maybe due to Tim's presence, Linda hadn't told Karen to get in the car to the graveyard. Or maybe it was because Karen was useful restraining charging wheelchairs.

Karen didn't have to ask who the wheelchair woman was.

Despite the useless, wire-thin legs beneath her skirt, Mimi Niebel acted far from helpless. With worry lines radiating from her eyes and lank brown hair going early to gray, she was someone who had suffered much, expected to suffer more, and made others join in her suffering. "My poor brother," she said fiercely. "Linda tossed him out. Like garbage. Human garbage."

Karen said, "I'm sorry about your loss. I was the one who discovered your bro—"

"You're that reporter who made Linda famous. I looked you up on the Web. What does she want from you? She'll use you."

They put Flo's coffin in the hearse. In a trice, the two-car funeral cortege solemnly moved away. Karen released the wheelchair's armrests and took a step back.

"Mimi," Karen said, "Albert was stalking Linda. Didn't a judge rule he had to stay away?"

Albert's sister reacted as if Karen had asked what year it was. "How dumb can you get?"

"Humor me, then. What do you mean?"

"Linda Reiner," Mimi said in a singsong way, as one might teach a slow child the alphabet, "obviously killed her own sister, then tried to blame it on poor Albert. He wouldn't hurt a bug."

"Why would Linda want to kill her own sister?"

"So she'd have Goldring to herself. The other sister, the math professor, she'd better watch out."

"Who told you about Goldring?"

Mimi waved dismissively at her stupidity. "Albert knew about Goldring. Come on."

"How did he know?"

Pulling a folded piece of paper out of her jacket pocket, Mimi said, "Because Linda told him. Duh."

"How did Linda tell him?"

She waved the paper at him. "Read this. That's assuming you know how to read."

Karen plucked the paper out of her hand. It was an e-mail to Albert from an America Online address belonging to Linda Reiner. The message said:

Dearest Albert,
The path is clear for us at last. I no longer have to hide my love for you. We can go off together and live in love, entwined in each other's arms forever. I have to tell you a secret and I need you to perform a task, my darling. For us.

The secret is that my horrible sisters and I have gained our wealth from a computer program loaded on a laptop, which we call Goldring. Goldring predicts which stocks are about to rise in price, before they do. So we buy them early and sell after they rise. The laptop has a gold ring embossed on it and is powerful magic. Think what it can give us, a life of luxury together until the end of time. But we have to be smart now, my darling.

On the night of Oct. 13 at 7 p.m., be waiting in the street outside my office. Wait until River leaves. Then go up to the office.

The door will be unlocked. Goldring will be in plain sight. Take Goldring back to your place and wait for me to come. Don't call me in the meantime; that's too dangerous. Then we will fly away and be rich and happy in love.

The note was signed: "Your true love, Linda."

"Can I keep this?" Karen asked.

"You can shove it up your nose for all I care," Mimi said. "Now you know what the beautiful Linda Reiner is really like. I dare you to print it." She rolled her chair away from Karen and the church. Traffic buzzed by. The spires of midtown caught what remained of the afternoon sun. In the west, sinister clouds were forming. A wind picked up, the herald of more wicked weather.

Halfway down the block, Mimi stopped and called over her shoulder, "The cops found this on his e-mail file and gave me a copy, asking what I knew about it. I said nothing. They said they had to turn it over to the FBI. I called the FBI and got the runaround."

As Mimi wheeled furiously away, Karen called Frank and told him the latest.

"That e-mail could have come from anybody," Frank said. "Or not. Trouble is, I'm not well-sourced in cracking AOL addresses."

"My head is spinning," Karen said. "Who else would have sent this e-mail and why?"

Frank cleared his throat. "Meanwhile, Friday also found a confirmation of a stock purchase on Albert's computer. From Merrill Lynch Direct. Seems like he opened an account there and put ten thousand bucks into a stock called Corsine Industries. Ever heard of it?"

"Yeah. Maybe."

"The stock has started to rise, which is odd," Frank said. "There's no apparent reason for this. No big earnings increase, no big new product announcement, the kind of things that usually make a stock jump. And Corsine stock has gone nowhere for years. Suddenly, boom."

"A classic Reiner-style value stock that sat like a lump, then soared. So Goldring had started to work for Albert, just as it did for the Reiners."

"The cops, who got that anonymous tip on Albert's real address, found something else. Are you sitting down?"

"I'm standing on a New York City sidewalk. No, I'm not sitting down. What is it?"

Frank said, "They found a .45-caliber pistol hidden in Albert's apartment, with his fingerprints on it and no one else's. One round had been fired. Ballistics matches it with the gun that killed Flo. When Friday reported this, his superiors told him to turn it all over to the FBI and to drop the case. They were mad he hadn't dropped it already."

"I don't get the picture of Albert killing Flo," Karen said. "Couldn't Mikhail Beria have planted the gun? Couldn't he have wiped the gun clean, put dead Albert's fingers on it to get the prints? Faff is involved, I tell you."

"Maybe, maybe not," Frank said. "Given the e-mail, how do you know Linda didn't do it?"

"Linda wouldn't risk it. She might break a nail. Besides, she has an alibi."

"Maybe Linda is more ruthless than you think. She could've hired a killer. She didn't blink at grabbing hold of your husband, did she?"

To restore his spirits, Jack Faff summoned what energy he could muster and picked a triumphal passage across the gold-stippled casino floor. The customers dropped their slot machine handles, their cards, their dice, and their watery drinks to behold the passing of a shining celebrity. One who had just decamped from the hospital to grace their drab lives with a brief walk-through. They applauded wildly.

"We love you, Jack!"

"Welcome back, Jack."

"Jack, I want to have your children!"

As he neared his private elevator, the last waitress he had bonked—named Denise or Deidre or maybe Donna—

intercepted him. The bodyguards moved to stop her, but he signaled them to stay back. She had a blazing smile for him.

"Jack," she said and laid a hand on his chest above his problematical heart, "I missed you. Want me to come up later?"

He flinched at her touching his sore ribs. Her smile went out. She was the wildcat type in bed. Too much for him now. "No, darling. Kind of busy."

The elevator whooshed him to his office. He paraded past the fawning underlings and closed the doors behind him. Mikhail sprawled on the couch. An edgy Solter—much more anxious than usual—perched on the edge of a chair, knees together.

Shucking the act of bold conqueror, Jack slowly crossed to his desk and sank into his chair with a groan. The sky outside his panoramic window churned ominously. "Storm coming. I'm not doing any driving tonight. Who has Goldring?"

Mikhail sat up straight. "We have not found it yet, Jack. But we will."

"Strike one. What about the Reiners?"

Unsure about the baseball reference but aware it wasn't positive, Mikhail hardened his stare. "We are watching them close. They go to Flo Reiner funeral today. We are on them like shit on fly."

"Uh-huh. Ball one. And those alleged feds outside Niebel's apartment building?"

Mikhail smacked a meaty fist into a meaty palm. "Touchdown. I got an old-time KGB guy now in the Russian embassy in Washington. He is on my payroll. He says he hears this American spy agency is doing some counterterrorism operation in New York. But this is not a real counterterrorism operation in New York. He knows this is phony baloney. They pose as FBI."

"Spy agency? You mean the CIA?"

"No. This is a branch-off of CIA. Called the Federal Reclamation Authority. They are bad dudes. Got big secret place out in Virginia."

Faff's eyes narrowed. "Never heard of the agency. In Virginia, you say? Where?"

"Outside the Beltway. In the sticks. Valhalla."

A sly smile came over Faff's lips. "Back in the nineteen eighties, we had a government construction contract for this massive building. Went deep into the earth, to survive nuclear strikes. Supposedly for the Pentagon. All very classified. We couldn't talk about it. It was the Reagan defense build-up time. The money was good."

"Bad time, the eighties," Mikhail said. "I served in Afghanistan. Young soldier, Red Army. People there were crazy nuts in the head. Wanted to kill every Russian."

Jack turned his attention to Solter, as a tiger would to a cringing monkey. "A high-level spy agency. This explains a lot. See, as I lay in my hospital bed, I had nothing else to do but think about how my secrets are getting spilled. How could these fake FBI types find out about Goldring when only I had the inside knowledge of it? How could detailed information about my finances leak to the press? The only logical answer: someone around me likes to talk. As they say, we got a mole in our own ranks."

"A mole," Mikhail said. "Very bad, a mole."

A film of sweat had formed on Solter's upper lip and forehead. "I'm sure that's not true, Jack."

The sweat was enough. But Solter's familiar lying tone— *"No, I didn't tell Pop-pop about your dope and that girl. Honest."*—made Jack doubly certain. "I want Mikhail to ask you some hard questions, Solter."

"No, Jack. Please."

Jack stood up stiffly. "I'm gonna relax. No women. Just

some light supper and some wine. Good for my heart. And when Mikhail has dealt with you, then you and I will talk."

Solter was hysterical. "Jack, for the love of Christ. I'm your brother. Don't do this."

Linda's old apartment in the Village had been a one-bedroom third-story walkup with a tiny kitchen whose window opened to the brick airshaft, only one cut better than Karen's new abode. Linda's best piece of furniture then was a Barcelona chair that she kept in the living room. A few Impressionist reproductions, bought at museum gift shops, decorated the walls. Stylish, but inexpensive was how Karen remembered it. Before her glory run with Goldring, Linda had spent a bigger chunk of her salary on clothes than on home decor.

Her new place, however, bore none of the hallmarks of single career gal. The cathedral-sized lobby, with its brigade of doormen, featured a long rectangle of water reminiscent of the Reflecting Pool in Washington. The elevator was almost as big as Linda's old apartment and Karen's new, post-Tim one. Although Linda answered her door herself, Karen knew that was only because she hadn't yet hired servants. The vast penthouse showed the nighttime city beyond through acres of sheet glass. Skyline lights shimmered in the rain, which splashed the sweeping patio beyond the glass.

A grim Linda looked with distaste at the dripping slicker Karen held in her right hand, then saw the shopping bag she hefted in her left. "What's that?"

"Food. Ginny wanted me to cook."

"I figured we'd order in, but if you insist." Linda acted as if she were doing Karen a favor by allowing her to cook for them. She beckoned for Karen to follow her. Even though she carried a load of woe, Linda's carriage was as dignified as always.

Karen deposited the food in the magnificent kitchen, which obviously hadn't been cooked in. (Linda, as the old joke went, didn't make dinner; she made reservations.) She then trailed Linda into the understated opulence of the living room. Ginny was pleased to see Karen, brightening at her entrance, then dimming, sinking back into a linen sofa with a large tumbler of scotch.

"I can't believe she's gone," said Ginny, full of both booze and melancholy. "So young. Whole life ahead of her. In computers, the best ones show class when they're young. Like athletes. Like mathematicians. Flo was a genius at computers. Her screwed-up psychological state stopped her."

Karen swept a hand to take in the room, "What a lovely place. All of you have worked hard for your money." Nothing like a little sucking up to start off. She demurred Linda's offer of a drink for the moment. She had an agenda.

Then, with a start, she heard her husband's voice. Tim paced impatiently in the next room, pouring his displeasure into the phone. "I don't care. . . . No, you're not listening to me. I don't care." Before her Billionaire Boys Club story, Tim never had showed such stress on a work-related call. Here, his preppy cool had fled faster than a WASP when the booze runs out.

"A little while ago on the phone, you said Tim wouldn't be here," Karen said.

"His meeting got cancelled," Linda said.

"We couldn't have created Goldring without Flo," Ginny said.

"Let's not discuss Goldring," Linda said, as if delivering an imperial edict.

"Who would have stolen Daddy's friendship ring from her finger?" Ginny went on. "That is so low. My God."

Karen said, "Anyone at the medical examiner's could

have stolen the ring. Frank says stuff goes missing a lot from there."

"Maybe we should check Father Finagle's hand," Ginny said. "He got everything else that belonged to Flo."

"Stop it," Linda said. "This isn't the way to remember Flo's life."

"I know this time is difficult for you guys," Karen said.

"We loved her, even though sometimes she was hard to love," Linda said, and hoisted her scotch glass. Thunder rumbled outside like divine ill will.

Tim trooped scowling into the living room. "I can't believe that stupid ass hasn't gotten the pro forma financials." Then he remembered why he was there. He moved back into charming mode. "Sorry." He ran a hand gently across Linda's cheek, which he used to do to Karen.

Linda summoned a smile for her boyfriend. She tossed her hair back like strong liquor.

Karen unclenched her teeth. "I'm going into the kitchen to start."

Tim spun around at her voice, surprised. "What are *you* doing here?"

"I told you I invited Karen over, Tim," Linda said. "She's helping me. Remember?"

Karen said, "On second thought, I should go."

Ginny's eyes widened. "No, don't, Karen. We want you here. You can help us when no one else can. Please stay."

"How can this reporter do you any good?" Tim declared, catapulting out of his feigned compassion at the sight of Karen. "Reporters do nothing but cause trouble. I can tell you that from personal experience."

" 'This reporter' happens to be your wife," Karen said.

"Not for long." Tim snatched his scotch glass from the steel-top coffee table, where Karen hadn't noticed it. "You got a lucky break with the Billionaire Boys Club story.

You're only good at writing cutesy stories. The idea that you can find Flo's killer and Goldring is ridiculous."

"What are you drinking there?" Karen said. "The milk of human kindness? And besides, my cutesy stories made people pretty happy in the Reiner family. Or doesn't that matter to you?"

"You're no investigative reporter," Tim said. "You're a fraud."

"Stop this," Linda told Tim. "I buried my sister today and all I hear from you is your issues."

"Are there any other kind?" Karen said.

"I'm tired of your mouth," Tim growled at his wife. "For once, shut up, Karen."

"Tim," Linda said, "if you can't behave yourself, then get out of here."

Her boyfriend's stormy expression rivaled the foul weather outside. "Fine. I'll go." He spun on his heel with the precision of a Prussian duelist after a drawn match. He said to Karen, "You started this."

"The only thing I'm starting," Karen said, "is dinner."

At least Linda had the proper complement of kitchenware in her glass upper and lacquered lower cabinets. The cooking island had a limestone counter that matched the floors. Karen rubbed the steaks with garlic and grilled them lightly under the stainless steel hood. She quickly tossed the salad with oil and vinaigrette dressing, sliced the sourdough bread, flash-baked the potatoes. She had learned to cook because her mother was a master at ruining food. Ma could make canned tuna taste like something the cat yucked up.

Karen summoned the sisters to dinner at the black cherry dining room table. Ginny dove into the food while muttering her satisfaction that Father Finagle wasn't on hand to ruin the meal: "He got free sex, free money, but not free food. Not tonight." Karen made sure they both had ample wine, atop the already large amount of scotch they had consumed. *In vino veritas*.

The rainstorm flailed at the floor-to-ceiling window that gave onto the patio. Linda had turned silent after the scene between her boyfriend and his wife.

As they ate, Ginny presented a morose monologue on Flo's hapless life. No friends. No romance. Always getting fired. Forever in disputes with neighbors. "That Albert was as close as she got to a friend, but look at him," Ginny said.

"Were Flo and Albert a . . . couple?" Karen ventured.

"Never," Ginny scoffed. "She had *some* standards. River was the one she had the hots for, but he rebuffed her. She had no love in her life." Ginny broke into sobs, one hand clasped to her eyes, the other still firmly gripping her wineglass.

Linda reached over and stroked her sister's back. "Hey, it'll be okay. I know it hurts. It hurts me, too. But we have to move on. To think of the future."

Ginny dropped the hand from her eyes. Her face remained contorted in anguish. "I don't have your strength, Linda. I don't have your guts. I couldn't have thought up Goldring like you did."

"We're not talking about Goldring, remember?" Linda tried to say soothingly. A bit of hardness could be heard around the edges.

"I hate this," Ginny said. "I want my life ordinary again. Predictable. I don't want to be rich. Never have. I tried to maintain a brave front, especially with Flo. But it terrified me that what Goldring does is illegal. We could go to prison. You and me both, Linda."

"Be quiet," Linda commanded. "You've drunk too much. You don't know what you're talking about, Ginny. Get a grip."

They had finished eating and were into the third bottle of wine. Now was the time.

"I'd like to talk about this." Karen retrieved the e-mail from her pocket and put it on the tabletop.

"What is this?" Linda asked.

Karen was studying her hard. "Read it."

"Linda? Ginny asked, on the brink of fear.

Tapping the e-mail emphatically with her index finger as she examined it, Linda said, "This is a lie. A damn lie. I have no AOL account. I never sent this to Albert. Someone else did it."

Karen told her how she had gotten the e-mail and that Detective Friday had it, too. Not to mention the FBI. "You're telling me the truth?"

Linda gave her an angry glare. "Of course I am, Karen. Friday already has shown this to me, and I told him the same. And if you don't believe me, you can go straight to hell."

"Linda," Karen said, "you are going to have to share information with me for this to work. Why didn't you show me this?"

Waving her finely boned hand to and fro, Linda said, "Fine, fine, fine. I was going to. But I've been a little tied up, what with burying my sister." She seethed for a moment. "This e-mail is obvious crap. Friday checked with AOL. He confirmed they have no account there in my name. This was a hack job into the AOL network. And I'd never tell a man I'd 'live in love' with him. I don't believe in love."

"Well," Karen said, "I'll believe that." She nodded. "Sorry. I had to be sure."

"Fake e-mail addresses aren't that hard to do," Ginny said. "Not that I could do one."

"Who would?" Linda said, partly mollified.

"Whoever snatched Goldring, to throw the cops off track," Karen said. "What's interesting is the e-mail seemed to assume that no one would be in your office when Albert was there."

Linda said, "This e-mail in my name appears to trick Albert into taking Goldring."

Karen shrugged. "Maybe Albert was working with someone else." She told them what she had learned about Corsine, and the gun in Albert's apartment. "Our two sets of suspects are Faff and his hoods, and these spy characters, the Federal Reclamation Authority, for whatever reason. Albert is tied to them somehow."

Linda said, "I don't know what to make of the fact that Flo was a trainee at that place before they fired her and sent her to jail for hacking them. But that was years ago and she surely had no remaining ties to the agency. Flo didn't have friends anywhere."

A hammer blow of thunder made them flinch. Karen drew in some breath. "There has to be a connection. Someone spilled the goods to both the spooks and Faff. Who?"

"River," Ginny said. "Has to be. He didn't have any alibi for the police for when Flo died, right? The girl down the hall, who River angrily blew off when she made advances, said our office door was open after he left for the night. River thought she told the cops that as revenge."

"He has flipped out, for sure," Linda said. "After he rather rudely rejected Flo's attentions, she was mean to him. But could River be involved in killing Flo?"

"Maybe Albert and River were working together," Karen said.

"I doubt that," Linda said dismissively, as though Karen had suggested Islamic jihadists were in league with Zionists. "Albert hated River. River threw him out of our office."

"Right now," Karen said, "given the gun in Albert's apartment, they'll say Albert did it and close the case. That's what Frank hears."

"Poor Flo," Ginny said, and glugged more wine. "What Daddy did to her. No wonder Flo—"

"Ginny," Linda said sharply. "None of that. Let's leave the past alone."

As she refilled her glass, Ginny said, "Why? What happened in the past has a relation to today. Like, Flo always was mad at you, Linda—and Lord knows at me, as well— for not being around when she needed us with Daddy. If only—"

"Enough, Ginny," Linda said.

Karen wanted to press for more, but decided to lay low on the Daddy subject for now. She said, "Who else besides the people in this room know about Goldring?"

"Who doesn't?" Ginny chortled. "Mimi Niebel, Tim, Detective Friday, your editor, most of Wall Street, Frank Vere. . . ."

"River is holding something back," Karen said. "I'll start with him. Then Faff—I have to find a way to draw him out and also keep his goons at bay. The spooks? I'm not sure how to find them, meaning I go at them last."

"What's this 'I' business," Linda said. "Let me help."

"Linda, really . . ."

"I was with you at Albert's place."

"Okay," Karen said with resignation. "We hit River tomorrow."

"You two should be very careful," Ginny said.

Linda put on her sly smile. "Karen's a tough city girl. She used to box."

Karen helped Ginny, decidedly in her cups, to the elevator. Despite Linda's protests, Ginny insisted on going home to her own bed. "They're redoing my building," Ginny slurred. "Gotta keep my eye on them. Gotta be near campus. Love my students, though it's mostly boys. Why can't girls like math? I got one pretty girl in my class. Danielle. She has these adorable freckles. I want to kiss every one of them."

Linda watched them from the hall. The brass elevator doors closed with a solid thunk. Karen gripped Ginny's arm to keep her upright. She staggered with Ginny through the lobby, realizing they both looked plastered. The doorman's expression was amused. He blasted his whistle for a cab.

"Why is Goldring illegal?" Karen asked, now that Linda wasn't standing guard on her sister's drunken utterances.

Ginny shook her bowed head. "Linda says we don't talk about it."

Amazingly, a taxi pulled up. Unoccupied cabs in the rain were scarce as love in Linda's heart. Karen told the driver Ginny's address in Morningside Heights and got her seated. As she leaned across her to fasten her seatbelt, Ginny suddenly hugged Karen. "Thank you for helping us, Karen."

The taxi sloshed onto the puddled side street. In the streetlights, rain fell in silvery curtains. Telling the doorman, in a decidedly sober voice, that he wouldn't get lucky hailing a cab a second time in such weather, Karen adjusted her slicker and set forth into this wet world. The subway station was many blocks distant. Perhaps she could snag a bus.

A block away from Linda's, she felt the eyes on her. Stopping and turning around, she saw a solitary man headed toward her, face covered by a hat. Something told Karen the man's fast and purposeful gait had nothing to do with the rain and everything to do with her. She squinted.

Lightning turned the entire lonely street stark white and lit up the man's face. He was the one in the back of the church, who had been lurking outside the hair salon.

Karen began walking fast. World-ending thunder cracked overhead. No one else was on the long block, filled with tall and silent residential towers. No one would hear her cry out.

She reached Lexington Avenue, where the gutters were running brooks. And . . . yes, there was a bus waiting, filled with welcoming light, its door open. Karen ran for it, but the door folded shut and the bus engine roared in a departing salute.

Checking behind her, Karen found no one. Surely, another bus would be coming along.

From nowhere, the powerful arm snaked over her shoulder and across her throat.

CHAPTER THIRTEEN

The man's lips tickled Karen's ear, intimately, dangerously. "Pay attention, my girl," he said with an upper-crust English accent. "You're beginning to be a bother. I don't enjoy bothers. So you'll do what I say. Understand?"

Karen's slicker hood had fallen off her head and the rain spattered her face. The arm encircled her neck with a python's strength. Although her voice came out a croak, Karen could only respond as she normally did. With a question. "Who are you?"

"Never you mind. Will you do what I say?"

"Who are you working for?"

The arm tightened more around Karen's throat. "Will you do what I say then?" the man said.

"What's your name?"

"One more question out of you and you die. Are you listening?"

Karen's strangled reply: "I'm listening."

"You're getting a chance. One chance. This is a warning.

If there's a next time for you and me, your chance is up. You are to leave the Reiners and their laptop alone. Drop the entire pursuit. I will be observing to ensure that you comply. Am I clear?"

"Yes." As the pressure eased on her windpipe, Karen added, "Are you with Faff or the Authority?"

"I'm with Satan, my girl."

The arm slowly and sensuously slid back out of Karen's view. With exquisite caution, she turned around.

Yet the Englishman was gone, as though he had melted into the concrete, leaving no trace of himself on the empty sidewalk on a night full of rain.

Morning mist shrouded the church, which was locked up like a treasury vault. Amid the gloomy confines within, behind the door to the office marked FATHER FINNEGAN, the priest logged onto Goldring. The laptop sprang into electronic life, filling the darkened office with an unearthly glow.

Yes, the computer showed Corsine Industries as a sure buy. It had just started to move, but the priest knew the rise would not be sudden. There still was time to get in.

The priest had signed up with an online brokerage using the pseudonym Simon Scratch. There had been an actual Simon Scratch, who had died two years before in a road rage incident—at a traffic light, he had called another driver an asshole for almost sideswiping him; the other driver had replied by shooting Simon Scratch five times. That taught Simon a lesson. Since the brokerage required a Social Security number, the priest used Simon Scratch's.

This morning, Simon Scratch bought five thousand dollars worth of Corsine, not enough to drive the price up or to be noticed by others. Simon would make numerous such piecemeal Corsine purchases before the stock really took off. Then he would tell the brokerage to unload the stock at a nice profit. Sweet, lovely, perfect.

The Corsine order confirmation popped up on the brokerage's Web site, accessible only to customers who had a password. "Nice," the priest mused, "to be an investing genius."

Deep under the beachfront casino was a sub-basement where you could hear the movement of the ocean. This was a dingy place, full of dampness and shadows, far from the glitzy world above. Sound stayed here, trapped. No one above could hear the screaming.

Jack Faff, ribs still afire, gingerly made passage along a dripping corridor, Mikhail at his side to guide him. At the end, in a dungeon-like room, a semicircle of large Russians stood around Solter, who lay on the floor like a broken dog.

Most of Solter's front teeth were gone. One bent inward, another hanging precariously. Old blood caked his face and new blood dribbled from his chin. His clothes were shredded and the blackened pustules from the burns were vivid. Solter's fingers were twisted at odd angles. He sobbed in pain.

"Get Jack a chair," Mikhail commanded, and one of his thugs hopped to obey.

Jack inspected the seat for dirt before sitting. Solter looked expectantly at his brother.

"Mikhail delivered some disturbing information about you," Jack said coldly.

"I'm sorry, Jack," Solter whined. "Please."

"Why did you betray me?"

"I met Karen Glick at this party with Linda Reiner over the summer. She'd done the Billionaire Boys story. I needed a media contact. Later, I gave her a summary sheet about our finances. But I never gave her the full document set on our finances."

"Not 'our finances,'" Jack said. "Mine."

"I was angry at you, Jack. So angry. You don't treat me like Pop-pop wanted you to."

"Pop-pop," Jack said, "is dead and he is in hell. What about the Authority? Why did you go to them?"

"This man, this Kingman Wooton, he contacted me. He already knew about our—your—finances. He wanted to hear about your plans, and paid me for what I told him. Better than you pay me, Jack. Your own brother."

Jack turned to Mikhail. "Who's Wooton?"

"Top bigshot at the Authority. My man in the Russian embassy says he is very, very powerful. Not a guy to mess with. They say he can read minds."

"No kidding. Mind readers aren't good to do business with. I'll bet a shiny nickel that Wooton is acting on his own behalf, using the resources of the spy agency to enrich himself, not for the flag-flapping glory of the United States." Jack stood up slowly and pointed at Solter. "Take care of him."

Everyone knew that didn't mean medical help. They could hear the ocean moan.

"Jack," Solter wailed, "I'm your brother. Flesh and blood."

"My experience?" Jack said. "Never trust relatives. They'll tear your flesh and drink your blood every time."

"You're going to be nothing when it all crashes down," Solter said. "When the money's gone, what will you have?"

Jack Faff bent over his brother. "I always win. I'll have everything."

"I'll haunt you, Jack. Me and Pop-pop."

As Jack headed down the corridor, he heard his brother crying his name. Until he didn't hear it anymore.

Standing outside Manhattan Muffin in the East Village, Karen told Linda of her late-night run-in with the man who was in the back of the church and watching outside the beauty salon.

"What does he want?" Linda asked.

"Me to quit. I guess not everyone agrees with Tim about me as a bad reporter."

"My Lord," Linda said. "What are you going to do?"

"Be more careful. That means you should be, too."

Linda winced. "Karen, my building has terrific security. But yours doesn't. You don't have a doorman; I've got a bunch. If the Englishman knows where I live—and my phone is unlisted—he surely knows where you live. You're listed."

"I like people to be able to find me to give me story tips. And maybe someday someone will call me for a date. Sitting by the phone is such fun if it's listed." Not that Linda would know about waiting by the phone for a guy to call.

"Didn't you say these men who seemed like law enforcement types were asking questions about you in your neighborhood? They talked to that bum who knows you."

"Rocky is not a bum," Karen said. "He's a gentleman of leisure." Rocky's favorite panhandling line was: "You don't have to be Rockefeller to help a feller." Hence his name.

"Then they probably were from the Authority."

"To be honest," Karen said, surprised at self-absorbed Linda's concern, "maybe this isn't such a smart idea to have you accompany me. Being near me is not a good idea for you."

"You need me to help you with River. He doesn't know you. And I can control him."

The muffin shop had a steady flow of customers. Unlike other New Yorkers en route to work, this group wasn't dressed in suits. A bohemian collection of artists, musicians, and actors, they dressed as they pleased. Karen's favorite was the woman clad in ostrich feathers.

"So River comes here every morning, huh?"

"Religiously," Linda said. "A deep-seated need for a bran muffin. Necessary, he informed us more than once, for the proper functioning of his bowels."

"Charming. I can see why Flo found him attractive."

"She was always pathetic around men. Trying, Ginny thinks, to win a substitute for her Daddy. . . . Never mind." She pulled her suede jacket closer around her. The morning's damp chill penetrated to the bone.

Karen was nursing the coffee she'd gotten from the muffin shop. It seemed to have been brewed in the holding tank of the Bayway heating oil refinery. "You must have considered in the past what would happen if someone stole Goldring."

"We kept it locked up. And it was one of several laptops we had in the office. It was an old IBM ThinkPad, built back before the Chinese bought the brand. The golden ring embossed on it identified it, to us. As an additional precaution, Flo—and this was pure genius—booby-trapped the program. If someone tried to copy it, the program would spew out these horrible viruses. Destroying itself and totally corrupting the hard drive of the poor fool trying to copy."

"Is that River?" Karen recalled him from when she was interviewing the Reiners for their story. Even in the bulky down jacket and a stocking cap he wore this morning, he was tongue-lollingly handsome.

"Where, where?" River had almost reached the muffin shop by the time Linda picked him out. "Oh, oh. Let's go get him."

Placing a restraining hand on her arm, Karen said, "We want him when he comes out. When his hands are full."

"He looks tense and strange. Like when he came to Ginny's office."

Once River emerged munching his muffin and holding his coffee cup with his other hand, he almost collided with Karen and Linda.

"I need to talk to you," Linda said with the correct mixture of womanly kindness and manly firmness.

River took three beats to register what was happening. His reaction wasn't one of anger. Rather, of sarcasm. "What, you're slumming this morning?" He pointed at Karen. "I remember you. The fluff reporter who doesn't dig too much. That's why Linda chose you to do the story."

Linda's face turned as icy as a charity benefit swan sculpture. Karen stared at her.

"Flo didn't like you," River said to Linda. "She didn't care too much for Ginny, either."

Linda eyed him as she would bad hair. "Your opinions are not what I'm here about, River."

"You know, I'd even say Flo hated you."

"That'll do. I need to find out some important information."

"Jesus Christ," River said. "For the umpteenth time, I locked the damn door after me."

"You're sure?" Karen said.

"Yes, I did, Little Miss Reporter. But here's something you've forgotten: how Linda played you like a twelve-string guitar."

Karen kept a poker face. "Why don't you tell the cops where you went after you left the office?"

"Because it's none of their damn business. And none of yours."

"You don't have to be ashamed," Karen said.

A chunk of muffin fell unnoticed to the ground. "What the hell do you mean?" he snarled.

"What I said." Karen sipped the horrible latte to show how low-key she was, even though she wanted to throw it on both of them. "Sexual preference isn't a big deal."

"It still is to a lot of people. . . ." More muffin escaped River's grasp. "Who told you and what did they say?"

"Doesn't matter," Karen said nonchalantly. "What goes on in your personal life should stay in your personal life."

"Damn straight. I don't want the details of what I do plastered all over the tabloids."

"You weren't sure Detective Friday could be trusted?"

"Cops hate gays."

Karen leaned forward. "You can trust me."

After taking a savage slug of hot, bad coffee, River said, "Can I?"

"Yes," Karen said. "You sure can."

With a defiant look at Linda, River said, "I tend bar at Alexander the Great nights. That's where I went the night Flo was killed. Yes, that's a gay bar."

"I bet you have witnesses at the bar," Karen said.

"Loads of them, lady. Happy waiters, happy bosses, happy customers. Hey, I can't let it get out I'm gay. A boy's gotta make a living. The Reiners never paid me much." He pointed at Linda. "Someday, I want big paydays. I want a film career. Tomorrow's Brad Pitt has to start somewhere. I don't want to be marginalized as a gay actor. I can act, I can dance, I can sing."

"What do you know about the missing laptop?"

"I know it had their trading system. The infallible system that supposedly couldn't miss. You work in an office, you hear stuff. At the bar one night, some big guy with a broken nose came in and bought me drinks. Bruce, the owner, doesn't allow that, but Bruce wasn't in. This guy was hunky, though a bit rough trade for me. He was more interested in my work than in me. I got sloshed, kinda. The guy asked me if Goldring really could predict stocks. I said, 'I guess. The Reiners sure are rich.' " He made a face at Linda. "So spread it around, Linda." With that, River walked off into the morning cool.

As he sauntered down the street, Linda said, "How did you know about him?"

"I didn't. I had a hunch to play. You guys told me that he didn't like Flo touching him, showing sexual interest in him. And he was nasty about shooting down the girl down the hall from your office. Men have turned me down before, but they were nonchalant about it, not angry. So I know. I guess you wouldn't."

"You bluffed him."

"Not bad for a little puff-piece reporter, huh?" Karen threw away her bilious, half-consumed coffee. "Sounds like the Authority sniffing around. Somehow, I believe River locked the office door after him. But if so, who opened it? How did Albert get in?"

Linda summoned up a smile as genuine as her old apartment's artwork. "But listen, those lies he told about my view of you as a journalist . . ."

"Linda, you don't fool me. You see me as the gateway to Frank Vere. And you're right. But you're going to see I can deliver, too."

"Oh, I'm sure," Linda lied.

"My next stop is Atlantic City, tomorrow, even though my editors wouldn't approve," Karen said. "I'm going without their permission. I know Faff will be there."

"I'm coming with you."

"No, you're not. Faff's Lair casino doesn't quite attract the glamour set, so you wouldn't fit in. You are too much of a distraction. I'm going to be digging deep, Linda. Very deep."

Back at the office, Karen stopped by Frank's desk and filled him in. "It may be of no importance, but this question of the Reiners's father keeps coming up. He was mean to all the girls, but seemed to have this special affection for Flo. He gave her that ring. The one that's missing. The one whose replica was embossed on the Goldring computer."

"So Linda said Godfrey Reiner was murdered." Frank sprawled in his chair. "Did you do a clip search from twelve years ago when this happened?"

"I didn't see the point, because poor Flo is dead and now buried. But since we have no idea who took Goldring and how they got access to the Reiners's office, maybe I can find some clue."

Frank hoisted himself in his chair to something akin to good sitting posture. "The cops don't really care about investigating the death of a nobody like Albert Niebel. Especially since they're under federal pressure to lay off the whole business. But I heard about the medical examiner's report of how he died. Very interesting."

"Very interesting how?" Karen shifted her weight, alert for Skeen or Christian.

"The killer broke Albert's neck with a single blow. Meaning the killer was skilled in martial arts. That doesn't sound like Mikhail Beria's style to me. He prefers sharp objects. He's a cutter, not a karate black belt."

"What does this tell us?

Frank slumped in his chair again. His spine really could use a hinge. "From a good source I have, it points to the Authority. Karate is one skill the spooks use."

"Maybe. Though Beria could have a black belt on his payroll. I would love to talk to just one of these sources of yours."

Gene Skeen wafted up to them. "Bill McIntyre specifically instructed that Frank Vere was not allowed to aid you."

"Aid me?" Karen said. "We're only chatting, Gene. It's called friendship. Maybe that's a new term to you."

Wendy smiled ruefully as she passed by. The parrot on her shoulder, at the sight of Skeen, made its customary strangling sound.

"I'm watching you," Skeen said to Karen, then cast an annoyed look at the parrot.

"Very innocent here, Gene," Karen said. "We were talking about how much we admire your interpersonal skills."

"You're on thin ice," the editor said and marched away like the landed gentry.

Karen shook her head, waved to Frank, and returned to her cube. She called up the news database from Defiance, the Reiner sisters' hometown in northwest Ohio. She found a brief newspaper item from a dozen years before about how Godfrey Reiner, fifty-five years old, prominent owner of a local insurance agency, had died after falling down the front stairs of his home around nine P.M. He had alcohol in his system. His youngest daughter, Flo, a high school senior, was the sole person at home. She called 911, but Godfrey was dead when the rescue squad arrived. Defiance police ruled it an accident.

"But Linda said he was murdered."

That night, Karen sat with Gran and watched the same casino heist flick on video-on-demand. Gran was working on her sixth viewing. Karen's mother was out on a social work visit to some poor soul. Her father, paper hoisted in front of him, had grunted twice when Karen had come in—relatively effusive for him, since he usually gave a single grunt. As Karen settled into the TV room, she heard Maury growl at the paper: "Fascist bastards . . . damn racists . . . no justice."

The credits started rolling on the screen. "Can I order up that old silent movie with Douglas Fairbanks?" Gran asked. "You know, *Robin Hood.*"

"I'm sure you can," Karen said. "Gran, I think I'm in danger again."

"They're not firing you, are they?"

"No, not that. Someone really bad is following me. Threatening me."

The old lady, back in her Communist days before she turned Republican, was accused of espionage and on the lam from the FBI, so she was a good person to ask about what to do here. Gran turned from the screen, where the crooks were escaping by causing pandemonium on the casino floor. "You want another safe house?"

When Karen was handling the Billionaire Boys Club story, she took refuge from some homicidal maniacs in the basement of one of Gran's tenements. Gran had many tenements, which to Maury Glick made her a loathsome capitalist. Maury did manage to temper his disdain since he and Emma lived with Gran rent-free.

"I'm not sure." Living in that cockroach-friendly basement was hellish. Karen now lived in a comfortable little studio apartment, also in a building Gran owned. But anyone could get into the building Karen called home. Karen had first met Rocky the panhandler when he was roaming her halls, cadging spare change to buy, he said, food—actually, Schlitz Malt Liquor. "But I am scared," Karen said.

"Listen, in 1946 I had to stay one step ahead of the G-men, until the American Civil Liberties Union got my case thrown out and I was off the hook. In the Party, we were like Robin Hood, robbing from the rich, giving to the poor. Except the rich were the slumming society kids who wanted to save the world, and the poor were the rest of us in the Party. Did I ever tell you about how I got away when they trapped me in the ladies' room at the Apollo Theater? All these girls primping in the mirror and two of J. Edgar Hoover's boys waiting outside the door."

"A zillion times. You shouted fire and got away in the stampede from the john. I told you about those FBI-like guys asking questions about me in my neighborhood. Sounds like the Authority. What do I do? I can't give up. Too much is at stake. I'm not this twerpy little girl they can intimidate."

Gran nodded sagely at the TV. "Always look for an escape."

"These people are professional killers, Gran."

"Racist pigs," Maury exclaimed in the other room.

"So you be smarter. Trick them good."

The walls in Linda's old apartment were so thin that neighbors could hear each other making love. That wasn't a problem in her new penthouse. After she chastised Tim for tardiness at the funeral and bad behavior in her home, she accepted his apology and accepted him back into her bed. "Lie down," she instructed him and got on top. Afterward, Linda lay with her head on Tim's chest and watched the galaxy of city lights out her window.

"Maybe I could help," he said as he stroked her hair.

"But you're too busy."

"No. I want to get involved."

Linda rubbed his broad chest, buffed from workouts with his personal trainer. "I have to work with Karen. It'd be touchy with you involved."

"Working with Karen. How's that going?'

"It has its ups and downs."

Usually mellow in the afterglow, Tim put a little urgency into his tone, "Don't cut me out. If this is important to you, then this is important to me."

"How sweet." She lifted her head to look at him. "The problem is that you two can't stand each other."

"She drives me crazy. Why, though, do you need her? She's not exactly a world-class investigative reporter."

Linda moved away from him and laid her head back on her own pillow. "She's got Frank Vere helping. And he *is* a world-class investigative reporter. Besides, Karen turns out to be a tough and resourceful chick. That's good, except when she's shooting her mouth off."

"I worry when you go with her to unsafe spots. Like to see Albert. And River. Both nut jobs."

"We had to make those visits with me. I knew both those guys. Tomorrow, you'll be pleased to learn, Karen is going by herself to Atlantic City. Not me. She thinks I'd be a distraction among all the lowlifes in Jack's casino." Linda told Tim about what had been uncovered, including the suspected involvement of the Federal Reclamation Authority, and about the Atlantic City plan. "She isn't supposed to go, because her superiors are afraid about the legal situation. She's stubborn. Karen figures she can get Faff to reveal more. He has a big ego he likes to display."

"These people are very dangerous, Linda," Tim said.

"Yes, they or someone like them killed Flo, whether Albert pulled the trigger or not," Linda said. "And they have my trading program. The Reiner trading program."

Tim got up and announced he must leave. Big meeting early the next morning.

She grabbed his hand. "No, you're not. I'm not finished with you." Linda pulled him down on the bed and straddled him. "Now you do exactly what I say."

"Don't I always?"

A half-hour later, Linda stood naked at the door and blew him a kiss as he left. "Take me someplace fun tomorrow night," she said.

"I thought we were going to Jack Faff's masquerade ball tomorrow night. The party of the season. The one you can't wait for."

"How can I go when he might have killed Flo?"

Tim looked distressed. He took her in his arms. "I really want to go. You don't know that Faff was involved in her death, just because he wants Goldring. Everyone will be there. This is your chance to show the world you are bearing up well after Flo's death."

"I'll want to rip his face off. I hope Karen traps him good."

"Besides," Tim said, "I need to get to Jack and sell him on signing up with Dewey Cheatham for his next underwriting. This is my chance to climb out of the hole that Karen has dug for me."

"I guess," she said into his shoulder. "But I'm not talking to Jack."

Tim grinned as he pulled the ornate door shut.

As she headed back to the now lonely bed, she recalled Karen's assessment of Tim. He was a good ornament and no threat. But a help? Well, that remained to be seen. He seemed to lack the generosity gene. His support after Flo's death was minimal, and he couldn't even appear on time for the funeral. While he might surprise her yet, she'd keep him on probation. As Linda told herself, men were like buses: another one would come along soon.

Down in the cathedral-like lobby, Tim waved off the doorman, saying he didn't need a taxi. At the next corner, he whipped out his cell phone and called the number he had memorized. He wasn't allowed to write it down. "I have the information you wanted about what Karen and Linda are getting into," Tim said into the cell. "It's disturbing."

"I don't get disturbed," the person at the other end said.

CHAPTER FOURTEEN

Karen never had been much good at gambling, where luck was no lady but sure was a bitch. She never understood Tim's zest for late-night poker with the boys, considering his own lack of good fortune. He always slunk home in the wee hours, reeking of good booze and bad cigar smoke, mumbling about how he needed to visit the ATM before he could show his face at Starbucks for his morning jolt of overpriced latte. Tim's Dewey Cheatham pals sometimes dragged him to Atlantic City or to Indian casinos, where all afterward claimed they emerged as winners. Karen knew better. She had read of a poll showing that a commanding majority of casino players contended they either won or broke even. If so, the Las Vegas Strip and the A.C. board-walk would be post-Apocalyptic wastelands.

The odds favor the casino, so Karen decided she must tilt things in her favor at Faff's Lair. She resolved to stay in pub-lic this time. Mike Riley, who gambled a lot and actually did win—he'd won their Hamptons summer house in a hi-lo split hand—told her before she left the office that every casino had cameras and state inspectors galore, meaning it would be hard for Faff to try rough stuff on the gaming floor. And taking a page from Gran, she bought some extra insurance. Before setting out, she visited a Broadway theatrical supply house. Then she aimed the Ford Escargot for a second time at Atlantic City.

Faff's garish casino wasn't first on her list, though. She had one lead: the casino parking attendant, Major Darcy, who had witnessed Karen getting into the passenger seat of Faff's Jaguar. Frank had turned up that old Darcy lived with his daughter, Regina, in Atlantic City. Regina's husband was a cop, which usually meant the phone would be unlisted. But Regina herself was a social worker, and felt that she should be accessible to clients, for much the same reason Karen listed hers. So the phone was in Regina's name. Frank also discovered that the husband, Darnell, was a bit of a hot head. Frank had disagreed with Karen's decision not to call first to see if she would be welcome.

"Don't worry," Karen reassured her friend. "I'm sure Darnell wouldn't hit a girl."

Karen found herself at the front door of a rowhouse in Atlantic City. The block was respectable. People scrubbed their stoops. No garbage was in the streets. She was the only white person in the neighborhood, which meant Mikhail Beria's thugs would stand out if they were around.

The woman who answered the door had the deadpan look of someone who had seen bad, awful, horrible, and back again.

"Hi," Karen said, flashing her press credentials. "I'm Karen Glick, from *Profit* magazine. I'd like to speak with your father." She weighed whether to say her mother was a social worker also, but rejected the notion as too fake-friendly.

"I know who you are, and he's not here," Regina said. She had on a nice Sunday worship dress. Karen figured she had just returned from the church where Major Darcy was a deacon. She was very pretty and the demure Sunday dress couldn't disguise her shapely figure.

"Your father witnessed me getting in the passenger seat of Jack Faff's Jaguar, the night of the accident. Faff lies and says I was driving. The police believe him and I've been charged. I need your father's help to get the truth out."

"My husband will be back from the store in a minute. He'll be very unhappy to find you here," Regina said.

"Faff's store-bought judge will crucify me, Regina. My reputation is at stake. I need your father's help. He doesn't have to go public. I just need to talk to him."

"My father's life is at stake, miss." A child called from within. "I'm coming, Keesha. You tell Lionel to hush up."

"They say your father is an honest man."

"Why make himself a target for those nasty-ass Russian hoodlums? Your promises are worth nothing. No thank you, miss. No thank you. My husband's in law enforcement, but there's no law in this town that will protect that old man. Jack Faff's got too much money and too much power. He can squash my father like a fly."

As if on cue, her husband came up, grocery bags under each arm. His church-going tie was twisted around. The outline of his service revolver was visible through his jacket. "Who are you?"

"The reporter lady who took the car ride with Faff," Regina said, as if Karen were deceased.

"All you people do is cause trouble. You get your fucking ass off my doorstep, you hear?"

"Darnell," his wife said, in protest of his language.

"I mean it," her husband said, the way he would to a drug pusher on a corner.

Karen pressed two cards into Regina's reluctant and clammy hand. "Here's my phone, cell, and e-mail. Please pass my card along to your father. He can contact me, night or day."

"It'll be a cold day," Darnell said.

Regina smiled apologetically to Karen and gestured at her leather jacket. "Nice," she said,

Karen trudged off into the shadowless light of an October midday, confident she'd done what she could. She looked back at Regina's house. An old man's face was in the window, lined like a fossilized riverbed with the passage of the world's ancient regrets and sorrows.

This time, Karen didn't park her car at Faff's Lair. She walked toward the monstrous casino from the municipal parking lot and wondered whether they would detect her before she announced herself. She entered the place and drew a short breath. Everyone was badly dressed. Mike Riley had told her that Faff's Lair gamblers were the worst. "They'd trade their heart transplant money for another turn at the roulette wheel. The sight of cash puts them into heat."

Karen had on jeans and Nikes, in case she had to run. She wore the leather jacket with the studs and zippers, given to her by the boyfriend before Tim—a peevish accountant who belonged to a weekend motorcycle club that he took too seriously and that Karen called (to his irritation) Hell's Yuppies. Karen figured that if she landed in the Atlantic City jail again, the jacket might give her a biker chick look and keep the skeevy inmates at bay. She felt around in her Kenneth Cole shoulder bag to ensure every little thing was in order.

The casino buzzed around Karen, oblivious to her. Spasmodic pings came from the phalanxes of slot machines. Bellows of joy and despair rolled over from the craps tables. In the blackjack and poker sections, gamblers bent studiously over the green felt and let the cards drop along with their bankrolls.

Karen spotted an officious, disagreeable-looking man who stood six-three and had on an obnoxiously red blazer. Mike Riley had told her the floor managers at Faff's Lair wore these eyesore blazers and were dauntingly large. This one resembled a man on a foxhunt who enjoyed tearing apart the prey with the hounds.

"I'm Karen Glick, from *Profit* magazine." She looked defiantly up at the manager. "Tell Jack Faff I want to talk to him. Now."

"I'm afraid Mr. Faff is busy, ma'am." The widening of the manager's eyes showed he knew who Karen was. He was almost as big as Beria's hoods, but American.

"I'm busy, too. Tell him I want to talk to him."

First excusing himself with exaggerated politeness, the manager picked up a red house phone nearby and mumbled into it. The manager returned, saying, "I'm to take you up to Mr. Faff's office."

"Not a chance. I speak with Faff in public. Not where his goons can do whatever they want."

The manager clumped away and Karen took a seat at a vacant poker table nearby. She plunked her bag atop its felt surface. It was early afternoon, but with no sight or sound of the outside world allowed in the casino, the hour could have been midnight. Karen knew from the casino Web site that at 3 PM. Faff would be cutting the ribbon at the wax museum down the boardwalk. His handsome likeness was the most prominent exhibit, although it wasn't an accurate replica. The Faff wax figure stood almost as tall as his red-jacketed manager.

The gamblers floated past like desperate souls in search of their lost lives. A World Series-winning cheer exploded from the nearest craps table. Karen tried to pick out the overhead cameras and couldn't.

Faff's approach reached Karen as might the heralding winds of a coming storm. Small swayings grew into wild thrashings. People swiveled their heads, stood up from tables and craned their necks, pointed and chattered excitedly. The hubbub ended the noisy craps game as its players trotted over to see. Then came the applause.

Faff, clad in an exquisitely cut double-breasted jacket and a silk ascot, was flanked by enormous bouncers. His well-combed head came as high as their lowest ribs. He moved with the slow caution of someone whose own ribs ached. "You want to talk to me?" he said with menace.

Not eager to endure Faff's overly manly grip a second time, Karen didn't offer to shake hands. She remained seated at the table. "About that night in your Jag."

"I own this joint, smartass, meaning *I* set the agenda." Faff motioned for the bouncers to stand back. He eased himself carefully into a chair beside Karen and eyed her like a chicken that needed to be plucked. "Want to play poker?" he said to Karen. "At a hundred dollars a hand."

Other large Faff retainers pushed the gathering gawkers away, out of earshot.

"I'm not much of a card player."

"You're also," Faff said, "a loser."

"Why did you lie about me the night you crashed the Jag? Why did you say I was driving and that you saved my life, when the opposite was true?"

"You want me to change my story? Well, I won't."

"Then let's talk about Goldring."

"Why should I talk to you about it?" With his index finger, Faff lightly touched the felt near her bag.

"Because I know things about Goldring you don't."

Faff didn't take the bluff. "You," he said, "know nothing about Goldring. You don't know how it works. You don't know why Linda and Ginny Reiner can't recreate it without Flo. And you don't know where it is."

"Where is Goldring?"

Faff showed his teeth in something between a grin and a snarl. "I don't know."

"Sure you do. That night you crashed your car, Goldring was the most interesting tale I'd heard all day. Did Mikhail and the boys have much trouble when they took Goldring from Albert Niebel?"

"I don't know what you're talking about."

"They broke Albert's neck. How good are your lawyers at defending homicide cases?"

"More of your wild accusations." Faff spread his hand on the felt. "You want to talk about court cases? Put that in your magazine and the libel judgment will be so big, Templar Media will be auctioned off down to the last mop and bucket."

"I only print what I can prove. And when I do, the stuff is solid," Karen said.

"Solid? Like the financial statement my brother slipped you? A phony. He was jealous of me. He had a hate fixation on me, like you do. And he wanted to hurt me. But I found him out."

"Where's your brother?" Why did Faff use the past tense in reference to Solter?

"I fired him. Who cares where he is?"

A chill went through Karen. The ever self-possessed Faff's eyelids had given a liar's flutter. "Did you harm him?"

"My own flesh and blood. What a silly question." Faff tapped the felt tabletop. "Since you're too much of a wimp to play poker with me, the bet's still available on Linda Reiner. At my masked ball tomorrow night, Linda is invited. A hundred bucks says I bang her like a cheap gong."

Karen's hands balled into fists. "You? I doubt it. She has a boyfriend."

"Sure. Your husband. He was too good for you and not good enough for her."

"Your ascot's a little too tight, Faff. It cuts off the oxygen to your brain."

"Women are whores. Every one. They use you for money and whatever you can give them. I can make a recording of me with Linda, to prove I won the bet."

"Are you sick or are you sick?"

His eyes narrowed. "Say, are you recording our conversation?" He stood up and grabbed her bag. As she protested, he reached in, rummaged around among her cash, flashlight, comb, lipstick, makeup (recently used to cover her face scratches), and Altoids.

"You can't do this," she insisted and grabbed for the bag. But the big red-jacketed manager caught her wrist. The bouncers moved forward to loom over her.

"Let go of me," she told the manager. He did.

Faff pulled out a rectangular plastic object from Karen's bag. "Aha. It's against the law to record me without my permission. And against our clearly posted casino rules to bring any recording device here." He peered at it to see the buttons and frowned.

Karen reached over and hit the lever that pulled the case open to reveal three neatly furled tampons. "If you needed one, all you had to do was ask," she said.

Then Faff went back into her bag and extracted the tape recorder. "Here we are."

"Give that back," Linda demanded, popping to her feet. "That's mine." The bouncers took hold of her arms.

"You've broken the law and you've broken Faff's Lair rules. We must deal with you." Faff turned on his heel and handed the tape recorder to the red-jacketed manager. The bouncers unhanded her and followed him. As he moved into the crowd, Faff turned jolly and signed a few autographs.

Karen recognized the two Russians as they shouldered

past Faff's entourage. They were even larger than the bouncers. She picked up her bag where Faff had dropped it on the floor and cast her head around for the best flight path.

Josef, the biggest one, stepped in front of her. "You come with us."

Kingman Wooton sat in his Eames chair, quietly munching a chicken salad sandwich with watercress on a sourdough roll, heavy on the mayonnaise. Normally, this was among his favorites. But he couldn't taste it, merely ate by rote, the mayo-slathered gunk sliding down his throat and unleashing armadas of fat globules into his bloodstream. His computer sat nearby, the power off.

The sounds of his wife having sex upstairs in her bedroom were vivid. His ears being quite acute, he could hear their bellies slapping. Erica's final cries stirred an old memory. Mick's stirred an even deeper sentiment. Wooton had quietly sent the operatives, stationed in the basement, outside the house. This was Erica and Mick's first assignation in Wooton's home.

At last came the bump of feet moving down the stairs.

"Do you have to go?" Erica said. "He won't be back for hours."

"Things to do, things to do, babe," Mick said. He was buttoning his shirt when he passed Wooton's study. "Holy hell."

"Get out of my house," Wooton said from his chair. His deep voice was at its most sepulchral.

"Hey, man . . . I mean, no biggie here . . . like—"

"Get out of my house," Wooton repeated, louder.

Mick exited rapidly, not bothering to say farewell to anyone, least of all Erica.

She stood nonchalantly in the doorway to her husband's study, one hand resting on the jamb. She wore a short silk robe and looked good. Very little fazed Erica. She had kept on her wedding ring, which had been pressed against the flesh of her lover's back.

"I suppose you'll be wanting a divorce, Kingman," she said in her blasé honeysuckle accent.

"He's much younger than you are."

"Kingman, *I'm* younger than you are. And my Mick is gor-Jesus. That's what he's here for, now isn't he? To be gor-Jesus."

"You also like that he's coming into his inheritance so he can keep your store going, aren't you?"

Erica smiled dreamily, as he'd first seen her do on a summer's eve long ago. "Until we get tired of the store."

"Until he gets tired of you."

"He won't, Kingman. No one can get tired of me. Except maybe you."

The director wanted to tell her how easy it would be to have Mick snuffed out. Hell, Wooton still had the stuff to break the creep's neck with a single blow. Wooton could hear his father-in-law saying to him every Christmas: "Lucky for you, boy, you're a god on my daughter's dollar."

"Kingman, you're not supposed to be home now. You're never home. When did you ever have any time for me? Or the kids? Or anything other than your dumb, paper-pushing bureaucratic job? Mick has a whole wide world full of time for me."

"Since the Colonel's money evaporated, that's all you think about. I know you, Erica. Money's what talks as far as you're concerned."

"Poor Kingman. Life is such a mystery to you."

"I'm going to come into a whole load of money soon, Erica. Then you'll see."

"Oh, please." Erica left, and Wooton was alone.

Josef had Karen by the collar. Nikita lumbered alongside. The gangsters trooped the reporter through the casino like a naughty schoolgirl.

The goons had left their prisoner's hands free. Karen pulled the thick envelope from out of her bag. Luckily Faff hadn't pulled it out.

"What you do?" Nikita said at her sudden movement.

Karen tossed a fortune in cash into the air. "Free money," she shouted. "Come and get it."

Gamblers ravenously attacked the fluttering twenty-dollar bills, elbowing each other, cursing and yelling. They slammed into the two massive Russians and threw them off balance.

No one noticed the bills were stage money with Groucho Marx's picture instead of Andrew Jackson's. Courtesy of the New York theatrical supply house. Karen would have to tell Gran that some stuff you saw in the movies actually worked.

Karen zigzagged through the casino. She hunched low as she ran so she was not visible to Nikita and Josef. She threaded through the slot machine banks, then sprinted for a wide door that gave onto the boardwalk. Once on the wood, she didn't stop, darting through the passersby, and down some stairs and onto the beach.

Panting, she crouched beneath the boards. Strolling feet moved overhead. She pulled the second recorder out of her jacket pocket.

CHAPTER FIFTEEN

Linda, in a midriff-baring T-shirt from Agnes B. and tight, shiny, creased pants, her hair fetchingly arrayed in a pony-tail, glided across the cold, hard floor of the Reiner Capital office. She had consented to opening the office only be-cause Karen wanted to see it. "I'm never coming back here again," she said. "I can't bear this."

"I understand. We won't be long." Karen took in the wide loft space. "It must have been horrible to see Flo's . . ." She decided to shut up.

"Yes, the police say they are closing the case and blam-ing Flo's death on Albert. The gun they found in his place clinched it. Albert's fingerprints were on the gun, the bullet that killed Flo matched to the gun. Detective Friday gave broad hints he thought there's more to the case, but his hands are tied." She stopped at the huge dark floor stain— Flo's blood. "I don't know what to do."

Karen eyed the dried bloodstain and wondered why Linda hadn't ordered it scrubbed away. The police were through with the office as a crime scene. "So you're going to that masquerade ball of Faff's tonight, huh? You and Tim."

"Tim wants some face time with Jack. He'd like to land Jack as a client to restore his name at Dewey Cheatham. . . ." Linda sucked in her taut belly. "Otherwise, I wouldn't go, even though I had been looking forward to this party. This is the big social do of the fall season. Jack's opening his new building."

"The one that has driven his company to the brink. I question whether he has any real business to give Tim. Unless Tim wants to move over to Dewey Cheatham's bankruptcy adviser section, that is."

Linda swiveled her marvelous torso around. "He's in trouble at Dewey Cheatham because of you. He needs a win somehow."

"Tim wants to be filthy rich like you. He wants someone to love him for his money." Karen tugged down her sweater, which had ridden up to expose part of her not flat belly. "He idolizes Faff. You could tell him anything about Faff and Tim wouldn't care. I know Jack Faff had his brother Solter killed, although I can't prove it."

"Jack could order someone killed. I know it. He has no moral sense."

As if Linda did? Karen kept the thought to herself.

Karen had spent the morning, following Frank's guidance, trying to track down Solter. "I feel it. Can't prove it. Look what kind of hoods Faff surrounded himself with. No one knows where Solter went. He hasn't been home to his townhouse in Carnegie Hill." Frank's friend at the phone company had turned up Solter's address; Solter, like most rich folks, had an unlisted number. Then she had worked the street. "I checked with the neighbors and the postal delivery woman. Nothing."

"I want to avoid Jack at the party tonight, which won't be easy," Linda said and sashayed that marvelous torso. "I know he *likes* me." She lowered her voice a sexy octave on the word "likes."

"I'll say. In fact, he wants to jump your bones tonight."

Linda gave one of her half-smiles as if to say: *Every creature with Y chromosomes wants to jump my bones.* "He may want to, but he wouldn't try it. Tim will be there."

"Oh, no? Maybe I should play you the tape I made of him in the casino. I draw your attention to the matter of the hundred dollar bet. It's not about cards." Karen produced the tape recorder from her bag, plopped it on Flo's old desk, and hit the Play button.

As Faff's swaggering remarks filled the large room, Linda fought a titanic battle to maintain her composure. When the tape had finished, she said, "That arrogant bastard. What a pig. Who does he think he is?"

"The rich guy who always gets the girl. Should I have taken the bet?"

"Please," Linda said with disgust. "If that slime killed my sister . . . Well, I have to stay focused." Then to change the distasteful subject and regain her all-important aplomb, she asked, "Isn't it illegal to record someone secretly?"

Karen shook her head. "In New Jersey and New York, you can do it as long as one party knows a recorder is running. That party here was me. Too bad Faff didn't admit what I wanted. I'd hoped his hubris would be enough for him to blurt out an admission he'd been driving the Jag. Or anything about Goldring. A longshot, I know." Karen pressed the Rewind button and the machine emitted a squealing sound. "Faff did point out I don't know how Goldring works or where it is. But he also raised an interesting question. Why can't you and Ginny recreate the Goldring program?"

Linda's gaze settled again on the bloodstain. "Flo was the key. She got input from me on how the market works and from Ginny on the abstruse math. But Flo was the programmer. I can't tell you more."

"Can't tell me more. Don't you want to be trading right now? Getting even richer?"

Linda gave a grimace. "Of course. Did you notice what's happened to Corsine stock?"

"Yeah. Taken off like a rocket to the stars. I bet someone is making a pile from it. Now what's this about Goldring being illegal?"

"I told you: Ginny was drunk and didn't know what she was saying. How Goldring works is off limits. I'm not going to repeat myself on this point."

"I think you should tell me all . . ." Giving up, Karen scanned the empty loft space again. The office was spacious and, even in daytime, filled with shadows. "I realize that the police case is closed. But how could someone get in here and surprise Flo?"

"I wish I knew. The lobby door downstairs is always locked after six. Daytime, a security man is on duty. There's a loading dock at the back. That door is locked, as well. Delivery people need to arrange with a tenant to open it from the inside. And our office door is locked after hours. And was the night of Flo's murder, if you believe River."

Linda's cell phone trilled. It was hooked to the waistband of her pants, hanging against a perfectly formed hip. She checked the caller ID and didn't answer. "The lawyer again. Ginny really believes she can stop Father Finnegan from getting Flo's money. Not a chance legally. I'm trying to give the lawyer enough courage to tell Ginny that."

"Are you feeling courageous today?"

"What do you mean?"

"You can get Faff to talk at his party tonight. Remember, he doesn't know we're working together." Karen told Linda of her plan. "See, lust can be a good truth serum. Besides, he has sore ribs. I doubt he's as frisky as he thinks."

"Karen, I told you, I don't want to get near that man."

"Linda, if we want to get to the bottom of this, we have to get to Faff."

"Well . . . what would Tim say?"

"I never needed Tim's permission to do anything," Karen said. She cocked her head to the side. "Do you?"

"I suppose, if it were in the midst of his party . . ."

"Don't worry," Karen said. "Forget Tim. I'll be at the party to protect you."

"You? How?"

Tim Bratton sat impatiently in the reception area outside Faff's Manhattan office. The walls were decorated with striking photos of Faff buildings, including the recently completed edifice looming over Central Park. Snobby architecture critics already had panned it, as they always did Faff projects. Faff didn't care. Nor did the fawning people who paid top dollar for the privilege of filling up his buildings.

Faff enjoyed keeping others waiting for him. It put them in their place. Tim, at least in his business life, was punctual. He tried to fill the time now by making calls from his cell. At last, he had no more calls to make. On the beautiful teak coffee table before him was an old copy of *Profit*, the one with the article about Linda, her sisters, and their seven thousand percent return.

He fumed about the little alliance smart-mouthed Karen had talked Linda into. Karen probably was busily tearing him down to Linda. The thought chilled him down to his wingtips. Although bothered by Linda's bossiness and coldness (except in bed), he rather enjoyed squiring around a famous, wealthy beauty, who had been Larry Ellison's and Garner Chase's girlfriend. The guys at Dewey Cheatham were impressed, even if Tim were otherwise in foul odor there.

"Mr. Faff will see you now," said the secretary, a model-perfect creature, the type that Tim used to date before Karen came along. Even Linda wasn't as pretty as Faff's secretary.

Faff's vast office was a monument to wealth and to himself. Crossing the expanse of finely carpeted floor to the tycoon's corner desk, Tim passed a Botero sculpture. The walls held a vast photo collection of Faff and the world's other celebrities. Entertainers, royalty, the rich, politicians, authors, the rich, scientists, athletes, the rich. How many of them, particularly the pols, had Faff bribed?

Faff's imposing old desk, which everyone knew once belonged to Benjamin Disraeli, overlooked a magnificent Oz-like panorama of midtown towers. The sky was cloudy, depriving Manhattan of its afternoon sparkle. Faff was reading e-mails on the screen and didn't glance up as Tim approached, let alone rise to meet his guest.

Tim stood before Faff's desk for a full minute before saying, "Would you like me to sit, Jack?"

"No," Faff said, eyes still on his reading, "you're not going to be staying long."

Tim waited.

A couple of uncomfortable minutes later, Faff finally deigned to look at Tim. "Do you know that Disraeli coined the term 'millionaire'? That was in 1827. He couldn't imagine 'billionaire.' But guess who owns his desk now?"

"You do, Jack."

"Yes, I do. So you're coming to the opening party for Faff Towers tonight?"

"I wouldn't miss it for the world, Jack."

"What are you coming as? A preppy?"

"That's very funny, Jack." Tim tried not to sound offended. "My costume is that of a Roman general."

"Well, you're not conquering squat tonight. That's reserved for me."

"I don't understand you, Jack."

"It's bad business for you not to understand me. Well, understand this: you didn't tell me that Karen Glick, your wife, located Major Darcy, the parking attendant."

Tim feared the displeasure of the mighty. "Linda didn't tell me that."

"We're going to have to watch Darcy now. Let's get this straight: I don't like receiving partial information from you. Understand me?"

"I understand you, Jack." Tim had not blushed like this since the sixth grade. His cheeks burned as if napalmed.

"Don't think that you get special points from me because you told me about Goldring," Faff said. "This is a game of What Have You Done for Me Lately? What is Linda dressed as?"

"Marie Antoinette. With powdered wig. Period dress."

"Period dress? We'll see about that."

Tim didn't know what to make of Jack's remark. "Linda told me in a call only an hour ago that Karen Glick is coming to your party. Unclear why. I had to talk Linda into coming. Linda thinks you might have had Flo . . . uh, well, you know . . ."

"Killed?" A special light came over Faff as the cloud cover parted and a sunbeam caught him. What it showed in his face wasn't heaven sent.

"Karen," Tim said, "is using an invitation you sent to the chief executive of Templar Media. Karen's the type who knows all the assistants at work. I guess she got one of them to do her a favor. She's coming as Robin Hood. This has something to do with an old movie her grandmother wants to watch and . . ." He stopped when he realized that Faff was no longer listening to him and he was babbling. Tim knew he must be rattled. Brattons never babble.

"She's sneaking in, is she?" Faff pondered the information. "Let's review what's at stake for you, in case you don't understand me. Goldman Sachs made big fees floating my last bond issue. Am I right or am I right?"

"You're right, Jack."

"And as I told you, my next bond issue will be for twice as much. And I'm going to insist that Dewey Cheatham be lead underwriter and that you be the firm's chief investment banker on the deal, which means you pocket personally a humongous bonus. Good for you since, thanks to your wife, you are in the toilet at Dewey Cheatham."

"I appreciate that, Jack."

"Appreciate this, pal. I want to have a word with Linda at the party tonight. In my suite at the top of Faff Towers. No one else there."

Tim nodded sagely. "Very well, Jack."

"You bet 'very well.'" Faff turned back to his e-mails and waved a dismissive hand. "Now you understand me."

The throng swirled around Faff Towers, thrilled to be at the big scene. Searchlights swept the sky. Heads bobbed. Limos arrived. Costumed partygoers waved. Was that the mayor, dressed as Fidel Castro? Good thing New York had no Cuban voters, like Miami. People chatted and laughed. What a perfect night for social Manhattan to go to a costume party. For many of them, dressing up for a Halloween bash was a snap; they'd spent years pretending to be someone they were not.

The building soared up and up and up over Columbus Circle, a massive monolith of sheeted glass that reflected the city around it like a mirror. It outshone even the neighboring Time Warner Center and Donald Trump's hotel. The massive dark rectangle of Central Park lay before it, dotted with lamplights that picked up the lush fall hues of the trees. With no city lights in the park to reflect off the mirrored skin of Faff Towers, the side of the building facing the park was dark, yin to yang.

Karen, clutching her toy archer's bow, presented the invitation. No Beria goons in sight. She ventured into the immense lobby, where the party swayed and bubbled. A fifteen-piece band played jazz. Masked white-jacketed waiters moved between the partiers, bearing silver trays of food and drink. People giddily lifted their masks to show who they were. That sometimes produced delight, sometimes disappointment.

The masked Robin Hood, also known as Karen Glick, certainly didn't belong. She used to have to go to shindigs like this with Tim. No longer. Another benefit of divorce. Here, she didn't have to mingle and smile. Everyone around her wore a fake chimpanzee smile. Her quiver bumped against her back as she navigated through the party, alert for Marie Antoinette.

Various Faff underlings shouted for silence. Faff's amplified voice filled the lobby. Karen couldn't see him, but given his height, she was not surprised.

The developer bid his guests welcome. "This will be the premier residential address in Manhattan," he went on. "I insist on nothing but top-of-the-line design elements. This is the best condominium building on the face of the earth. No expense was spared." Karen could see the mayor, who was trying to keep a straight face. Faff's superlative-filled speech rolled on at a Fidel Castro-like length. When Faff blessedly finished, everyone took to chatting about what an egomaniac their host was, although they happily drank his champagne.

Then Karen spotted an old friend, Denholm Brassard, the theatrical producer, who was dressed as another fabled archer, William Tell. A thin, fey fellow, he usually had his adorable boyfriend with him. Not tonight.

"How are you, Denholm?" She could tell who he was despite his mask.

"I'm sorry, I don't . . ." The man's face lit up when Karen

briefly lifted her mask. He gave her an enthusiastic hug. "Great to see you, Karen. You don't even have to ask: I'm fantastic. I heard you're getting divorced. Tim's a louse. Good move."

She had written a favorable story about the producer in the past, and later saw him at swanky parties she'd attended with Tim. Hearing people disparage Tim was like a sip of good champagne. "I'm not so fantastic."

"I read about your problem with Jack. I'm surprised he still invited you tonight."

"I'm crashing."

"How notorious of you," Denholm said. "I should be back at the theater casting my next production. But no, I'm here, trying to have a good time. It's difficult and giving me a headache."

"Say, I like your costume, but we should have called each other before we came."

"You'll have the archer thing all to yourself." Brassard brandished his William Tell crossbow and slurped his champagne. "I'm thinking of splitting. I'd like to complain to Jack, but I can't get near him for all the people kissing his ring."

"Complain about what?"

"Since you and I are both wearing essentially the same costume, maybe you can explain this." The producer gulped more champagne.

"Well, I'm Robin Hood and you're William Tell. But go ahead."

Brassard gestured with his bow. "These gorillas manhandled me and took me into this back room. Like I was a common criminal. They kept calling me 'lady' and 'bitch' and other less printable words for women. What homophobes."

"Really?" Karen checked behind her to see if anyone was watching her.

"I've been a well-behaved lad here. It's not like I was trying to shoot an apple off someone's head. My arrows have suction cups. I showed the louts my invite. I had to show them my driver's license before they believed I was me and let me go. Good security is fine, but this goes too far. Jack should be alerted to this."

"Did the gorillas say what they wanted from you or who they thought you were?"

"They could barely speak English."

Karen scanned the crowd. She recognized the three very large, very mean, very uncostumed men heading toward her.

And they recognized her. How could they know?

Leonid pointed at Karen. They quickened their pace.

CHAPTER SIXTEEN

Linda, with Tim in his imperial Roman armor posted protectively beside her, was talking to Woody Allen when the disturbance started. Allen was wearing a Woody Allen costume: flannel shirt and rumpled pants. Despite his mask, it was obvious who he was.

In her Versailles regalia, Linda looked every bit Marie Antoinette. The telltale beauty mark rode on her cheek. Her white-powdered wig rose a foot into the air. The jewelry dazzled, none of it fake. Her dress was a cascade of ruffles and lace befitting a queen. Woody Allen told her how much he admired her investment record and how sorry Flo's death made him feel, while he peered down Linda's décolletage.

Linda spotted the three huge, uncostumed men hustling through the crowd as if answering an emergency call. Faff's security men? Next, she saw—with alarm—that they were headed toward a guest dressed as Robin Hood. "Karen," she exclaimed.

"Is something the matter?" Allen asked Linda.

Tim, star-struck by Woody Allen, looked around in confusion.

Then Linda saw that another sylvan archer figure stood beside Karen. With his crossbow, he more resembled William Tell. Robin Hood said a few quick words to William Tell, and they both put arrows into their bows, pulled back on the strings, and aimed at the oncoming security men.

The three hulking guys stopped short, ten feet from their quarry, as though covered by deadly weapons. The crowd near them grew silent, unsure if this were a show or not.

Karen used that opportunity to scoot into the swirling crowd, as Robin might have slipped away from the Sheriff of Nottingham. The crowd applauded Robin's exit.

"My Lord," Linda said and put her hand to her chest, thus obstructing Allen's view.

She felt Jack Faff's presence before she could see him. Woody Allen and Faff exchanged terse pleasantries before the comedian slumped off.

"The clown tried to stop one of my buildings from going up," Faff said. "Change is inevitable. So I won." He gave Linda a triumphal grin. "I bet that's Linda Reiner in there."

"I hear you like to bet, Jack." Linda turned her most brittle smile on him.

"Why not? I own a casino." Faff stood half a head shorter than the queen of France. Appropriately, he had come as Napoleon. He even had slid his right hand between the buttons of his tunic.

"I need to talk to you, Jack. About Goldring."

Several well-born well-wishers swarmed up to Faff. He greeted them with grand bonhomie and put his hands all over the women. When they had left, Linda said she needed to talk to him without interruptions.

"Napoleon ruled France long after Marie Antoinette had lost her head to the guillotine," Faff said. "I hear you like to get your own way. This is my party, and any talking we do is on my terms."

More celebrants surrounded Faff. When he had done with them, he said, "If you want my undivided attention, you'll have to accompany me to my suite on top of this building."

"Let's go off to the side and talk," Linda said.

"No," purred Faff, long used to staking out firm negotiating terms. "It's my suite or nothing."

"Tim goes with us," Linda said.

Faff turned his gaze to the Roman general. "Ancient Rome's ruled the world. Now Rome is only a tourist spot. The good general will stand watch at this party while we go upstairs."

Tim said nothing.

"Jack, you're aware of Flo's violent death," Linda said. "I feel a little on edge. I'd be more comfortable with Tim beside me. I insist he come along."

"Do you insist?" Faff tapped Tim on his plastic breastplate. 'How about it, general? Do you insist, too?"

"Well . . . I . . . You see, Jack . . ."

Linda watched incredulously as her boyfriend stammered. "Tim, what's the matter with you? Of course, you're coming with me."

"What about it, general?" Faff smiled as he did just before the opposition to a deal crumbled.

"I'd better stay down here," Tim managed.

"Tim," Linda said. "For God's sake."

Faff offered his blue-uniformed arm, which Linda reluctantly took. With his free hand, he made a circular gesture to indicate the two of them. "Vive la France."

As the emperor and the queen walked away, Linda glared at Tim over her shoulder. Tim bowed his plume-helmeted head over his sandaled feet. Then a waitress in a white jacket and mask appeared beside him.

"Tim? Where's Linda?" the waitress asked him.

"Who the hell are you?"

The waitress briefly flipped up her mask.

"Oh, it's you," Tim said to his wife. "She went up to Faff's suite. With Faff." He tried to appear blasé about the idea, but Karen could see he was bubbling inside with anger.

"What?" Karen said from her new disguise, snatched after she'd retreated to the serving area. "And you let them? What's wrong with you?"

"I don't need to answer your stupid questions." Tim badly wanted to lash out at someone.

"Here's another stupid question: Why did I ever marry you? I'll see you at the lawyer's." Karen scanned the milling party for Faff and Linda. Were they at the elevator already?

Faff's private elevator rose up the side of his building like a fly, its glass exterior offering a peerless view of the city. "No one else uses this elevator."

"You're impressing me to death."

"That's what I like about you, Linda. You have spirit."

"Somehow, I doubt that's all you like about me."

"I like that you have made a lot of money. Money is the measure of a person's worth in this world. Like it or not."

The elevator opened onto an immense living room, filled with a wealth of design touches that beggared the imagination. Much of its walls were glass—and the city view made the one from Linda's penthouse paltry. Tailored armchairs and couches, exquisite wooden tables, profusions of flowers from ancient Mediterranean vases. Linda knew the effect was meant to dazzle. It worked.

She passed her hand over the knap of an armchair. "Liaigre did these, I understand," she said. "Natural fabric."

He stroked her bare arm. "Skin is the best natural fabric."

Linda jerked her arm away. "I'm not interested in anyone's skin."

Faff removed his Napoleon hat and leered at her. "I can make you very interested."

"I doubt it. And you're not winning your hundred-dollar bet."

"Karen Glick has a big mouth." Faff began unbuttoning his tunic. "Oh, I know you're working with her."

"I want to know about Goldring."

He took a step toward her and looked up at her randily. "There are many more fun things to know about."

Linda feigned a laugh. "Oh, please. I'm bigger than you. Watch yourself."

"Taller, but not stronger. Did you know I was a very good wrestler in college? Haven't lost my touch."

Karen, the waitress, wheeled the cart with the champagne bucket and the caviar around the edge of the party, in search of an elevator. She passed many a famous name. Jake Crayfield, whom she knew socially through Tim, dressed as a buccaneer—apropos for a Wall Streeter. His new wife, Anthea, had come as a slave girl; she displayed an alluring amount of flesh. Karen stopped for them and identified herself.

They were overjoyed to see her. "Great costume," Anthea burbled.

"You know Jack?" Jake asked. "Wait, didn't I read . . . ?"

"I know Jack too well."

"We heard about you and Tim. We're so sorry," Jake said without sorrow.

"I hope you're getting a good settlement from him," said Anthea, on her third marriage to a rich man.

"Enormous, beyond belief," Karen lied. Anthea wouldn't understand the truth. "Say, you didn't happen to run across a service elevator hereabouts, did you?" When Jake said he hadn't, Karen hesitated before rolling away. Without Tim to bounce Wall Street matters off of, Jake would do. "By the way, did you see what happened to Corsine stock?"

"Yeah, go figure," Jake said. "I heard. Fidelity decided it fit their investment profile and bought heavily. Others followed. They do that."

As Karen had told Gran, a giant mutual fund group like Fidelity could get a stock moving with the stroke of a computer key. After excusing herself, Karen rattled the cart along until she encountered a homeless guy with the plastic trash bag full of cans and bottles. She'd seen him earlier at the party. This character looked worse than Rocky. The homeless guest talked to no one, merely drifted around, watching and listening.

"You're Karen Glick," he said.

"Who's she?" Karen said, alarmed at being identified.

"Relax, I'm not one of Faff's brutes. I'm better at seeing through masks than they are. My friend, Frank Vere, told me to keep an eye on you tonight."

"Who are you, sir?"

"Welles."

She peered at him closely. "Welles, as in . . . Welles?"

Frank once had told her about his friendship with Welles, one of his many high-placed contacts. Welles, the world's richest person. A man who floated about the earth with no bodyguards and no entourage, his face seldom in the news, passing himself off as an ordinary soul. Kings used to disguise themselves as commoners to discover what was transpiring in the realm; Welles, his economic power vast, pursued the same wisdom. He hardly ever made the social scene.

After fiddling with her mask to ensure it was in place, Karen said, "I'm surprised you came."

"I get invited to everything," Welles said. "I go to very little. Frank tells me you're working on a story about the Federal Reclamation Authority."

Nodding, Karen said, "Sure. What do you know about them?"

Welles settled his bag of beverage containers on the floor and accepted a glass from a passing tray. "We rub up against the Authority from time to time on the international scene. Big business and our nation's intelligence services have, shall we say, a sometimes symbiotic relationship."

"They're after a certain computer program that—"

"I've heard about Goldring. I hear the agency's director, a man named Kingman Wooton, is running a rogue operation using the Authority's capabilities to somehow restore his fortune. It would make sense for him to pursue Goldring. Wooton, you see, married a wealthy woman and now the money's gone. He lives a lush life in Georgetown and wants to continue."

"I've never heard of him."

"You're not supposed to. He's a formidable man. Overweight from indulgence, he has a distinctively deep voice that commands attention and a razor-sharp intellect. They say he reads minds. He certainly notices the details others miss, but he lacks a facility for personal relations. His wife, Erica, a rather attractive middle-aged woman, has a foolish food store called Ratatouille and is having an affair with the young fellow, named Mick, who runs it for her."

"Hey, thanks a lot. Now I need to find the service elevator." Karen bent to resume rolling her serving cart.

"Through that double doorway to the right of the band, second hall on the right," Welles said. "But be very careful."

Karen followed Welles's directions. The double door wasn't locked and she pushed the cart through. The corridor beyond had been freshly painted. Down the second hall stood stainless steel elevator doors. The champagne bottle clanked against the silver bucket as she shoved the cart toward the elevator.

The indicator panel said that the elevator shaft went

halfway up the building, where the elevator car was now. Once up there, she'd have to find another elevator to take her the rest of the way. She hit the button and the elevator car began descending.

The elevator doors opened to reveal Mikhail and his nasty, sharp-toothed smile.

"The cameras Jack has got around here work pretty good—I saw you coming," the gangster said. He inserted his index finger underneath Karen's mask and pulled it off. "Think you fool Mikhail, huh?"

"Jack, I'm almost thirty-five. Too old for you." Linda kept the timbre in her voice just right to show she wasn't scared. Or at least to try to show that. "Let's talk."

"You have a few months until your birthday. I checked." He indicated a long couch that faced a large iron cube of a hearth that contained a crackling autumnal fire. The couch was long and wide enough to accommodate two prone people. "Why not sit on some of my natural fiber? And we can . . . talk. A good idea to . . . talk. We have lots to talk about."

"I'll try this," she said and sat in an armchair.

Faff sat alone on the couch. "Part of my success is knowing who is right and wrong for a job. You want Goldring returned to you. Find a good ally."

"You don't have Goldring?"

With a predatory dealmaker's smile, Faff said, "I don't have Goldring. Someone killed Albert Niebel and took the laptop from him. I've been trying to find it ever since."

"Did the Authority take it?"

"Maybe."

"How did you hear about Goldring? We'd been very careful to keep it under wraps."

"Linda, you can't keep such a thing a secret. Word gets out."

"Exactly who told you?"

"Doesn't matter," Faff said.

"Was it Tim Bratton?"

"Doesn't matter."

"I've wondered sometimes if my seeking publicity brought on Flo's death."

Faff shrugged. "I hear Goldring is a miracle."

"It is a miracle."

"How does it work?"

"Doesn't matter," Linda said.

"Fair enough. For now." Faff watched her with a smug smile and a keen interest that went beyond the sexual, as if he faced her over a chessboard.

"There's this frightening Englishman, gray-haired, dapper dresser. He keeps popping up. Observing us. At the hair-dresser's. At Flo's funeral. He threatened Karen and told her to stop chasing Goldring. Who is he, Jack?"

"Beats me. First I've heard of him."

"Then he must work for the Authority," Linda said. "And it stands to reason that the Authority has my computer."

"And it also stands to reason," Faff said, "that you're not going to crack a powerful government intelligence agency with the help of a little reporter like Karen Glick."

"For your information, Jack," Linda said, "she's taller than you."

"When you're rich, you're eight feet tall. I'm the one who can help you, not Glick. I've got the assets and the people who can track Goldring down and grab it away from James Bond or whoever the hell has it now."

"Do you, Jack? The people? A bunch of two-bit hoods. The assets? Karen says you're standing on the brink of financial disaster."

Faff sat back on the couch and crossed his legs, as if untroubled by her insolence. His smug composure stayed intact. "Linda, Linda, Linda. You've wasted so much time. You spent years trying to sell stocks to ignoramuses and going to parties as arm candy for the likes of Larry Ellison and Garner Chase. Don't waste any more time."

"Jack, Jack, Jack. I spent my time perfecting Goldring. Now I'm spending time getting it back. You should be spending yours talking to a good bankruptcy lawyer."

"Everyone in business has temporary setbacks," Faff said. "Pay mine no mind. Mikhail Beria and his men have more resources and connections than you can imagine." Faff's face was alight with unpleasant amusement. The demon fire in the iron cube hearth made his eyes flash. "Glick is about to get canned, and she's a clueless pipsqueak. The Authority has a fortress in Virginia. I ought to know—I built it, years ago. The place is better guarded than a nuclear weapons site. How can Glick possibly get inside it?"

"You underestimate her. A lot of people do."

Faff spread his hands. "What's in this for you? Let's say you get Goldring back and Glick writes about it in her magazine. Your secret is really blown then."

"We'll simply have to have better security to ensure there's never another tragedy like we had with Flo. She gave her life for Goldring."

Faff barked a laugh. "Spare me, Linda. You're saying Flo was a martyr to the cause of you getting rich? You're just like me. You want more and more wealth, and the public adulation. And your sister can rot in her grave."

Linda lost her cool. "Don't you dare speak about my sister like that, you bastard," she shouted.

Faff stood and marched across to her chair. "I'll speak any way I want." He gripped the armrests, hemming her in. "And your father gave Flo a 'friendship ring.' Some friendship they had. A little too close, I hear. Good thing smalltown cops are dumb."

"This is none of your business." Snarling, Linda thrust her face defiantly into Faff's.

"I know everything."

"You know very little, you creep."

"Let's see about what I know." He gripped the low-cut neck of her dress to tear it off.

Mikhail produced a long, cruel knife. He poked it at Karen's face. Karen flinched. The point hovered an inch from her wide right eye.

Other than the muted party music and chatter, the only sound to be heard was Karen's rapid breathing. Mikhail held his mean smile as steady as his blade.

"Jack, he likes privacy," the gangster said. "You got no respect for a man's privacy. That's your problem. It is a big problem. I gonna cure it for you."

The far doors opened and the party's roar enveloped them. A homeless man with a bag of cans and bottles entered, followed by several of Faff's managers.

"Whatever you want, Mr. Welles, I'm sure Mr. Faff would honor," one of the managers was saying.

Mikhail had slipped his knife out of sight.

Welles gestured toward Karen. "I want her to accompany me out of the building. And I want no interference from this thug or any of the others. Understood?"

"Yes, sir, Mr. Welles," another manager said. "Mikhail, could I have a word with you?"

"You doing what?" Mikhail said. He was ready to bite the managers' noses off.

"Do you appreciate who this is?" a third manager whispered to Mikhail, tilting his head in Welles's direction.

"Come with me," Welles said to Karen. He handed the clattering sack to a manager and guided Karen by the arm back into the party.

"But Linda," Karen protested.

"Can take care of herself."

*   *   *

With both hands, Linda pushed against Jack Faff's ribcage. His rage-filled face contorted in anguish. He collapsed to his knees.

"You'd better be telling me the truth, Jack," she said as she got up. "That steering wheel did a number on you ribs, huh?"

She took the private elevator down, ignoring the magnificent scenery. Linda glided out into the party. Tim stood by himself, in his armor, swilling straight scotch.

"Faff got to you, didn't he, Tim?"

The Master of the Universe swagger had left him. "Well . . . Linda . . . very complicated . . . hard to explain . . . You must approach this, well . . . ah—"

"This isn't too complicated," Linda said. "I never want to see you again."

Holding the dress so she wouldn't trip on the hem, Marie Antoinette swept out of the gala and onto the nighttime New York sidewalks. She drew pedestrians' stares as she headed several blocks south.

At Carnegie Hall, their prearranged rendezvous point, Karen was waiting in her white-jacketed waitress outfit.

"You're okay? Did Faff hurt you? Did he—?"

"I'm okay. He's not." There was a certain bloodthirsty euphoria about Linda. "What happened to your Robin Hood costume?"

"I donated it to the clothing drive for poverty-stricken real estate developers."

"I kept my clothes on, and he wouldn't have won his bet. I couldn't see where he had the camera in his suite, but he couldn't see mine, either." Linda pulled the towering white wig off and reached into its tresses. Her bejeweled hand emerged with a small video camera. It was one of the many electronic toys Flo had lying around the Reiners's office.

"Did he admit anything?"

"Either he's a very good liar, or the Authority has Goldring."

"He's a very good liar," Karen said. "If you're right, it's time to go after the Authority."

CHAPTER SEVENTEEN

The door opened, the retainers produced the chair, and Wooton made his grand entrance. His eyes had a strange, wounded quality that Logie found worrisome. He settled his well-dressed bulk into the chair and silenced Logie with a gesture before she could speak.

"Ms. Logan," Wooton said with a peevishness Logie hadn't heard from him before, "don't start with me. I know you're going to ask me about your daughter again. She is being well taken care of. You have my word. You will be united with her at such point as we secure Goldring."

"But, Director, I must—"

"We will discuss this no further, Ms. Logan," Wooton said in his thundering bass. "You think you're the only one with problems? Do you?"

"Director, I—" Logie couldn't tell where this came from.

"Well, you aren't." Wooton looked furiously to Logie, then at Donner, then at Logie again. "Now, you have news of Siegfried Wolfe?"

Thwarted, Logie set her lips primly. Then, "Yes, Director. He is staying at the Plaza Hotel in Manhattan under one of his customary aliases."

The director had gotten hold of himself. He contemplated her in silence. "An extraordinary man, isn't he, Wolfe? And to think that I saved his life once. Well." Wooton turned to Donner, who sat bolt upright in his chair. "Mr. Donner, I want a team scrambled. You will seize Goldring from Wolfe. If he does not have possession of Goldring, he will be apprehended and will undergo interrogation at our alternate command post in New York."

"Director," Donner said, "shouldn't I go up there to supervise the operation?"

"Mr. Donner, I appreciate that you feel stir crazy here. Nevertheless, you shall remain here until further notice." Wooton hoisted himself up to leave.

"We'll get the laptop, no sweat," Donner said. "Goldring is probably in his hotel room. Wolfe shouldn't be a problem. Hey, he's getting old. My guys are young and strong."

"Don't be so cocksure," Wooton said. "They seldom come as skilled as Wolfe. You've already failed once, Mr. Donner. Let's not go for two, okay?"

"You're not going to hurt this guy, are you?" Logie asked.

"Stupid question," Donner said.

"Ms. Logan," Wooton said as he strode out, "Wolfe has committed murder."

"That doesn't give *us* the right to be murderers," Logie said.

The next morning, Karen waited for Linda in Bryant Park. And waited. And waited. Fog embraced the trees, dulling their autumnal hues. A bagpiper played off in the mist. Karen was the only one in her family to like bagpipes. Her father, the peacenik, thought them too military. Her mother, the feminist, thought them too masculine. Her grandmother just plain objected to the music ("In heaven they hand you a harp. In hell, bagpipes."). This misty morning, they sounded mournful. As time wore on, she grew more irritated.

At last, a half-hour late, Linda strolled nonchalantly into view. In no hurry, she sipped her Starbucks.

"I thought we were meeting at eight," Karen said, and ostentatiously looked at her watch.

"What kind of a watch is that?" Linda said, as if Karen's wrist were circled with dung.

"The kind with the minute hand that says you're thirty minutes late."

Linda sipped her coffee. "I had to deal with my new housekeeper," she said.

"Oh, well, that explains everything. I had to deal with mine this morning, too, except it was quicker since I'm the housekeeper. I used to call my husband—excuse me, your boyfriend—'the late Tim Bratton.' I guess what he had is catching, huh?"

"He's not my boyfriend anymore. So you don't have to bother bringing him up."

"I've watched the video again and again. You think people 'underestimate' me, huh?"

"So that's what's bugging you this morning," Linda said.

"What's bugging me this morning, Linda, is that for this partnership to work, we need a little mutual respect and cooperation. Tim told Faff that I'd be there and that I'd be dressed as Robin Hood, didn't he?"

Linda shrugged minutely, as if Karen's question were hardly worthy of a response. "Who knows? I am over him. I hope his deal with Jack falls through."

"Did you tell Tim what we were doing?" Karen said. "Did you, Linda? Tell me."

"Well, of course I did. He was my boyfriend. I don't like your tone."

"And I don't like your broadcasting our plans to my husband, who would swallow broken glass to land a big deal and get back in his boss' favor at Dewey Cheatham."

"Don't be so melodramatic," Linda said and fixed Karen's gaze with her Arctic glare. "I trusted him. Didn't you trust him once?"

"Linda, you can't simply—" The phone rang in her pocket. She turned her back on Linda and answered it. "Mr. Prince," she said, "thanks for calling. Frank Vere said you might."

"Vere says he has faith in you," Harry Prince said with his precise diction. No one called the natty Securities and Exchange Commission investigator Harry, according to Frank. Even his wife called him "Mr. Prince."

"This involves a stolen computer that—"

"The one belonging to the Reiner sisters that predicts stocks."

Karen laughed incredulously. "You've heard about this, too?" Linda, sipping her Starbucks coffee, was pacing nearby, close enough to be in earshot, far enough to indicate displeasure.

"A rumor. I hear lots of rumors. Most of them unfounded. Predicting the future? I prefer a Ouija board."

"Mr. Prince, Flo Reiner died in the theft of this laptop. Whoever has it now, I suspect, has ordered lots of Corsine stock, which then took off for the moon. I need to know who has been buying Corsine lately." The SEC has the power to retrieve trading records.

"Let me get back to you."

When Prince hung up, Karen said, "That was one of Frank's confidential sources. Frank was initially reluctant to share any with me, but now he figures I deserve at least one."

Linda took another sip of coffee. "Why? Frank has dug up everything for you."

"Oh, please. Last night I learned a lot about this Wooton guy at the Authority."

"From Welles, who is Frank's friend."

"For your information, Linda, I uncovered the fact that Faff is in financial trouble in the first place." Karen began wondering how Linda would look with that Starbucks dumped on her head.

By some unspoken agreement, Karen and Linda walked wordlessly into the park. The electricity of ill will between them was almost visible. They sat at opposite ends of a bench near a pigeon-bombed philosopher's statue.

"Linda, we need to be on the same page here. I need to know what you know."

The fog had lifted and the park lay placidly beneath its bright October foliage. The fountain splashed happily. The bagpiper had left with the mist. Painters were posted about, standing like sentries before their canvases and easels. A V formation of birds flew over, headed south for the winter, and disappeared beyond the autumn palette of trees and the midtown skyline.

"God," Linda said. "Jack Faff might have a point, you know. How on earth can you—can we—crack this super-secret intelligence agency, with all its power? I don't know. Do you?"

"Nobody is cracking anything until you level with me. For instance, how was your father murdered when the news account said he died in an accidental fall? What did Faff mean about the local police being dumb?"

"I fail to see how that is relevant to going after this Wooton man." Linda sighed. "But if you insist. One day, when she was a teenager, Flo took a bus the whole way to Ohio State and collapsed in my arms, sobbing, hysterical. Said she'd just pushed Daddy down the basement steps, then said he had been having sex with her ever since I left for college. I'd told him to stay the hell away from Flo when I caught him pawing her. I thought that had worked, but then I was gone off to school. Our mother didn't want to know. Are you happy now?"

"And the police were satisfied with the accident story?"

"Yes. Who knows how Faff found out about what really happened. I kept our secret. I only told Ginny. Trouble was, from then on, Flo developed this deepening resentment toward me."

"Because you were popular and pretty."

"Still am," Linda said with conviction. "A lot of women resent me. Like you."

"I don't resent you," Karen lied.

"Sure. Well, I think Flo was angry because I was no longer at home to protect her. I always had bossed her around, and Ginny. Flo came to depend on it as a teenager. Without me, she fell under Daddy's spell. They had this love-hate thing I can't fathom."

"What's strange to me is that becoming rich didn't make Flo one bit happier."

"It made me a helluva lot happier," Linda said. "I was sick of holding myself in and letting the guy be in charge. I was sick of just being someone's pretty date. And all of them were so into sports. How boring. I remember, when I was seeing Garner Chase, sitting in the skybox at the Super Bowl, pretending I was having fun. Please."

"Tim's like that. When he'd park himself in front of the tube to watch football, I pissed him off by asking: 'Why don't they give each team one of those funny-shaped balls and then they won't have to fight over the one.' But I did watch with him. I actually like sports."

"I forbid Tim from watching football in my presence. I told him it was either sports or me. I won." Linda clapped her hands on her thighs. "Look, I'll get another malleable boyfriend to replace Tim. Do you know what prompted me to create Goldring?"

"What?" Karen said, mulling the image of arrogant Tim meekly obeying female orders to stay clear of sports.

"That jackass boyfriend, Garner Chase. The last one

from my arm candy days. His family has more money than anyone this side of Bill Gates, Welles, and maybe God. I mean, their name is on a bank. Garner makes Tim look like Saint Francis of Assisi. Beneath Garner's old-money savoir faire, I saw what a mean man he was. He asked me to marry him. I turned him down. How could I keep up the smiling pretense of a trophy for my entire life? Nobody says no to Garner. He told me all I was good for was to show off in public. Since I had no money, he said, I'd better play my cards right before I got too old and couldn't snag a wealthy man. That's when I realized I needed to get rich on my own."

"Well, you surely did," Karen said.

"Still, what haunts me is that, if I had married Garner, then Flo would be . . ." Linda turned away and bowed her head.

Karen reached over and patted her shoulder. "Hey, it's okay."

Linda whirled around, her lovely face a mask of annoyance. "I'm not crying. I don't cry. I don't love anyone. Understand?"

Aghast, Karen managed, "But you love Ginny. You loved Flo."

"They are my sisters."

"Okay. Fine. Whatever you say." Karen tilted her head back and saw another V formation of migrating birds. "Right now, the priority is Wooton. I have a plan to draw him out of his haunted house."

"How do you propose to do that?"

"Through his weak spot."

"And that would be what?"

Three operatives broke into Wolfe's hotel room at the Plaza. They were solid-looking young fellows—broad in the shoulder, square in the jaw, linear in the mentality. They no doubt had done good work combating terrorism and serving their country. They meant well. They had no idea what was on the laptop they sought. And they didn't deserve what they'd get.

Two of them went inside his room and closed the door to the hall; the third stood guard outside in the hall. Wearing disposable gloves, the two operatives rummaged through Wolfe's belongings. One was particularly impressed by Wolfe's wardrobe hanging in his closet.

"This guy can dress," he said. "It's like *Gentleman's Quarterly* around here, Johnny. He's like the director. After a good diet, that is. Did you hear the director is splitting from his wife? He caught her latest boyfriend in the act."

Johnny grunted. "Who is this guy, Wolfe?"

"We don't have the need to know, Donner says."

"Donner is such a dork, Terry. Why isn't he up here?"

"Likes to stay near the throne, I guess."

Out the window, the sun poured like butter over the rich coloring of Central Park. Street noise was muted.

The secret door in the wall popped open. Wolfe held the Glock in firing position, silencer affixed. Johnny received a perfect three-shot group clustered in his chest, blowing his heart into useless tissue.

Terry was good. As his partner fell, his hand sped from the clothes in the closet to the weapon under his left armpit. Wolfe had the element of surprise, though. The Englishman blew apart both the young man's shoulders before he got his gun out. He had hardly hit the floor before Wolfe was on him, squelching his screams with duct tape over the mouth.

"No, your comrade out in the hall can't help you," Wolfe told the writhing wounded man, who emitted muted moans. "He's dead. I took the precaution of hauling him out of sight."

Wolfe wouldn't take long to pack. There was no telling if

another team was posted nearby. This was the first time he had used the special feature this room provided—a secret door that led to a private stairway. Fearful of criminals in the hall, the rich and well-connected of the 1930s had insisted on this escape path. Memories of it had since faded. Few were aware of its existence. It added quite a bit to the room rate. Wolfe got this room at the Plaza on every New York visit.

"Pity I have to leave," Wolfe said. "The Plaza is my favorite." He injected the wounded man with morphine and, when the drug took effect, ripped away the duct tape.

"You're after a laptop, aren't you?" Wolfe said.

A blood bubble formed on Terry's lips. He closed his eyes. He was trained not to talk.

"Dirk Donner's involved, eh?" Wolfe said. "I've heard of him. He's formidable. If he'd come to my room, I might be the one on the floor."

The operative's eyelids opened at the sound of Donner's name.

"I'm not going to kill you," Wolfe said. "I need you to be my messenger. To Kingman Wooton." Wolfe jotted on Plaza stationery with an old-fashioned nib pen. "Here's where he should phone to reach me. It's in Iran, but they can link us up. Tell him that he and I need to meet. About the Goldring laptop. I have it."

Wolfe folded the paper and stuck it in Terry's inside jacket pocket. "You should get into another line of work. Where they hire the handicapped."

"The director will get you," the young man managed to say through his druggy haze.

Wolfe turned to his packing. "Did you know Wooton saved my life once? Good of him, wasn't it? How disappointing he'd try reversing the process now."

CHAPTER EIGHTEEN

Ginny, late for a 9 A.M. department meeting, left her apartment and had reached Broadway when she checked her briefcase. She had absentmindedly left the copies of her proposal at home. She didn't trust herself to wing it at the meeting without the comforting support of a written document for her colleagues to peruse—or to pretend they were perusing. She had twenty-five copies sitting on her desk at home. Getting Freddy to make the copies had been a minor miracle; the only task he performed well was to fetch her dry cleaning. She rushed back to her building and took the stairs two at a time.

The stairs in Ginny's apartment building had been stripped of the old rug, which had been there since Pythagoras developed his theorems. On the landing below her floor were buckets of glue to lay the new carpeting. The university, which made a featherbrained landlord, had told tenants nothing about the work schedule. No workmen were in evidence this morning. Or anyone else.

When Ginny turned the key to her apartment, she realized that the door hadn't been locked. At first she figured she might have forgotten to lock it when she left. Flo's death had unsettled her to such a degree that she was overlooking little details of life lately.

Once in the apartment's foyer, she understood that she wasn't alone. Someone was in her bedroom, beyond the half-open door. She heard rustling sounds, sinister, alien.

Urban dwellers are taught to flee if they encounter an intruder in their apartment. No one wants to tangle all alone with a psycho or a dope fiend.

But Ginny couldn't move. The quickening, thudding tempo of her heart was deafening. Her mouth became arid and she couldn't swallow. Sweat popped out on every square inch of her face. Her feet were fused to the floorboards. Ginny was transfixed by the half-open door to her bedroom. She caught a glimpse of a form stealing past the opening.

She willed herself to look at the rest of the apartment. Every drawer of her desk was out. On the wall, the Escher prints hung askew, as if the intruder had checked the back of them. The living room rug had been partly rolled up.

Ginny drew one ragged breath and lifted a leaden left foot, the beginning of backpedaling out of there to call the cops.

The bedroom door opened.

Ginny whimpered.

It was Freddy. The shock he showed equaled Ginny's.

"Freddy . . . what—?"

"I got your dry cleaning," her assistant said.

Her surprise overwhelmed any anger, let alone fear. That was right: he had a key, as well. "Freddy . . . why on earth did you . . . what's this?" She gestured toward the desk and the rug and the wall paintings.

"I saw a mouse in here and tried to catch him. Maybe

ripping up the old carpet on the stairway stirred him up and he got into your apartment. You never know with mice."

"But—"

"Excuse me, Professor Reiner. I got a class." He shouldered past her.

Ginny lacked Linda's air of command. Maybe he was sharper than she thought. She let him leave unchallenged.

At the office, Karen had finished making travel arrangements when the phone rang. She grabbed it, hoping for the SEC's Harry Prince.

"Is this Miss Glick?" said a reedy, somewhat familiar, man's voice.

Miss? "Only to my friends. Who's this?"

"Father Finnegan. We met at Flo's funeral mass. I don't know if you're religious . . ."

Maury Glick had brought up Karen without religion, which he considered hypocritical and fraudulent. When she was twelve, Maury took his daughter to a community meeting at an opulent Upper West Side synagogue. The topic was how to help the homeless. Maury declared stridently to the crowd that the whole show of concern was a sham, and that tax-exempt places of worship, such as that one, should be taxed to provide more money for the neglected street people. The rabbi leading the meeting told her father: "Sir, if you care this much for the homeless, why don't you take in a few at your house?" That shut Maury up.

"Depends," Karen said to Finnegan. "I worship Brad Pitt and George Clooney, but that's it."

"The reason I'm calling is that I hear you have influence with the Reiner sisters."

"I bicker with Linda periodically."

"Ginny Reiner is talking about taking legal action to

thwart Flo's will. Miss Glick, the money is going to our parish. Could you please convince Ginny to stop?"

"Father, some of Flo's money went to you personally. Ginny thinks you had a romantic involvement with Flo and she didn't use sound judgment."

"That's absurd," the priest said. "I've taken a vow."

"We're all human," Karen said. "Hey, I didn't take any vow, but I've been celibate for a while myself. It's called a bad marriage."

"You have a smart . . . take on life, Miss Glick."

"God's gift, I suspect," Karen said as he hung up.

Wooton had been living at headquarters lately to keep himself from thinking too much about Erica, which proved impossible. He hadn't been out for a decent meal, and that only added to his ill humor. From his chair planted in the command center, he was a rumbling volcano of discontent. The disasters were piling up.

"The sheer incompetence," Wooton thundered at Donner, who stood before the director. Donner's corded arms were crossed, as if afraid his body would be blown apart. "An entire three-man team. You assured me this would be easy. Totally bungled. And now Wolfe, and presumably Goldring, are God knows where. Wolfe surely has assumed a new alias. Probably one we don't have on our list."

"They . . . director, you see . . . We had a good team." Donner spread his hands imploringly. "The after-action report may—we're ready to interview Special Operative Granger in the hospital. He had surgery. Maybe then—"

"Terry Granger has a lot to answer for," Wooton said. "Such as how three professionals can get themselves shot, leaving us with a lot of explaining to do to the NYPD."

"Those poor guys," Logie said. "John Donatello was engaged, I hear. And they died pursuing our agenda, not thwarting terrorism. Nothing noble."

"As far as the world is concerned, Ms. Logan, they were indeed part of a counterterrorism campaign," Wooton said. "In light of some of the people he has worked for, I consider Siegfried Wolfe tantamount to a terrorist."

"Terry Granger probably won't have full use of his arms anymore," Donner said quietly. "The doctors are seeing what they can do."

"All three of these men gave up their old lives and became Authority operatives," Wooton said. "They were fully aware that this is a hazardous life. At least Granger confirmed Wolfe has Goldring."

"I'm sorry for what happened to them—they didn't deserve it," Donner said.

"Perhaps you can explain to me," Wooton said seethingly to Donner, "precisely how you permitted this to fall apart."

Donner began, for once, to gather some courage. "By not being in New York, Director. These were three good men. But somehow Wolfe was a step ahead. I'm a field operative. Cooping me up here does us no good."

Wooton regarded him for a long moment. Then, "You weary me. Go sit down."

Logie looked between a sullen Donner and a steaming Wooton. "What about calling that number in Iran and setting up the meeting with Wolfe that he's after?" she said. "That's the clearest path to him. Maybe he wants to make a deal. Maybe he can hand over Goldring without anyone else getting hurt."

"I'm considering it," the director said, with no hint that he really was. "But bargaining with Wolfe hands him a psychological advantage. He's setting the terms, not me. I'd rather surprise him, as we were supposed to do at the Plaza."

"So we set up a meeting with Wolfe that's really an ambush," Donner said. "We sweat him until he tells us where he has stashed Goldring. End of story."

"This death and violence sickens me," Logie said. She didn't bring up her anxiety over her daughter.

"Get used to it," Donner said.

"Mr. Donner," Wooton said, "when I want you to speak, I'll ask you to speak."

Logie wished for the millionth time that she'd never gotten involved. When she'd heard about the shootings in the Plaza, she had gone to her little room to cry. Facing her husband's legal travails would have been much easier. No one had died because of them.

The lunch bunch at Ratatouille wasn't impressive. Only a couple of customers, overdressed lobbyist types, who stood impatiently at the counter. Located a block from Washington's Dupont Circle, the store had been smartly—and expensively—decorated, with good tile on the floor and a glass front that admitted abundant fall sunshine. The two sullen young women behind the counter firmly believed that the customer was always wrong.

"How's the ratatouille today?" Karen asked after the two other customers had huffed out, empty-handed. She spotted a man in the back of the place but no middle-aged woman.

"Who gives a rat's ass?" said the girl with the ring through her lower lip. "I think we're out."

"Yeah, we're out," said the other one, intent on a handheld video game. She hadn't washed her hair in a month.

"Is that Mick?" Karen asked.

"Yeah, in the back. You're not a lawyer for his father, are you?"

"Do I look like a lawyer?" Karen said. "Where are my horns and tail?"

Inside the small office to the rear, Mick also was playing a video game, although on the computer. A handsome fellow on the sunny side of thirty, he had a mischievous air about him, as if the world were one big joke. His cowboy boots were hand-tooled. He wore a single earring.

"I'm Karen Glick, a reporter with *Profit* magazine."

Mick grinned. "The press? We need some good publicity. How about an article about the hottest new take-out joint in the Dupont Circle area?"

"Actually, I'm trying to find Erica Wooton. I'm writing a story about her husband."

That made Mick chortle. "Her husband's a boring bureaucrat. What's to write about? Actually, she probably doesn't want to talk about him. They're getting divorced."

"That's too bad."

More chuckling from Mick. "Yeah, her old man isn't too happy with me, either. He caught us doing the humpty dance in his own house. Looks like I might end up a party to the divorce proceedings. Them's the breaks." He seemed quite proud of himself.

As long as Karen had been a journalist, she was perennially amazed at what people blurted out. "That's a shame."

"Hey, Erica likes the young meat. What can I say? She's pretty good for an older babe. You know how they are when they get to that age. It's great. They don't swell"—he patted his stomach—"they don't tell, and they're grateful as hell."

"Interesting assessment." Karen felt tempted to rip his earring off. "How did you meet her?"

"She used to go out with a friend of my father's. Oops, here comes Erica now. I'd better shut down the video game. Got to pretend I'm working."

"Yoo-hoo," Erica called from the front.

Mick's grin wavered. "If she calls me 'gor-Jesus' once more, I'm—"

"Doesn't sound too bad," Karen said.

"It wasn't," Mick said, "the first five million times."

Erica, who had a good two decades on Mick, still looked damn fine. She had a shapely, gym-toned body and wore tight leather pants well. Many Southerners lost their accents when they moved north; Erica's had no doubt become more intense. With her wide mouth and toothy smile, she made a more earthy version of Scarlett O'Hara.

"Now Mick, who's this lady," she said when her boyfriend hesitated. Despite her smile, she eyed Karen with possessive suspicion.

Mick's concerns encompassed three things: himself, himself, and himself. The petty details of others' lives didn't interest him. "Uh . . . this is Ms. . . . I didn't catch the name."

"Glick. Karen Glick. I'm a reporter for *Profit* magazine, ma'am."

Erica feigned delight. "Oh, my. That is one of my favorites. I read it cover to cover every month."

"Actually, we appear weekly."

"Ms. Glick is going to write an article about Ratatouille," Mick said from his chair.

Erica moved over to his desk and motioned for him to get up. After all, he was addressing his elders. She was as bossy as Linda, but Karen wasn't sure which was worse. She slid a hand in the back pocket of Mick's jeans. "That would be simply lovely," she said.

Mick dutifully laid a tentative hand on her shoulder.

"Not quite," Karen said. "I'm writing a story about your husband, Mrs. Wooton. I need to talk to you about him."

"Kingman?" Erica slid the fingers of her other hand into Mick's shirt and fondled his chest hair. "Who would care about him? We're splitting up. And I got myself a new man." She smooched her lover on the lips. Mick gave a weak smile.

"Congratulations," Karen said.

She stroked his chin. "Yeah, isn't he simply gor . . ."

"A gourmet," Karen said. "To run an establishment like this, he'd have to be."

A young blonde woman, barely out of college, wearing a headband and a Fair Isle sweater, had entered the store. When she spotted Erica and Mick, she spun about and walked briskly away.

Erica seemed displeased by the sight of the preppy girl. She unhanded Mick and turned serious. "What's happening with Kingman? Is he in any trouble?"

"Let's talk in private," Karen said.

She snatched her bag from Mick's desk and told him: "I expect you to be here when I come back." She marched Karen out the front, past the indifferent counter attendants, and lit a cigarette. Erica blew out the first puff in an angry gust.

"Who's the blonde girl in the headband?" Karen asked.

Erica's Southern charm had dissipated as rapidly as her exhaled smoke. "Some little slut who works on the Hill. Now, you wanted to talk to me about Kingman. What about him?"

They were traveling west along P Street. "Your husband is a very powerful man. And he's misusing that power."

"I can't imagine what you could mean. Kingman is a midlevel paper pusher at the CIA. Working there is not as glamorous as it sounds. And they pay him joke wages."

"You're wrong about what he does for a living." Karen told her about the Federal Reclamation Authority, the murder of Flo and Albert, and the search for Goldring. She told her about Jack Faff. And she told her that Kingman Wooton was wrongly marshaling federal resources for his own private gain. By the time Karen had finished, they were standing on the bridge overlooking Rock Creek Park.

Erica lit another cigarette. "Kingman had the potential to

be a real somebody. Say what you want, the man is smart."
She shook her head. "He's very impressed with himself,
which doesn't make him much of a husband. But that kind
of an ego would work well for him playing bigshot. I just
never thought he'd gone very far. How about that?"

"Mrs. Wooton, how do you get along with your husband?"

"We're getting divorced. How do you think we get along?
We've led separate lives for so long. I'd volunteer for this
cause or that charity. I'd see friends. Travel. On my own. Or
with a man I'd met. Kingman was too busy for me. At home,
we have a live-in cook. Or did, till our money began running out." She explained about how the Colonel's estate
had evaporated, all the while staring off into the void beyond her cigarette. "Kingman would dine alone. I'd go out.
Couldn't stand sitting at the table with those silences.
Those awful silences."

"You have a nice house?" Karen hadn't been able to find
a trace of it in Washington real estate records she's scanned
online. There was no trace of a Wooton phone number,
listed or unlisted. Frank Vere's phone company pal had
come up empty.

"Beautiful. In Georgetown. Big enough for Kingman and
me to avoid each other. Paid for with my father's money.
Kingman contributed exactly zilch."

"Your financial situation is bad?"

Erica took a deep drag of her cigarette. "It's bad. It's bad
as bad can be."

"You've got the house to keep up. And the store."

"Well, Mick's about to come into his trust money, unless
his father monkeys around with the thing. That'll bail out
the business. I can depend on Mick."

Her sincerity was heartbreaking. "Where are you living?"
Karen asked.

Erica closed her eyes for a spell. "Mainly at Mick's. Kingman is sleeping at the office. Still, he comes home occasionally. So do I. I try to avoid him, though I can tell when he's been there. Dirty dishes he doesn't bother to wash." She laughed dryly. "He loves the house and the whole life of luxury it provides, or used to provide. His whole world is falling apart. The money, gone. Me, gone. He let slip they may force him to retire. He's changed lately, but I'm not sure how. He talks about how he is going to make a lot of money for some reason. I think he's trying to win me back somehow. I just brush the idea off. This laptop thing of yours sounds like a tall tale, frankly."

"Do you still love your husband, Erica?"

"So now it's 'Erica'?"

"Do you?"

She flicked her cigarette butt into space. "Don't ask me that question. What more do you want from me?"

Karen handed her her card. "If you have feelings for him in the slightest, I want you to talk to your husband about our conversation. He could go to jail for what he's doing. I want him to call me."

"Jail?" The enormity of the bad publicity potentially headed her way dawned on Erica. Her face darkened. "You could really hurt Kingman. And me. Can I trust you to do the right thing?"

More than you could Mick, Karen thought. Instead, she answered, "Yes, you can."

Waiting for the shuttle to board, Karen sat in the airport departure lounge and called Eudell to report in. She listened while Karen described the visit.

"Even though she's estranged from Wooton, I'm betting his wife will get to him," Karen told her editor. "This is the best means I see of smoking this guy out."

"Linda Reiner will want you to grab Goldring from this powerful character somehow and deliver it to her. Let's say

you do get to interview Wooton. The chances of him bringing Goldring along for you to admire are two: slim and
none."

"If I can tie Wooton to Goldring, then I can write a story
about the whole deal. If others in the media pick this up,
then it should force him to relinquish the computer to its
rightful owners, the Reiner sisters."

"A lot of 'ifs' there," Eudell said. "He could stonewall us,
claim it doesn't exist and hide it in a safe somewhere until
the heat dies down."

"As Mike can tell you," Karen said, "life's a crapshoot."

"Speaking of crap, I had to beat back Christian and
Skeen again today. They tried to convince Bill to pull the
plug on your whole project for lack of results. He didn't go
along. But we have to make some real progress or, I'm
afraid, he might shut it."

"I hear you." Karen disconnected the call and repeated,
"I hear you."

When the loudspeaker announced that the plane was
boarding, Karen's phone rang.

It was Harry Prince. "We've had initial activity in Corsine
stock in the days leading up to its rally," the SEC man said.
"Four purchases of five thousand each for a total of twenty
thousand dollars. Since the individual purchase orders
weren't large, they didn't affect the stock price much or
draw any notice on Wall Street. But then came a wave of
heavy buying from Fidelity funds and the stock soared. Our
stealth buyer just sold his entire position. He quadrupled
his money."

Other passengers were shuffling toward the departure
gate. Karen ran her hand over her face and asked the big
question. "Who did the initial buying for twenty thou, Mr.
Prince?"

"This is odd. The activity comes from a new online account in the name of one Simon Scratch. We ran the Social

Security number of Simon Scratch and determined that he sells plumbing supplies in Tampa, Florida. Or once did. He was shot dead in a road rage incident two years ago."

"So someone has appropriated his identity? Who?"

"We know little more, alas. The online account he opened with the stock brokerage lists his old Tampa address but instructs that the proceeds from the trading be wire-transferred to a bank in Andorra. That's a tiny country in Europe that protects its clients' privacy, like the Swiss once did. Unless we can prove Scratch is a terrorist or a drug lord, we have little chance of getting the Andorrans to cooperate."

"Thanks, Mr. Prince."

"Thank Frank Vere."

Karen floated over to the gate, adrift in thought. Wooton, with his intelligence resources, certainly could find the particulars on a dead man and steal them to cloak his doings.

Through the confessional screen, the priest appeared displeased. Wolfe seldom saw clergymen bare their teeth in animalistic menace.

"Where have you been?" the priest demanded. "You left the Plaza with no notice to me. How am I supposed to get in touch with you? I have to wait for you to waltz into this church when you feel like showing up? Who is paying your fee? Me."

"Father, isn't anger one of the seven deadly sins? You have too many sins listed on Saint Peter's ledger already. Why add any more?"

The candlelight from beyond the curtain made shadows shift inside the confessional. And it showed the priest's face tightening even further.

"I'm losing patience."

"Father," Wolfe said, "Wooton's operatives are after me. The assignment has gotten more complicated. I am rather fond of my continued existence. Thus I had to leave the hotel. I can furnish a phone number to reach me indirectly. It's in Iran."

"Why not give me your cell phone number?'

"Cell phone? Too much technology for me. I don't know how to turn on a computer, remember? What I need is more money, father."

"Whatever. You are behind schedule. Kill Ginny. Kill Linda. Kill Karen Glick. Now."

CHAPTER NINETEEN

"Karen Glick told you this?"

Wooton disliked getting upset in the middle of a meal. His half-eaten breakfast lay before him. He had come home with a hankering for some good old-fashioned, horribly unhealthy pancakes and bacon, which he was forced to fix himself. The fattening fare wasn't as good as Consuela's, but with the cook gone, he had no choice.

"That's what the woman said, Kingman." Erica, in a smart sweater and slacks set, stood at the other end of the long dining room table. No one had ever eaten at it besides her, the children, and her husband. She was going with Mick to a tailgate party at the University of Maryland football game; Maryland was one of several colleges Mick had attended.

"Why have you come back home to tell me this?"

"Because I need fresh clothes." She shook her head sadly. "And because you might want to know about the reporter."

"I see." Wooton glowered over his cooling Saturday breakfast. "Hasn't this gigolo of yours received his trust money yet? Why don't you have him buy new clothes for you?"

She let the insulting questions pass. "Are you really such a bigwig, Kingman?"

"That surprises you?"

"And this computer really can predict the stock market?"

"It can solve all our financial problems, Erica."

Erica gripped the table's edge. "We have more problems than financial."

Kingman Wooton's lower lip trembled for an instant. Then he regained his bearing. "Give me another chance, Erica."

"Kingman, I . . ." She fished in her suede bag. "Here's Karen Glick's card. She wants to talk to you." Erica placed the card on the linen tablecloth as gently as a falling leaf.

"Give me another chance, Erica," he called after her.

When she had gone, he summoned Frohlich from the basement and ordered a motorcade to headquarters. Unlike Frohlich and those in the Authority, Erica didn't know her husband could read minds. He certainly never had been able to read hers. But then, he never had tried.

So Karen Glick knew about his quest for Goldring. And actually knew about him. Wooton had arrangements to make regarding Karen Glick.

Leaving his breakfast, Wooton went over to the card Erica had left at the table's far end. He held the card in front of his face as if it were Glick's soul in his grasp.

"You stupid, reckless girl. You don't comprehend what you've done."

Wooton crumpled the card.

Karen, returning to her neighborhood, was enjoying a slice of Gino's pizza. The air had a good pre-Halloween crispness to it. She'd slept at Wendy's, where presumably no one could find her. Later, she would go to Tim's lawyer's office and finalize the divorce. That's why she needed some Gino's pizza now. The sign of good pizza was being able to fold it and not have the goopy end droop. Gino boasted a gift for erect pizza.

Rocky spotted her from the sidewalk and hustled in. The panhandler said, "You remember them FBI-type guys asking questions about you around here?"

"You told me about these characters. Are they back?"

"Worse." Rocky peered up and down the street. "This time, it's hard-ass hoodlums. Russians, I reckon. Been asking about you. Saw them nosing around the front door of your building. I hightailed my ass when they gave me the evil eye. That's bad."

"And that ain't good." Karen gave him some money for pizza. Rocky pocketed the bills and sauntered off to buy Schlitz Malt Liquor.

Her cell phone rang. "Is this Karen Glick?" came an older man's voice.

"Speaking. Who's this?"

"This is Major Darcy, young lady. The fella who put you in the passenger seat of Mr. Faff's Jaguar."

Karen almost swallowed her tongue. "Major Darcy? As in the parking attendant at Faff's Lair casino?"

"Well, I'm not the CEO. We gotta get together. I'm in New York. I got big news for you."

Karen asked him if he knew where Bethesda Fountain was in Central Park.

"I got me a map and a good pair of feet," Darcy said.

"You'll remember what I look like?"

"I remember what every innocent person looks like."

Why was he changing his story now? Well, stranger things had happened. Like Karen's falling for Tim Bratton. Next, maybe Linda would wake up with a big zit on her nose.

* * *

The door to the command post opened and the director made his entrance. But before he could enthrone himself in his chair, Logie said, "Siegfried Wolfe called for you."

"Whatever do you mean he called for me? How?"

"Well, I took the initiative to phone the number he gave in Iran. They said he'd call back. I talked to him. He said for you to call him any time. The Iranians would patch you through."

"What in the name of God?" Wooton swung around to Donner.

"Don't blame me," Donner said, spreading his hands. "I told her not to unless she got your permission."

The director turned to her, on the verge of leonine wrath. "How dare you act without my order."

"Why not? Are you afraid of him, Director?" Logie stuck her jaw out defiantly. Someone needed to move this to a conclusion so she could get her daughter. She had scoured the Authority's intranet for a sign of Alexandra's whereabouts. Nothing thus far.

"Afraid? I'm afraid of no one, Ms. Logan."

Logie held out the telephone receiver. Maybe Wooton could read her mind, but she could manipulate his. "Show me."

Accustomed only to deference at the Authority, Wooton stood stock-still beside his chair, flummoxed.

Logie pushed the phone at him. "Show me."

He grabbed it. "Put the call through." After she tapped out the number, an accented man came on the line and asked what he wanted. "This is Kingman Wooton," the director said. "I wish to speak to Siegfried Wolfe." A crackle followed, then came a series of electronic sounds.

"Hello, Kingman," said an upper-crust English voice, the same one recorded by the bug at Albert Niebel's apartment. It had changed only slightly with the years from the young MI-6 agent Wooton had met in Prague in 1968. "How the calendar does turn. Been well?"

"Let's move on from the pleasantries," Wooton said. "Do you really have it?"

"Whatever do you mean? 'It'? Do I have my old roguish charm? I dare say. Do I still have my appreciation for a good wine? Of course. Do I yet have my eye for fine tailoring? Definitely. We share that."

"Don't be cute with me. You killed three of my men."

"Only two," Wolfe said. "The other will live, if in a diminished state. Fortunes of war. Besides, we shouldn't discuss delicate matters over an open line. Never know who could be eavesdropping. We must meet and discuss a topic of mutual interest."

"How about in the federal courthouse in Foley Square, Manhattan. Tomorrow, Sunday. Agreed?"

"My heavens, no. You'll probably have them clap me in irons. I suggest neutral territory. A restaurant. That should please a man of your appetites. As a gesture of good faith, I'll even let you order dessert. You obviously love dessert."

"Which restaurant were you thinking of?" Wooton asked.

"And here you're supposed to be reading my mind. I figured you'd know what I was thinking. Well, all right. One of New York's best and newest. On East Fifty-fourth between Fifth and Madison. Tomorrow noon, for a proper lunch. The establishment is called Fate. Apt, no?"

"I'll be there."

"Outstanding," Wolfe said. "Love to your delicious wife. But then I'd have to join the queue, wouldn't I?"

Wooton contemplated the disconnected phone in his hand as if it were an artifact from an alien civilization. He handed it to Logie and sat heavily in his chair.

"You're really going to meet him, Director?" Bonner

shifted his eyes back and forth from the slumping director to Logie.

"We're moving our operations to the alternate command post in New York," Wooton said wearily.

Donner brightened, primed for cosmopolitan delights. Logie felt she too should be happy about leaving the imprisonment of this windowless bunker. But Wooton's subdued behavior worried her. What was the matter with the director?

"You're right, Mr. Donner," Wooton said. "You need to be in New York to be on top of events. The same goes for us all."

"Whatever you say, Director." Donner was grinning wall to wall. "New York, it is."

Wooton's eyes grew vacant. "I can't stay here." His words were difficult to hear. "Not here." He lowered his chin to his chest and his jowls bulged out. "I have to get Goldring. Have to."

"Are you okay?" Logie asked.

The director lifted his head. "Mr. Donner, I have a task for you."

Donner, while puzzled by Wooton's melancholy revery, kept smiling gamely. "What, sir?"

"Karen Glick has learned of Goldring and my involvement with it. She is a threat to our operation. Eliminate her." Wooton pitched his bulk to his feet.

"Consider it done," Donner said.

Logie spread her hands. "Wait a minute. You promised me we wouldn't harm anyone. This is wrong."

"Change is inevitable," Wooton said. "Eliminate Glick."

"She's as good as gone," Donner said with carnal enthusiasm.

"Are you sure this is all you want, babe?" rasped Sasha, a half-hour since her last cigarette.

Karen and her lawyer had been waiting too long in the regal conference room of Tim's hotshot law firm, which did dirty work for Dewey Cheatham's financiers. Behr, Hawke & Fox had a special matrimonial division to handle everything from prenuptial agreements to adultery detection. When a Dewey Cheatham partner's kids told him that mommy took naps with her handsome personal trainer every Thursday afternoon, a Behr, Hawke & Fox photographer burst in on them.

"All I want from Tim is enough money to fund a decent retirement," Karen said. "I don't want to end up like my parents." She checked her watch. "Where are they? I have to meet someone in Central Park. Then I'm helping a friend pack her stuff."

Finally, Howard Fox blasted into the room, bearing a pile of documents. He exuded the malevolence of a plutonium plant about to explode. "Okay, let's get this done," he said. "I have other things to do on a Saturday."

"Well, maybe you could've shown up on time," Sasha shot back.

"I bet it's Tim's fault they're late," Karen said.

While Fox obliviously sorted papers across the table from them, Karen heard her husband approaching. "For the tenth time, no," Tim was saying into his cell. "No, no, and no."

"It's your positive attitude I always will treasure," Karen said as Tim slipped the cell phone into his blazer pocket and sat next to his lawyer, not meeting her gaze. She wanted to confront him with his treachery with Faff, but then decided to swallow her anger.

"This should be easy since you don't want much," Fox said, contemptuous that they weren't demanding a fortune for Karen.

"Why don't we cut to the chase, Mr. Fox?" Sasha said. "I've reviewed the documents. So has my client."

Once they had finished signing papers, Sasha popped to

her feet. Karen slowly and wordlessly followed her out. Karen suddenly felt herself awash in sadness. At the conference room door, she paused to look at Tim. Their eyes met, then he turned away.

Down on the street, Sasha lit a Virginia Slims and inhaled gratefully. She was blatting about the cash settlement transfer, but Karen wasn't listening.

Then Tim came striding out of the building. Despite Sasha's protests, Karen charged over to him as he hailed a cab.

"Not even a good-bye?" Karen said to him.

"How about 'good riddance'? You hurt me at my firm. And you sabotaged my relationship with Linda."

All the sweet sadness Karen had felt now turned to vinegar. "I did? You were the one who sold her out to Faff."

"That's your warped perception." Tim swept his hand dismissively. "Ah, who cares? Linda's a cold bitch anyway. Always bossy. She wouldn't let me watch sports."

"Oh, poor Tim. Well, now you can watch all you want. By yourself."

"You want to know how I hooked up with Linda? I sought her out. I wanted to get under your skin. And guess what? It worked."

"You told Faff I was coming to the party as Robin Hood, didn't you? A new low for you."

"I don't have to listen to a mouthy bitch like you anymore, Karen," Tim said.

Sasha had galloped up with the zeal of the rescuing cavalry. "Watch your own mouth, Mr. Bratton," she exclaimed.

"I'm not stopping there," Tim said. "How about dumb bitch? You don't even know how Goldring works, do you, Karen?"

"Okay," Karen said. "If you're the smart guy, how does it work?"

"You spent hours and hours with the Reiner sisters and

you don't know? Pathetic." Tim shook his head with drama. "Goldring is a hacking program that gets into the computer networks of Fidelity and other big mutual fund houses. The houses screen for value stocks, ones that are out of favor but have a lot on the ball." He spoke with the smug cadence she knew too well. "The houses list these stocks on their order entry books to be bought later. Goldring tells the Reiners what's on the order entry books, and they buy ahead of time. When Fidelity starts buying, and others jump in, the stock price heads for the sky."

"How do you know this?"

"Unlike you," Tim said, "I keep my ears open. The sisters rented a house on Nantucket a few weeks back in September. Flo was talking to Ginny about it downstairs. Linda had gone out for a walk. They must've thought I was still sleeping. So they're breaking the law." He raised his hand again for a cab. "And you want to be an investigative reporter?"

Numb at the news, all Karen could say was: "I do." The right two words to end her marriage with. "I do."

Ruminating on the revelation about the Reiners's law breaking, Karen passed along the lip of the Central Park lake, alert for Major Darcy. Ordinarily, she would revel at being outdoors during this fine fall day. Over at the band shell, there was a kids' Halloween party. Happy parents led their excited, costumed offspring by the hand toward the festivities. Small goblins, ghosts, werewolves, and vampires wafted through the tunnel arcade joining the lakeside and the band shell. Inside the acoustically enchanted tunnel, they passed a classical ensemble playing a spooky rendition of *Night on Bald Mountain*.

Spotting Major Darcy was easy. He stood hesitantly at the top of the long sweep of stairs that led down to the fountain plaza. Karen waved at him. Darcy took a moment to see her. Then the old man smiled and, in a spirited trot, headed down the stairs and past the sandstone obelisks carved with woodland scenes. He pumped Karen's hand eagerly.

"Comes a point in every person's life that he's gotta make a choice," Major Darcy said. "I'll help you. But keep my name out of it. Mr. Faff could get to my family. My son-in-law is an A.C. cop, which means he works for Mr. Faff's spit-lickers."

Karen had a handheld tape recorder going. "I appreciate this. Believe me. Right now, we'll talk about what happened that night. No one will hear this other than the magazine's editors."

Darcy settled onto the long, curving sandstone bench that bracketed the fountain and the angel statue that rose from it. He smiled indulgently at the passing children in their costumes. "I love Halloween. Used to dress up my Regina and take her trick-or-treating. Now I do that with my grandkids." His smile faded.

"I love Halloween, too. I always have treats for the kids."

"Let me tell what happened the night you got in the Jaguar with Mr. Faff." Major Darcy described how Faff was driving. "No doubt about that. He'd never let anyone drive his cars."

"What happened to his brother, Solter?"

"Dunno for a fact. Poor Solter always was one brick shy of a load. Couldn't care for hisself. Grapevine is that Mr. Faff ordered Mikhail Beria and his bad boys to torture Solter. Made him fess up he been talking out of school. To you. And somebody else. Somebody from Washington. Government type. Then Mr. Faff had them kill poor Solter, kill him dead as a dog in the road."

"My God," Karen said.

"Solter, he never was much in the smarts department. But he made nice to the folks working the casino. His brother Jack ran his behind off the livelong day. They say he was cut up and buried in pieces out in the Pine Barrens. Legend is that, when your murdered body is buried in the pine forest, the Jersey Devil digs you up and eats you. Either way, Solter'll never be found. When I heard about Solter, I knew I had to help you."

"My sweet God."

A child, dressed as a witch, passed by and made faces at them. Major Darcy waved at her. Darcy clasped his hands, which were mottled with age. "Listen to me. Every last movement in Faff's Lair casino is captured on video. There's pictures of you getting in the passenger side of that Jaguar."

"Where is the video kept?"

"In that central computer main brain they got." Major Darcy took in the lovely setting around them and filled his lungs with fresh autumn air. "Get your hands on that, and you're home free."

As Karen watched the old man trudge back up the stairs, she reached for her phone to tell Eudell what she'd learned. Eudell was at work this weekend, preparing a special investing edition along with other editors.

"Honey," Eudell said after listening to the Darcy story, "how can we get our hands on those photos? We can't simply order them from Amazon, now can we?"

"I'll come up with a plan." Karen knew she stood a stronger chance of breaking into the Fort Knox vault. Maybe Frank could . . .

"Honey, you better do it faster than a bunny. We are running out of time."

A troubled Karen made her way up to Ginny's Morningside Heights apartment.

They had packed three hard suitcases and four soft bags for what Ginny called her "temporary relocation." Linda remarked that her sister was bringing enough for a round-the-world cruise. Ginny told Linda to quit trying to push everyone around in her home. Karen said she didn't mind humping the luggage down the stairs.

"How can we fit this stuff into a taxi?" Linda asked. "Maybe we could rent a tractor trailer."

"Remind me why I'm coming to live with you," Ginny said, struggling to be civil. Both sisters were on edge about the Freddy situation.

"How about because of your assistant? The one you for some reason haven't fired, even though he's a damn spy. Just like Tim."

"Let it go," Ginny said. "I'll deal with him. I only wonder who Freddy's working for. Faff or Wooton?"

"About Tim," Karen said. "I saw him this morning, while signing our divorce papers. And he told me the most interesting story about how Goldring works."

Ginny, who'd been delving into a desk drawer, stopped. She visibly blanched. "He told you?"

"It's an illegal hacking program. Violates securities laws. Gives you advance warning of mutual fund buying." She related Tim's tale in full. "Now I know."

Linda put down the soft bag she'd been hoisting. "No, you don't know. Tim is lying out of spite for me. Goldring predicts the market in a perfectly legal manner. No more on this subject."

"Karen knows," Ginny ventured. "We should—"

"No more, damn it," Linda said. "Let's get moving."

Too bad none of Ginny's neighbors were around to help. The landlord, Columbia University, had posted a sign saying the carpet laying for the halls and stairs would occur today, so everyone had vacated for the big academic symposium on campus or for the fall glory of Riverside Park or for the football stadium. Columbia at long last had a good team. The workmen hadn't shown up yet, and Ginny predicted they wouldn't come at all.

"Hey, check this out," said Ginny, going through her

desk. "Halloween, twenty-five years ago. Look at us. Daddy took the picture."

Karen sidled up to examine the old snapshot. Faded with time and lined like ancient papyrus, it showed a sad-eyed Flo at six, an ebullient Linda at ten, and a scowling, chubby Ginny at fourteen. Flo was dressed as Dracula with blood-tipped fangs, Linda as a fairy princess, and Ginny as a mortified teenager in jeans and a sweatshirt.

"I was so bummed," Ginny said. "Forced to take my little sisters trick-or-treating. Gross."

"Well," Linda said as she plucked the photo from Ginny's hand, "it's not like we kept you from going to the school dance that night. You never went out."

"Watch it," Ginny said. "I had a boy interested in me. This was before I came to terms with my real sexuality."

"You mean Jimmy Egbert, the math nerd?" Linda laughed and said to Karen, "Jimmy had specs so thick that he practically could use them as a magnifying glass to burn ants."

"Don't laugh," Ginny told Karen, who wasn't in a laughing mood. "Flo snatched his glasses and actually tried to do that. She usually used Daddy's magnifying glass for the ants."

"That's a little twisted," Karen said.

"Daddy taught her how to do it," Ginny said.

For once, Karen's seldom-used verbal brake engaged. She wanted to say: *The family that slays together, stays together.*

Linda smiled over the picture. "Look how the flashbulb from Daddy's camera gave us red pupils. How Halloween. Like the undead."

Ginny peered over her shoulder. "Speak for yourself. The flash hardly affected my pupils. I was taller then you twerps then."

"Yeah," Linda said. "Flo's are the reddest, like stoplights.

Guess that helps when you go as Dracula. She was closer to the ground."

Pointing at Flo's long-ago image, Ginny said, "She never was a happy girl, was she?"

"I tried to make her happy," Linda said.

"By running her life," Ginny said. "Go on this diet. Listen to this music. Buy this skirt. Have your hair done this way."

"For her own good." Linda didn't want to discuss sad, tragic Flo anymore. "Karen, get that bag and the one over there. We'll make two trips."

"As you wish, madam."

"Have I forgotten anything?" Ginny said. She snapped her fingers. "Let me put the blinds down and put on a light. Freddy will think I'm home at night. He's disappeared lately, but who knows?" Ginny stood at the window and played around with the stubborn cord for the blinds.

"I can help you," Karen offered.

The bullet smashed through her window and burst Ginny's head open like a cantaloupe.

CHAPTER TWENTY

"*Nooooooooooooo,*" Linda cried.

Karen stumbled backward. Linda grabbed her arm.

Ginny's body had toppled to the floor, where it lay twitching. An enormous halo of blood spread from her head.

The world froze. Life stopped. Except for Linda's gasps. And Karen's painful swallows. The blood spread. When the blood seeped over to their feet, Karen moved Linda away like an awkward dance partner.

"My God," Linda breathed. "Who did this?"

"We have to call the cops."

"Who did this?" Linda repeated, louder, angrier.

"I . . ." Karen put a hand on Linda's shoulder.

Linda shoved herself from her. "*Damn it.* Who did this?"

"Don't, Linda."

Linda bolted for the smashed window and shouted into the sunny afternoon outside: "Who the hell did this?"

Karen lunged for her.

She yanked Linda from the window an instant before a second bullet whizzed into the apartment.

Karen pulled her to the floor. They lay next to the desk, Karen's body shielding Linda's.

"Let me up, Karen."

"Okay. But stay low. Don't go near the window."

Linda pressed her palms against her eyes and shook from the trauma.

Karen reached up to explore the desktop for the phone, which she had seen there earlier. She brought it down to floor level and hit 911. When she put the receiver to her ear, she discovered the phone was dead.

"No dial tone."

Linda removed her hands from her face. "This is her only phone," she said.

"The bastard must've cut the line. How did he do that?"

"Cut the line?" Linda said, bewildered.

Karen, staying low rapidly crawled over to her bag, which lay in the corner. She flipped open her cell phone, only to discover no signal. "He must be blocking it somehow. We gotta get out of here."

"Why?"

"He's coming. Any minute. Why else would he cut the phone? He figured that if he missed with the rifle, he'd need to come here."

Siegfried Wolfe examined the empty window across the street through his sniper scope. What untrammeled luck. Before, he couldn't tell who was with Ginny Reiner. But now he knew: Linda Reiner and Karen Glick had actually shown up in the same killing zone as Ginny. People had heard about the luck of the Irish. But the luck of the English? Well, why not?

He hoped he wasn't slowing down with the years. The

surprise of seeing Linda suddenly framed in Ginny's window had stopped his usual reaction—to squeeze off a well-aimed round. That instant of hesitancy had allowed the Glick woman to pull her from harm's way.

"Such a lovely creature you are, Linda," he said to himself. "Only fitting that you should be allowed a few more moments, I suppose."

He didn't relish killing Linda. But a job, as the Calvinistic Americans would say, is a job.

The Americans had many failings, but firearms manufacture wasn't one. Wolfe gently laid aside his M40A1 rifle. Standard issue for U.S. Marine snipers, the weapon was a marvel. He adored its adjustable butt plate and its dead-on accuracy at up to one thousand yards. The 10-power telescopic sight was perfection. The last time he'd used the M40A1, he successfully had splattered an Israeli general's head. Head shots were more difficult than chest ones. That was why he went for the head.

What a shame that idiot boy Freddy had been caught by Ginny in her apartment. In retrospect, Wolfe knew he shouldn't have asked the lout to go there in search of keys to Linda's home. Living in a high-rise, doorman-guarded building, Linda's place would be harder to crack, though not impossible.

Wolfe checked the action in his Glock pistol and returned it to the holster under his suit jacket. For the remainder of the job, he needed a sidearm, not a rifle. This would be close-in. More personal. Perhaps let lovely Linda beg a bit.

Leaving the rifle by his window, where he'd collect it later, Wolfe hurried out of the small apartment he had rented. Nothing like the Plaza, this. No nice views, no plush bed, no concierge.

Reaching the street, he pulled from his pocket the keys that Freddy had provided to Ginny's place.

Wolfe, filled with the scent of the hunt, ran across the street, Linda's face alive in his mind.

Karen delved farther into her bag and extracted her compact. She opened it and discarded the powder puff used to hide her facial scratches. Then she ran, hunched, into the kitchen, where she quickly found a pair of tongs.

Sliding along the wall under the Escher prints, she crossed to the window. She needed an enormous step to clear the lake of blood. She avoided looking at Ginny and the gory, shattered skull.

Linda, on all fours by the desk, watched Karen with intense eyes. "What are you doing?"

"I saw this in a movie I watched with my grandmother."

Crouched under the windowsill, Karen clamped the compact mirror with the tongs and hoisted it up into the sunlight. A good sniper-denying periscope. She angled it to scan the side of the adjacent building, in search of a rifle barrel. Nothing. Then she pointed it downward.

That was when Karen saw the Englishman, dapper in a charcoal gray suit, loping across the street. Headed for the front door of Ginny's building. In his hand he held what looked like . . .

"The Englishman's got keys and he's almost to the front door," Karen said.

"There's a fire escape out the bedroom window," Linda said. "The window has a bar gate, but the key to that's in the top drawer of the nightstand."

"We're four floors up. If we're still on the fire escape when he gets up here, he'll lean out the bedroom window and shoot us before we've reached the ground. We'll be in the open. Easy targets." Karen tried to keep the desperation out of her voice. "We have to buy time for the fire escape."

"How?"

Karen vaulted over the blood pool and reached the apartment's front door in three bounds. She flipped the locks open and rushed over to the stairwell, which dim bulbs lit poorly.

Three large white cans of carpet glue stood by the railing, awaiting the long-promised workmen. A screwdriver sat atop one of the cans.

The street door opened, she recalled, with a telltale whine. Now, that whine carried up the four flights of stairs like a demon's cry.

Karen bolted down one flight and jumped to smash the landing's overhead light bulb with her fist. Then she clambered back to the fourth floor landing to do the same to that bulb. The last stretch of stairs before Ginny's floor was really dark now, like Albert's had been. She didn't want to think about what had happened to Albert.

A hurried tramp of feet sounded on the first flight.

Karen tried to pry off the lid of a glue can with the screwdriver. The lid, as stubborn as Calvin Christian, wouldn't budge. Why was Karen thinking of Christian at a time like this? Linda stood behind her, anxious to help, although uncertain what to do. If Linda had a plan, she would've issued an order.

Footfalls on the second flight.

The lid gave a fraction of an inch. Karen wedged the screwdriver in deeper and pressed down with every muscle in her body. Would another can give less resistance? Too late to try.

Footfalls on the third flight.

The lid popped open. Karen caught it before it clanged on the bare floor. She tipped the can over and let the clear glue wash down the steps. Invisible in the dimness.

A pistol, held in a two-handed shooter's grip, appeared first. The Englishman came into view.

Karen pulled back, shouting, "Hey, asshole. Up here."

"No need to be crude, my girl."

Grabbing Linda's arm, Karen hustled her back to the apartment.

The pursuing footsteps sounded different now. Squishy. Then came a wild yelp of confusion and alarm. Next, the thud of a person tumbling painfully to the landing below. And a loud shout: "Damn you to hell forever."

Karen locked Ginny's door behind them. Linda now was ahead of her; she had unlocked the barred gate in the bedroom window to the fire escape. The steel scaffolding trembled and clanked as they spiraled down to where the fire escape ended, one floor above the street. Linda threw the catch to send the last-leg ladder shooting toward the pavement. She negotiated the ladder swiftly with Karen right after her. The final eight feet was a matter of hanging and dropping to the concrete. The two of them landed around the corner from the building's front door.

They pelted down the street. Linda motioned Karen into a dry cleaner's. The small Korean man behind the cash register smiled at the pretty girl, but Linda put a finger to her lips and scrambled behind his counter. She and Karen burrowed among the plastic-sheathed array of hanging clothes.

In a few moments, the Englishman limped past the shop's broad window. As Karen had hoped, the fall had slowed him down. His mouth was a taut line of contained pain. The gun was hidden. He peered inside the dry cleaner's.

The Korean shopkeeper, who had lived under a dictatorship, wore a blank, tell-nothing expression.

The Englishman passed on.

"Sir," Linda whispered to him. "Call 911. That man's a murderer."

*   *   *

They had brought the director's chair to New York. And now he sat in it, gripping the arms as if on a theme park tilt-a-whirl ride. As Donner briefed him, Wooton almost seemed nauseated.

"The English gunman on the police report has to be Wolfe," Donner said.

"Mr. Donner," Wooton said, "you are a master of the obvious."

"Hey, no need to be nasty." As soon as the words escaped Donner's mouth, he adopted a stunned look of regret and fear.

"I'll be whatever I choose to be and don't you forget that," Wooton said. "Get back to your seat, Mr. Donner."

Donner, whipped pup eyes trained on the floor, did as instructed. He plunked gloomily behind his desk.

Their alternate command post was identical to the one down in Virginia headquarters. The main difference was they had windows—bulletproof and tinted to obscure any outsider's view, to be sure. Their windows showed the intricate facade of an old building across the street. The Authority's Manhattan satellite office was in a 1910 office structure near City Hall. Wooton was staying here, too. One floor below. Logie and Donner hadn't been allowed to see the director's quarters, although his surely were more spacious than theirs.

"Very well," the director said. "Now, Ms. Logan, we know that Karen Glick is at the police precinct. What we need to know is where she goes to hide next. I want you to invade her magazine's e-mails and find evidence of where she is living, since she has left her own apartment."

"Why don't we let Wolfe take care of her?" Donner ventured, trying to reingratiate himself.

"I doubt Siegfried Wolfe has the resources to discover where she and Ms. Linda Reiner will be hiding," Wooton said. "I doubt it will be Ms. Reiner's plush apartment. Too obvious."

"I bet she's headed out to that group house in the Hamptons. We learned about that place on the phone taps." Donner attempted a grin on Wooton, hoping for validation. "I bet."

"I've given you no permission to place any bets, Mr. Donner," Wooton said. "Well, Ms. Logan, can you manage to follow my instructions? Should I repeat them slowly for you?"

"I need a walk to clear my head," she said. "Some fresh air."

"I don't care to discuss with you what you perceive as the morality of our dealing with Karen Glick," Wooton said. "Time is of the essence. We must find her."

Logie knew better than to raise this subject. "I haven't had much sleep," she said. "I've been cooped up for a long time and need to get some fresh air."

They had been whisked in the depths of night from headquarters to an Air Force jet and flown to New York, where they touched down at LaGuardia. The motorcade had briskly delivered them to their new command post. Her gulps of fresh air outside of cars and planes had been too brief.

"I'll arrange an escort for you," Wooton said. "Later."

"An escort?" she said. "Donner can gallivant around outdoors. Do you think I'd run away? You have my daughter. Get real."

"I'll escort her," Donner said.

"Dirk? Did you hear what I just said?"

Donner looked hurt. "Why not me?"

Wooton thundered his wrath, the bass notes almost shaking the walls. "What's the matter with the two of you?" He rose. "I'm offering you vast riches. Glick is on our trail. We have her pinpointed right this minute, and have no plan to get her. And you want to go for a stroll? I will not stand for this nonsense. Do you understand, Mr. Donner?"

Donner raised his hand like a child in class. "Director,

about the vast riches. Why do you get a full half and we each get a quarter? Why not divide the money equally?"

"No," Wooton intoned. "The division is as it is because I am who I am. You are wasting time here, Mr. Donner. Glick is in play."

Donner smacked the desktop. "Damn, I just came up with a terrific plan to bag Glick." He related it with zest and finally got Wooton to agree with him.

Logie rose off her chair in alarm. She hated her so-called friend Donner for his eagerness to kill Karen Glick. And she hated when Wooton read her mind. As Donner rattled on to the director, she dared to glance at the printout sitting on her desk, the fruit of an internal hacking job. It showed that sweet little Alexandra was in an Authority facility not very far from New York, in an isolated patch of forest called the Pine Barrens.

Detective Friday sat coiled in his chair across the long, gray metal table. He looked like a linebacker poised to slam into somebody. Karen and Linda were across from him. Karen did most of the talking. Linda stared dully at Friday, fixated on the military tattoo decorating his thick forearm, the one about killing them all. Karen wished he preferred long sleeved shirts.

Eudell was at the table's end, a knot of motherly concern. The editor took notes even more prodigiously than did Friday.

"See, we got no way of proving this English hump works for Wooton or anyone else," Friday said. "He could be some nut working solo. The shooting came from an apartment recently rented by a British gentleman who paid cash." Friday nodded. "Gave his name as Guy Fawkes. Does the name jingle your jangle?"

"He tried to blow up Parliament," Karen said.

"An IRA guy?"

Karen told him it was in 1605. "He failed, too."

"When we got to Fawkes's place," Friday went on, "he'd cleaned out pretty good. We found gunpowder residue near the windowsill, where he had his firing position. No evidence of prints yet, but the crime scene guys are gonna go full-tilt."

"What about Wooton and the Authority?" Karen asked.

"Hell, I'm expecting a call from the feds any second telling me to back off this murder, too," Friday said, then added, "Forget what I just said. You didn't hear that."

"What should we do now?" Eudell asked.

"My advice to you," Friday said, "is that Ms. Glick and Ms. Reiner here"—he sarcastically elongated the "Mizzzzz"—"should stay out of sight. Maybe get out of town. Whoever is after you is a pro and seems to have a line on you. I mean, Fawkes had that key to Virginia Reiner's apartment."

"That has to be Freddy's doing," Linda said. She explained how shaken Ginny had been to find Freddy searching her apartment.

"So that maybe explains it," Friday said, and rubbed the back of his neck. "Meant to tell you. Frederick Fannon's body was pulled out of the river earlier today. Bullet through the back of the head. Glock round, nine millimeter."

Linda hugged herself tightly.

"If Freddy was working for the Englishman," Karen said, "I bet he told the creep that Linda and I were headed to Albert's. And that the Englishman gave you the anonymous tip where Albert lived, Detective."

"Well, enlighten me then on why he would do that," Friday said.

"So you could discover Linda there and she could get tangled up in Albert's death, what with the e-mail she supposedly sent to Albert," Karen said, as Friday shrugged.

"Templar Media can put you two ladies up, on the company," Eudell said. "Anywhere that's safe. I've already cleared it with Bill."

"Did Christian and Skeen object to the cost?" Karen asked.

Eudell sighed in answer.

"I'd feel better if we were someplace we knew the territory," Karen said. "I'd say Mike Riley's summer house in Hampton Bays. That's our group house. How could the Englishman or anyone else know about that?"

Linda, her lips dry and her hair in her face, said, "Listen, it's obviously me the Englishman is after. He killed Ginny and probably Flo. I'm next. But I can hire bodyguards. Leave the country. I'm the target."

"Hey, I'm a target on my own, not only when I'm with you," Karen said. "The Englishman told me that he would get me if I stayed on the story. I stayed on the story. No, Linda, I need you around. We need a new strategy, and I'll need you to help. The first priority, though, is to take cover while we figure it out."

"The Hamptons, huh?" Linda said.

"Not the fashionable Hamptons," Karen said. "Hampton Bays."

"I'm not sure where that is." Linda looked down at the cashmere sweater and designer jeans she was wearing. "I should go back home and get some clothes."

"Don't risk it," Karen said. "There are clothes out there that will fit you fine. Wendy is about your size."

"Wendy?" Linda said, as if Wendy carried bubonic plague. "Tim told me about her. Doesn't she own a parrot?"

Friday tilted his head. "You sure you'll be safe there?"

After the phone call to Regina, Major Darcy was happy. He stood on the subway platform and hummed a kids' song to himself. His grandchildren were so cute. They wanted him back to play with them and take them for ice cream and trick-or-treating. Regina had sounded upbeat when he told her he'd take the next bus home.

"I'm coming home," he repeated to himself. The roar of an approaching train filled the station. "As soon as I can, I'm coming on home." He had told her not to worry, that he trusted Karen Glick to make what was wrong right.

He was headed down to Times Square, where he wanted to buy two *Lion King* T-shirts for his grandkids. He wished he could afford tickets to take them to the stage show. After he got the T-shirts, he'd ankle over to the Port Authority bus terminal.

The train rolled up to the platform. The door slid open and a woman's automatic voice welcomed them inside. The car was clean and bright, nothing like the filthy, graffiti-scarred boxes he remembered from his New York days in the funky 1970s. To him, those had seemed like coffins on wheels.

The car was half full. After a few stops, a batch of parents and costumed kids got on, evidently from the Central Park Halloween party. The youngsters were very excited.

At the next stop, an adult boarded, clad in a sheet with holes for eyes and mouth. A ghost costume, Darcy guessed. At first, the ghost seemed like a Klansman, but he had no separate hood.

The ghost stood next to Darcy as the doors closed. A couple of kids nearby goggled at the ghost and stood behind their mother.

Major Darcy tried not to look at him, but the sheeted figure trained its eye holes on Darcy.

After a while, Darcy said to him, "What you looking at?"

A Russian accented voice said, "I'm looking for you, son of a bitch."

Stepping backward, Darcy said, "You stay away from me, hear?"

The sheet moved as if arms were busy beneath it. In the mouth hole, Darcy could see sharp teeth. "Been talking to people you shouldn't be talking to. Not good. Very, very bad."

Darcy knew those teeth. "Stay away."

The passengers around them shuffled uneasily, not sure what was unfolding.

A corner of the sheet lifted to reveal a hand holding a long, mean knife.

"My God," somebody shouted.

Serpent quick, the knife flashed out and under Darcy's ribcage, then up into his heart.

Amid the passengers' wails and screams and shrieks, the train reached the next station. The ghost floated out the door onto the platform. Major Darcy writhed on the subway car floor until he subsided. His last thoughts were of Regina and his grandchildren. He felt so sad. He couldn't give them their T-shirts.

Frank Vere drove his Ford Escargot to the car lot next to the station house. But the cops wouldn't let him see Karen, so he left. While Linda went to the restroom with Eudell, Friday told Karen in an undertone, "Nice move with the glue."

"Thanks," Karen said.

"You realize this ain't exactly a weekend getaway," Friday said. "Stay on your tippie-toes. You never can tell what's out there."

When the cop left, Karen leaned wearily against the institutional green wall and rubbed her temples. She tried to think of what they could do next, but nothing came. The image of Ginny's head exploding invaded her every thought.

Eudell emerged from the ladies' room. "You going to be okay, honey?"

"I'm fine, Eudell. Don't forget, I ran into plenty of death and violence with the Billionaire Boys Club." She had been repeating that to herself and wanted to believe she was thus immunized.

"You're a strong lady." Eudel shook her head. "This is hard on anyone, anytime, anywhere."

Karen produced her best game smile for her editor. "Linda's a strong lady, as well. We should do fine."

"I'll say. Maybe a bit too strong. If my sister had been shot dead in front of my eyes, I'd be bawling like a baby. This Linda is touching up her makeup, blithe as you please."

"I don't think Linda does crying."

Linda came out and summoned her own brave smile. Her cheeks were dry. She almost seemed ready for a date.

Karen and Linda went out into the golden hue of the late afternoon. Cars buzzed by in the street. Pedestrians cruised past on the sidewalk: adults carrying just-bought pumpkins, kids in Halloween regalia, everyone happy and unworried. An autumn sun caught the wispy overhead clouds with an iridescent glow. The contrails of a jet sliced upward toward eternity.

"Mr. Escort's in the lot around to the side," Karen said. "Frank left it."

"We're taking that heap?" Linda said.

A white, blue-striped police van lurched up to the curb and three uniformed officers piled out. They were big, even for cops.

"Ms. Glick?" said the one with the broken nose and sergeant's stripes. "We got the shooter in custody and need you to identify him. The English guy."

"You've got him?" Karen exclaimed. "Where?"

"One Police Plaza, ma'am," the sergeant said.

"I want to see this dirty, filthy piece of evil," Linda said.

Dirk Donner grinned at the pretty woman. "Come with us. In the van. Won't take long."

CHAPTER TWENTY-ONE

Donner turned his eyes to Linda Reiner, where they lingered for more than the two seconds he needed to assess someone. Her classically lovely face, recently made-up, compelled him to gawk. This Reiner chick was exactly as advertised. Even better than her photo.

"We're sorry to hear about your loss, ma'am," said Daniels, also busy ogling her.

The distraction the woman provided made Donner miss the commotion at the precinct house door until too late. Friday came trundling onto the sidewalk, belly bobbling, followed by two plainclothes and two uniforms. "Where you going?" the detective shouted.

If Donner had hurried Glick and the Reiner babe into the van, they would have been off by now. Special Operatives Daniels and Fisher traded what-do-we-do-now glances. Donner stoically faced the oncoming phalanx of cops. Friday charged up to stand two inches from Donner's face.

"We're going to see the Englishman in custody at One Police Plaza," Karen said.

"What kind of horse hockey is this?" Friday said.

"Orders from the commissioner that we transport these individuals there for positive identification of the suspect, Detective Friday," Donner said.

Friday squinted at Donner. "Do I know you?"

"I know you," Donner said, doing his best to contain his adrenaline, which Friday's belligerence had stoked to a high burn.

"Who do you work for?"

"The commissioner himself," Donner said. "We are under strict orders to transport these material witnesses. And we're late."

"I don't give a flying fandango if you're early, late, or right on time," Friday said. "Procedure is, *I'm* the primary here. That means I get notified of any arrests made by you, the commissioner, or my grandmother. And I don't have that notification."

"We're late."

Friday had positioned himself to shield the two women, and his coterie of cops stood like a firing line a few feet behind them. The Authority operatives were outnumbered and outgunned.

"That truly does disturb me deeply," Friday said. "But tough toenails. I am personally acquainted with every worthy human being working for the commissioner. And you are not one of that fine group of public servants. So you're not taking these two people anywhere."

"You're going to be sorry for this," Donner said.

"Yeah, yeah, yeah. Who are you, really? Show me some ID besides those very authentic-style badges."

Donner showed Friday something else. His pistol flew out of his holster and into a two-handed shooter's position in a nanosecond. Fisher and Daniels drew their own weapons behind him. The line of cops quickly displayed a brace of guns, too.

"Drop your pieces and no one will get hurt," Friday commanded. The women stood frozen.

Donner backed toward the van. Fisher, gun still aimed, dropped onto the rear seat. Daniels squirted around to climb behind the wheel. The motor, per procedure, was running.

One-handing his weapon, Donner opened the passenger-side door and eased into the van. Then Daniels mashed the accelerator and the van sped away from the standoff. The cops weren't about to open fire on a busy street.

"Code purple, situation corrupted, hot pursuit expected," Donner barked into the radio mike as he slammed his door shut.

"Roger," came the reply. "Reception will be ready."

Daniels expertly wheeled them around the block. The traffic lights were with them and he didn't activate the siren. No need to alert anyone of their route. Thankfully, no police patrol cars were in sight.

The van sped down a long and mostly unpopulated street of warehouses, where a truck awaited with twin ramps connecting its bed to the pavement. Cohen and Milton flanked the ramps, dressed in workmen's coveralls, as if set to load cargo. The van rolled up into the truck. Cohen and Milton rapidly folded the ramps inside and closed the doors.

"We're okay," Donner said to his men. He gripped the scrambler-enhanced radio mike, agonizing over what to tell the director. Procedure dictated that he report in. The truck rumbled to life, ready to sneak them the hell out of there.

"Okay?" said Daniels, ever the smart-ass. "We were an inch from a fire fight with the NYPD. Where are the terrorists? I didn't see any terrorists. What's the deal with the cops?"

"You don't have a need to know," Donner said.

"This whole operation doesn't add up," Daniels said. "We're tracking this reporter and these sisters. And the computer freak out in Queens who got neck-snapped. And trying to find the missing laptop. What does all this have to do with a terror cell?"

"Rumor I heard was that this actually isn't a counterterror operation," Fisher said from the backseat.

"What's the rumor?" Daniels asked.

"That the director is doing freelance stuff for himself. That he wants to get his hands on the laptop because it has a program with great stock market tips. Everybody's heard about his financial problems." Fisher shook his head.

"And that he's out of a job by the end of the year," Daniels said. "I didn't join the Authority for this kind of crap. Sounds wrong as hell. Two of our guys died at the Plaza and one will never regain use of his arms. What's going on, Donner?"

All Donner could do was reiterate that they lacked the need to know.

Mr. Escort sputtered through heavy traffic with an unmarked police car trailing. Karen drove with the care of a cat in a dog run. Linda closed her eyes to keep out the world.

"We'll be safe in Hampton Bays," Karen said.

Linda opened her eyes. "Who were those three guys dressed as cops?"

"My guess is they come from the Authority. They pulled off a very good impersonation of cops. Something that spooks could do. The one with the sergeant's stripes had a broken nose. The guy who River talked to in the bar about Goldring—he had a broken nose, as well."

"Can we trust anyone?"

"We can trust each other."

"That's reassuring," Linda said, her sarcasm as unsubtle as the maniac cabbie next to them, who thought his horn would magically clear the clogged road.

"Hey, what's with the attitude?"

"Something occurred to me just now. I was wondering if your going to Washington stirred up the Authority, and this Wooton sent the Englishman as a result."

"Cut it out Linda. They were involved long before I came along. The broken-nosed guy questioned River at his bar. Besides, let's not forget who saved your life today. In case you have, it was me."

"I suppose," Linda said. She shut her eyes again.

The taxi beside them gave another hallelujah chorus with its horn.

Karen agreed with Eudell that Linda could act more upset. Well, the best course would be to act kindly toward Linda, Karen vowed to herself. Linda surely was upset deep inside her lovely self where no one could go.

"Could you get away from that obnoxious taxi with the horn?" Linda said. "It's giving me a headache."

"We're kinda hemmed in here," Karen said.

The unmarked car fell away around the Queens-Nassau line. Karen and Linda rolled along the asphalt ribbon of the Long Island Expressway through a glorious colorful profusion of maples and oaks. At another time, Karen would've appreciated the scenery. She never had much enjoyed the long summer drive to the Hamptons in Tim's BMW. He drove as impatiently and dangerously as the adjacent cabbie, who thankfully exited at Great Neck.

Linda opened her eyes again. "Why are you driving so slowly? The traffic has thinned out. At this rate, we'll never get there."

Karen could see why Flo was permanently pissed at Linda. "The car is old. I don't want to blow the engine."

"We should have rented a new car."

"It's Frank Vere's, remember? He wanted me to have it."

Linda, used to taking a rich man's private helicopter to the Hamptons, said, "This is one gift I'd have refused."

"Well, other than we sing 'Ninety-nine Bottles of Beer on the Wall,' there's not much I can do here to make the trip ideal for you."

Hampton Bays is a working community, where the tradespeople and shopkeepers live, serving the toffs like Jack Faff. Mike Riley's house was as Karen had last seen it on Labor Day: an undistinguished saltbox with a deck, a stone hearth, and a skylight. The kitchen wasn't the best, revolving around an old range and an oven whose temperature fluctuated with the unpredictability of weekend weather or Karen's bosses' moods.

A Weber grill sat on the deck; Mike Riley, the self-appointed grill master because he owned the place, insisted on outdoor barbecuing with charcoal, not gas. "It gives the meat a campfire taste," he had insisted, right before the Razz drunkenly dropped the steaks onto the coals, where they soaked up dirt like a vacuum cleaner. Unlike everyone else, who ordered pizza, the Razz insisted on eating his filthy steak.

"What a cute little place," Linda said as they drove up, making no effort to sound sincere. "How many of you are out here on a summer weekend?"

"Six to ten. Tim never liked it here and wanted us to stay with his pals in Quogue. I think he secretly liked it here, though. Where else could he feel superior to everybody?"

"How crowded. I never cared for group houses. Too much aggravation." Linda spoke as though describing a Third World shantytown.

Karen fished out the house keys from her bag. "We have a lot of fun. Frank Vere is a house member."

"Isn't that remarkable? I'd heard that. It's really true? He would come to a place like this?" Linda made it seem like the famous Vere must be barking mad.

"Yeah, the neighbors love it. His presence has doubled property values. It'd be okay, except for all the tour buses coming by."

Inside, the house hadn't changed, either. The picture window and sliding glass door onto the deck could stand a washing. Unlike the large-lot estates elsewhere in the Hamptons, the houses in this neighborhood sat closely together. They all had garishly grinning jack-o'-lanterns in the yard.

"Halloween's tomorrow," Karen said, after a sweep through the house and onto the deck.

"I should have kept that old picture of my sisters and me at Halloween. I hope the cops, when they scour Ginny's apartment, don't lose it the way someone lost Flo's ring."

"I need the softball bat." Karen reached into the closet and pulled out the bat.

"What for?"

"Protection," Karen said.

"I thought we were safe out here."

"Oh, we are. Merely a precaution. I'll put it in my room. I'm staying in the bedroom downstairs. I always use that one. Take one upstairs. There's bedding for you in the closet."

"I'm hungry. When will you fix dinner?"

So now I'm her servant, Karen fumed. But she held her tongue. "We have nothing in the house. Want to come out with me and shop?"

"No, thank you," Linda said airily. "I'm going to take a shower."

"Sure. Wendy's clothes are in the room upstairs to the right. Top two drawers in the dresser."

"Now, about this Wendy. She's a bit of a misfit, right?"

"No more than the rest of us. And Wendy's parrot is very clean." Karen headed out.

From the window, Linda watched Karen walk out to the car. She greeted the next-door neighbor. Linda had heard about him, as well: a porky guy who rode motorcycles with a pack of over-the-hill outlaws, did carpentry odd jobs, and grew marijuana in his garden. Everyone called him Stoner. He and Karen had a serious conversation before Karen drove off.

Tim had given Linda a complaining earful about the summer house: "They are weird, weird, weird. One guy lies on the floor and recites Rudyard Kipling. This woman has a parrot on her shoulder, night and day. What is she, a pirate? And even Frank Vere, who is a big name, is strange. He can't get any women. He's a dork, basically."

Linda made the shower nice and hot. She lathered herself up. As she washed her hair, the soap got in her eyes. When Ginny was a kid, she hated the soap getting in her eyes. Ginny's eyes were so sensitive. Linda sank down the wall tiles and huddled on the floor with the spray dousing her shaking shoulders. She cried and cried and cried.

After a while, she picked herself up and with shaking hands finished washing. Then she raided Wendy's drawers. Linda sniffed the clothes and examined them for traces of parrot poop. She chose a shapeless pullover and well-worn jeans. Wendy had the wardrobe of a bag lady, but Linda was in no mood to be glamorous.

Heading down to the kitchen, she checked her watch. Karen had been gone for a good forty minutes. Did shopping take that long? She wasn't sure whether to be worried. Linda paced around the downstairs. *Where was Karen?* Now she'd been away for fifty minutes. Should she call Friday? But they were three hours outside of New York. What good would calling the NYPD do?

Linda bolted into the yard. Her feet swished through the leaf-strewn grass. The wind scattered more leaves from the trees. She went to the roadside and peered down the street. A car approached. And it passed. Not the Escort. The jack-o'-lanterns leered at her.

What was Karen's cell phone number? It was in Linda's bag upstairs. She headed back for the house and gripped the front door knob. Damn. Locked. How had she locked herself out?

Linda started to circle around, bound for the deck. Maybe Karen had left the sliding door open when she went out to examine the grill. When Linda rounded the corner, she almost collided with a large shape waiting for her. Linda cried out, "Oh, my God."

"Hey, take her easy, lady," Stoner said. "I'm your friendly neighbor." He smiled with stained teeth.

"I'm sorry. You see, I'm a little on edge here. Karen has been gone for a long time and I'm afraid—"

"She'll be back," Stoner said. He wore a plaid jacket opened to reveal his gut and a nasty sweatshirt from Metallica's 1988 world tour. "Karen told me some bad-ass dudes are on your case. You can always call on old Stoner for help."

"Thank you." She turned toward the street to see if the Escort was returning. Nothing.

Stoner gave her a grease-lined paper bag. "Take it. A pretty lady always should be able to protect herself."

"Thank you." She accepted the bag and finished her trip to the deck. The sliding door was locked.

"If you want to wait at my place, old Stoner wouldn't mind," the neighbor said from the lawn. Mercifully, he didn't trail her onto the deck.

"No, thank you. Very kind, but . . ." She slumped onto the bench next to the barbecue.

Stoner left. Darkness began creeping, lengthening the tree shadows, moving relentlessly, malevolently. A chill invaded the air. She clasped her arms to herself and tried to stay warm.

The Escort's headlight beams announced its arrival. She ran to the car. "I was locked out," she said. "Where the hell were you?"

Karen stifled the urge to fire back at Linda and her sense of entitlement. "Sorry I took so long. They're not stocked like in summer. I had to visit a few stores to get the goods."

Linda made no move to help bring in the groceries. Karen loaded herself up with four sacks of provisions and awkwardly unlocked the front door.

"Hurry up, will you?" Linda said. "I'm freezing."

Karen put away the food while Linda, wrapped in a blanket, leafed through old magazines. Karen made a robust fire and settled her in front of the hearth with a brimming wineglass. Karen asked what music she wanted and she said Wagner—the one German composer Tim detested.

They ate a great meal while the fire crackled and the music soared. Karen's chicken Marbella had long been a house favorite. She baked a pumpkin pie in honor of the season, even though Mike's house lacked the marble counter Karen had back in her own kitchen to make pastry. Actually, it was Tim's kitchen now. Linda drank a lot of wine and said almost nothing. Karen didn't feel like talking, either.

The only remark Linda uttered was to complain about the absence of low-fat margarine. "You have only real butter? I can't eat that."

"I asked if you wanted to go shopping with me," Karen said, trying not to sound testy.

The meal over, Karen asked her if she wanted to watch a

movie. Linda said, "I looked through your titles. They're ghastly. Listen, I am exhausted." Without thanking Karen for dinner or saying good night, she retired upstairs.

Linda tried to sleep and couldn't. The wind-whipped shadows of the trees outside played around the bedroom—spectral presences, scary.

She came back downstairs and knocked on Karen's bedroom door. Karen opened it. She had on a dumb pair of flannel pajamas.

"You look like you have enough room in that bed," Linda said, more like giving an order than making a request. "I'm on edge being alone right now."

"You'll feel right at home sleeping here," Karen said, losing the battle to hold back the asperity. "Tim and I used to share it."

"How lovely for you." Linda eyed the sheets for cleanliness.

Both of them settled in on the farthest reaches of the bed. And they fell fast asleep.

Logie walked the vast city by night. Leaving the Authority's building had been blissfully easy. No one challenged her. The director's order that she be escorted outside hadn't taken. Costumed adults cruised past her occasionally, bound for Halloween parties. White gases rose ghostly from gratings and spiraled into the chilly air.

She felt jazzed. She just had downed a small pizza and a beer at a noisy joint filled with post-collegiate revelers, most in costume. They all were friends, calling each other by name, happy to be together. Many of the young women were dressed skimpily despite the dropping temperature, aimed at interesting the men. The young men had good physiques, well-styled hair, and ready smiles.

Logie's running shoes, made for sudden departures,

moved silently along the concrete. Hidden in Logie's pocket was a brochure from Avis, whose all-night outlet sat next to the bar where she'd eaten. All she had to do was rent a car and go fetch Alexandra. Except for one problem: could she wrest her daughter from whatever Donner-like guards were posted there?

Logie returned to the Authority's building, passed through the eye scanner, and took the clunky old elevator to the alternate command post. She could hear the director before she reached their floor. Her hand dove into her pocket to ensure the brochure was in no danger of falling out, into Wooton's view.

"Incompetence of the worst kind," Wooton was booming from his throne of a chair.

Donner was leaning back in his chair, head tilted toward the ceiling, working his jaw.

"What possible excuse do you have now, Mr. Donner?"

"Glick got lucky. That's my excuse." Donner gave the director a challenging look. "She won't be next time. All right?"

"It's not all right. You are a magnet for bad luck," Wooton said.

"Oh, yeah. How about you? The rumor's hot around here that you're freelancing. People have heard about Goldring. They're asking why we sacrificed operatives at the Plaza to make you rich. Talk about incompetence. I didn't leak word one. Did you?"

Wooton grew silent. He contemplated his exquisite tie for a moment. "We can contain this. Our operatives will do what they're told, as they have for years."

"You better hope," Donner said. "I'm not going to jail."

"No one is going to jail," Wooton said quietly. "Now, we have confirmed Glick's location?"

"Yeah. She's out in Hampton Bays. We stuck a transmitter

on her car. Didn't have time for a bomb. I'm going out there tonight. Without anyone else. Too many of the men are suspicious of me."

"No, you're not, Mr. Donner. Remember the lunch tomorrow with Siegfried Wolfe. I want you along. We will snatch Wolfe if he doesn't cooperate. After that, go to Hampton Bays."

"You said you wanted me to ice Glick."

"You no doubt also are eager to see the gorgeous Linda Reiner again." The director gave the arriving Logie a withering look. "And where, Ms. Logan, do you think you've been?"

Logie's hand tightened on the rental brochure in her pocket. "Out to get some food. Is that a crime?"

"You've been drinking."

"One beer with my pizza. A real bender."

"I required you to have an escort," Wooton intoned.

"Well, read my mind: I didn't need one." Logie watched the director's round form leave. She said to Donner, "I'm glad you're finally standing up to him."

"I can only take so much crap."

"Here's another way of standing up to him: leave Karen Glick alone. Seriously."

"I've been given a direct order."

"You're not going to harm Linda Reiner, too, are you?"

"If she's near Glick, what do you think? Wooton may think I'm stupid, but I'm smart enough not to leave witnesses."

Sunday. Cool noon air coursed through Manhattan's sunny streets, tossing loose newspaper pages and bags and leaves about with devilish abandon. People wore scarves and the wind moved their hair around. Children laughed, eager for the coming evening's trick-or-treating.

Wooton, with gun cars fore and aft, arrived at the restaurant on time. "The detail is in place?" he asked Donner.

Donner, sitting glumly across from him in the car, said, "Yes, Director. You asked me that twice before."

"The rear door, the kitchen, the basement, and the front?"

"Yes, sir. And half the busboys are ours. How many times—"

"As many as I want to, Mr. Donner. For your own good, you will refrain from any more attempts at speaking out of turn. It's a bad habit you have acquired from Ms. Logan. In fact, you will say nothing until I tell you to. Understood?"

Donner grimaced. "Do you want me to stay with the car?"

"No, I don't. You are about to have the rare privilege of meeting Siegfried Wolfe. You will be at our table."

"Me? Wouldn't it be better if I coordinated the arrangements to bag this sucker? I can't do that at the table with Wolfe."

"Let Spinelli handle coordination. Your best utility is at my side. Do you know why?"

"I guess in case he tries something, I wax him."

"Very good, Mr. Donner. For once a sign of life in that brain of yours. Congratulations. Let's go in."

Wooton heaved himself out of the car and made for the restaurant's door. Donner preceded him, hand inside suit jacket, ready to produce his weapon if needed. The Sunday brunch bunch was crowding the foyer, attracted by the great reviews. A woman with garish lipstick complained loudly about having to wait even though she had a reservation.

But Wooton was special. Official government arrangements, made in the name of the FBI, had seen to it. The maître d' had thought the notion of clandestine law enforcement activity deliciously enticing, cachet enhancing. Wooton and Donner were waved past the panting others.

The day glowed brightly outside, but here a night-like, funeral parlor chic reigned. Heavy, dark red curtains hung from every wall. Little spotlights, set high in the ceiling, cast small ovals of illumination on the tabletops. They followed the maître d's shaved head and clinking earrings through the maze of tables filled with animated, black-clad customers.

Wolfe sat to the rear against the wall. He wore a newly tailored tweed suit and an old regimental tie. He rose from the table to offer first Wooton, then Donner, a handshake.

"It has been a while, Kingman," Wolfe said as he jauntily assumed his seat, theatrically flounced his napkin out, and settled it over his lap.

"It has, Siegfried. You're looking well. For someone who fell down a flight of stairs, that is."

"Fully recovered from this and other calamities. I hope you won't reiterate that tiresome business about how you saved my life. I never mix reminiscing with a good meal. If you're at all decent company, I may pay." Wolfe turned to Donner. "Kingman has an overly serious side."

"Mr. Donner isn't talking today," Wooton said.

"Has Kingman entirely emasculated you?" Wolfe said to Donner. "How dull."

Donner's grimly set mouth gave a wormy wiggle, as if suppressing the urge to bite.

A soignée waitress appeared. She had a plunging neckline that attracted the eye and black lacquered hair that repelled it. "And?" she said with one raised eyebrow.

"Since I discovered this delightful establishment for us, I will do the ordering," Wolfe said. He ordered arugula salads, tuna tartare, and a Rhineland white for the table.

"Mr. Donner isn't drinking," Wooton said.

"Got to keep his wits about him in case I pull out a firearm, eh?" Wolfe opened his suit jacket to reveal his bone-white shirt. "Nothing here. You can frisk me, Donner. That would be a thrill."

"You watch it, pal," Donner said.

"Be quiet, Mr. Donner," Wooton said. "Now, Siegfried, let's talk about Goldring."

"Let's not," Wolfe said. "Discussing business before a meal is unhealthy for my digestive system. Particularly in view of all these hulking busboys, who seem so out of place here." He proceeded to regale them with his opinions about the absurdities of U.S. life: Bloody Marys at Sunday brunch ("dredging up an unfortunate period in British history, best forgotten"), professional football ("in the American version, hardly anyone's feet come into contact with the ball"), and trick-or-treating ("the little urchins don't actually deliver any tricks").

"Perhaps we can speed your passage out of this dreadful country," Wooton said.

"I'm not complaining, dear Kingman. Merely being amused."

"You never amused me."

"I understand you never amused your wife."

Wooton's plump cheeks reddened. "How can you possibly know the first thing about my marriage, you damn twit?"

"There are no secrets, Kingman. About you. About Goldring."

When the salads arrived, Wolfe switched plates with Wooton. "I'd hate to think anyone put a little surprise in mine," Wolfe said. He chattered on and consumed most of the wine. When the main course came, he again exchanged plates, but with Donner.

With the tuna consumed, Wooton raised the matter of Goldring once more. "Do you have it?"

Wolfe savored the last of the wine. "No. Although I know who does. Some sly boots who's not sly enough."

"You're working for this 'someone,' aren't you?"

Wolfe held up an index finger. "You and your marvelous clairvoyance. How can a simple English lad like me hope to compete with such powers?"

"MI-6 wants to hunt you down like a dog for killing your own people."

"How sweet of them to care. I still retain my British passport, even though it's revoked. And I still root for my sceptered isle in the World Cup. Real football, that."

"Back to Goldring," Wooton said. "We'll pay you a lot of money to deliver the laptop to us, in good working order."

"I have a question of my own about Goldring," Wolfe said. "And this is the reason I wanted to meet with you. You would know the answer, if anyone does."

"Very well. What's your question?"

First patting his mouth with a napkin, Wolfe said, "I am skeptical about the stock market. Too many fools chasing the latest rumor. No better than a casino and perhaps a lot worse. But people have gotten rich from it. Especially when the game is rigged. Tell me: does Goldring really work?"

"Yes," the director said. "We examined all the Reiner sisters' trades. Somehow, they knew beforehand what stock was going to take off. They never were wrong. Not once."

"*How* does it work, Kingman?"

"We don't know. It simply does."

"Why should I want to sell it to you?"

Kingman leaned over the table. "Because you don't know how to work a computer, so it's of no use to you. And because, if you kept it, we'd join MI-6 in tracking you down. Not an appetizing thought after a good meal, is it?"

"Given that you're a lame duck at the Authority, I'm not sure that's such a potent threat," Wolfe said. "Another question. I can appreciate that a man of your gifts, Kingman—flattery intended, as a concession to the man who once saved my life, which we won't get into—a man of your gifts could operate Goldring." He fluttered his fingers in Donner's direction. "But a certified dolt like Dirk Donner here? Doubtful. Correct?"

Donner's fist slammed the tabletop, bouncing the empty plates and soiled cutlery. "Do you think you're actually gonna walk out of here on your own, shithead?"

Wolfe gave him a strange little smile. "Oh my, yes."

He pulled the small electronic device out of his suit jacket's inner pocket. A small explosion came from the basement. The lights went out. By the time the emergency lighting kicked in, Siegfried Wolfe had left nothing but an unpaid lunch check and a swaying wall hanging.

Karen prepared a fine Sunday breakfast. Linda plunked herself down at the table under the skylight. She said she had drunk too much wine last night and had slept too long. She dug into her mushroom-and-brie omelette. Karen had squeezed the orange juice herself and baked the croissants. There was plenty of strong, hot coffee.

"You snuck out before I awoke," Linda said.

"Had to do a bit more shopping."

Linda spread strawberry jam on a croissant. "Where's the low-fat margarine?"

Squinting at her in annoyance, Karen made do with: "I forgot."

"Did you get the newspaper today?"

"No," Karen said. She had read parts of it at the deli.

"Why not?"

"All the papers have stories about Ginny." Also, each had a small item about the ghost-costumed thug's knifing to death an elderly man from Atlantic City on the Broadway Local subway, a man named Major Darcy. "I didn't think—"

"You're right." Linda wordlessly finished her meal. "Take me to the beach."

"The beach? It's cold there now."

"I want to go to the beach."

"Ooooookay. Let me clean up first."

"I want to go now."

"Fine," Karen said evenly. "Then when we get back, maybe you can help me clean up."

"That's a one-person job. Let's go."

The ten-minute drive took them past the treeline, over the causeway, and into the sandy seaside world along Dune Road. Karen parked in a huge empty lot. As they got out of Mr. Escort, a polar wind stung their faces and whipped their hair around. The sand was as white as on a summer's day. Gulls glided overhead, crying like lost souls. The Atlantic, gray now and cold as death, boomed powerfully onto the shore.

"I used to come to the beach with Garner, off to the east near Montauk," Linda said, burrowed into Frank Vere's down jacket. "The Chase family owns a whole stretch of beach, fronting their compound. It's lovely. No other people around. You can sunbathe nude. Have sex in the daytime on the sand."

"The only time I ever did that, it was at night, hidden in the dunes," Karen said. "A seashell gouged my butt."

"Once this mess is over, I'm going to buy my own beachfront property. With Goldring back, I can buy the whole coast."

Karen, toeing the sand, said, "Must be nice."

"It is nice. Very nice."

Unable to contstrain herself any longer, Karen said, "Holy hell, Linda. If it were me and I retrieved the laptop, I'd destroy the damn thing. Thanks to Goldring, your sisters are dead."

"How dare you," Linda said. A wave hit the sand with a bomb-like crash. "And you most definitely are *not* me."

They avoided each other the rest of the day. Karen tried to read an old paperback, but couldn't concentrate. She went outside to do yard work. Linda took a long walk.

That night, Karen grilled a marinated lamb shank on the Weber. That, mashed potatoes, peas, mint jelly, and home-made peach cobbler constituted a fine meal. Linda ate plenty and drank plenty of the good merlot. A haunting silence continued to reign.

Linda was heading for the bathroom when the doorbell rang. Karen was out on the deck cleaning the grill. Linda tentatively opened the door. No one was there. She opened the door wider.

A gaggle of phantoms jumped out at her. Linda shrieked.

"Trick or treat!" the kids chanted.

Karen bounded up. While Linda caught her breath, leaning against the hall wall, Karen smiled and handed the youngsters candy.

"That was simply . . . ," Linda patted her chest as Karen closed the door, "too much."

"A few kids came by earlier, when you were up in the shower."

"I should get to bed."

"See you tomorrow," Karen said.

"Are you kidding me? I'm going to your room again. I am too weirded out."

The house settled down for the evening. The air outside was calm. Linda snuggled in. Karen eventually did, too. They didn't speak. Soon they were asleep. A midnight Halloween stillness enveloped them.

They didn't hear the glass cutter working on the door from the deck. A handheld suction cup on the square-cut section of glass pane kept it from falling to the floor and disturbing the night silence. They didn't hear the click of the lock as a hand reached around for it through the opening. Nor the soft movement of the door sliding open. Nor the rubber-soled steps of the man entering with a gun.

CHAPTER TWENTY-TWO

A harsh wind roared off the Atlantic and tossed the water about angrily. Karen gingerly walked along the beach with Tim, near where the dangerous waves crashed. Then Karen noticed that Linda was with them. And they were all naked. Karen looked down at her belly: its small amount of pudge had ballooned. She was fat. Linda insisted on walking closer to the waves, even though they might be swept out to sea. Tim and Linda now had their arms around each other. Tim told Karen, over the wind, that Linda was so hot-looking. Linda informed Karen that she and Tim were going back up the beach to have sex on the sand, but that Karen had to stand by the smashing waves.

The cell phone on the nightstand sounded.

At first, Karen wasn't sure whether this was part of the dream. She unglued her eyes. Linda lay sleeping, blonde hair arrayed fetchingly on the pillow.

The phone rang again.

Linda stirred. "Wha . . . ? Hmmmm. Uh . . . wha . . . ?"

"Lemme . . ." Karen groped for the cell. Linda turned over. Karen mumbled into the phone: "H'lo?"

A woman's voice, urgent, panicked: "Get out of the house. Get into your car and leave there. Right now."

"Excuse me?"

"You're in danger. A man is coming to kill you."

"Who is this?"

"It took me a while to find your cell phone number," the woman ranted. "Hours. Phone company's new system is harder to break into than a Swiss bank. Would've called earlier, but didn't have the chance. People watching me. I'm not kidding. Get out."

Karen passed her free hand over her face and peered about in the darkness. All seemed still. "Your name?"

The woman was shouting louder still. "Wake up. Get moving. He knows you're in Mike Riley's summer house. Your Escort has a GPS tracking transmitter affixed to it."

"How do you know this stuff? Who is coming?"

"Get out, get out, *get out*. He'll kill you, and Linda Reiner, too."

"Calm down. I need to—" But the woman hung up. Karen returned the cell to the nightstand.

"What's going on?" Linda asked, her words muffled by sleep and the pillow.

"How strange." Karen turned on the bedside lamp. "I'm going to have a look around." She swung her legs onto the floor and reached under the bed for the softball bat.

Linda lifted up her head. Her hair was tousled and her eyes open a millimeter. "Who called?"

"Dunno. Some woman." Karen stood up and hefted the bat. "Stay here."

"What's happening?" Linda said petulantly.

The bedroom door swung open.

A large man in a black leather jacket stood there, a bizarre set of goggles covering his eyes. He gripped something with both hands. It was a big gun with a fat silencer tube. Pointed at Karen.

"Jesus," Linda said. Karen was closest to the gunman. She stood with the bat.

The man in the doorway disengaged his left hand from the pistol grip to remove the goggles, evidently a night vision device that the bedside light disrupted. The goggles dropped to the floor.

This was the same man with the broken nose who had posed as the police sergeant. He looked malevolently pleased with himself.

"What do you want?" Karen asked.

"Drop the bat," the gunman commanded. "Or I'll drop you now."

Karen tossed the bat onto the bed. With the gun on her, its muzzle a black circle of death, she started to breathe heavily, as if in a race. "Who are you?"

"Because you dropped the bat, you get to live for a few more seconds."

"Is this about Goldring?" Linda said, crouching on the bed. "We don't have Goldring. Is that what you want?"

The man stared hungrily at Linda, who wore a torso-baring half T-shirt and bikini panties. "I don't have Goldring either, baby," he said. "Wish we did, but we don't."

Karen licked her dry lips. "Are you alone?"

"You're gonna go first," the gunman said to Karen. "Then blonde chickie-poo is gonna get a royal sendoff. Take everything off, baby."

"Leave her alone," Karen growled. "You don't have to do this."

"Sure, I do."

Karen went into journalist question overdrive. "Are you with the Authority?"

"What a smart bitch you are." The gunman seemed to savor his utter control of the women.

"Why didn't you send the Englishman out here?"

"Do you think we'd hire that fruit? Gimme a break. You're not that smart after all."

Karen, though panting, kept up with the questions. "He doesn't work for you? If you don't have Goldring, who does?"

"Whoever hired the Englishman. Beats me who that is. It's not us and it's not Faff." The intruder gestured with his gun at Linda. "I told you to take them off. Do it." He ogled the outline of Linda's nipples through the thin T-shirt fabric.

With the gunman preoccupied by Linda's bod, Karen launched a massive punch at his stomach, summoning every ounce of her teenage gym training.

But his left hand, with inhuman speed, caught Karen's fist in midflight. Still holding the gun with his right, the man twisted Karen's arm behind her back. He leaned over her pain-etched face. "Want me to break your arm before I wax you?"

Linda reached into the bag Stoner had given her, which she kept beside the bed, and brought out the neighbor's pepper spray. Before the gunman could react, she blasted him in the face. His gun hit the floor right before he did. On his knees, heavyweight frame jerking as if electrocuted, he clasped his hands to the white-hot coals in his eye sockets and filled the bedroom with demon wails.

Released, Karen clasped her aching shoulder and started to speak.

Linda grabbed the bat from the bed and gave a Major League swing that connected with his bucking body. It hit him where his thick neck joined his mountain range of shoulders. He toppled the rest of the way to the floor with a skull-smacking sound.

Karen looked down from the bed at the prostrate gunman. "Is he dead?" She felt the side of his tree-trunk neck. "Just unconscious. You whacked him pretty good."

Linda straddled the big man and rifled through his pockets. She lifted a wallet out of his pants and fingered its contents. "He has credit cards and driver's licenses. All in different names."

"Hey, the guy's a spook."

"Should we call the cops?" Linda was smiling, as if at a party.

"After we put some distance between him and us. This guy and his buddies had no trouble posing as cops, so who knows what'll show up if we wait around." Karen marveled at how Linda's vanquishing of the gunman had brightened her, much as she'd been after smashing the amorous Jack Faff in the ribs. "Let's get a move on. We gotta get dressed and haul ass."

Linda dropped the pepper spray and the gunman's pistol into the paper shopping bag. Karen pulled her pajama top and bottom off and, as she reached for her clothes, saw Linda giving her nude self a critical appraisal.

Karen said, "And quit looking at me like I won the ugly contest."

"I've got a great diet for you. I tried to get Flo on it."

"Enough with the compliments. We've got more urgent things to do than chat about diets, for God's sake."

"I never need to diet myself. Another reason for you to resent me." Linda got into Wendy's shapeless togs. "I can't believe this Wendy dresses so badly."

Karen dropped her cell phone into her handbag. "Are you finished insulting me and my friends? Let's move it."

"No, I'm not. Wendy makes Björk look like Cindy Crawford."

They stepped over the Authority operative, cracked the front door, and peered out into the night. Linda started to lunge forward, but Karen restrained her. She waited until her eyes adjusted to the darkness. All appeared quiet. No one lurked nearby. Giddily heading for the car, Linda fairly skipped through the grass, past the leaf bags Karen had stuffed that afternoon. Linda swung Stoner's shopping bag as if she'd just cleaned out the Hermes collection at Henri Bendel.

"Are you always this happy after you've hurt someone?" Karen said.

"Only if they wanted to rape me, sweetie."

Karen had gotten out the keys to Mr. Escort when a powerful black car materialized, gliding to a stop beside the driveway. The driver's door opened and a man's silhouette emerged. He was as sizable as the Authority guy.

"Who the hell is that?" Linda exclaimed. She slid a hand into the shopping bag for the gun.

The shadowy man sprinted for them. In his hand was a knife. A very long, cruel knife.

"Shit," Linda said. The bottom of the bag ripped open. The gun and pepper spray hit the driveway and skittered away.

"You going somewhere?" Mikhail said through his sharp teeth. "You going nowhere." He wore a dark shirt and white pants, as if he'd been out club-hopping. And he loomed over them.

"What do you want?" Karen gauged the distance to the gun, which lay at the lawn's edge. Mikhail's knife would stick her before she could hustle over there.

"You to die," Mikhail said, and drew back his blade.

"Hold your damn self," said someone to Karen's left.

They all turned to see Stoner advancing on them. He held a shotgun aimed at the gangster.

"Ain't nobody gonna hurt old Stoner's friends, long as he's around," the neighbor said. "Drop the frigging knife before Stoner blows you to hell."

Mikhail's jaw hung open and his eyes bugged. His knife clattered to the asphalt.

Stoner chortled and indicated the Russian's midsection with a poke of the shotgun muzzle. "Hey, did you just have an accident in your trou?"

While Stoner covered Mikhail, Karen gathered up the pistol—she couldn't find the pepper spray—and unlocked the car. Linda kissed Stoner's furry cheek, which made him smile as though his year had been made.

"How did you know we were here?" Karen demanded of the gangster.

Mikhail showed his wicked teeth. "I got ears everywhere. Next time I see you, first thing I do, I cut yours off."

"Watch your damn mouth," Stoner said. "You're smelling real bad, man."

"We need to get scarce," Karen told Stoner. "What will you do with Mikhail here?"

"Stoner's not gonna give him a bath," Stoner said. "Stoner's got lotsa cop pals who buy his wacky weed and they'll be over before you can say, 'Boo.' Old Stoner can feed this hump to them with no problem. In the Hamptons, they hate troublemakers."

"Another one's inside," Karen said. "Downstairs bedroom. Out cold. Linda clocked him with a softball bat. Hard."

"And pepper spray to the eyes," Linda added.

Stoner guffawed. "You got your wind back, lady. Don't pay to get on your wrong side."

Karen and Linda piled into the car and took off, pistons clattering. Before sliding onto the highway, they stopped at an all-night gas station and, lying on its concrete apron, Karen beamed a flashlight underneath Mr. Escort. In the left rear tire well, she found a rectangular object stuck to the chassis by magneticism. She threw it far into the woods.

"Let them try to find us now," Karen said.

"Where are we going?" Linda said. "Someplace nicer than your group house, I hope."

"Linda, my tongue's got a hernia from me holding it back. Let's get a little attitude improvement from you."

"You don't know who you are messing with," said Mikhail, his arms aloft, Wild West style.

"Seems you already messed yourself," Stoner said. "Say, what's wrong with your teeth?"

Movement near the house distracted Mikhail. Stoner looked. Another large man came shambling around the corner, lurching like Frankenstein's monster. As he drew closer, Stoner could see the long metal object in his hand. It was a MAC-10.

"Where's Glick?" asked the guy, sounding as if he were in great pain. His eyes were extremely puffy, barely open.

Stoner swung the shotgun on him. "Stay where you are."

Gritting his teeth as if each movement were excruciating, the newcomer brought up his automatic weapon. "One twitch of my finger and I cut you in two, dumb ass."

Stoner backed toward his property, shotgun still aimed at the MAC-10 guy. "Don't get yourself excited."

Mikhail lowered his arms. "You maybe, by some chance, work for the Authority?"

"Not that I can see too well," the MAC-10 guy said. "But you look like that Russian who works for Faff—Beria."

"I think this fat asshole is gonna call the cops. We better beat feet, no?"

"I hate fat people." He footdragged after Mikhail to the black car. Once inside, he said, "I parked my vehicle over by the railroad tracks. It's a humvee."

"Bit of a walk." The Russian twisted the ignition and wheeled noisily away.

"Strange cars attract attention in residential neighborhoods. A good rule of tradecraft."

"I like my automobile where I can jump in it. Why did

you not use the MAC-10 on Glick? You wouldn't even have to enter house. Shoot through her window. Make Glick dead now, big-time." Mikhail checked about for police cars as he swung onto the main road.

"I wanted to use a sidearm with a silencer. Like, to keep it quiet for the neighbors? Dunno how fatso was alerted. And I wanted to have a little fun with the Reiner chick before I did her. I kept the MAC-10 hidden out on the deck."

"I like the blade," Mikhail said. "You slide a blade in and you got this moment, like sex, where the guy surrenders to you. His life on end of your blade. Not the same with MAC-10."

"U.S. military doctrine is what we use," the Authority man said. "Go for superior firepower. You win every time."

"That didn't work this time. The Reiner woman, she did a number on you."

"Tricky bitch," the Authority man said. "When I wasn't looking." He caught Mikhail's mocking grin. "Hey, she made your boss do the hurt dance."

"He's not my boss. I do work for Faff cuz I like his money. He's a little shrimp weenie. Big money, little dick."

"I wouldn't know about the dick. What smells in here?"

"Guy who loaned me the car, he's a real pig. Smells bad. No shower." They wheeled up behind a humvee. "This yours?" Mikhail asked.

"You kidding? It's the government's." The Authority man slowly pulled open the door.

"Government—you got a shitload of people. Why just you out here tonight?"

"I don't trust anybody but myself to get this job done."

"I feel the same," Mikhail said. "My men can't find their asses with both hands sometimes. Hey, you don't have the Reiner laptop, right?"

The government agent, halfway out of the car, thought for a moment. Then, "Not a chance."

"Maybe we do a deal. Work better."

"How do you mean?"

"Get our bosses together. Join the forces. Two heads better than one." Mikhail nodded eagerly, as if seeking to induce the spy guy to start nodding, too.

"Two swelled heads. Well, hell. Worth a shot. Let me pass this along to the fat bastard. Provided he'll still listen to me after this screwup." The Authority man tried to walk, but stumbled. "Damn it, I feel real bad."

"But I get to kill Glick first, okay?"

The sickly yellow light of morning came through the window into Father Finnegan's office. Like a pianist poised to play Rachmaninoff, the priest sat with fingers hovering above Goldring's keyboard. The digital clock on the desk flicked to 9:30. The market was open. And a new order from Simon Scratch was entered—this time for Tarnhelm Tool and Dye, another sleepy stock. How little they knew on Wall Street.

The phone rang. Normally, he would allow the machine to take a message. But this might be Wolfe. The priest had tried to reach Wolfe through the Iran number, trying to tell him that Linda probably was with Karen Glick and probably in the Hampton Bays summer house. And the priest wanted the delicious details on Ginny Reiner's death.

In the news reports about the "shocking sniper murder" of the second Reiner sister, the police were quoted as saying only that Linda had been taken to an undisclosed location for her safety. Officially, no one would draw a connection between the two sisters' deaths, other than to note that the methods differed: the first sister got shot at close range with a .45, the second from a distance with a rifle. Both head shots.

"Good morning, Our Lady of Perpetual Suffering. How may I—"

But a woman's voice interrupted. "Father Finnegan, this is Linda Reiner."

"My goodness, yes. I've heard about your tragic loss. I was filled with sadness. Is there anything I can do to help you?"

"Why, yes, father," Linda said. "I have to make arrangements again, of course. And although Ginny wasn't very religious—the communion we had at Flo's mass was her first in a long while; mine, too, actually—she grew up Catholic."

"I understand. Perhaps you would like to stop by the church and we can discuss the arrangements."

"A lot is up in the air now, father. Someone is trying to kill me. And Karen Glick, that reporter, whom you've met. We have to be very careful." Linda sounded as she had in the past: strong, willful, centered. Hardly traumatized.

"Certainly. Let me come to you. If you could give me an address where we could meet." The priest scrambled for a pen.

"No, not now, father. The reason I called was to let you know we'd be needing you and to ask you to be flexible. You're the only priest I know. My family back in Ohio are all gone."

"I see. I'll be available for whatever you need. Yet I'm worried about you. Is Miss Glick with you now?"

"Absolutely. I can assure you we're in a safe place. Oh, about that attempt of Ginny's to thwart Flo's will? Forget it." Linda expressed her thanks and hung up.

The priest took the Lord's name in vain. The Authority could trace such a call, not the church.

A tapping came from the thick wooden door, then an insistent male voice: "Let me in."

While using Goldring, Simon Scratch wanted the door deadbolted shut. The priest closed down Goldring and hid the computer in the desk's large bottom drawer, and carefully locked it.

More tapping. "Let me in. I need a priest."

"Why do you need a priest?" The priest stood next to the door now, fingertips caressing the wood, tone low and purring.

"To do bad things with."

"Priests are supposed to be good. I'm a man of God. How can I do bad things?"

"Because you're a rich priest. And rich priests can do whatever they want. Why shouldn't Father Finnegan do what he wants?"

"Why shouldn't he?" The deadbolt snapped open.

The director sat in his chair, fists balled, fleshy face twisted in fury, a thwarted potentate surveying the ruin of his imperial designs. "Astonishing," he rumbled.

Donner was in a small chair a few feet away. He had difficulty standing. He leaned forward abjectly, supporting his head with his large hands planted under his chin. "I think I have a concussion. Head hit the floor. Maybe cracked vertebrae on my neck, too, from the bat. Thought it'd be better by now. Getting worse."

Wooton had no sympathy. Even though Donner had delivered a detailed report while in pain, including Mikhail Beria's demented suggestion that they form an alliance, the director could express only contempt for his subordinate's latest mess. "Mr. Donner, I lay in the bush on the Plain of Jars, calling in B-52 strikes while I had a sucking wound in my stomach from a Pathet Lao bullet." Wooton looked at him incredulously, as though Donner was an abomination in God's eyes. "You're so incompetent that you defy categorizing."

Logie watched Donner's latest humiliation from her desk. If Donner hadn't tried to kill innocent people, she would feel sorry for him. Fortunately, the telepathic director hadn't traced calls from their command post to Hampton Bays, like the one Logie had made last night.

"Fool isn't good enough," Wooton said. "There's a comical aspect to a fool. You are tragic."

"Can't walk straight."

"Idiot might do. But an idiot has a small child's level of intelligence. While you're no genius, you at least have enough mental power to rise to a senior operative's rank."

A cow-like moan came from deep inside Donner. "Maybe I have bleeding in my brain."

"You disgust me," Wooton boomed. "I turn the entire power of the Authority over to you. I offer you the chance to become rich beyond comprehension. And you repeatedly bumble every task."

Logie jumped to her feet. "Stop this. He needs a doctor. What's the matter with you?"

Wooton looked at her, his mouth a small zero of surprise, as if a household appliance had spoken. "What did you say?"

"You heard me. I've had it. Two of our people lie dead and a third crippled because of this nonsense. Now Donner is critically injured. Let's just give up, before more harm gets done."

"Ms. Logan, I have not solicited your opinion."

"You promised to hurt no one. Sending Dirk to the Hamptons to kill somebody violates that promise, wouldn't you say?"

"Oh, please, not this again," Wooton said. "You are not in command. Let me remind you, Ms. Logan, that I am."

"Are you?" She crossed over to Donner and knelt beside him. He stared listlessly at the floor with eyes bloodshot from the pepper spray. His pupils were unequal, the sign of a concussion.

She touched his sleeve. He put a hand over hers.

"I've never been hurt like this," he said. After he had run off the road trying to enter the Long Island Expressway in the wee hours, Authority operatives had fetched him.

Wooton hadn't let him be taken to a hospital. He wanted Donner back at the New York command post for debriefing.

Logie took a certain pleasure that a woman had bashed Donner before he could kill her, and then escaped. But now was the time to retire him from this insane game. And retire the game itself. "You'll be okay," she said. "Is there someone we can notify for you?"

"Got nobody. Nobody has me for Christmas. No New Year's party. Birthday? Like any other day."

She realized she knew very little about him. "No relatives? Parents? Brothers? Sisters?"

Donner put his hands over his wrecked eyes and began weeping. "I had my funeral. Remember?"

"This is too much," Wooton said.

Logie rubbed Donner's back and murmured that he'd get medical attention in a minute.

"You and I could work well," Donner said, the unaccustomed tear tracks standing out on his cheeks like tattoos. He clasped her wrist. "I like you. We got a lot in common."

His sudden affectionate display struck Logie speechless.

"I had a sucking wound in my stomach, and I could do my job," Wooton thundered. "You never saw me crying. You never saw me going gooey emotional. You are a disgrace, Mr. Donner."

"All you think about is your stomach, you fat bastard," Donner said, barely audible. "You want to hog half the Goldring money. You don't deserve it."

"I will not tolerate insubordination from either one of you," the director bellowed, the force of his voice almost shaking the bulletproof windows.

"Forget your ego," Logie shot back. "He needs a doctor."

Wooton was a loud lump of frustrated rage. "He needs many things. He needs common sense. He needs operational competence. He's a pathetic specimen."

Donner focused his damaged eyes on Wooton. "You fat, ungrateful prick."

"What are you daring to say to me?"

Like a volcano in slow motion, Donner rose. "Dare? Who are you to talk like this to me?" He took a lurching step toward the director. "You, who lost his wife to another man." Another step. "You, who's running out of money." Another step. "You, who the president is gonna can."

Wooton's belligerent expression lapsed into amazement. "Where did you hear this?"

"It's everywhere," Donner said. "Everybody knows. And everybody's laughing at you. Asshole." Another step. Now he was a matter of feet from the director. His pain-twisted face radiated murderous intent.

"No one laughs at me." Wooton's chubby yet dextrous hand slipped inside his suit jacket and emerged with a small, snub-nosed pistol. It put a small and perfect hole in Donner's forehead.

Logie hollered in horror. Donner jig-stepped back and crashed to the floor like a felled bull.

Hopping froggishly over to the big man's corpse, Wooton swiftly placed the gun in Donner's hand. He took care to slip Donner's index finger through the trigger guard.

Sounding hysterical now, his deep voice breaking like that of a fat boy entering puberty, Wooton said to Logie, "You saw, you saw, didn't you? You saw how he pulled out the gun and shot himself? You saw, you saw. Tragic. We tried to stop him. The pressure he's been under. You saw, you saw." The hopeful, open-mouthed cast of his porcine face was obscene.

The operatives from the director's detail were pounding on the locked door from outside. None had the entry code.

Logie bolted for the door.

"Let them in and tell them," Wooton called after her. "You saw. You did. Tragic."

When Logie undid the door, the operatives and their waving guns piled in. The director was midway through his story to them when he realized she had kept going. He ordered them to seize her.

But Logie got the elevator before they did. And in the chaos, no one thought to alert front-entrance security to stop her. She had a destination.

CHAPTER TWENTY-THREE

Preferring her own company, Linda was strolling the grounds of Denholm Brassard's estate when Karen caught up with her. The euphoria of vanquishing the gunman had worn off and Linda had plunged into silence

The lordly trees, which had borne silent witness to generations of human strife, swayed gently in the autumn breeze and sent flights of red and yellow leaves swirling into the air. Denholm lived in a robber baron's manor house on the Long Island Gold Coast, a few miles from the Queens line. When Karen had reached him by cell phone as they fled from the Hamptons, Denholm had been intrigued and eager to harbor fugitives.

"Let's figure out where we are," Karen said, absently rubbing the shoulder that the Authority guy had twisted. "I need your help on that."

"We're nowhere, as far as I can tell," Linda said in a maddeningly blasé way.

Karen pressed on. "If we believe what the gunman said,

Wooton and the Authority don't have Goldring. Nor does Faff. And the Englishman's employer does. He's the missing piece."

"Pardon my bad attitude, but how is this 'missing piece' to be found?"

"I just got off the phone with Frank. He found out that the Suffolk County cops reported that Mikhail and the Authority guy escaped from Stoner. Now Frank is trying to check into the Englishman through his contacts with the FBI. The espionage world is hard to penetrate."

"Okay, we'll play your little game as if we had a chance in hell of finding this 'missing piece' of yours," Linda said. "Let's say the Englishman was behind Flo's death and the framing of Albert, whom he also killed. We are certain he murdered Ginny. And he tried to kill us. Why did he *warn* you first? The night after Flo's funeral, on the street outside my building, he told you to back off, stay away. Why?"

"That bothers me, too," Karen said. "Why would he want to give me a chance?"

"Maybe he likes you. Everybody likes you, Karen."

And, Karen was tempted to say, *nobody likes you. Except, of course, the boys.* "The easiest thing, when he had me in that grip from behind, was to kill me on the street. Doesn't add up." She brushed away a red leaf that fell against her chest. "For your information, Wooton doesn't like me. Nor does Faff."

"You may be a pain, but I have to hand it to you," Linda said. "I can hardly believe you were asking the Authority jerk questions as he was getting ready to shoot you."

"Got information we wanted, right?" Karen rubbed her shoulder again. It was feeling better, not that Linda had asked. "So I'm a pain, huh?"

"Let's not go there," said Linda, who already had gone there. Her verbal drive-by shooting complete, she looked up at the blue sky with its wispy clouds. A hawk circled overhead, poised for prey. "The question I have is why my sisters and I have been targets. What did we do? The Englishman's boss has Goldring. Isn't that enough?"

"From what I can tell, you're not a target of Faff or Wooton, who want to stop me from exposing them. If you're in the way, like at the Hampton Bays house, the Authority or Mikhail want to kill you."

Linda said, "That woman who called your cell phone in Hampton Bays—she saved us. Who could she be?"

They had reached the end of Denholm's property, marked by an old stone wall from the Revolutionary War. The land rolled downward from there, a multihued treasury of gorgeous woodland that joined the Sound. The water, calmer than the Atlantic, sparkled like fine gems in the afternoon light.

"My guess," Karen said, "is she's with the Authority. She spoke of finding my cell number by breaking into the phone company. I assume, electronically. Sounds spy-like to me. And she knew what the Authority gunman was up to. And about the GPS transmitter on the car."

"Why would she go against them?"

"Good question."

"I'd like some good answers," Linda said.

They started back toward the house. The afternoon had taken on a crimson quality. In the sunlight, the red leaves were intense corpuscles. The hawk, aloft on dragon's wings, cruised by lower.

Karen had had her fill. "Well, we're going to get them, Linda. With time and diligence. But I'm not your servant. Understand?"

"How much more 'time and diligence' will your editors allow you, Karen? Maybe Tim was right about you. I have a slender reed of hope with Frank Vere. If he can't deliver, I'm going to take other measures. I can hire first-rate investigative help."

"Well, pardon me for breathing. But you committed to me. And I committed to you. I keep my word. Do you keep yours?"

"I'm not having this conversation anymore," Linda said. "I'm going back to to the house." Meaning: alone.

Karen watched her stride purposefully across the leaf-strewn greensward. More leaves fluttered down about her. Karen followed, keeping a distance. She came upon the parked Escort and, with her hand, swept dead leaves from the hood and windshield.

Hidden within the car, the Authority's GPS device—still in place, because she had instead removed Frank's magnetic key holder hidden in the wheel well—beamed its location to a spy satellite high in orbit.

Karen glanced up and saw the sharp-beaked hawk coasting along above, silent as death.

An exhausted Jack Faff fell asleep in his chair, high above the Atlantic City boardwalk. Floors below, the slot machines twirled, the cards slapped on green felt, the dice careened. Faff dreamed of his father's grave—and his own. Solter visited him in the dream. Somewhere his mother was telling Jack to spit in the eye of a lion. And the Jersey Devil hovered in the mist.

Faff awoke just as the Jersey Devil's talons were about to clamp on his skull. He was sweating, his French shirt spotted with blotches of moisture. His chest ached more than ever; the damn doctor had said his ribs would be fine and they weren't. He cursed everyone.

The phone rang. It was his secretary, who normally didn't show exasperation. Faff hired secretaries for beauty—and coolness. "Mikhail's here, sir," she said, "asking where his money is."

"Give him an evasive answer. Tell him to go to hell."

The office door opened and, amid the secretary's outcries, Mikhail strode in. He pointed behind him to the secretary. "Hey, Jack, I think I want to date this one. Got a lot of fire."

"All you think about is your ding-dong."

"Jack, all I think about is that big money you owe me. You hear me?" He loomed over Faff like the Jersey Devil.

Faff was used to the mighty wall money built around him and wasn't intimidated. He glanced up at Mikhail. "I'll get you the money by Wednesday. Happy now?"

Mikhail withdrew. "Damn well better get the money."

As the gangster headed for the door, Faff said, "*Maybe* Wednesday."

Mikhail whirled around. "Hey, you know you are sweating like a pig? You don't get me my money and you really are going to sweat. Sweat so much you drown in it."

Karen spent the rest of the afternoon deboning a turkey, a duck, and a chicken. This was tricky work: removing bones, cutting tendons, leaving the birds' skin and flesh intact. Denholm and his boyfriend, Niles, enjoyed a novelty meal, and Karen would give them one. Terducken was on the menu, the chicken stuffed inside the duck, then stuffed inside the turkey.

Night had fallen when Denholm sailed into the kitchen, full of bonhomie. "Niles is going to be beside himself," the producer said as he eyed the main course.

"Good," Karen said, busy now preparing the dessert pastry.

"I've been dining out on the story of how we faced down those thugs of Faff's with our arrows."

"Just don't tell anyone we're dining here. Or staying here."

"The cat has my tongue," Denholm said. "Speaking of which: Linda isn't exactly chatty, is she? She was so charming when I met her, back when she was Garner Chase's squeeze. Now she's like a sullen teenager."

"Well, she's been through some real trauma. Seeing Ginny shot and all. Being targeted for death herself. That can affect morale." Karen was reluctant to unload all her feelings about Linda to Denholm, who liked life to be as cheery as his Broadway productions.

"I tried to brighten her up." Denholm sighed. "I told her to examine the wardrobe in Diana's Room if she wants something nice to wear for this evening." Princess Diana, shortly before her own tragic death, had stayed there. "Linda is rather the clothes horse. Maybe this will work."

"Worth a try. Dinner will be ready at seven."

At six-thirty, they assembled in the Blue Room, so named for its electric blue motif. Denholm had had the room done to resemble a 1930s art deco cocktail lounge, with blue walls, blue carpeting, blue upholstery, blue lampshades. The only thing not blue was the chrome trim.

Niles, a slender fellow with slicked-back hair, sat playing at the baby grand. He greeted Karen effusively. "You look lovely."

Karen, in her sweater and jeans, smiled at the fib. "Wait till you see Linda."

"What a vision," Denholm exclaimed as Linda swanned into the room. She had on a little black dress, a single-strand necklace of gold mesh, and extreme high heels.

"Diana wore that dress once and left it here," Niles said. "She wasn't one to wear something twice, now was she?"

"I'd like a large scotch, Denholm," Linda said.

Denholm signaled to the manservant, Colin, who moved toward the bar.

"Isn't Diana's Room marvelous?" Niles said. "How are you liking it?"

"It reminds me of my new place in the city, and how eager I am to return there," Linda said, watching Colin pour. She regally perched in a chrome creation of a chair, swathed in silence.

"Yikes," Niles said. He launched into a medley of his standards, such as "Stormy Weather" and "Someone to Watch Over Me." Able to charge large sums for his concerts, he restricted private recitals to Denholm's friends, A-list Hollywood celebrities, and British royalty. By the time Niles arrived at "Good Morning, Heartache," Linda was on her second scotch.

It was seven. "Time for dinner," Karen said. She and Denholm applauded Niles.

"I'm glad you permitted me, at least, to choose the wines for tonight," Denholm said to Karen as he rose from his chrome-rimmed sofa.

"Another scotch, please, Colin," Linda said.

The candelabra on the dining room table was Niles's gift to Denholm; it had belonged to Liberace. Karen carved the terducken by the pulsing candlelight.

Niles asked Karen how she had come by her culinary skills.

"My mother was such a lousy cook, I had to learn out of self-preservation," Karen said. "Ma cooks the bejesus out of any remotely edible item, with the goal of making it taste like day-old cardboard."

"You also were a food critic for that newspaper," Denholm said.

Karen smirked. "For a short time. I got bounced because I was a bit too harsh. For one overpriced bistro, I wrote: 'This restaurant is perfectly consistent. I get sick every time I eat there.'"

"Marvelous," Niles said as Colin served him his plate. "This truly is fowl play." He clapped his hand to his mouth. "I'm sorry, Linda, I didn't mean . . ."

Linda stared at him. "I better be able to trust you, Niles."

"Linda, dear," Denholm said, "of course you can trust us. We'll give you whatever you need."

She rolled around the ice in her glass. "What I need is another scotch. Colin?"

"Maybe more scotch isn't such a good idea," Niles said. Colin hesitated.

"More scotch is a great idea, Niles," Linda said. "A truly fucking marvelous idea."

"Colin, go fetch Ms. Reiner a scotch," said Denholm, more tactful than his boyfriend. "Linda, dear, we're here to support you."

"Denholm, staying here puts you in harm's way. What if our enemies show up?"

"I assure you," Denholm said, "we have a state-of-the-art security system. Anyone trying to get in a door or window will bring the police."

Linda grimaced. "Our enemies are more sophisticated than some burglar."

Niles looked about wildly. "Are we in danger? Denholm, you didn't tell me that."

"Niles," Denholm said, "calm down."

Linda accepted the fresh glass from Colin and downed half of it in a gulp. "I wouldn't be calm at all. Face facts. We're fugitives. Powerful people want us dead. And we have no plan to turn the tables on Faff, Wooton, or the Englishman. None. Zilch. Zippo."

Karen speared a green bean on her plate. "Once I get more information, I'll have a plan."

"Great." Indicating Karen with her thumb, Linda said to Denholm, "So far, her plan is that we run like rabbits."

"I don't know what your plan is," Karen shot back, "other than to whine and complain."

"What a thoughtful comment," Linda said. "If not for me, sweetie, you'd be lying dead in your Hamptons slum housing."

"Which I *thoughtfully* brought you to as a refuge and to let us keep working together. And I'm sorry if you don't like me around, but let's not forget that, if not for me, you'd be lying dead in Ginny's apartment."

They ate the meal in silence. Linda picked at her food, even though it was delicious.

The front door chimes sounded. After a moment, Colin appeared in the dining room and said, "Someone to see Ms. Glick."

"Who is that?" Denholm asked.

"Someone from the Federal Reclamation Authority."

Linda flung away her heels and barefooted up the back staircase. The Hamptons gunman's weapon lay hidden beneath the frilly pillow where Princess Diana had laid her celebrity head.

One of Linda's wealthy rat ex-boyfriends, Danny, was a gun enthusiast who taught her to shoot. She flicked off the safety and stalked back downstairs, the way she had come. In the pantry, she passed Niles, who cowered against the wall. He blanched at the sight of the gun.

"Are we in danger?" Niles croaked.

At the front door, across the marble floor of the entrance foyer, Karen stood talking earnestly to a woman dressed in a sweater, jeans, and running shoes. They were dressed alike.

The woman saw Linda and the gun. She yelped.

Karen turned around. "Put the gun down, Linda."

"Like hell. She's with the Authority."

"Put the gun down, Linda," Karen repeated, more forcefully.

"Why should I do that?" The gun, aimed at the newcomer, didn't waver in Linda's grip.

"Because we can trust her," Karen said.

"We can? How can we be sure there's not a bunch more Authority creeps outside."

"Because there aren't," Karen said.

"How can you be sure?"

"Because she's telling me the truth."

"Oh," Linda said. "She's telling the truth. The human lie detector says she's telling the truth." But Linda lowered the gun to point at the floor.

"God," the woman at the door gasped, "you could've shot me."

"This is Trixie Logan," Karen said. "She hacks computers for the Authority. Or she did. Now she has left them. She hates what Wooton is doing. She wants to help us."

"Help us?" Linda said. "What's the catch?"

The woman drew herself up. "You will aid me in recovering my daughter."

CHAPTER TWENTY-FOUR

A wind was up. Hard air shook the finely carved front door, a beast seeking entry. The threesome stood in the elegant foyer with its antiques and its ancient sentiments, a perfect triangle formed. Their hearts tripped along at different rhythms.

"I prefer to be called Logie," the Authority woman said. She gave Linda an assessing gaze. "You're even better looking than your pictures."

Linda, used to compliments on her appearance, never responded to them. Linda appraised Logie, who was a nondescript woman in her thirties with a bad haircut. An afternoon at Antonio's would do her good. She could stand to lose a little weight. "My pictures?"

"I know a lot about both of you—comes with the territory," Logie said. "Could you put the gun away, please? Makes me nervous."

"Sorry, sweetie," Linda said. "Your people tried to kill us. The gun isn't going anywhere."

"Dirk Donner—that's his name, the gunman out at the summer house—he won't try to hurt us anymore," Karen said.

"And that," Linda said, "would be why?"

Karen and Logie exchanged a glance. Linda caught the instant rapport; it puzzled and disturbed her.

"He's dead," Karen said.

"Oh." Linda's eyes narrowed. "From me hitting him with the softball bat?"

"From the bullet Wooton put through his head," Karen said. "Put the gun away, Linda."

Linda's expression grew fierce. "Hey, I was there when Ginny was shot. And I saw Flo's dead, murdered body. And I'm supposed to trust Loopy here?"

"It's Logie." Logie shook her head. "The Authority didn't kill your sisters."

"So now you're Eagle Scouts?" Linda said. "Well, what the hell was this Donner up to last night? Not trick-or-treating."

After tilting her eyes at Karen, Logie said, "I have a lot to tell you. About Dirk Donner. About a lot of stuff." She gave the short version of how she had joined Wooton's effort to obtain Goldring. "I insisted that no one be hurt as we pursued Goldring."

Linda laughed sarcastically. "Hey, Logie, you are a real saint. What's a little theft here or there? It's only somebody else's laptop. By the way, how'd you find us? Karen tossed away your GPS locator."

"Not really," Logie said. "She probably tossed away Vere's hidden magnetic key holder."

"That's simply brilliant, Karen. Good job," Linda said.

"You're safe," Logie said. "I remotely disabled the GPS after I tracked you here. It's so small you'd never spot it."

Logie drew back her shoulders. "We're safe? How did Mikhail Beria track us down in Hampton Bays? Lucky guess?"

"We think Beria has a spy in the police department," Logie said. "Maybe elsewhere. Besides, the summer house was a logical destination for Karen."

"No kidding?" Linda said. "Good choice, Karen."

"Back off, Linda," Karen said. "We need to plan, not to dump on others. Put the gun away."

Linda pulled open the drawer of a century-old French armoire and placed the weapon there. "Okay, but I'm keeping it near me. It goes where I go."

Denholm and Colin appeared in the archway from the vast living room beyond. Not Niles. Karen motioned for them to leave, which they did.

"I'm on your side," Logie said to Linda, trying for some peace.

"Uh-huh," said Linda. "Where's Goldring?"

"As we suspected, either with the Englishman or whoever he's working for," Karen said.

"You sure got a lot out of this woman in a few short moments," Linda said, with a flick of her head toward Logie.

"That's why she's such a good reporter," Logie said.

Linda pointed at Logie. "How can *you* help?"

"I can help you expose Wooton and Faff and the rotten stuff they've done," Logie said. "I know a lot and have the technical skills to learn more."

"Then help us get the Englishman," Linda said. "And Goldring."

"Get Goldring? Don't you have enough money?" Logie asked.

"Why, no, Logie dear, I don't," Linda said. "No one ever does. Goldring is Reiner property. When you were trying to steal it before to get rich, that didn't bother you?"

"Yes, it did," Logie said. "I made a bad moral compromise. First, I'd be stealing from you. Second, with Goldring, I'd be breaking the law. After all, it's an illegal hacking pro-

gram that gives illegal advance notice of what mutual funds
are going to buy."

"Karen has made the same ridiculous accusation," Linda
said. "But, as you say, you wanted the riches Goldring
brings. And you tell me I can't have it?"

"I needed the money to take care of my daughter," a defiant Logie retorted. "But I don't want it now. I'll find another way. Goldring has blood on it."

"How noble of you," Linda said.

"Ladies, ladies." Karen suggested they all sit down in
the other room. "I have lots of questions. Have you eaten,
Logie?"

Logie said, "I understand you're great in the kitchen."

Linda tossed her hair. "Yeah. She made a good little
wife."

Wind rattled the old windowpanes. Logie gobbled ravenously from the plate Karen gave her, sometimes using her
hands. She laughed when Karen told her about terducken.
She glugged two glasses of Denholm's fine wine like water
in a desert. Linda sat, magnificently long legs crossed, and
observed the Authority woman eat as Martha Stewart might
a pig foraging in her garden.

They were in the Red Room, which Denholm had mod-
eled on the White House's. The producer had advised his
good friend, Hilary Clinton, when she was First Lady, on
how to renovate the original. The wallpaper was deep
crimson, picking up the red and gold motifs in the upholstery; the draperies were sapphire blue.

"There's dessert," Karen said. "I did the cinnamon phyllo
tart shells, and had Colin buy the rum ice cream that goes
inside them."

"You are such a good cook," Logie said.

"You missed your calling, Karen," Linda said.

"You did, too," Karen said, "in the diplomatic corps."

Linda switched from sarcasm to seriousness. "I have a question of my own: how does the Englishman, this Siegfried Wolfe, fit in?"

"That's the puzzle we never solved," Logie said. She addressed the room at large, not Linda directly. "What I can't figure out is why Wolfe wanted to meet with Wooton at that restaurant. Other than to prove he could be surrounded by a crew of Authority operatives and still escape."

"Maybe to get assurance from Wooton that Goldring works as advertised," Karen said.

"His boss, evidently the one who trades under the name Simon Scratch, should know that it works," Logie said.

"Maybe Wolfe operates at arm's length from Scratch," Karen said. "Maybe Wolfe wants Goldring for himself."

Logie shrugged. "Wolfe has no facility for computers and hates the stock market. We know that because the British gave us his file."

Karen passed her hand over her face. "But who sent the fake e-mail to Albert, supposedly from Linda? Trying to paint Linda as Albert's accomplice in Goldring's theft and Flo's murder?"

"Not the Authority," Logie said.

"And who," Karen went on, "took Flo's ring from her hand when she lay in her coffin? And why? Did it happen at the medical examiner's? Or . . . hey, or at the church?"

"That's sad about Flo and her father and the ring he gave her and the incest," Logie said. She was looking at Linda now, fiercely.

"You're a first-class little snoop, aren't you?" Linda said.

"Stop it, Linda," Karen said. As Logie took another glug of wine, Karen moved to change the subject. "By chance, did you break into the Faff's Lair mainframe and come across any photos of me and Faff getting into his Jaguar?"

"The car that crashed." Logie reached for the wine bottle,

although Karen beat her to it and poured her another glass. "That's no longer on the Faff casino computer. I searched for it, believe me. They must've scrubbed it quite thoroughly."

"Speaking of your wonderful facility with computers," Linda said evenly, "did you run across my sister when she was in the Authority training program?"

"I spoke to her class but didn't meet her," Logie said, speaking to Karen, not Linda. "Flo was a discipline problem. Her mimmicking her superiors wasn't appreciated. She punched a fellow student, female, over some petty comment involving her father. Had a crush on an instructor, male, whom she stalked. Then she broke into the Authority server to lower the test grades of classmates she hated. A troubled woman. They bounced her. Got a conviction on her."

"We have a lot to accomplish, starting tomorrow," Karen said.

"Oh, joy," Linda said. "Karen has a plan."

"Yes, I do. So listen to it."

Wooton noticed it in their faces, from a twist of the mouth, a narrowing of the eye, a hesitancy of speech. He had lost that vital quality. That towering sense of awe. An awe that he required. They behaved as might well-reared children whose father had gone mad—they obeyed, after a pause or two, and might call the grandparents if he really crossed the line.

"There must be some way to track her down," Wooton thundered. "She's not a trained field operative." The large pizza sat next to his computer, cooling like molten glue.

"We understand that, Director," Spinelli said with care. "But nothing has popped. She only used her credit card for the vehicle rental. Not for a hotel room, where we could get her. She hasn't tried to contact her husband, who is out on bail. She hasn't boarded an airplane, a train, or a bus, as far as the NYPD can tell. We have to assume she has remained in the New York area."

"I must conclude she has gone over to join Wolfe," Wooton said. "As such, she is dangerous to us. And to national security. A hacker of her talents. Lord knows how Wolfe would use her."

Spinelli had the gaunt, stiletto-eyed look of a guerilla who had spent years in the jungle, fighting for a cause. "Director," Spinelli ventured, "could you at least tell us what exact terror threat Wolfe poses?"

"He killed two of our men and crippled another for life. Isn't that sufficient, right there?"

"We want revenge as much as you do, sir. But if Wolfe is plotting a terrorist act, giving us a clue would help."

Wooton gave Spinelli his best telepathic stare. Then, "You're buying that nonsense—that terrorist disinformation—about the Reiners's computer being some kind of stock market oracle. And I want to get my hands on it for my own selfish ends. Nonsense, man. No one can predict the market. The laptop has the plans for a terror operation. In code. That's why it's vital to acquire the thing."

"I see," said Spinelli, who plainly didn't.

"That's why Ms. Logan is so dangerous on the other side. That's why we have to find her. Find that damn reporter, Glick. Find Wolfe. And find the damn computer. Do I make myself clear?"

"You do, Director." Spinelli turned to go, but stopped. "The cremation of Senior Operative Donner occurred earlier today. How would you like the ashes disposed of?"

"Bring them to me. They will be put in a place of honor. Even though Dirk Donner took his own life, he really did die for his country. He sacrificed both his sanity and his life."

"Very well, Director." He headed off and halted again. "Oh, almost forgot. Senior Operative Erder is holding for you."

Wooton watched Spinelli march out of the command post. He could have offered Spinelli the deal that Donner got, cut him in on the Goldring boodle. He simply didn't know if he could trust Spinelli. That man had no appetites and went to church a lot. How could mere wealth tempt him?

"Ms. Erder," Wooton said into the receiver, "how is our young charge this evening?"

"Fine," Erder said warily. "We made fudge, and we did some coloring. Alexandra wants a computer for games, but we don't have one." She cleared her throat. "How much longer do I have to play babysitter?"

"Not long." He described how Logie had deserted. "I appreciate how you've taken charge of Ms. Logan's daughter, although the child is no longer of use to us. We will get rid of her."

"What do you mean, get rid of her?"

Wooton quickly reassured Erder. "No, no, no. We'll put her up for adoption. She can't go back to that ne'er-do-well father. He's headed for jail. And her mother has joined the terrorists."

"Don't get me wrong," Erder said. "I resent the fact that I drew this duty because I'm a woman. And I want to be back in the field."

"When you're done, you can come work directly for me again. You were good at management."

"With all due respect, sir," she said, "I wouldn't want to end up a suicide, like from that small pistol you carry."

Sweat bubbled up on Wooton's rind of neck. A subordinate had made him sweat? "What do you mean, Ms. Erder?"

"Oh, nothing, Director. Will that be all for tonight?"

Seething, Wooton returned the phone to its cradle. What

savage impertinence. When Spinelli returned, carrying a small container before him like a burnt offering, Wooton utterly lost his composure. "Give me that and get out. Now."

Spinelli registered no emotion at the volcanic outburst. He unflappably deposited the container on Wooton's desk. "The ashes are still hot, Director." And he left.

Wooton grabbed the container and, belly wagging under his vest, quick-stepped across the room. The container was almost too hot to hold.

He dumped Donner's ashes in the toilet. "Incompetent," he said, and returned to his pizza.

"We're not staying here beyond tonight," Karen said. "We have three things to do. First, we have to rescue Logie's daughter. Second, we have to expose Faff and Wooton, and stop them before they can cause more harm. Third, we have to find Goldring, Wolfe, and Simon Scratch."

"I have some good hacker software out in the all-terrain vehicle I rented," Logie said. "That can help."

"Dare I ask?" Linda said. "Does someone have an actual idea how we accomplish all these objectives?"

Logie pulled a paper from her pocket and unfolded it on the red carpet. Kneeling over it, she pointed. "I got this from an Authority database. This is a map of the safe house in the New Jersey Pine Barrens where they're holding my daughter. It's in the middle of nowhere."

Karen crouched beside her. "This is pretty detailed."

Linda did not join them on the floor. The last time she had sprawled on a floor was with a corporate titan who insisted. "People like Dirk Donner are guarding her?"

Logie said, "One operative is. A very good one named Gwen Erder." She told how Erder had killed two knife-wielding al Qaeda terrorists with her hands. "They thought she was merely a girl."

Linda said, "But this means she can take care of the three of us just as easily."

"That's why we have to be smart," Karen said. "You're a crucial part of this, Linda."

Linda held up a well-manicured finger. "Hold on. Isn't this putting the cart before the horse? Once Wooton is exposed, we can free your daughter and nobody has to take any chances getting shot dead by Lara Croft in East Nowhere, New Jersey."

"Linda, you want my help, we get my daughter first," Logie said. "That's my condition."

"Entirely reasonable," Karen said. "Are you with us, Linda?" She squinted at her. "Linda?"

"If I must. I'm dubious."

"You don't have a daughter," Logie said. She gave Linda a laser-burning stare.

Karen said, "Okay. Now, about Wooton and Faff. I've got an idea that's going to involve your skills, Logie. And I need to talk to my friend, Frank Vere, to set up this up." She told them her plan.

Linda leaned forward. "You really think that will work?"

"That's a terrific plan, Karen," Logie said.

"Is it?" Linda said. "Risky and far-fetched, yes. Terrific?"

Karen continued. "I have a hunch that Our Lady of Perpetual Suffering Church also bears examination. Flo said she was headed there the night she died. Her 'friendship ring' from her father went missing, maybe at the medical examiner's, but maybe at the church. And that Father Finnegan gives me a bad feeling."

"That twerpy priest is a criminal mastermind?" Linda said. "Come on, Karen."

"He and his church were the beneficiaries of Flo's will," Karen said. "What's that about?"

Linda uncoiled herself from her seat and headed away.

"Beats me. I'm going to bed. In case we have any visitors to-night, I'm keeping the gun with me."

"Everyone get a good night's sleep," Karen said. "We move out early tomorrow for New Jersey. Erder will be tough. Let's hope we don't run into the Jersey Devil, too."

"Karen," Logie said. "What's the Jersey Devil?"

CHAPTER TWENTY-FIVE

Autumn's colors don't come to the Pine Barrens, where nothing changes. On this windy Tuesday morning, the vast ranks of evergreens swayed all the way to the horizon. The battleship-like clouds scudded quickly through the sky as if in panicky retreat.

Karen, Linda, and Logie were by Logie's rented ATV, which was parked in a firebreak near the safe house. The strong wind flapped their hair around. With the binoculars she had borrowed from Denholm, Karen scanned the house down the hill. There, through the bobbing firs, she could see a one-story clapboard dwelling with a satellite dish on the roof and a Jeep Cherokee out front.

"No movement," she said. "Although the Jeep sure suggests someone is home."

"Isn't there a better way to do this?" Linda said.

"We're going through with our plan," Karen said.

"*Our* plan?" Linda said with asperity.

Logie said, "We must be careful. They have sensors in a radius of fifty meters from the house. Only when we've distracted Erder can we penetrate that perimeter."

"Wait," Karen said. "Movement."

"What is it?" Logie said eagerly.

"In the kitchen window. A child. Seems to be seated at a table. Someone, an adult, is bringing her a plate. And a glass."

Logie hovered near Karen. "Is it really her?"

"That's the girl whose picture you carry."

Karen passed her the binoculars. Logie jammed them against her eyes. Her lips quivered. "Sweet princess," she said. She lowered the binoculars, then, through her numb grip, dropped them. She covered her eyes with the crook of an elbow. Her shoulders shook.

Karen placed her arm around Logie.

"Isn't she precious?" Logie said in a small voice.

"She's precious," Karen said.

Linda picked up the binoculars at Logie's feet. She trained them on the house. "Very cute," she said matter-of-factly. "So I'm risking my life for cute. Great."

"Shut your entitled mouth." Furious, Logie took a step toward Linda. "I know you only care about yourself. But that's my daughter there."

"Guys, don't do this," Karen said.

Under Logie's smoldering stare, Linda's face turned into a haughty mask. "I guess I have no choice." She turned to Karen. "Are the keys in the ignition of that rattletrap car you drive?" When Karen nodded, Linda sashayed off to the Escort, parked twenty yards away beneath some trees.

"Why is she such a bitch?" Logie asked Karen.

"Because she's not in charge," Karen said. "She can't stand not being in control. And let's face it: this Gwen Erder is a trained killer."

* * *

The old Escort bounced along the unpaved road leading up to the safe house. At the wheel, Linda tried to quell her fear by distracting herself with fuming over what ninnies Karen and Logie were. As the safe house drew nearer, the roadside pines moved to and fro like crazed sentinels. She parked beside the Cherokee and waited a moment. What would Gwen Erder look like?

Linda drew in a deep breath. Her heart had hit a marathoner's rate. They hadn't been able to see Erder well through the window.

When she twisted the ignition off, the car shuddered spasmodically. Linda opened the car door and, as she stepped out, stumbled. The hard metal knocked against her side. In a deep pocket, within the L.L. Bean ski jacket Denholm had lent her, lay the gun Karen had told her to leave behind.

Time to be cool, she told herself. Poised. Self-possessed. She walked toward the house, as the hornet buzz of anxiety sounded in her head.

The front door opened. A black rectangle lay beyond, impossible to see into.

Linda halted and gawked at the empty doorway, as if it held the wicked and supernatural.

A form stirred in the dark doorframe. Took shape. Faded in, faded out of view. Then nothing.

Linda swallowed. What was going on?

Gwen Erder strode out the door with the purpose of an athlete taking the field. Despite the fall chill, she had on a tank top that showed her well-muscled frame. Otherwise, with her good jeans, tasteful earrings, and smartly cut hair that the wind ruffled, she could pass for a soccer mom. Sort of. There was an undefinable earthy quality about her. Certainly womanly, certainly powerful.

"What can I do for you?" Erder asked, her tone friendly.

Erder couldn't be concealing a gun in that outfit.

"I'm lost. Can you tell me how to get to Atlantic City?"

"You must've taken a wrong turn."

"I know. I'm late for an appointment. If you could help me, I'd really appreciate it."

Erder was still standing too close to the house. "This sounds hard, but isn't." She gave a spiel of lefts and rights and landmarks to return to the Garden State Parkway.

"That's where the trouble started, the Parkway," Linda said. "Listen, I'll never remember all that you told me."

"Let me get a pencil and paper in the house."

"No, no, no. I, uh, have those in the glove compartment."

"Not a problem." Erder's panther stride moved her in an instant to Linda's side. They headed for the car. Erder walked as Linda did in a social setting, with grace and utter command. And she was moving away from the house.

As Mr. Escort bounced up to the front of the house, Karen and Logie sprinted for the rear, gambling on the timing. When someone breached the perimeter, Logie knew, a sensor would flash a message inside. A beep would sound at the control panel. Three beeps at once, in their case, for Karen, Logie, and the Escort. They counted on Erder not picking up the difference. Karen and Logie flattened themselves against the house's rear wall and waited.

"There goes Erder out the front," Karen said.

Karen whipped over to the back door and gripped the knob. Thankfully, the door wasn't locked. She had been prepared to break the glass pane, at the risk of Erder's hearing it, to undo the lock by reaching inside. She opened the door and let Logie in first.

A child with Logie's eyes sat at the kitchen table eating a

sandwich, a half-consumed glass of milk before her. Those eyes widened. The sandwich hit the plate.

"It's Mommy, sweet princess," Logie managed.

"Mommy?" Tears welled in the little girl's eyes.

Mother and daughter rushed together over the linoleum tile. Logie bent over and embraced Alexandra. They sobbed together.

"Come on," Karen said. "We gotta go."

Linda spread the roadmap on the Escort's too-hot hood, holding it down so the wind wouldn't lift it. "Okay, you say I should go one exit south of where I left the Parkway."

"I'd think someone like you would be driving a better car than this," Erder said, still all friendly.

Someone like you? "Well, it's what I can afford." Linda leaned over the map.

"But that weapon you have hidden in your jacket is really top of the line," Erder said, as pleasantly as she might appreciate Linda's choice of clothing.

Linda froze. "What weapon?"

Erder plucked the gun from Linda's jacket with superhuman speed. She examined it and said, "Looks like Dirk Donner's."

"I beg your pardon," Linda said, attempting to summon indignation, where fright was more apropos. "That's for my own protection."

"Silencers are illegal. No, it's Donner's, for sure. What a pig he was, may he rest in peace."

"Give that back to me, please."

Erder unscrewed the silencer, slipped it into her pocket, and shoved the barrel of the gun into the waistband of her jeans, its butt hard against her bare, muscled stomach. "A battered old Ford Escort? See, I figured Linda Reiner is a BMW kind of a girl."

"I . . ." Linda was transfixed by the gun, which was as far from her as Mars.

"They snuck in the back of the house, didn't they?" Erder said. "Not a bad plan."

"Well . . . I . . . well . . ." Linda lost her hold on the map, which went cartwheeling away in the wind.

"You don't normally get flustered, do you, Linda? Can't blame you." She turned to the house. "I better go back inside before this gets out of hand."

Linda clutched Erder's shoulder. "Don't."

In a millisecond, Linda found herself lying on the pine needle-strewn sand, dazed. And Erder was going through the front door. Linda weakly tried to call out a warning to Karen but the wind drowned her out.

Logie hoisted Alexandra. "You're getting to be such a big girl," she said.

"Mommy," the girl cried out.

"Welcome to New Jersey."

Karen whirled around to find a woman with a gun butt protruding from her jeans.

"Look, Gwen," Alexandra shrieked in delight, "Mommy's here. Mommy came to get me."

"I know all about your Mommy," Gwen Erder said. "She's very good at computers. She was teaching you about computers, wasn't she, Alexandra?"

"I like computers," Alexandra said.

"And this lady is Karen Glick," Erder said. "She's a reporter. She digs out stories about bad people and prints them in her magazine, to stop them from doing more bad things."

"She's Mommy's friend," Alexandra said.

"Let me keep my daughter," Logie said.

"It's what's right," Karen said.

Erder patted her denimed hip, near the gun butt. "Kingman Wooton would not be pleased if that happened."

"Let me keep my daughter," Logie said, more shrilly.

Alexandra looked scared. Logie stroked her daughter's hair and put the girl's head against her chest. "You don't have to do what Wooton says."

Erder smiled. "This is true. His days are numbered, once Karen writes about him and that business about the stock market-predicting computer. The president, at whose pleasure he serves, will accelerate his retirement. And throw him in the clink." She crossed the kitchen and rubbed Alexandra's back. "And there's not a chance he'll keep this little muffin from her Mommy."

"Really?" Logie said.

"Hey, I never liked Wooton," Erder said. "He's been at this for too long. Got a bad case of hubris. Then the wife addled his judgment. Not good. He wanted Alexandra to be put up for adoption. I'll simply tell him that's what happened."

"What's adoption?" Alexandra said.

"Nothing," Logie said. Then to Erder, "God bless you."

"I served as the Authority's chief of operations for five years, but couldn't stand Wooton, so I transferred back to the field," Erder said. "I liked that story about the Billionaire Boys Club, Karen. It's good when arrogant, powerful people get theirs."

"Thanks." Karen craned her neck to look back through the house. "Where's Linda?"

"Oh, I gave her a little martial arts demo. She'll be fine. No bruises, which is important to a chick like Linda."

"So we can go?" Logie said.

"Let me say good-bye to Alexandra first," Erder said. "We've gotten to be good pals." Logie put her down and Erder hugged her. Then Logie told her to go fetch her belongings.

"Did Dirk Donner really commit suicide?" Erder asked as the child scampered off.

"Of course not. I was there," Logie said. "Wooton shot him."

"Mommy," Alexandra said from the doorway, "Daddy said you did suicide. What's suicide?"

Wednesday morning moved over Manhattan in a swirl of fall winds that made overhead traffic signals move like pendulums. The air was brisk and brought a skin-bracing blast of winter. The gloomy sky spoke of hard weather coming in.

"What's all this about global warming?" Friday said. "Is that a crock, or is that a crock?"

The gorgeous secretary ignored him. How did they grow women who looked as good as her? Friday had given up trying not to ogle.

The phone chirped. She listened for an instant. "Mr. Faff can see you now," she said.

"What, he's been blind?" said Friday, who had been waiting for an hour. "Never mind."

Friday entered Faff's inner sanctum and traipsed along the exquisite carpeting, swiveling his head to drink in the artwork and the wall photos of the great man and his renowned pals. Faff was seated at his fine old desk, scowlingly intent on the computer before him. He was as handsome as he was in his picture on the billboards advertising his casino. But in those, he was smiling.

Not one to play Faff's status games and wait for the great man to acknowledge him, Friday dumped himself in a chair unbidden. "Hey, Faff, that's Disraeli's desk, right? Did you know Benjamin Disraeli invented the word 'millionaire'? Doesn't that rock your world? Especially since, according to that reporter, Glick, you're broke."

Faff allowed his gaze to lift from the computer.

"Detective, I don't have time for this." Faff consulted his watch, which gave off a glint of gold even on a gloomy day. "In fact, I have a meeting."

"You bet your bippy you have a meeting. You're in it right now." Friday shrugged his burly shoulders.

"What can I do for you, Detective?" Faff said with a put-upon expression.

"Your brother, the screwup. Solter. He's been gone missing for a while. People are starting to wonder. And I'm here to wonder in an official capacity."

"Did Karen Glick put you up to this? If she did, her legal problems are only beginning."

Friday poked a tongue in the side of his cheek. "I put me up to this. One of the prominent citizens of our fair town has done a vanishing act. He's your flesh and blood. Aren't you worried?"

"Not a bit. I fired Solter for incompetence. He's probably licking his wounds down in the islands. Probably with a woman after his money. With luck, there won't be a paternity suit. My brother, as you say, is a screwup."

"Well, by the power vested in me by the city of New York, I am hereby commencing a missing persons investigation concerning your brother. We're gonna be asking a bunch of questions of you and your people. Both here and in Atlantic City, where he last was seen alive. Okay by you?"

Faff processed the information beneath a stormy brow. "What? Atlantic City's not in your jurisdiction."

"Good thinking," Friday said. "We got a special deal with the New Jersey State Police, who'll handle that end. Not that I don't trust the A.C. cops or nothing. But I *don't* trust them."

"You really must be going," Faff said, making no move to rise and bid him farewell with a handshake, firm or otherwise.

Friday swung to his feet. "Yeah, I must. Say, the state cops will want to ask you about those Russian hoodlums on your casino payroll as security. Did you realize that employing members of organized crime can lead to the loss of your gambling license? That could ruin your whole day."

"We briefly employed some temporary help and they gave us false credentials. I have no knowledge of criminal affiliation. But we fired them. No harm done. We're clean."

"Clean, huh?" Friday nodded and steered for the door across the richly woven carpet.

As he reached the door, Mikhail Beria burst in, followed by the secretary, her aplomb gone. "I'm sorry, Mr. Faff, but . . ."

"Hey, Jack, you bastard, where's my damn money?" the gangster yelled. "Today's payday. You promised."

Friday stuck out a hand, which Beria automatically took. "As I live and breathe, Mikhail Beria. Been following you for a good while now. This Faff character here deserves a hard time." He clapped Beria on his leather-clad back and edged past, winking at the secretary.

"What did you say?" Mikhail called after him.

Friday turned around. "Were you, by any chance, wearing a ghost costume on the West Side subway Saturday? And sticking a knife in this nice fella named Major Darcy?"

"What did you say?"

"Never mind, we'll talk about that another time—you got a meeting with Jack Faff here," Friday said. "Catch you later."

"Who's he?" Mikhail said as Friday popped through the door.

"A cop, you idiot. I told you to stay out of sight."

"You are not giving me orders with no money paid. Now, where is my money? No more dumbass delay crap."

Faff tapped a key on his computer. "You have to wait. Until Monday. Small cash flow problem."

"I've had it up to my ears, and you, you're gonna get it up the ass, you cheap bastard, no good guy with small dick."

The secretary stood frozen in her loveliness.

"Watch you language," Faff said.

"You watch yours," Mikhail said.

After Mikhail tromped out, the secretary said, "I'm sorry, sir. He just barged in."

As she left, a pain spread through his chest. He massaged it, to no avail. If he couldn't rely on Mikhail and his men anymore, he'd have to use his own security guys. But they were an even bigger bunch of buffoons than the Russians.

Intent on ignoring the pain, Faff turned back to his computer.

Then he opened the next e-mail and found a still greater dilemma. "Holy God," he said, and wondered what to do.

Amid the tomb-like silence of the New York command post, Wooton finished his reuben sandwich. The fat globules did the danse macabre through his arteries. Ordered from the local deli, the reuben had great zest. He wished he did.

There was no one else in the room. No Logie working her databases. No Donner setting up street operations. His own computer blinked before him, next to the telephone.

He had been hovering over the telephone all afternoon. Wanting to call home. Fearing that she would be in. Fearing worse that she wouldn't. How she used to look at him, years back.

Wooton dextrously tapped out his home number.

Erica picked up on the first ring. "Hello?"

He could say nothing.

"Mick?"

He snapped off the connection.

Spinelli entered the room, and Wooton barely heard

what he said. "Director, Glick must have disabled the GPS device on her car. We can't pick up the signal."

"What's that?"

Spinelli repeated his news.

"Find her. Now. Let's go. Hurry."

Spinelli refused to scurry away. When he had sauntered out, Wooton looked at the computer. The newly arrived e-mail made him catch his breath.

"That's incredible."

"What do you mean, they could be anywhere?" The priest's face was pressed up to the confessional screen.

"Father," Wolfe said with maddening nonchalance, "I can't even say where Ginny Reiner is."

"What are you talking about? She's in the morgue, awaiting burial. You killed her, right?"

"I was chatting with Satan last night and he wouldn't let on whether Ginny Reiner has been dispatched to hell. He can be such a tease. Flo Reiner is a good bet for hell. Linda Reiner . . . Ah, father, you know my feelings about Linda. Measure her for a halo in the afterlife."

"Well, put her in the damn afterlife. There's no excuse for letting Karen and Linda get away."

Wolfe chuckled patronizingly. "Linda Reiner will be coming to see you soon about Ginny's burial. It won't do to delay the funeral forever. I'll be ready then."

The priest's clerical collar was too tight, as if it didn't belong around this particular throat. "I'm sick of the delays."

Wolfe smiled as a shark does before striking. "Wooton and Faff have made the assignment more complex. As they thrash about, they drive Karen and Linda further into hiding."

"What are you saying?"

"That if I had a little extra incentive, I might track down Karen and Linda much sooner."

"Outrageous. I'm paying you a fortune. And I'm sick of waiting."

"Priests who go to hell are very unhappy there, Satan tells me. Talk about waiting an eternity, father."

"You want more money? Is that the holdup? Okay—half a million more, with two fifty in your account today, the rest upon completion. What does it take?"

"I'll take that. I'm no socialist."

"Kill them, damn you. Before the week is out."

CHAPTER TWENTY-SIX

Linda wandered through the topiary of the rooftop garden. Most of the flowers were gone, but a few roses clung stubbornly to the trellis despite the wind's buffeting. She reached the parapet and leaned against it, huddling the L.L. Bean jacket around her. The roofs of Tribeca spread out below, ready for the next rainfall.

She saw Karen approaching and looked out over the cityscape, uneager to talk with her.

"You okay?" Karen said, seemingly solicitous about Linda's run-in with Gwen Erder.

Linda could tell that Karen and Logie found it funny that Erder had dumped her in the dirt. "I'm wonderful. When I'm not scared, I'm bored. Like now."

"We've been playing video games with Alexandra. You should join in the fun."

"Playing Donkey Kong and singing nursery rhymes— sounds like a blast." One song they sang in particular

grated on Linda—it included the line: "The more we stay together, the happier we'll be."

"Logie is putting her down for a nap. I'm going into the
office."

"Wait," Linda said. "Let me get this straight. You're telling
me to stay holed up here to stay safe, then you go off galli-
vanting around the city."

"Linda, I have lots to do. My editor says trouble is brew-
ing on the political front at the magazine. If I don't calm
them down at the office, I might not be allowed to proceed
with the story. I will be very careful out on the streets."

"Hold on. This doesn't make sense. Frank Vere, one of the
greatest reporters of all time, is on this story with you. How
on earth could your higher-ups cancel a story that Vere is
doing?"

Karen took a deep breath. "Well, Frank isn't supposed to
be helping me with this. But he is behind the scenes. So in
the eyes of the editors, I'm on my own. And if I don't
deliver—"

"What the hell? You never told me this. You led me to believe that Frank Vere was powering the whole operation.
And now I hear that it's just little you?"

Hell, she had a point. But Karen was sick of trying to
deal with her. "Let me bite my tongue and leave. You see, *little me* doesn't like to keep people waiting."

"Can I believe anything you say? Like, I find it impossible
to believe that this place belongs to Welles, the world's richest person. It's decorated no better than a Motel Six. The
furniture is from Ethan Allen, for God's sake."

"Sorry it doesn't meet your standards," Karen said. "Frank
Vere arranged this for us. Now, you try to be nice to Logie.
She is a good person."

After Karen left, Linda saw Logie coming toward her,
past the bare flowerbeds.

"How are you feeling?" Logie asked, suffused with motherly warmth after snuggling her child in for a nap.

"Never better," Linda said with bite.

"No bruises showing. That's good." Logie, at Karen's behest, was trying for a truce. "Aren't you cold out here? Come inside and I'll make you some coffee."

Dark clouds, poised high above, gave occasional rumbles, but nothing more.

Linda welcomed the overture, in her fashion. "Make me an espresso. I'm dying to go to Starbucks, but that's not an option."

"Uh, Welles doesn't have that kind of a machine. Only an old Mr. Coffee."

"Well, forget it then." Seeing she was acting ungracious, Linda said, "When this is over, I'm taking you to Antonio's. The best hairdresser in the city. Bar none."

"You don't like my hair?"

"You'll thank me."

"In other words, no." Logie hesitated. Then, "When Alexandra wakes up, we'll read *Mother Goose*. Frank Vere thoughtfully sent a bunch of kid stuff here. Maybe you can join in with us."

"That's not my scene," said Linda, who viewed children as little better than rabid ferrets.

"Oh, I'm sorry I asked," Logie said, resentment creeping into her tone. "Alexandra can read."

"What an accomplishment."

The sky offered a dyspeptic groan.

"Alexandra adores Karen," Logie said pointedly. "After she's through at the office, we're meeting her in Central Park, at the Alice in Wonderland statuary. Karen told Alexandra all about this: Alice, the March Hare, the Dormouse. She's seen the Disney video. Alexandra is excited. You could join us, but I suppose that's not your scene, either"

Linda brushed windblown hair out of her face. "You're going out, too? And taking the kid?"

"I hope the rain doesn't come."

"Logie, sweetie, aren't we supposed to be in serious danger? And you want to go tripping down the sidewalk singing nursery rhymes?"

"We're taking a cab. No one will see us. Alexandra needs an outing. I don't want her turning stir crazy. I know I feel that way and we've only been here a day."

Linda pulled the gun out of the jacket. "Take this, then. Erder gave the thing back to me. She felt sorry for hitting me. Sort of."

Logie's mouth hung open and she took a step back. "No. No. No. No more guns. Not after what I saw Wooton do. No."

"Don't be stupid."

"I'll put my faith in Karen."

"You will?" Linda said. "Well, in her nice plans, I don't see how we are going to catch this Wolfe. Or most important, get back my Goldring. Can you think of a way to find them?" When Logie didn't reply, she added, "My patience is growing thin. Maybe I should get out of here, too. This place is a dump."

"I haven't been in a place this nice since my honeymoon," Logie said.

Linda angrily watched Logie head back through the garden.

"Still nothing," Skeen said. "This story is going nowhere. Time to cut the cord."

"Gene," an exasperated Eudell said, "have you been listening to one word Karen has said? Logan, the Authority lady, has a lot of what we want. She even saw Wooton kill Donner."

"What I heard," a petulant Skeen said, "is that some

woman has come forward making reckless accusations. But pardon me, I don't see her here today. Where is she? Does she truly exist?"

Karen sat staring malevolently across the conference table at Skeen. "She's with her young daughter. They've been separated. I didn't see the point of bringing her here now."

"And when will that great day be?" Skeen said.

"This is getting too drawn out," Christian said. "Gene is right."

"When she's ready," Karen said. "Shouldn't you trust your own reporters?"

Christian motioned for Karen to be quiet. The managing editor spoke as if she weren't present. "The fact remains that Karen Glick faces very serious charges in New Jersey, and her hearing is next week. Rather than have her continue to roam around the country, we need her in court, where the case against her is not good for us. And, in fact, is rather strong in Faff's favor."

"That tape recording she played us from a man purporting to be Major Darcy?" Skeen said. "The man on the tape could be anybody."

"You really think she's making up all this?" Eudell said. "In case you didn't notice, Karen almost was killed by the assassin who shot Ginny Reiner. And then there was the business with the fake cops who tried to capture her. Led by Dirk Donner."

"We have no hard evidence on anything, such as that Glick was the target of the assassin," Skeen said. "And what happened at the precinct is murky—NYPD is releasing no details."

Karen's hands were balled into fists. "As I've said in the past, Gene: they ought to arrest you for impersonating an editor."

"This is gross insubordination," Skeen squawked.

A presence loomed in the doorway of the conference room. They went mute by instinct.

Bill McIntyre gave his snaggle-toothed grin. "We-e-e-e-e-e-ell, I got to have me a little chat with Karen. Y'all mind if I borrow her for a spell?"

Karen silently walked out into the newsroom with Bill. At the sight of the editor-in-chief, the guys stopped chucking around the football. Wendy cruised past with her parrot, who was reciting a dirty limerick; the parrot went quiet before the final line. The Three Musketeers were arguing over the latest market news; they, too, shut up.

Bill threw an avuncular arm around Karen's shoulders as they moved over the ugly industrial carpeting, dozens of eyes on them. "See, we're in a bit of a bind. Top management at Templar Media, who sign our paychecks, is in a snit about the Faff auto wreck charges. My managing editor and a senior editor think you're making up wild stories, trying to ride the Reiner sisters' tragedy and divert attention from your Faff problem. And I got no solid facts to prove you're in the right. And we've given you a lot of time to provide them. What would you do in my situation?"

"Give me a little more time."

"Today's Friday," Bill said. "We're putting the magazine out today. You got a court date in Altantic City on Tuesday. I need you to vindicate yourself real quick-like. Like by Monday. In time for us to run your story on how you were right. And it better be airtight. Got me?"

Karen watched him walk away as the newsroom held it breath. "I got you," she said.

A few rain specks tickled their faces, but Logie pumped up a smile for Karen, who seemed lost in thought. "I know the rain will hold off for us," she said.

Karen smiled back, wanting to shake away her moodiness, and took Alexandra's hand. "Check out those sail-boats, Alexandra."

The little girl jumped in delight. They were drawing near to the Conservatory Water—a long basin where young and old gathered around to radio-direct elaborate model ships, the sails of which caught the November wind and scooted merrily along. Occasional raindrops made small circles on the water's surface. Karen and Logie pointed out different boats to Alexandra: Chinese junks, Yankee clippers, Span-ish galleons. The three of them strolled past the lip of the basin, the adults holding Alexandra's hands.

"That Linda," Logie started. Then, with a glance at Alexandra, "Let's talk about her later."

"Much later," Karen said.

The bronze statuary awaited them to the north of the wa-ter, with a tangle of nearly leafless woodland beyond. Alexandra pulled free of them and bolted for it. She clam-bered up on a giant mushroom and sat next to Alice.

"Do you recognize all the characters?" her mother asked.

Giggling, Alexandra named each of them except for the Cheshire Cat. "There's a kitty, but he's not the Cheshire Cat cuz he's not smiling," the girl said, pointing to the sober cat statue.

"He only does in the Disney movie," Karen said. "This Cheshire Cat isn't smiling because he's afraid it might rain. Kitties don't like to get wet."

Alexandra nodded, as if great wisdom had been im-parted. "I like cats," she said. "Daddy said he'd get me a cat, but he didn't."

"I'll get you one soon," Logie said.

As Alexandra crawled over the mushroom, Logie turned to Karen and said, "So we both married charming, sexy guys, who turned out to be no good."

"I'm sure good men are out there for us somewhere."

"How about that Frank Vere? He's single."

"For a reason." Karen laughed. Then she thought about how Frank looked at her sometimes, with this adolescent yearning.

"You're worried about tomorrow, aren't you?" Logie said. "It'll work. It is a fine plan."

"If it does work . . ." Karen examined her feet. "You really don't mind if we write about you and your husband, Jeff, and the Authority? You realize that makes you vulnerable to prosecution, along with your husband? In addition to tax charges, they could go after you for using government resources for your own gain."

"I did prepare the joint returns, even though I thought our information was genuine. Maybe I should have known better. And yeah, with Wooton, I broke all kinds of laws and rules mounting a fake counterterrorism action. We plainly were conspiring to commit theft. Maybe they'll throw the book at me. But the truth must come out. Isn't that what you believe?" Her eyes blinked.

Karen folded her hands. "Yes, that's what I believe. I don't want you hurt, though."

"I'll stand up for—" Logie looked at the statuary. "Where's Alexandra?"

They circled the large bronze work. No sign of the child. They both called out her name. They anxiously scanned the boat basin for her. Nothing.

"Maybe she went up the hill," Karen said, gesturing at the wooded expanse that spread beyond the statuary.

They trotted up the slope, calling "Alexandra," swiveling their heads in an effort to spot her. The trees and their stark branches spread before them.

At the top of the hill, amid an outcropping of dark, primeval rock, they saw Alexandra. Mikhail Beria kneeled beside her, one hand over her mouth, the other around her twig of an arm. Her eyes were wide with fear. Amid his crazed, moss-like beard, Mikhail's sharp teeth grinned.

"Let her go," Karen and Logie shouted, as one.

Mikhail's beast grin widened. "You gonna call the cops? They'll take a while. I can bring out my knife real quick and you better go buy a small casket. Or I can twist off her head with my hands."

Her fists ready, Karen stalked toward the Russian. "You hurt her and I will kill you."

Alexandra's sobs came from beneath Mikhail's paw. Her eyes spilled tears, which trickled over his knuckles.

"Don't harm my daughter," Logie pleaded.

"You'll kill me, huh?" Mikhail said to Karen. "I do not need a knife to tear you to rags."

"Let the girl go," Karen said with menace.

Mikhail guffawed. "I will if you sit down and talk to me."

"Whatever. I'll do it. Only let the girl go."

"Okay. As a good will business thing." He released Alexandra. She ran for her mother, who grabbed her in a hug. "Now, you and me talk business, Karen Glick."

Karen said to Logie, "Take her home."

"But, Karen," she said.

"Please. Now. Do what I say." Karen watched Logie as she carried Alexandra away and looked back at Mikhail reluctantly.

The gangster sat on a rock and patted the spot beside him. "Now for business. Come sit and let me show you."

Still poised for action, Karen perched next to him. "What the hell do you want?"

Mikhail held up his hands. "See, I got no knife out. I could kill you easy, like you deserve. Instead, how about a little transaction?"

"Faff sent you?"

The Russian preceded his answer with a loud snort. "Faff? Tiny midget shitball, he stiffed me money he owes me. And he fired my guys on his casino payroll. I'll do no more business with that no-good deadbeat guy. Here." He withdrew an envelope from a pocket within his leather jacket. "You are going to like this."

Karen took the envelope and opened it. Inside was a batch of photos. She thumbed through them. Evidently taken from a video camera, they were high-resolution shots of a certain night in October at Faff's Lair. The date and time were printed in the lower-right corner. The photos showed the Jaguar, its plates visible. And Major Darcy, holding the passenger-side door. For Karen. And Jack Faff, jumping behind the wheel. And the sportscar zooming into the rainy night.

"Wow," Karen said.

"It is what you want, no? We took it from surveillance data. Before they washed it out of the computer, my men were doing security at the casino. I told them to get photos in case I wanted to make Jack Faff look like a piece of crap. And I do."

"How did you find me here in the park today?"

"I figured you'd go back to the office sooner or later. Vlad was waiting outside and saw you. He called me on the cell and followed you. Bingo. Like magic."

"Are your men around now?"

Mikhail snorted again. "Nearby. But I need no protection. You do."

Karen put the pictures back in the envelope. "Well, thanks for this."

"Not so damn fast. You need to get ten thousand big ones before you take them. I don't care if it comes from you or your company. In cash." That carnivore's smile appeared.

Nodding her head in agreement, Karen stood. "Sounds like a good starting point for negotiation."

"No negotiation, you witch. You are due in court, where Faff will leave you bleeding. Worse than from my knife. You better—"

That was when Karen swung hard and hit him flush in

the stomach, just as Mikhail had hit her the night of the Jaguar crash. He bent over, wheezing like a dying locomotive. Then he vomited.

"These aren't yours to sell," Karen said. "I can return them to their rightful owner. Once I've made copies."

She left Mikhail gasping for air on the hillside, and she clasped the envelope as firmly as if all the world's wealth rode inside.

The Cadillac sped down the Garden State Parkway, Nikita driving, the windshield wipers taking occasional swipes at the spatterings of rain. The headlights cut through the nighttime mist. Mikhail sat in the back, holding his stomach. He felt a bit better, and could use a drink.

Vlad, whom Mikhail had found outside the park on Fifth Avenue, stuffing a hot dog in his mouth, had been placed under strict orders to find Glick. Mikhail's men were pouring into the city from New Jersey. If the other New York gangs didn't like that, too bad. His men had a job to do.

"Who is left back at bang-bang house?" Mikhail asked Nikita.

"Only Pasha, boss. And a woman. We got you one, like you said. Black. Pretty."

Mikhail grunted. Pasha was a good eighty years old. He spoke nostalgically of Stalin, but preferred to live out his last days amid the comforts of the West. Pasha would be no good scouring Manhattan for Karen Glick.

The Cadillac left the Parkway, flashed past the treeline, and arrowed along the causeway toward Avalon. Friday was seeking to question him, so Mikhail needed to be far away. The seaside resort was quiet now that the summer crowd had gone. The only action on the Jersey Shore in November was up the coast in Atlantic City. Mikhail hopped out of the car and into the liquor store, to establish his presence in town for when Glick was killed and the cops asked about his whereabouts.

Then Nikita drove his boss to the bang-bang house, a modern, glass-walled structure that stood on pillars by the dunes. There were no neighbors for a hundred meters. Mikhail usually had guards posted around it, but tonight they were up in New York on a manhunt. No matter. He feared no one.

Mikhail got out. Two of his other cars were still parked there: a Ford Explorer and a Nissan Maxima. A small Kia was by the curb, probably belonging to the girl.

He leaned in Nikita's window. "You go back to New York. Vlad will put you to work. Find that Glick whore and kill her dead."

"Will you be all right here, boss? You have only Pasha."

Mikhail didn't answer. He headed for the house, feeling much better. Anticipation stirred in his loins. He climbed the stairs to the deck. Pasha was waiting at the front door. His withered hand, slightly shaking, handed Mikhail a drink.

"Where's the girl, old man?"

"Pretty girl, watching the waves," Pasha said, and he took Mikhail's leather jacket. "Dinner warming. Ready when you want it, boss."

Grinning, Mikhail strode with his drink through the stark white interior, past the many bedrooms. By his count, he had bang-banged six dozen women in this house, only two of them black. Which bedroom should he use tonight?

He saw the girl before she saw him. She was standing with a drink by a broad floor-to-ceiling window and was surveying the waves smashing foam on the sand. Too bad no moon or stars were visible. A lightning bolt flashed, far out at sea. She wore a tiny skirt and had fine legs and a pert ass.

"Good," Mikhail said. "You got a drink."

She pirouetted around. Her sumptuous breasts almost spilled out of her plunging neckline. She had a smile for him that somehow didn't match her eyes, which were narrow. No matter.

"You're so big," she said as he neared her. She put a hand on his broad chest. "And I'm so lucky."

He guided her to a long sofa and settled her next to him on the right. The girl's left leg, long and shapely, nestled against his. She clinked his glass.

"You have trouble finding my house?" Mikhail asked.

"Everybody in A.C. knows where your place is, sugar. You're a legend. They say you're a magician with a knife."

Mikhail laughed gruffly. "That not all I'm a magician with."

"Your knife is part of your legend," she said. "Let me have a look at it."

Obligingly, Mikhail withdrew the knife from the sheath he kept inside his pants, against his left hip. He held it aloft like a king's conquering sword. It was as long and mean.

"My God," she said. "When's the last time you used this?"

"On a no-good bastard on the New York subway. This is the best knife in the world."

The sight of the blade captivated her in an almost sexual way. "Can I hold it? Please?"

He offered the knife's handle to her. "Don't cut yourself. It is very sharp. Like a serpent's tooth."

She fondled the knife, then wiped it with the hem of her short skirt, as if to shine it. Then she grasped the handle with both hands and drove the knife deep into Mikhail's chest.

As he writhed on the floor like a dying insect, she bent over and said to him, "The name's Regina. My father was Major Darcy. And he was fifty times the man you ever were."

CHAPTER TWENTY-SEVEN

The priest laughed giddily at the laptop's message. It said the Tarnhelm stock, which had soared angelically, now had all been sold. Profit: $510,000. Since the position closed out Friday, the money had zipped safely and electronically to Simon Scratch's offshore bank account. There was enormous virtue in easy money.

Switching into the search program, the priest grew as quiet as the church beyond the locked study door. Goldring flashed up more intriguing news. At T. Rowe Price, the big mutual fund house in Baltimore, they were preparing to buy stock in Goaderdam Enterprises, a long overlooked company that made drill bits for deep sea oil exploration. The fund house's massive buying wouldn't start for another week, levitating the price then. Come Monday, though, Simon Scratch would be in the market for Goaderdam shares, adding more on Tuesday and still more on Wednesday.

The study's wooden door creaked open. The priest started, then yanked open a desk drawer. Inside lay a .45.

Wolfe stood in the threshold, behind the priest's large-backed desk chair. He was dapper in his tweeds and sporting an amused smile. "Good morning," he said.

"You're only supposed to see me in the confessional." The priest lowered the .45 and got up to face him, with the chair manuevered to block the intruder's view of Goldring.

"I can see why, father. You look so much better through the confessional's small aperture. Whoever gave you that ghastly haircut? My, my. That .45 is very much like the one I planted on poor Albert. I guess they didn't buy the ruse."

The priest returned the pistol to the drawer and closed it, taking pains to keep Goldring hidden behind the chair. "Let's not talk here."

"Oh, let's not." Wolfe craned his neck. "But first, isn't that the famous Goldring? Been making some trades, have we?"

The priest recovered the presence of mind to assert some command. "How did you get into this office? I locked the door."

"Yes, I know you do that when you're playing with the computer. Well, in my profession, doors don't stay locked for long."

The priest managed to summon up a fierce expression. "Get out. You're making me very angry. I'm paying you a fortune to—"

"Yes, yes, yes." Wolfe straightened his tie. "I'll meet you in the confessional."

After he left, the priest slammed the door, shut down Goldring, and locked the laptop away. Cursing, the priest stalked over to the booth, footfalls slapping the tiles of the sacred ground. The priest slid past the curtain to find Wolfe's smug face floating on the other side of the screen.

"I've been calling you through the Iran number and have heard nothing. I'm paying you extra, and this is what I get in return?"

"I've been busy tracking down our quarry, father. And I hear tell that Linda Reiner is paying you a visit tomorrow afternoon, after Sunday mass, to discuss Ginny Reiner's funeral. That would be an excellent opportunity to minister unto her, eh?"

"How do you know this? That's what I've been phoning to tell you." The priest glowered at Wolfe.

"Why, Satan told me."

"I'm paying you extra money to find her and Karen Glick. Now Linda falls into your lap, and you act like this is your doing."

"I work in strange and mysterious ways, father. After I deal with the delicious Linda, I still have to find Glick. But I will. Extra money, yes. Regardless, what's the extra money to someone with Goldring to continuously churn out more?"

"I told you to get them both before the week is out. Tomorrow is Sunday."

"It is? Alas, my least favorite day."

Spinelli rode in the car beside the director and tried to give him a good brief. But Wooton was distracted and irritable. "The office where you'll meet appears to be uninhabited, sir. People, mainly tech types, are working today in adjacent offices, even though this is Saturday. Gonzalez and Simmons are up in the meeting site now, as the advance party. They say the third-floor office's door already was open when they arrived. No sign of Faff or his people."

"No one is up there other than our two operatives?"

The guncar in front of them sluiced through a large rain puddle, splattering their windshield.

"No, Director. As I said, the office is uninhabited. A handful of desks. Disconnected phone lines."

Wooton rested his chin on his chest so that the flab bulged out from under his jaw. For a moment, Spinelli thought he would nod off to sleep. Then the director said, "Mr. Spinelli, do you have any notion who owns this building? Is it Jack Faff?"

"As near as we can determine, sir, the Meeker-Grubman Building is owned by a syndicate in which Faff has no interest."

With a grumble that almost represented approval, Wooton turned to gaze out the side window at the rain as they motored through a washed-out Manhattan day. Donner would not have been sufficiently sharp to investigate the ownership of the building. Wooton lamented anew that he couldn't risk enlisting Spinelli as a Goldring partner.

"What is Faff going to be talking to us about?" he asked the director.

"You don't have the need to know," Wooton replied. "Once I'm inside the office, I will meet with Faff alone."

Their motorcade stopped in the West Thirties outside the industrial loft building, many of the windows alive with light. "Any one of these occupied spaces could contain a threat to us," Wooton said.

"We have canvassed each of the other offices, posing as FBI. Nothing but geeks and computers. No threat situation."

The side door opened and Wooton stepped out under the large dark halo of the umbrella that Holstein held.

Two operatives stood post by the building's front door. With Spinelli and three others running ahead, Wooton crossed the lobby's filthy terrazzo floor and climbed a series of metal stairs. A young man with thick glasses hurried past them, oblivious to all but the computer code forming in his head.

As they reached the landing for the third floor, Wooton

signaled for the group to halt until he had caught his breath. "I used to be more fit," he said. "In Laos, Plain of Jars, I had a bullet in my gut. And yet I could call in B-52 strikes."

Some of the operatives discreetly exchanged glances.

When Wooton was ready, they proceeded down a hallway past metal doors with oddball company names like Headfake.com.

Gonzalez and Simmons flanked the expensive teak door at the end. As Wooton drew closer, he saw that a sign had been pried off the door. He stopped.

"This was the Reiner sisters' office," he said. "Why does Faff want to meet here?"

"I beg your pardon?" Spinelli said.

"Never mind." Wooton consulted his fine watch. "We're right on time. I'll wait inside. Alone."

He ventured into the office, past a seven-foot partition from which a logo had been removed. Three widely spaced desks stood on the vast concrete expanse. One for each sister. The bloodstain was barely visible on the floor. Someone had taken pains to scrub it away.

Since there were no chairs, Wooton settled his copious rump against one of the desks and waited. And waited. He was hungry. To occupy himself, he thought about wealth and food and Erica. Where was his wife right now?

A half-hour later, Spinelli poked his head around the partition. "Faff is here. He has five people with him."

"Not those Russian gangsters?"

"They look more like lawyers and accountants."

"Only Faff comes in here," Wooton said. "Make sure the door is closed. Him and me—alone."

An unpleasant hubbub ensued out in the hall. At last, Faff came swaggering past the partition. The door was closed loudly behind him.

"Your goons won't let my people stand near the door,"

Faff said. "Of course you and I will meet alone. I want my people nearby in the hall, though, in case something goes wrong."

"Mr. Faff, I desire only a civilized discourse. As I'm sure do you. No one is in danger here."

Wooton noted that Faff, as handsome as in his photos, was amazingly short. The developer wore brightly shined loafers, superbly pressed chinos, and a silk sweater. He folded his arms in a gesture of ownership. "Don't try to intimidate me with your psychological ploys, Wooton. I'm not in danger? Meaning I could be if you chose? Government bureaucrats don't scare me."

Wooton felt he was off to a good start. His game was back. His operatives' show of force plainly had gotten to the rich—that is, formerly rich—man. "Psychological ploys? Now, now, Mr. Faff. Arriving at an appointment a half-hour late is not only rude. It's a crude attempt to show how important you are. But with your finances collapsing, that's an empty gesture."

"Oh, yeah? I'll be back. Meanwhile, I heard you're going to be out of office very soon, Wooton. And hey, I heard you were a snappy dresser. Bad information. Where did you get those shoes?"

Taken aback, Wooton said, "These are Allen Edmonds."

"Store bought? I get my own shoes made. And that watch of yours? Nobody wears a Patek Philipe anymore. You don't get out much, do you? Who are your friends?"

"I have no friends, and neither do you." The director wanted to crush the little man's neck, right at the opening of his natty sweater. "Quit baiting me about my appearance."

"With that gut of yours, you need a good tailor."

"Don't be deceived by my weight. I could crush you with one hand."

"Civilized discourse, huh? Hey, when you're rich, you're

eight feet tall," Faff crowed, as if he had won points. "Let's talk business."

"Business? Very well. You're aware of the considerable intelligence resources I can bring to bear in locating Goldring. The Authority can commandeer the ultimate in federal power. What do you bring to this party?"

Faff took a step toward Wooton. "Great wealth, as you'll learn if you get some, gives great resources. I've found out all about you—and you're supposed to be so secret that you don't really exist. Remember who built your headquarters in Virginia? Me."

"But you don't have any more muscle." Wooton shook his head. "Were you aware that Mikhail Beria was reported murdered on the Jersey Shore this morning? His killer is unknown. News to you?"

"Huh?" Faff took a moment to absorb this, then pushed on in the spirit of letting nothing rock him as he negotiated. "No matter. I fired the asshole."

Feeling he had the opponent at an advantage once more, Wooton said, "Beria and his men murdered your brother, correct? Who will do that kind of work for you now?"

Faff squared his shoulders, the sturdy bantamweight. "I should have killed Solter myself, instead of leaving the job to Mikhail. Damn traitor was talking to you and Glick. My own brother. He deserved what he got. No, I'm close to locating Linda Reiner and Karen Glick."

"Really? Where are they?"

Faff flung up a hand to show that didn't matter. "I'll know soon. Okay, if you say you can supply muscle now, how good is it? I mean, that broken-nosed jerk of yours—Linda Reiner took care of him pretty quick with pepper spray and a baseball bat. And this clown is a trained killer? Please."

At the mention of Dirk Donner, Wooton sensed his momentum slowing. "He was weak and incompetent. And I got rid of him."

"We have to get rid of some more pests around here. As in kill them. And Karen Glick is at the top of the list. She wants to destroy us both. You say you have resources. Do you have the balls to use them?"

"In abundance, Mr. Faff, in abundance. Dirk Donner was a failure. I put a round through his worthless excuse for a brain. We are not playing pattycake here. For however long I have at the Authority, anyone who crosses me will not remain living." As he rumbled this out in his deepest voice, Wooton thought he saw Faff betray a flicker of intimidation, at last.

Faff showed the tension by jamming his hands into his pockets. "Listen, Wooton, I'll locate Glick. And you have the bitch killed. And that damn Linda Reiner along with her."

The director decided now was the time to seal the pact, although he had to be careful. "Agreed. But then we must find Goldring."

"I'm working a back channel to get my hands on the laptop very soon. Then we'll share the information on the trades. And both make more money than God. Do we have a deal?"

"Indeed we do, Mr. Faff. Now, I know you're thinking you'll work the laptop alone and cut me in on the proceeds. Wrong. That will tempt you to cheat me. We'll make a copy of the Goldring program. Then each man can go his separate way."

Wooton, perched against the Reiner desk, watched Faff frown. The director's telepathy was dead-on again. Yes, Wooton was back.

Faff shrugged. "You know what I'm thinking? Oh, yeah, you're the mind reader. Count me as slightly impressed by you, as opposed to not at all. Know what I was thinking when I came in here? That your e-mail proposal sounded weak. Practically begging to meet me. I hate weak. Did your second sight tell you this?"

"My proposal? You were the one to e-mail me that you wanted this meeting here to explore working together."

"What the hell are you talking about? You e-mailed me with the time and the place. What are you trying to pull?"

As the hard rain drummed on the van's roof, short-sleeved Friday stretched his bare, burly arms and the tattoos on them danced. "I'd say we got the lowdown on these upstanding individuals. I love to watch a pillar of society crumble."

"I was afraid they'd start talking about the e-mails at the beginning, about who invited whom," Logie said. "That would've screwed everything up." They were jammed into the police surveillance van.

"I'm still amazed that you could disguise a Wooton e-mail to Faff, find out his e-mail address, and send it to him—and then do the same, Faff to Wooton," Karen said. "How did you learn to do all this stuff?"

"Time on my hands, lack of a social life," Logie said.

"Faff and Wooton are still dangerous," Karen said, huddled off in the corner near the door. "Faff might not have his gangsters anymore, but he can hire more thugs. And Wooton has his men."

"I really doubt," Logie said, "Spinelli or any of the others will carry out Wooton's orders to cold-bloodedly murder any of us. Wooton may say we're terrorists, but his credibility has worn thin."

The sound of the Reiner Capital door closing signaled the end of the Faff-Wooton meeting. A police technician fiddled with the sound level and shut down the taping system.

"I think you girls are home free, as far as the Russians go," Friday said. "We've been rounding up Beria's hoodlums, who have been roaming around the city—I guess searching for you. A lot have outstanding warrants. The Costanza mob fingered them. A turf thing, I guess. The Costanza guys didn't like Beria's style. All that biting off rats' heads."

"Thanks again for letting us come along," Karen said, bent on acting nice to what her father still called "the heat."

"Thank Frank Vere. He set this up. Vere's done me a good turn in the past. He's the man." Frank's intervention had miraculously transformed Friday's attitude toward Karen. The detective reached for his styrofoam coffee cup, perched on the corrugated metal floor. "Where is the fair Ms. Reiner?" Again, he elongated it: "Mizzzzz."

"With some friends on Park Avenue," Karen said. "She wouldn't say who. She didn't like where we were staying. Low-class company. Children. Tacky furniture. Second-rate coffee."

"She told me she'd take me to her hairdresser's," Logie said. "But she's probably forgotten."

"If you go to that hairdresser, you'd better be careful," Karen said. "The Englishman was watching Linda and Ginny there. Could he be staking the shop out now?"

"Wolfe doesn't have a broad intelligence network like the Authority's," Logie said. "He's alone and can't be everywhere." Her worried look belied her confident assertion.

"Not a problem," Friday said. "This Wolfe dork—we still haven't been able to find squat on him through the department—can be dealt with. I got two trusted uniforms I can send with you. They'll take you in a standard-issue cop car that does wonders at scaring away evildoers."

"Okay," Karen said reluctantly. "Well, maybe Linda has forgotten."

Smartly dressed people glided along Madison Avenue in the chill. The rain had stopped for the moment and they emerged from their well-appointed refuges to take the air. Clothing boutiques bearing classy European names invited them in with bright window displays. Some you couldn't enter without an appointment, but the Madison Avenue walkers had lots of appointments.

Sartorially, Karen didn't fit the mold of an Upper East Side grande dame out for a stroll. In her jeans and sneakers, she stood for a moment outside Antonio's. Many of the nicely dressed sidewalk passersby could be the Englishman. Finely shaped silver hair was a must among men over fifty. Across the street sat Friday's promised police car.

Karen ventured into the shop. A busy salon filled with exotic hair cutters, chic patrons, and sharp furnishings, Antonio's wasn't the kind of establishment Karen went for her haircuts. At the Cutting Room Floor, her usual place, gum-gnawing Estelle charged a fifth of what Antonio did.

Linda, wearing fashionable leather pants and a man-tailored white cotton shirt, sat on one of a bank of industrial modern waiting chairs and read *Vogue*. Several shopping bags were beside her.

"New clothes?" Karen asked.

"I took Logie to Barneys. We both needed things to wear. Wait till you see her."

Karen was taken aback that Linda was acting nice. "The cops went with you to Barneys?"

"Kevin stayed outside in the car. Dennis went inside with us. What a hoot. People didn't know whether we were under arrest or what." She patted the shopping bags. "Dennis even carried the bags. They have this cute contest over who will get to accompany me. I thought they'd be too out of bounds in here, which is why I told them both to stay in the car."

Linda's reveling in her power over men was far preferable to her behavior lately. "I'm cooking tonight at Welles's," Karen said. "We'll have me and Logie and Alexandra. Plus Wendy and her parrot. They have been great at babysitting Alexandra. You're invited."

"I can't. I've got plans." She might as well have said: *with better people than you.*

Feeling somewhere between relieved and disappointed, Karen said, "That's a shame. Well, where are Wendy's clothes you borrowed? She'll need them back."

Linda gave a throaty Kathleen Turner laugh. "No, she won't. I did her a favor. I threw them out."

"You what?" Karen decided not to pursue it. "Anyway, you're meeting with Father Finnegan tomorrow. How about I tag along? As I say, something about him bothers me. As for tonight, let's divvy up the police escort."

"But Kevin and Dennis must work together. They're partners. I'm sure you'll be fine."

"What?" Karen exclaimed. "You've expropriated our police escort, meant for the three of us, for yourself exclusively?"

"They don't mind," Linda said. "Oh, check out what's coming."

Logie approached, far removed from the plain computer nerd who sends doctored e-mails. Her bangs were cut asymmetrically and a silky wing of hair swooped across her cheek, with henna highlights that gave it all a red pop. "So?" she said.

"An improvement," Linda said, as if Logie had finally mastered toilet training.

Unnerved by Linda's faint praise, Logie turned to Karen. "So?"

"Makes you look great," Karen said.

"Well, consider yourself thanked for your contribution," Linda told Logie as she stood to go.

Antonio fluttered up, carrying a manila envelope. "I cut her myself. Such a nice head of hair." He kissed Logie's hand. "You listen to Linda, cara, and you can't go wrong."

Out of a wan sense of politeness, Linda introduced Karen to Antonio.

"I've heard a lot about you," Karen told the salon owner.

"Yes, you are the great journalist," said Antonio, used to exaggeration. "Since I have made this beautiful creature still more beautiful for the aesthetic delight of mankind"— he bowed toward Logie, who beamed—"perhaps you can do me a favor, Ms. Glick."

"If I can, I sure will. What's up?"

"Normally, Anna, a lovely Russian girl, cuts Linda. I myself get to do very little cutting anymore. Well, for some time now, Anna has been missing. The police, they only shrug. She's a club kid, out all night, drinking, drugs, boys. I've spoken to her, but she's young and laughed at me. She has no family in this country. I'm very worried. Maybe you could put her picture in the paper, give her some news coverage, and the police might get moving. This is a shame. A lovely child." He handed Karen the envelope.

Karen pulled out a glossy photo. Anna had a broad face and very short hair, evidently a high-end cut. Also in the envelope was a printed sheet with her personal information, including the last time anyone saw her, which was at work. "I'll see what I can do. I work for a business magazine, which wouldn't handle this kind of story, but I have lots of friends on the dailies I can call."

"This picture was very recent," Antonio said. "Made the day before she disappeared." He pointed to a wall containing all the stylists' framed pictures. "They're like my children."

"Anna is terrific," Linda said. "I liked her short hair a lot. I told her to give Flo a cut like it. Flo had the same features."

A misty rain had resumed. When they came out of the shop, Dennis wheeled the police car around to the curb. Kevin met them at the salon door. He took Linda's shopping bags and held an umbrella above her head as he led her to the car. Karen and Logie trailed, with Logie holding a newspaper abover her new hairdo and Karen carrying her Barneys bags.

While watching Linda's butt as she climbed into the back of the car, Kevin said to Logie and Karen, "Can I drop you ladies off before I continue on with Ms. Reiner?"

When Linda started to say that would not be necessary, Karen drowned her out with: "We'd love that. Say, officer, weren't you supposed to be guarding us all?"

Kevin gave her a wolfish grin.

Eyeing the other women with distaste, Linda scooted herself and her shopping bags over to give them room on the backseat.

"Where are you staying, Linda?" Karen asked.

"With good friends. Let's leave it at that." Linda brushed her lustrous hair back. "Oh, Karen, on second thought, it'd be inconvenient if you came to the church tomorrow. In fact, I'm going to be hiring private security and private investigators from here on out. But it's been interesting being with you. Best of luck."

"Huh?" Karen gave her an incredulous look. "You and I were in this together."

"Were we? I don't know," Linda said airily. "You and Logie have dealt well with Faff and Wooton. But you haven't a clue where to find Wolfe. Or Goldring. Sorry."

"Linda," Karen said, "you are such a pill that Merck, Pfizer, and Glaxo are scrambling for your patent rights."

"You self-centered harpy," Logie snapped at Linda. "Here. Keep your Barneys clothes."

As Logie proferred her shopping bags, Linda held up a well-formed hand. "I can't, sweetie. They're too big for me."

Thunder echoed across the sky as they pulled away from the curb. And Siegfried Wolfe stood beside the shop window, assessing the police car. The raindrops fell in volleys of divine wrath.

CHAPTER TWENTY-EIGHT

Outside, the wild night raged. Fusillades of rain attacked Welles's windows. The bushes on the billionaire's rooftop garden writhed in the wind as might souls in torment. Jagged lightning bolts sizzled through the sky. A good night to be inside.

Alexandra accepted the adults' reassurances that all was well and they were safe. Logie had told her that Mikhail was a funny clown and she shouldn't be afraid of him. Then, at dinner, she showed an adventuresome palate for a six-year-old. She liked the caviar on toast points.

For the main course, Karen served roast duck in green peppercorn sauce, accompanied by apricot glazed carrots, green beans and mushrooms, and wild rice. When she sat down and poured them some Chateau LaGrange, Logie asked, "Where is Linda tonight?"

"Wherever is cool," Karen said. "Not here."

"I hate Linda, and I've never met her," Wendy said. "She threw out my clothes. What a shit." Then the ever-ditzy

Wendy blanched when she remembered a child was present.

"Wendy said a bad word," a wide-eyed Alexandra observed.

"What a shit, what a shit, what a shit," the parrot repeated until Wendy shushed him.

After Wendy left and Logie put Alexandra to bed, Karen and Logie drank brandy and complained about Linda. Karen admitted she was flummoxed about what to do next.

"I think I can satisfy my cheering section at the magazine with the photos of me getting in the passenger's side of Faff's Jag. And we've dealt a blow to Faff and Wooton. But pieces are missing. I don't care if Linda ever gets Goldring. My concern is that I won't ever be safe from Wolfe unless he is caught. Even if I'm exonerated on the car-crash charges and can write about Faff and Wooton, I'm still a marked woman."

Logie held up her snifter in solidarity. "I'll do whatever I can for you."

"Logie, you've already done a great deal. Thanks."

Karen, somewhat blitzed, collapsed into bed. She soon fell deep into a soggy sleep. Then she heard a noise. There came another noise. Footsteps. Karen opened her eyes.

The Englishman was standing over her bed and leering at her. He held a .45, pointed at Karen's face. The same one that had blown Flo's head apart. "I gave you your chance, my girl," Wolfe said. "And you muffed it, didn't you now?"

Karen jolted awake.

In the morning, the storm kept dumping water and wind on the city. Karen chose not to tell Logie about her bad dream. She wanted mother and daughter to feel completely safe, especially since she had sanctioned their traumatizing visit to Central Park.

While Logie bathed Alexandra, Karen fetched the newspapers from a newstand on the sidewalk near Welles's building. She tucked the mass of papers under her slicker to keep them dry, then prepared a breakfast of pancakes, using bacon and fruit on Alexandra's to make a face. The kid was delighted.

Afterward, as Alexandra colored on the floor, Karen and Logie lounged on the couch and read the papers.

"Why did you want to go with Linda to that church?" Logie asked.

"I wanted to talk to Father Finnegan, and figured Linda would be a good *entrée*," Karen said. "Her appointment is in a half-hour. I'll get to him later, on my own. I have this funny glimmering about him and Our Lady of Perpetual Suffering. How he and it were beneficiaries of Flo's estate. Something . . ." She reached for Antonio's envelope and examined Anna's photo and the printed information.

That was when she noticed it.

"What's the matter?" Logie said.

"According to this . . . Anna was last seen the day Flo was killed."

"What does Anna have to do with Flo?"

"She did her hair. . . ." Karen examined Anna's photo again.

Karen hopped to her feet. "I've got to stop Linda from going to the church. She's in danger." Moving to her room so she would not alarm Alexandra, she hauled out her cell phone. For some reason, the call to Linda's cell wouldn't go through. The weather?

At the precinct, Friday wasn't in. Karen got a bored desk sergeant who told her that Kevin and Dennis were out on a special detail.

"Tell them to stay clear of the church. It's a trap."

"Right. A trap. I'll pass it along when they check in," the sergeant, who clearly wouldn't, told the nut on the phone.

"You don't understand—"

"I understand I'm kinda busy here, lady. Have a nice day."

Logie was standing at the door. "What can I do?"

"Stick here with Alexandra. Maybe I can stop Linda before she enters the church. She might have the cops with her, but I've got a bad feeling."

As Karen ran for the elevator, Logie told her to be careful.

With the rain cascading down in steely sheets, Linda sat in the rear of the police car and watched the church. Wind buffeted the car. Mass was long over and Our Lady of Perpetual Suffering brooded in the mist under a dark sky. Linda's eyes were a little bloodshot and her head throbbed. The Tylenol she'd gulped hadn't been equal to the task. The previous night, she had tried to drown out the nerve-shattering recent past with Vodka. She would have preferred to talk to someone sympathetic, but that proved an impossibility and she didn't try. Her "friends," a silly young couple with more inherited money than common decency, preferred to ignore her unseemly plight and babble about what they owned, whom they knew, and where they'd been.

"Well," Linda said to her police escort, "it's time. I better go in. Who's coming with me?"

Kevin and Dennis looked at each other. They began whispering furiously to each other.

Amused and able to hear everything, Linda said, "Why don't both of you go inside with me? You can leave the car alone, can't you? Do us all some good to go to church."

Linda opened the door and popped the umbrella open. The wind tried to snatch it from her two-handed grasp. The two cops simultaneously grabbed the umbrella to steady it. They trudged on either side of her, the rain lashing their faces.

They climbed the church's slippery old stairs and reached the wooden front door. The door opened into a dark interior, but a dry one. With some force, Kevin had to push the door shut against the invading wind.

A catacomb stillness prevailed inside, except for the tinkling of rain on stained glass windows and the demonic wind beyond. Linda caught her breath, remembering her last visit to this church, and why she was here now.

"I'm not a very good Catholic," Linda said. "I don't have my rosary anymore." She smiled to herself. "My sister Flo returned to the church in a big way. Ginny, the feminist, thought Catholicism was a cover for male domination. Still, in her heart of hearts . . ." Linda saw the holy water stoup and went over to it. She trailed her fingertips through the water, then crossed herself. "Ginny would want a funeral mass. She would."

The priest glided into view in his black shirt and slash of clerical collar. He'd been hard to spot in the gloom. His thin smile seemed pasted on. His eyes darted nervously between the two policemen.

"Father Finnegan," Linda said, taking his clammy hand. She introduced her two bodyguards. "In light of recent events, I'm sure you can appreciate why I have these fine gentlemen with me."

"Yes," said the priest, in his reedy voice. "But we do not want guns in God's house. I'm sure you can appreciate that. Perhaps you fellows could wait outside."

"It's raining like a bastard—" Dennis checked himself as soon as he uttered the salty language.

"We're under orders to protect Ms. Reiner," Kevin said.

"Father, I take my piece to mass, in an ankle holster, and the priest knows I do," Dennis said.

Linda treated them to one of her winning smiles. They made her feel miles safer than she'd felt in a long time. "Why don't you guys wait by the door? You can keep me in sight. The father and I can conduct our business in the pews here. Okay?"

Finnegan's forehead crinkled. His eyes richocheted between the two cops. "I suppose." His eyes clicked over to Linda. Or rather to her breasts. "But before we proceed, I should hear your confession. At your sister Flo's ceremony, you took communion and later told me you hadn't had confession in years. Now is the time."

Nodding slowly, Linda said, "Okay. If that would make matters easier, we can do that, father. Then we need to talk seriously about Ginny's arrangements."

"We have to keep our eyes on her every minute," Kevin said.

With a wave toward the confessional, not ten yards distant, the priest said, "We're not going very far."

"This will be fine," Linda said. She removed her coat and handed it to Dennis. Kevin looked annoyed that she had chosen Dennis. "You two stay right here. I won't be long. My sins are minimal."

The officers watched her and the priest go to the confessional. She stepped into her side. Finnegan hesitated, contemplating the cops oddly, then ducked to enter his side.

"Did you catch how the father was getting an eyeful of her?" Dennis said as he draped Linda's coat over the back of a stand whose racks held missionary leaflets.

"The dude's got taste."

The front door opened, admitting a gust of wet air and a man in a trenchcoat. "Excuse me, I'm looking for a friend," the newcomer said in an English accent. "He wouldn't normally come into a church, but this one's different. Any port in a storm, eh?"

"Not a lotta people in here now, chief," Dennis said. "Who's your friend?"

"Satan, actually. Seen him?"

In the dark, hushed confines of the confessional, Linda could barely make out Father Finnegan through the screen. She crossed herself again. The beast of a wind howled.

"Bless me, father, for I have sinned. It has been, oh, twelve or thirteen years since my last confession." She hesitated, then released a torrent of words: "I was in college, and my sister Flo came to me and said she'd pushed Daddy down the stairs, and he died. I told the priest in confession, but I don't think he believed me, and he said tell the police if you are really convinced of a crime being committed, yet how could I—Flo was my sister and Daddy was forcing sex upon her and she hated it and liked it at the same time. . . . How awful this was. . . . My God."

Linda sobbed and choked, covered her eyes with her hands. She tried to stop, regain her customary aplomb, but couldn't. She cried for several minutes. At last, her tears subsided and she reached for a tissue in her bag.

"You're upset." Finnegan sounded less than comforting, as if he disapproved of her emotions.

She dabbed her eyes. "Well . . . my sisters were all I had. Ginny was good and solid. Flo was . . . lost. Still, we made something, the three of us. We did."

"Which of your sisters did you prefer?"

"Excuse me?" What a strange question, far removed from the customary priestly words of comfort and healing. Maybe, Linda thought, confession had changed since last she'd been.

"Which," the priest said, "did you prefer?"

"Oh, father, please. I had no preferences."

"Didn't you? When Flo came here, she talked about how you bossed her around and treated her like a child. Ginny was your favorite."

"Father, this is hardly appropriate."

"We're trying to reach the nature of your sin."

Linda shook her head. "Listen, Flo never was wrapped too tight, okay? One failure after another. She tried to hurt me—sleeping with one of my boyfriends even. She needed some direction."

Finnegan began raising his voice, which seemed to change in timbre, as if belonging to someone else. "But your father really loved you, burned for you, and then you teased him. And went on to treat Flo like she was this dirty little slut. When you were the slut, with your boys hanging around, jumping to do your bidding. A stupid party girl who knows nothing more than how to manipulate men. You deserve to burn in hell."

Linda cringed at the sheer venom coming through the screen. "Father, what are you talking about? Are you crazy?"

"No," the priest shouted. "I'd be crazy to let you go unpunished. This is very sane."

"Kevin, Dennis, help!" Linda cried. She hustled out of the confessional, but stumbled backward when she saw who loomed outside.

The Englishman stood there. "They're not available, I fear. You'll have to settle for me."

The priest whirled into view. "Your time to die, slut."

And Linda saw. "Oh, no."

Karen found the empty police car parked near Our Lady of Perpetual Suffering. Linda, she assumed, must be inside the church. At least both cops were with her. As rain peppered her poncho, Karen pelted through the puddles and got to the church's front door. Which was locked. She pulled hard on the wet iron handle. It wouldn't budge.

Another entrance must be somewhere. She ran to the side. Nothing there. The windows were high above, out of reach and closed. She sprinted toward the rear of the church. In the back was an alley with a couple of cars—a battered Ford Focus and a spiffy Bentley, gleaming in the rain. And a steel door that led into the church.

She yanked its handle. The door opened.

Karen leapt up a small flight of stairs and found herself amid moldy old curtains, like some medieval backstage. She brushed through them and came upon a corridor and a closed door. The sign said that this was Father Finnegan's office. She shucked the slicker and pounded on the door. It too was locked tight.

She thought she heard a woman calling out in alarm. Somewhere else. Karen headed for the sound, which came from the other side of a thick fire door with a crash bar. She popped it open.

Father Finnegan himself was on the other side, propped up against the wall. He had a hand to his cheek, as if stunned. "This is evil. I can't stop it."

"Where's Linda?" She grabbed Finnegan by the shoulders.

"Evil. This is my fault. The call of greed and carnal desire was intense. I lost my bearings. Lost my faith. Blinded by all the money. An evil plan. When Wolfe distracted the police, I slipped out of the confessional and . . ." He acted totally zoned out. "I'm sorry."

Karen dodged past him and ran down another hall. She emerged by the altar. At the back, on the other side of all those rows of pews, there were three figures. She squinted in the gloom.

A priest. Linda. The Englishman. The priest was yelling. Like no priest ever should.

Karen raced down the side of the church, under the stained glass, past the pews. Calling, "Hold it. Hold it."

"Karen," Linda shouted, "run away."

"You see," Wolfe said to the priest, "a nice little delivery of our two packages. And here you doubted me. Customer satisfaction guaranteed, that's my motto."

The priest produced a .45 from inside the confessional and trained it on Karen. "Stop right there, you. We'll deal with you after Linda."

"Put the gun away, you lunatic," Linda demanded.

"You're through giving orders, Linda," the priest said, and shifted the pistol's aim over to her.

His expression amused, Wolfe stood with arms folded. He displayed no weapon. "Really, father. Why the gun? Since you've paid for my services, shouldn't I do the honors?"

Karen looked around frantically. "Where are the cops?"

"More of Linda's male admirers," the priest said. "You had a chance to stay clear of this, Karen. I told Wolfe to give you a warning first. You should've listened to him."

"Is that like the gun that killed Anna?" Karen asked the priest.

"Oh, aren't you the brilliant one, Karen?" the priest said. "At Albert's apartment, Wolfe planted the murder weapon. Did the great reporter figure that one out? Did you? Linda had you pegged as a second-rater. A real ninny."

"I can't believe you've done this," Linda said to the priest. "You're so twisted."

"Shut up," the priest yelled.

"Okay," Karen said. "You're skilled at hacking. You wanted it to look like Albert both committed the murder and stole Goldring. And you sent Albert that e-mail, purportedly from Linda, telling him to go to Reiner Capital at a certain time and grab Goldring."

"She's actually quite a clever lass," Wolfe said of Karen. "Hardly a ninny."

Karen fought to contain her anger. "You left the office door open for Albert to make the theft easy. Then when he left with Goldring, poor Anna, the hairdresser, wearing Flo's clothes, with Flo's same haircut—hell, she had Flo's same build—was trotted out and got shot dead. Friday said they found drugs in Flo's body. You must've had Anna hidden in the office when Albert was there. Drugged."

"I appreciate why you had the Russian girl give you her

same haircut," Wolfe told the priest. "That certainly enhanced the illusion that she was Flo. You know my opinion on this short-hair look, however. Most unbecoming."

"Poor Anna," Linda said. "She had nothing to do with us. She didn't deserve this."

"Poor Anna?" the priest said. "She worshipped you. She deserved every bit of it. She deserved to be put into a crate for Wolfe to bring up. He dressed like a deliveryman, delivering garbage. And after Albert left with Goldring, she deserved to be dragged over to the desk and propped up so Wolfe could take care of her with the gun. Too bad she came around and screamed at the last moment. Some people deserve to suffer."

"And you put Daddy's 'friendship ring' on Anna's finger, didn't you?" Linda said, showing more ire than fear, drawing out the words "friendship ring" with sarcasm.

The priest's right hand extended for everyone to see. "I got it back when Anna's body came here for the funeral mass. And it's never going to leave my hand, Linda. Never."

"Why," Karen said, "did you do these horrible things, Flo?"

"Aside from getting Goldring all to myself?" Flo said, the clerical collar circling her neck. "I did them because they were long overdue. The real question is: why didn't I do them sooner? Well, I finally had enough money to hire somebody like Wolfe, is why." She waved the gun between Karen and Linda, almost playfully.

"To be sure," Wolfe said, "our good Florence actually has what's required to take up my trade—viciousness, guile, love of money. And she has the added advantage of a talented gift for mimicry. I've listened to Father Finnegan at the pulpit, and my employer Flo impersonates him to a fare-thee-well. Flo restricted our contacts to the confessional, where you can't see very well, and for a while I was convinced she *was* Father Finnegan. Bravo."

"All I ever wanted to do was help you, Flo," Linda said.

"That assumes I needed your help," Flo said. "How nice for her majesty to deign to help me. My only regret is that my e-mail to Albert didn't get you in trouble with the cops. I wanted you splattered with some mud before Siegfried Wolfe ended your rotten existence. Let you appreciate how being reviled feels."

"And what about Ginny?" Linda said. "She never did anything to hurt you."

"Or to help me. She cared more about her equations. And she'd always side with you. You wanted to tell the news media about Goldring and become a celebrity—yep, Ginny went along."

"How will you be able to live with yourself?" Linda said.

"Quite well," Flo said. "I'll live under an assumed name, in luxury. After this, I'll get Goldring from Finnegan's office and say good-bye, New York."

"What about Finnegan?" Karen asked.

"He's not much of a boyfriend. Too much guilt about betraying his vow of celibacy. The money kept him in line, but this will be too much. He'll go to the cops, for certain. In the future, I'll buy some real choice companionship with my money. Hollywood handsome." Flo turned to Wolfe. "Once these two are gone, I want you to kill Finnegan."

"Father, please," Wolfe said with mock reproach.

"I'll separately pay you two hundred thousand for Finnegan. All bodies disappear, of course."

"Simply because he's a feckless and uncomely chap who's not good in bed doesn't mean he should come cheap," Wolfe said. "For Finnegan, I require three hundred thousand."

With Flo distracted by bargaining, Karen lunged at her. But Flo recovered and brought the gun up. It was an inch from Karen's eye.

"Back off," Flo snarled. "I want you to watch Linda die. I'll kill you first if you provoke me."

"If you do any shooting, I must be paid full fee regardless," Wolfe said. "A deal, as they say, is a deal."

"What?" Flo shouted, gun on Karen, eyes on Wolfe. "You haven't done a damn thing lately."

"As you're aware," Wolfe said, "I'm very reluctant to harm a heavenly being like Linda Reiner. Perhaps you could attend to her. The world needs more like her. Would you destroy a Matisse?"

"I'm paying you good money," Flo cried. "You've received a fortune up front already."

"Drop that gun, Flo."

It was Linda. She'd pulled Donner's weapon out of her bag and aimed at her sister.

Flo spun to fire on her.

Linda pulled the trigger. The bullet tore through Flo's chest and sent her sprawling on the holy ground. In shock, Linda and Karen stood over the body.

Linda turned the gun toward Wolfe. But he had vanished.

Karen pried the .45 from Flo's lifeless fingers. "Let's find Wolfe. He had to go somewhere."

"He didn't seem to have a gun," Linda said. She knelt beside her sister's body and the magnitude of what she'd done began to sink in. "Oh, Flo."

"No time for that. We can't let him get a gun."

"Flo can't pay him the rest of his money now," Linda said, numbly yet with perfect logic. "He may be gone."

They roamed through the dark church, guns at the ready. Past the plaster statue of the Virgin, through the pews. They found Kevin and Dennis on the floor among the pews, unconscious, yet otherwise alive. They came across Father Finnegan next to his office door, curled into a fetal ball. The door, previously locked, was ajar.

The priest gazed up at them. "The Englishman," he said.

"What about him?" Karen peered inside the office. No one there. A desk drawer yawned open.

"The Englishman," Finnegan said, "he took that laptop. He's left. In his Bentley. Do you know what that laptop can do? It's called Goldring."

CHAPTER TWENTY-NINE

Monday morning, Karen introduced Linda and Logie to the editors. Bill gallantly unwound himself from the near-prone position in his chair and warmly shook their hands, Linda's in particular.

"See, I really do exist," Logie told Skeen, whose eyes had narrowed.

Everyone sat down, with Karen, Eudell, Logie, and Linda across the table from Skeen and Christian. At the head of the table, Bill sat erect for a change.

"Let me fill you in on what has happened, and that's a lot," Karen said. She went through the weekend's events. She spread on the tabletop the casino pictures she'd taken from Mikhail. "The photos here definitively show that Jack Faff was driving the Jaguar, not me. He said in his statement that I took the wheel at his casino. Untrue. You can see the date and time designations."

"These pictures are private property from his casino security cameras," Skeen said. "He can challenge us on possesion of stolen property."

"These actually are copies I made," Karen said. "I have sent the originals back to Faff. Registered mail. I'm not responsible for making off with these from the casino. Mikhail Beria was."

"But Faff could still—"

Bill motioned for Skeen to be quiet. "What else you got?" he said to Karen.

"Tomorrow or Wednesday at the latest, Jack Faff will be arrested for ordering the murder of his brother," Karen said. "Aside from Faff's admitting it aloud in his meeting with Wooton, Detective Friday has testimony. He has arrested several of Mikhail Beria's hoods, who were roaming around New York, hunting for me. Three of them have implicated Jack Faff in Solter's death. With Beria gone, they aren't exactly maintaining any codes of silence."

"Who will believe a pack of hoods bargaining to save their own hides? Faff has powerful lawyers," Skeen said.

"He'd better," Eudell said. "Consórting with a gangster like Beria will cost him his casino license."

"What about Wooton?" Bill asked.

Karen nodded. "This is a federal matter, even though Wooton's murder of Dirk Donner occurred in the NYPD's jurisdiction. The fact of the Authority's existence is top secret. Logie has given her eyewitness account of Donner's murder to Detective Friday. The feds tell Friday's superiors that, since we are about to publish a story blowing the Authority's cover, its secrecy is moot. So Wooton likely will be arrested this week, as well."

"In time for us to get our story into the magazine," Eudell said. "The newspapers will have pieces of this. We'll have the whole blessed shooting match."

Bill had a way of looking soulfully at people. He did this

to Linda. "What about your sister? Flo. When'll they announce what has happened to her?"

Linda gave a half-smile at Bill's tactful wording about Flo's treachery and death. "Friday is holding off the announcement on Flo until the arrests of Faff and Wooton," she said. "A big manhunt is under way for Siegfried Wolfe."

"I got the license plate number for his Bentley, parked behind the church," Karen said. "The steering wheel is on the British side. The cops are searching for that combination. But Friday says he probably has a number of license plates."

Bill stroked his fringe of white beard. "With the Englishman at large, are y'all still in danger?"

"I think we're okay," Karen said, more out of hope than conviction. "Since Flo's dead, he can't collect the rest of his money. What's the point of coming after us for free? He is a businessman."

"Besides," Logie added, "he expressed his reluctance at the church to kill Linda."

"I want to see him fry for what he did to Ginny," Linda said.

"This is very nice, but it's hearsay," Skeen said. "If we write about the Wooton-Faff meeting in the magazine—and any of it turns out to be wrong—then they have terrific lawsuits against us."

Karen stared hard at him. "Well, Gene, I'm sorry you don't accept my account of their meeting. So I've got a little video presentation that will ease your fears." She showed them the police recording of the meeting in the Reiner sisters' office. Watching the TV, Christian kept shaking his head. Skeen grimaced as if he had just lost money. Bill had a smile that kept growing wider.

"This is official police property that they can challenge us on," Skeen said. "We have no right to possess this."

"Our lawyers can argue our holding the video is protected by the First Amendment," Eudell said.

"How did you get this?" Skeen said. "Did you steal it?"

"A source in the police department," Karen said testily. Frank floated past outside the conference room's glass. He looked at Linda, then Karen.

"Excuse me," Logie said to Skeen. "I can't believe you are trying to create roadblocks in the way of an incredible story about misuse of power and actual murder. Are you really a journalist?"

"Good question," Eudell said.

Skeen pointed at Eudell and shrilled, "I resent your innuendo."

"Honey," Eudell said, "you can stick it in you end-o."

Skeen slapped the table in front of the dazed Christian. "Calvin, speak up. Our legal liability is tremendous."

The managing editor spread his hands in bewilderment.

Gesturing at Logie, Skeen said, "How credible is she? She falsified tax returns to cover up her husband's crimes. Please."

Karen rose out of her seat. "Listen, you—"

Logie put a hand on Karen's shoulder to defuse her. "This morning, thanks to Frank Vere's friend at the SEC, Mr. Prince, I've received assurances from the IRS that they won't go after me for that. I prepared and signed the joint returns unaware that my husband had stolen money and was hiding it. Should I have known? Did I suspect? Sure. But this isn't enough for the IRS to hurt me. And the feds are giving me a pass on misuing government resources if I testify against Wooton."

"Vere was supposed to have nothing to do with this story," Skeen keened.

"It's a good thing that he did," Bill said.

The editor-in-chief's comment didn't dissuade Skeen. "That's not all," he went on. "I've been hearing that Goldring is this magical talisman. Is it? How do we know that Goldring isn't some device that breaks the law?"

"I'm not telling how Goldring works," Linda said to Skeen. "And I'm not speaking to you."

"Honey," Eudell said to Linda, "I'm worried that you'll go on out and build yourself another Goldring. Then won't some other bad guys be after you again?"

"I couldn't replicate Goldring," Linda said. "I'd need Ginny's math expertise and Flo's computer programming skills."

"How do we know this woman doesn't have a disc with the Goldring program copied on it?" Skeen said, referring to Linda. "We make her out to be some kind of martyr in our magazine when all she's doing is breaking securities laws, and will continue to."

Linda beamed hatred at him. "My sisters are dead, damn you."

"How can we be sure?" an overwrought Skeen declared. "Flo has turned up alive before. How do we know your sisters aren't sitting down in the Caribbean laughing at us and waiting for you?"

Karen jumped up from her seat and headed around the table to punch Skeen. All three women grabbed her.

Christian faced Skeen. "Karen has this story nailed down, Gene. We're hearing the complete truth from her. Goldring is gone."

"Gone where?" Skeen screeched.

"Boy," Bill said to Skeen, "be quiet for once." Then the editor-in-chief turned to Karen, who had grudgingly sat back down, and said, "You done made us proud. Congratulations."

"Thank you, Bill," Karen said, barely audible, touched.

As the meeting broke up, Karen thanked Linda for appearing. "I wasn't sure you'd show up."

"But I did," Linda said. "And I realize . . . now . . ." She drew in a ragged breath. "Goldring is indeed gone. And my sisters are, too. If Goldring were to fall into my hands today, I'd destroy it. Enough."

"How are you holding up?"

"Fine. As Ginny would say, I'm the strong one."

"Why don't I bring Frank Vere over? He was vital to this story. And he would love to meet you again, I'm sure."

"No, thanks," Linda said. "I'm not in the mood today for some unattractive man mooning over me. No matter how famous he is. When he asks me out, I'd just have to say no. He should focus his attentions on someone else." She arched an eyebrow at Karen.

"Oh," Karen said. "Pardon me for being friendly."

"We're not friends. But the main reason I came here today is to remind you that you promised me 'sympathetic' treatment when you write your story. I don't want to read anyone's hearsay that Goldring is an illegal hacking program that let us break securities laws. As that dweeb editor Skeeen would say, you wouldn't want a lawsuit from me, now would you?"

"I can't prove Goldring could spy on institutional investors," Karen said quietly. "So you're home free on that."

A smiling Logie approached them. She said to Linda, "How great you could come today to help Karen. I take it back. You're not such a bitch, after all."

Linda smiled and headed for the exit. "Sure I am."

Kingman Wooton sat in his Eames chair in his drawing room. What was left of the dead rose stems bobbed in the cool wind outside the French doors. Next to him was a thick roast beef sandwich, goopy with Russian dressing, reigning on the plate in artery-clogging splendor. A tangy potato salad was plopped to the side like lumpy paste. The two were coronary co-conspirators. He sighed. Hungry, he eyed his midafternoon snack and wondered if he should tuck into it before the phone rang.

Wooton was eating even more than normal lately. The previous night, he had told his top aides they all were going out to dinner at an important restaurant. On a government credit card, per usual. They each had a plausible-sounding excuse. He hadn't insisted. There was a time when they wouldn't dare refuse the director.

He heard someone walking on the old floorboards that William Seward once had trod.

"Frohlich?" he called out. But it wasn't any member of his house detail.

Erica appeared in the doorway. Her cheeks were crossed with tear tracks.

"I heard about the store," said Wooton, who didn't get up. "Did you?"

"They should have given you some notice before padlocking the place," he said. "Maybe I can help you."

"Maybe you can't."

"I'm waiting for an important call right now. But once that's over, I can have pressure put on the landlord. Maybe—"

"Maybe you can't, Kingman."

The rebuke sunk in. "I'm sorry." He eyed the phone. "Doesn't your . . . man have family money to pay the store's rent?"

"His father took legal steps to postpone that. He won't come into his money until he is married."

Wooton asked the painful question: "Are the two of you going to . . ."

"No. Mick has left me. For a little blonde cutey who graduated from college a year ago. She works on the Hill. Isn't that nice?"

Wooton heaved himself to his feet. "Erica, I'm sorry."

"No, you're not. You're never sorry."

"Erica, I'm serious. Give me another chance. We can work this out. I'm very close to getting Goldring." He was lying about Goldring, but he had to say something.

"Sure." She turned and walked out.

"Erica," he called after her. He crumpled back into his chair.

The phone didn't ring. His snack waited for him. He reached for the roast beef.

Then he heard someone approaching. His hand put down the sandwich and retreated to his lap.

"Erica?"

Dressed for business, Gwen Erder entered the room. Several people in suits whom he didn't recognize clustered behind her but didn't come in.

"What are you doing here, Ms. Erder?"

"Director, your telepathy didn't tell you?"

"Don't be insubordinate to me, Ms. Erder," he thundered. "I don't like your attitude. You're not on house duty. What do you think you're doing here? Who are these people?"

"I'm here to deliver a message," she said.

"It will have to wait. The president is about to call me. Go outside until I summon you."

"He's not calling," she said. "I'm here on his behalf. The people with me are FBI agents. They're going to arrest you for misusing the powers of your office. And for murdering Dirk Donner."

Wooton sat stunned for a moment. Then, "Nonsense. The existence of the Authority is top secret. The FBI has no jurisdiction over us. The Authority is above the law. You know that."

"Times change."

"And just who does the president fancy can head the Authority in my absence? There has to be an orderly transition. Even if I were to retire at year's end, I was to be kept on for a while to help my successor get into the job."

"Not going to happen," Erder said. "Since I'm your successor, I'll simply play it by ear."

Wooton placed his hands over his plump face. Hit by an inspiration, he dropped them and said to her urgently, in a low voice that the agents couldn't hear in the hall, "Listen, join with me in splitting the fortune from Goldring. We both can be rich."

"Siegfried Wolfe has the laptop, which means it could be anywhere. Even if you had it, I don't care. The stock market? I had a good day in Atlantic City recently. I'm quitting gambling while I'm ahead."

The agents began filing into the room.

"Would you like to finish your sandwich before you're taken into custody?" she asked.

"I'm not hungry."

Faff sat by the panoramic window, his piercing eyes studying the boardwalk below. Now that night had descended, patrons should be streaming into his casino. But they were headed elsewhere. Faff's Lair wasn't the place to be now for a gambler. Too much bad karma swirled around it.

First was Glick's magazine story. Now all the papers had picked that up. They also were writing that he was a fugitive from justice, holed up in his office. He had skipped out of New York before Friday could arrest him. Legally at least, Atlantic City, which he still controlled, was the best sanctuary for him. Apart from outside the country. But the airplane company had repossessed his private jet. There was no way he'd fly commercial. The airport guards would nab him at the gate, anyway. Besides, he wasn't made to run. As his mother had told him, he'd spit in the eye of a lion.

He rubbed his chest, where the pain wouldn't subside, and cursed all the fools who had let him down. His official statement was: "Of course I didn't order my own brother killed." The Atlantic County prosecutor had thus far kept at bay the New Jersey State Police, who were acting on information provided by the New York cops. The local prosecu-

tor, owing his job and his hidden wealth to Faff's largesse and connections, argued that the alleged murder of Solter Faff occurred within his jurisdiction, and only he could determine whether Jack Faff should be charged. This was buying time, at best. With the story being trumpeted in the media, despite Faff's threats of libel suits, the heat was on to resolve the standoff quickly.

He felt a presence in the room and looked up. A dapper man with silver hair and a superbly tailored tweed suit stood in the doorway. He held a Louis Vuitton briefcase. "Yes," he said in a fine Eton accent, "the suit was made for me. I figured you'd approve of the tailoring."

"How did you get past security? Where's my secretary?"

"They all must've gone to the loo." Siegfried Wolfe closed the door behind him and strode across the exquisite Persian rug that the Shah of Iran had given Pop-pop. "A few moments ago, I got off the phone with my bank in the Caymans. They received the two million from you. Very satisfactory. I assume those tales I read of your financial troubles are simple balderdash."

Faff didn't rise to greet the Englishman. "You assume right. Damn media invents crap to humiliate me out of jealousy. Sells newspapers and magazines, I guess. Anything for a buck." Faff had generated Wolfe's two million by unlawfully sapping his employees' pension fund.

"Horrible invention, the profit motive."

"I never pay all the money in a deal up front," Faff said, seeking to establish his dominance in the encounter. "But I'm making an exception in your case. You better have what I want with you."

"Have what you want with me? Well, I know you want as many tall women as you can get. Alas, I don't have any women available. And I know you like the adulation of the masses. But one hand is occupied"—he held up the briefcase—"meaning I can't applaud you at this moment."

"Don't be a smartass." Faff looked lustfully at the briefcase. "Is that it?"

"That, Mr. Faff, is decidedly *it*. Before you receive this, however, you require a wee lesson in manners. When a visitor enters your office, particularly one with whom you are transacting business, you stand and greet him."

"Cut the noise and give me the damn laptop, okay?" Faff said, not moving from his chair.

Still clasping the briefcase, Wolfe circled the desk at uncanny speed. With his free hand, he grabbed the knot of Faff's Italian silk tie and yanked Faff to his feet. Wolfe loomed over the developer and spoke down to Faff's frightened face: "I detest doing business with someone who is not a gentleman."

Once Wolfe released him, Faff stroked his throat and said, "Hey, I'm sorry. Didn't realize you were so touchy. May I sit down now?"

"But at times I must deal with such people." Wolfe placed the briefcase on the desktop as Faff resumed his seat. "If I were you, given the amount of publicity Goldring has received, I'd hide the infernal contraption. A whole circus troupe of lawmen will soon descend upon you, I fear, poking into every nook and cranny of your life. They'll find the thing in a trice."

"With the money this baby can make me, I'll buy the best lawyers on the planet to keep the whole world off my back." Faff undid the briefcase's clasp and peeked inside. He pulled out the laptop. An old and undistinguished IBM ThinkPad—undistinguished except for the golden ring embossed on it. He caressed the computer lovingly.

"You certainly need some money."

"You never can have enough."

Faff lifted his eyes from the laptop. But Wolfe was gone.

He opened the computer as he might a treasure chest. Booting it up was simple. Then he saw that it had but two programs: one was to trade online, the other was Goldring. He accessed Goldring. The top choice was called "latest pick." He went for that.

Before him was a panel saying that T. Rowe Price, the big fund house, was poised to buy shares of some company called Goaderdam Enterprises, a maker of oil drilling bits. He had a few days to amass a position before they went into the market and the stock surged.

"Oil," he said, drawing out the syllable. "Black gold, Texas tea. Money, money, money."

He laughed uproariously. Couldn't stop. He could barely stay on his chair. He was overcome by the sheer giddy delight of beating everyone. All those fools.

His secretary called and asked if he was okay. Evidently the sound of his laughter must have traveled out to her.

"I'm fine," he managed between chuckles, wiping away the tears. He was so fine he forgot to chide her for letting Wolfe enter without warning him. "No interruptions. No matter what you hear from me. I'll be busy."

Faff set down the phone and sat in wonder before Goldring. Wolfe was right. The cops might pounce on Goldring. If they had warrants, hiding the computer would be difficult. His office was the first spot they'd check. Stash it in the casino vault? His employees observed all he did and might rat him out if he put it there. The best course was to copy the program and destroy the laptop. He could order the Goederdam stock from his own computer.

Faff retrieved a fresh blank disc from his desk and slipped it into the Goldring laptop. Then he set about copying.

That was when he saw the screen go wild. Frantically, he tried calling up the Goldring program. Gibberish—a series of figures and exclamation points filled the screen.

And he realized that Goldring had been set to destroy itself if someone tried copying it. And that he had stolen two million dollars to buy a useless lump of fried circuitry.

The pain seared through his heart like a sword. He made a lot of noise as he fell to the floor, his chair overturning. No one dared come, per his instructions. He twitched and squealed. Were Solter and Pop-pop standing over him? He squealed more.

The Jersey Devil winged in from the Pine Barrens and attached its talons to Faff's soul.

Thanksgiving Day at Frank Vere's was one of the gang's best parties. His apartment was jumping with many friends. The enormous turkey, recently unloaded from the oven, sat on his kitchen countertop. People bustled about the kitchen, some helping with food preparation, others by being amusing. Karen, as always, presided over food preparation with Frank as sous chef.

"What's the difference," said the Razz, pleasantly plotzed, his hands busy holding his drink, "between Gene Skeen and a pig, both lying dead in the road?"

Mike Riley looked up from the kitchen table, where he was showing Alexandra card tricks. "Gee, I don't know, Razz," he pronounced in mock wonder. "What's the difference?"

Karen and Logie looked anxiously at each other, then at Alexandra. But she seemed to be ignoring the adult chatter.

The Razz took a sip of his drink for effect. "The skidmarks in front of the pig."

"I don't like pigs," Alexandra said.

"Pick another card," Mike said to the girl.

"You stole that one from me, Razz," Karen protested, laughing nonetheless as she filled the gravy boats. "Except it was about Calvin Christian."

"Christian has never been alive to begin with," said Wendy, over by the window. Her parrot was celebrating Thanksgiving on his own because he got too excited at big parties. Karen had told Alexandra that the parrot was afraid he'd be deposited in the oven and served for dinner.

"You guys are in charge of opening the wine," Frank called over to the Three Musketeers, who stood arguing in the doorway about the meaning of the latest consumer confidence report. "Can you agree on how to do that?"

"Phil here believes that the economy is so good, it's like wine that doesn't need a wine opener," Milton Brainard said. "So effervescent that the cork will pop on its own."

Phil Sarkasian looked skyward in exasperation. "Milton, you've predicted six of the last two recessions."

Thomas Dailey repeated his mantra: "Neither one of you knows what he's talking about."

Frank, en route to the turkey to inspect the meat thermometer, rubbed Karen's back affectionately. Perplexed, she glanced up from the big bowl of creamed onions she was fixing. He kissed her forehead. "How're you doing?"

"I'm doing great, I guess" she said. "Thanks again for your help. And I don't mean with the dinner. My cover story is more than I could have imagined."

"You broke the story," Frank said. "You're going to be a great reporter." He picked up a plate of canapés and went into the living room.

Sally shouldered through the gaggle of Musketeers at the kitchen door, calling Karen's name. She carried a grocery bag from the Korean market around the corner, where Frank had sent her to fetch more butter.

"What's up, Sal?" Karen said.

"Someone is here to see you. Wants you to come down to the street."

"Who is this someone?"

"Uh, he wouldn't give a name. He's distinguished looking. Has an English accent."

"Don't go, Karen," Logie said with alarm. "I'll call the cops."

"Go ahead and call them," Karen said. "I'll try to keep him occupied till they come."

"But it's too dangerous," Logie said. "Stay here."

Karen, though, bolted into the hall and took the stairs two at once.

A car waited outside Frank's building in the autumn chill. A Bentley. Karen had seen it before. The wheel was on the British side. The rear window rolled down.

A laptop held by a pair of gloved hands protruded from the car window. The machine had a gold ring embossed into it. Siegfried Wolfe's dapper countenance moved into view above the computer.

"Seems this monstrosity is not its old self," he said. "When Faff tried to copy its program, there was a boobytrap that destroyed everything. What a pity. I scooped it up from Faff's office right after he died."

"You filthy bastard."

Wolfe held Goldring out to her. "While it may be useless, there's a sentimental value attached. This would make a nice keepsake."

Karen grabbed the laptop and tried to smash Wolfe's head with it, but the Englishman was fast. His window zipped up. Made of some super-hard glass, the window was strong enough that Goldring bounced off.

Wolfe waved good-bye, wiggling his gloved fingers. His driver put the car in gear. The Bentley sped down the street.

Karen stood at the curb with the ruined laptop, swearing at the retreating Bentley. Then she dumped Goldring in the trash bin and went back upstairs to Thanksgiving.

LAWRENCE LIGHT

TOO RICH TO LIVE

They're known as the Billionaire Boys Club. They've made a fortune by taking over companies, ruthlessly firing their workers…and hiding their profits from the government. Financial reporter Karen Glick is determined to make a name for herself by exposing the club for tax fraud, but one thing is getting in her way—a radical group has targeted the Billionaire Boys for murder, one by one. As Karen keeps digging, she uncovers one particularly terrifying fact: she's become the group's latest target. Her story is no longer just a career-maker. Now it's a matter of life and death.

CAUSES UNKNOWN

LESLIE HORVITZ

It just didn't make sense. When Michael Friedlander heard how his brother had died, he couldn't accept it. So he started to look for his own answers. But every lie he uncovered or secret he exposed simply drew him deeper and deeper into a chain of cover-ups that has led him at last to the New York City Medical Examiner's office....

The ME's office is just one part of a widespread conspiracy. Shadowy figures have created a hidden power structure involving the city's most trusted agencies. Michael has come too close to a truth far more dangerous than he can imagine. If he isn't able to discover the conspiracy's final secret, he will become its latest victim.

THE BRIBE

WILLIAM P. WOOD

He was a war hero and a member of Congress. Now he's dead—shot down the day after he made a scathing speech blasting corruption in Washington. For Sacramento police detectives Terry Nye and Rose Tafoya, the investigation is a time bomb. They have just twenty-four hours to find out if the congressman was killed because of his speech…or something far worse.

Dennis Cooper is acting District Attorney during these critical twenty-four hours. He's in for the fight of his career and time is running out for everyone—and they know it.

DAVID HOUSEWRIGHT
TIN CITY

It started innocently enough. An elderly beekeeper asked Mac McKenzie to find out why his bees were suddenly dying. Asking a few questions isn't a big deal for Mac, but it looks like the beekeeper's neighbor, Frank Crosetti, doesn't like nosy people. Now he's disappeared, leaving behind a dead body... and a very angry Mac McKenzie.

With only a faint trail to follow—and some very suspicious federal agents gunning for him—Mac is forced to dive underground. But he'll find Crosetti even if it means sniffing around the Twin Cities' darkest corners. No one's going to stop Mac—unless of course they kill him.